BORN
IN
PARADISE

BORN
IN
PARADISE

Armine von Tempski

OX BOW PRESS
Woodbridge, Connecticut 06525

1985 Reprint published by
Ox Bow Press
P.O. Box 4045
Woodbridge, Connecticut 06525

Library of Congress Cataloging in Publication Data

Von Tempski, Armine, 1892–1943.
  Born in paradise.

  Reprint. Originally published: New York: Duell, Sloan, and Pearce.
1940.
  1. Von Tempski, Armine, 1892–1943. 2. Children—Hawaii—Biography.
3. Hawaii—Biography. 4. Hawaii—Social life and customs. I. Title.
CT275.V595A33 1985   996.9′03′0924 [B]   84–27345
ISBN 0–918024–34–X

To my beloved DAD *and the
people of* HAWAII,
*and to
my husband,* ALFRED BALL,
*who helped to build
this book*

*Certain characters appearing in this auto-
biography are composite portraits with
fictitious names. In no instance, however,
has authenticity of characterization been
violated.*

CONTENTS

BORN
IN
PARADISE

1. BORN IN PARADISE

A TTAINING Paradise in the hereafter does not concern me greatly. I was born in Paradise.

The first word I learned to say was Aloha—"My love to you!" —spoken from the fullness of warm generous hearts. That greeting is the key, the password of racial blends making up the colorful and varied pattern of Hawaii. Not until later, when I visited the sterner lands of more northern latitudes did I realize what a wonderful heritage was ours—we children of white parents born and reared in Hawaii. Unsullied boundless spaces surrounded us; music and mirth were eternally in our ears; the stir of creation filled water, earth, and air; the sweetness of wild ginger blossoms and ripe guavas weighted the wind. Savage silver rain, tawny sunlight over land and sea, flowers tearing from green buds in orange, scarlet, blue, and purple gave a sort of heady intoxication to the nights and days. The very earth underfoot was alive from lava seething through its veins. . . .

How can words convey the mighty flow and ebb of the leisurely, gracious existence of those lost regal decades which have no exact parallel in history. I had no white children to play with except my sisters, and later a brother, but my comrades were polyglot—amazing personalities ranging from the gutter to the Gods, who made the years and days rich beyond any telling: Ah Sin, the Chinese cook, whose mummy-like face, whose oaths resounding like gongs, invested him with the qualities of a magician. Tatsu, my Japanese nurse, who always warmed her hands inside her kimono before touching me, and who smelled faintly and pleasantly of incense and pale hot tea. Makalii, the old Hawaiian *paniolo*—cowboy—who carried me in front of him on a pillow while he made his daily round of the nearer pastures, who taught me the lore of the hills and of his people, who schooled me to understand the whispered language of nature. Aunt Lively, whose six feet and two hundred pounds of rich, brown flesh seemed to house all the fun and laughter of the world. Charlie Kaa, who had seen Mauna Loa erupt fifty times and who knew all the legends about the fiery Goddess of Volcanoes and her Sea-lover, Kamapuaa.

Lusty Hawaiian sailors, who manned monster whaleboats that brought passengers ashore from evil-smelling, evil-mannered Inter-Island steamers anchored outside the reefs. Lovely ladies, sugar planters, cattle ranchers, royal personages, visiting celebrities, who thronged our home over week-ends, singing, dancing, playing poker all Saturday night and sallying forth at dawn on Sunday to rope wild bulls, ride match-races, or loll on the lawns enjoying those typically Hawaiian celebrations called *luaus*. These were my friends and companions, the people I loved.

My Gods were Christ, Buddha, the Polynesian Creator, and hosts of lesser deities. Tidal waves, volcanoes, *kona*—southerly— gales walked beside me during the years of my childhood, investing life with an extra dimension that charged dawns and dusks with supernatural qualities and invested the most ordinary days with a sense of impending adventure.

The ranch where we lived bore the proud name of the great volcano on which it sprawled—Haleakala, The House of the Sun. Impressively simple in outline, like all Hawaiian volcanoes, wrapped in loneliness and mystery, the quiescent giant brooded like an aloof god guarding our world. The sixty thousand acres of throbbing soil, forming the ranch, sat like a mammoth saddle on the back of the ten-thousand-foot mountain. In places the land was robed with rich jungles, elsewhere it was scarred by black lava which had once streamed in molten scarlet to the sea. From the shimmering grasslands and eucalyptus groves at Makawao, at the two-thousand-foot level, rolling hills and cattle-dotted pastures went up to the summit of Haleakala. Down through the livid scar of the crater, up the battlements of the far rim, then down the far slope of the mountain, the wide acres poured like a green torrent to the sea.

Over this kingdom ruled my father—Louis von Tempsky.

There are people who seem to move through life with an invisible spotlight focused on them. Louis von Tempsky, of Polish and Scotch blood, was one of that breed. The way he moved, spoke, and held himself, the way he entered a room, printed itself on the memory of everyone he met. His gay eyes, filled with intense glee of living, the flash of his smile—which made a person feel braver and stronger—the quick ease with which he swung on to a horse or bent to pat a dog set him apart.

When Louis von Tempsky was eighteen he left New Zealand and started around the world in search of adventure. He stopped off in Hawaii on his way to Mexico to visit the island of Maui where his widowed mother, years before, had been governess in one of the great families, and young von Tempsky found in Maui a spot which he recognized to be his by right of an immediate and passionate love.

His father, known later to us wide-eyed children as "Granddad," was Major Gustav Ferdinand von Tempsky, political exile from Poland at the age of eighteen, who had left a globe-trotting trail of accomplishment in his wake. As a youngster he got mahogany out of the jungles of Nicaragua, braving fever, hostile tribes of Indians, crocodiles, and snakes. In 1847 he went to California and remained long enough to participate in the Gold Rush. But after a little, California grew too tame for him. Mounting his white stallion he rode from San Diego to Mexico City. In 1853, he visited the ruins of Mitla in Yucatan, and fought for a while under Maximilian. With his flashing eyes and flowing black curls, brandishing his guitar, paint brush, and sword, he was a welcome visitor anywhere—a scholar and a fighting man.

But through it all, artistic gentleman or ruthless warrior, he was a vagabond.

Quickly draining the delights of Mexico, he went on to the Corramandel gold fields of Australia. Within two years he was offered the leadership of the Mills and Boone Expedition being formed to cross the then-unexplored deserts of interior Australia with a camel caravan. Fearless, but intensely practical, he declined, convinced that the expedition would prove a failure. It did, for all its members perished in the attempt.

Later he enlisted as an officer in the Maori Wars in New Zealand. Until he came, the English had been unable to defeat the ferocious tattooed warriors. With the Forest Rangers, whom he organized and led, von Tempsky outmaneuvered the Maoris, carving a smashing and colorful career on the field of battle and, eventually, dying in action. Today children studying history in the Antipodes find him rated as one of the great heroes of New Zealand.

Small wonder that his second son, Louis, should succumb to the vital quality of Hawaii. But Louis had no material assets to gain a foothold in the Islands. His equipment was his joyous personality, his love for life, his driving force, and his ability to see through and beyond material things even while he utilized them. Like his father, he was a musician and a fearless and expert horseman. His inheritance gave him courage, vision, and tact; his youth added a wide-open mind and adaptability. When he ate rice or sipped tea with a Japanese or a Chinaman, he was Oriental; when he sang or danced *hulas* with Hawaiians, he was Polynesian; when he talked with Whites, his keen mind and vision enabled him to see through immediate problems to goals of the future.

Once in the Islands, Louis, despite his lack of funds, determined to go no farther. Overnight Hawaii fixed a stranglehold on his heart. In order to remain there he turned his hand to whatever work came his way. For a while, he drove an ox-team and carted supplies; then he worked as a butcher, ran a dairy, operated a corn mill—while he dreamed of someday planting stately groves of trees and raising blooded stock.

He found that contrary to common knowledge, cattle ranching was a major industry in Hawaii, long before it flourished in the great American West. Yet even today, if you ask a Hawaiian for a cow you will invariably be presented with a goat! Some early explorer visiting the Islands, promised that he would bring some cows on his return. During the long voyage around the Horn all the cattle died, while a small herd of goats survived. When the goats were landed the Hawaiians took them for the promised cows, and goats are still called *kaos*.

In 1792 Lord George Vancouver made his first visit to the Islands and established warm intelligent relations with the natives. On his second voyage to Hawaii, in 1793, he brought a number of longhorn cattle from California and presented them to King Kamehameha, who turned the animals loose to breed. Impressed by the gift, Kamehameha put a rigid *tabu* on them and for twenty years it was forbidden to kill them. The herd increased vastly and when time came to round them up the Hawaiians didn't know how to go about it. *Vaqueros* were imported from Mexico to instruct the natives in cattle ranching, and the Hawaiian word, *paniolo,* meaning cowboy, is derived from *Español* —Spaniard.

Louis von Tempsky speedily proved his ability as a stockman and when a corporation offered him the management of the Haleakala Ranch—on Maui, second largest island of the group— he accepted and proved his worth by getting the ranch out of debt and keeping it on a paying basis throughout the term of his management. Near the close of the nineteenth century he met and married Amy Wodehouse, daughter of Major James Hay Wodehouse, British Ambassador to the Court of Hawaii. He brought his young wife to the Haleakala Ranch to live.

Although the ranch was never his by right of ownership, it

was his by right of love. The hypnotic pull of that soil held his soul against all the rest of the earth. He gave his love, his mind, his strength and, finally, his life to the acres which were entrusted to his care. He had found his Paradise—and in it I was born.

2. MY FIRST RIDE

"A RE ALL the women asleep?" Daddy asked Tatsu, my nurse. Tatsu nodded. Lunch was over. The house was still. A hot afternoon lay over the island.

"Go softly into the nursery and bring Armine to me," Daddy ordered. "I'll be at the back door on my horse."

"But, Mr. Louis!" Tatsu protested. "Baby-san only one month old."

"I'm just going to take her for a short ride. It won't hurt her."

"But if Mrs. Louis and English sisters wake up and baby-san no stop inside crib they all-same crazy fellas. And if they find out you take for *holoholo*—" Tatsu could get no further.

"Hell, Hawaiian women take their week-old babies all over the island on horseback. My child's as tough as any of theirs."

Daddy had the gift of making things jaunty plus the ability to turn ordinary, or even upsetting, happenings into adventures. Tatsu was enslaved by him, like the rest of the help on the ranch. Shaking her head she went off, her straw sandals making soft slapping sounds on the matted floor.

She stole through the long lofty living room. Above the fireplace hung a pair of wild bull horns measuring five-foot-three from tip to tip. On the piano was an imposing array of silver racing trophies won by Haleakala Ranch horses at the Kahului track. Priceless vases three feet high flanked the hearth, presents from the Chinese Ambassador to Grandfather Wodehouse, who represented Great Britain in Hawaii. Deep rugs, ranked books, rich oil paintings, bowls of flowers, trifles of carved ivory and jade lent an air of dignity to the room which was like a deep warm heart in the careless sprawling body of the old house.

9

Like a quiet moth Tatsu flitted guiltily past closed doors behind which Mother and the English aunts were sleeping. Reaching the nursery, she flashed in. Going to the crib she wrung her
hands, her heart torn. Then with the unquestioning obedience
of Oriental women to masculine commands, she picked me up,
wrapped a blanket of Shetland weave about me, and laid me
on a small pillow. Hurrying out, she closed the door quietly and
started down the hall, glancing over her shoulder occasionally
as though she sensed *obakes*—ghosts—treading on her heels.

Daddy, mounted on his best horse, Buccaneer, was waiting impatiently at the back door. Buccaneer was darkly suspicious of
Tatsu's long flapping kimono sleeves and of the white pillow
with a squirming object upon it. Backing away, snorting, he
evinced his disgust and his unwillingness to be party to the
kidnaping.

"Orr, Mr. Louis, more better no make this kind," Tatsu said
tearfully. "Buccaneer too wild. Maybe buck you off and baby-san
get broke. Better get old, slow horse."

"Buccaneer's perfectly trained, he won't buck, Tatsu," Daddy
assured her. "He's just high. My First Born's first ride must be
on a real horse, not on an old plug. Fetch Ah Sin. He'll help you
to get Armine to me."

Frantic, but adoring, Tatsu trotted to the kitchen to enlist the
aid of the old cook. Grinning sardonically, the wrinkled Chinaman came out, exchanged a quick understanding man-look with
Daddy, then walked forward to take hold of Buccaneer's bit.
But Ah Sin's flapping apron, whisked about by the brisk trade
wind, fanned Buccaneer's fears to frenzy. Tatsu stood at a safe
distance holding me and crying as Japanese women do, without
a sound, with slow tears stealing down her flat rag-doll face.
After half-a-dozen unsuccessful attempts to get to the horse, Ah
Sin gave up.

"Me go get Makalii. Me no too smart for horse," he chuckled,
then added proudly, "But Sonna-pa-pitch I swell cook!"

"Damned if you aren't," Daddy agreed, grinning.

In a few minutes Ah Sin returned with the grizzled *paniolo* who had worked for Dad since he first landed in Hawaii. Expert in the ways of horses, Makalii soothed Buccaneer and got me to Daddy without further trouble. While the old Hawaiian held the spirited horse, Daddy settled the pillow and small baby in the crook of his right arm, then rode triumphantly off to the hills. With the sun and wind in his face, with his eyes filled by the rich beauty of the land he loved, Daddy forgot all about time, happy in the knowledge that someday, after he was gone, atoms of him persisting in the cells of my body would live on to enjoy the green ways of the earth.

Before he returned, my loss was discovered. Terrified, weeping, Tatsu attempted to explain. Mother had hysterics, the English aunts were scandalized. When gay young Dad came riding back with me, none the worse off for the jaunt, he was drowned in a flood of female fury.

"My baby, my baby, *give* her to me!" Mother wailed, rushing forward. "She might have been killed. Oh, Von, how could you!"

Alarmed by the rustle of her skirts, Buccaneer leaped backwards. Mother screamed. Aunts recoiled.

"Upon my word, how any father could do such an outrageous thing as to take a month-old baby for a ride *on a horse like that!*" one aunt said indignantly.

Daddy got Buccaneer quieted. "Armine's right as a bank. She liked it," he insisted, signing to Makalii to come and get me.

"*Like* it! How absurd. She's only a month old," the other aunt exploded.

"Well, she didn't cry," Daddy insisted, sliding me into Makalii's uplifted arms.

Daddy jumped off his horse. Makalii led Buccaneer away. Going to Mother, Dad put his arm about her. "Don't go off at half-cock, Amy. A short ride can't hurt any child. We weren't out for an hour. Week-old Hawaiian children are taken all over the Island."

Mother flung off his arm.

"First you risk Armine's life! Now you put her in the same class with Hawaiians! I don't ever want to see or talk to you again." Sobbing uncontrollably she started for her house.

Wise in the ways of women, Dad did not try to follow her, or attempt to justify himself with her sisters who swept along in her wake toward the nursery.

Of course, I was too young to remember it, but the episode was fed to me second-hand all my life. Dad's version. Tatsu's. Makalii's. Ah Sin's. And Mother's. Only poor Mother's had no chuckles in it!

Children's earliest memories are supposed to center about their parents, but my first hazy recollections, like those of most Island children raised on isolated ranches during the early 1900's, have as their pivot a very special sort of guardian and friend—Makalii, the old Hawaiian cowboy who had charge of my activities by day. Next in vividness is Tatsu, my mama-san who dressed and supervised my indoor activities; and third, Ah Sin, the old Chinese cook.

Outside these, in a widening circle, shadowy figures came and went. Daddy, who rode off before dawn and came back at sunset smelling of sunshine and horses. Mother who wore sweeping *holokus*—a glorified Hawaiian version of a Mother Hubbard, and a flower in her hair during the daytime, and at night appeared in evening gowns. For a while "Gan," Daddy's mother, a tiny gentle-and-steely Scotswoman who had trailed her adventurous Polish husband all over the world. Gwen, my roly-poly sister, and my adopted sister, Aina. Mother and Dad took Aina to rear when her mother, Annie Leialoha Cleghorn, died. Aunt Annie was related to the Royal Family of Hawaii and was briefly married to Hay Wodehouse, Mother's eldest brother.

But Makalii was the demi-god of a gorgeous and breathtaking world slowly taking shape and assuming solidity out of the mists wrapping infancy. The first memory-picture inked on my mind is that of being carried in front of Makalii over lava-flows in the moonlight. The occasion was probably one of the rare times when the family spent a week in Honolulu and was returning to Maui by way of Makena, the port-of-call at the southwestern extremity of Haleakala.

Other fragmentary impressions are tangled into the first realization of being on horseback. A steamer, which I thought was a restless house, smelling of hogs and cattle. Being carried down an unsteady gangway that hovered above a big whaleboat. Lanterns flashing on strong brown arms, pulling long wet oars. Roaring masses of water bursting over the reef which tried to overtake the boat and devour it. Hawaiians shouting. The hiss of the prow grating on a black volcanic beach.

Strong gentle hands grasped me and tossed me over churning foam to land in Makalii's dear arms. Daddy, Mother, Gwen, Tatsu kept getting lost and found in lantern beams as we walked over crunching sand toward a stone corral under cocoanut trees where saddled horses waited. After the bustle of mounting was over, there was only the sound of hoofs plodding steadily along a rocky trail which wound up long slopes culminating in the mighty dome of Haleakala, massive and solemn against the stars.

The volcano rearing out of our back yard in size approximated the craters pocking the moon. The pit at the summit, rising ten thousand feet above the sea, is twenty-seven miles in circumference and, roughly, two thousand feet deep. Haleakala in nature, and Makalii among humans, occupied center-stage during my early years. Every day the gentle old man took me with him on his rounds of the nearby pastures, where he watched thoroughbred mares about to foal, mended fences, and adjusted the floats in water troughs. And always the vast blue presence of the mountain filled half the sky. A blueness more solid than the blue arch of the heavens, a blueness which engulfed the jaunty figures of horsemen riding away at daybreak and which, faithfully, disgorged them at night.

I listened avidly while Makalii told me about the Cloud Warriors, *Naulu* and *Ukiukiu*—trade-wind-driven clouds split by the height and mass of Haleakala into two long arms. *Naulu* traveled along the southern flank of the mountain, *Ukiukiu* along the northern and they battled forever to possess the summit. Usually *Ukiukiu* was victorious, but occasionally *Naulu* pushed him back. Sometimes both Cloud Warriors called a truce and withdrew to rest, leaving a clear space between the heaped white masses of vapor looming against the blue of the sky. The space, Makalii told me, was called *Alanui O Lani*—the Highway to Heaven.

And somewhere in the gray mists of babyhood are recollections of a night when the island we lived on fought to ease the pressure of lava ripping out its vitals. I was roughly awakened by my bed slithering across the room and banging against the wall. Before I could call Tatsu it shot in another direction. The house seemed to have gone suddenly crazy, to be filled with lanterns and hurrying people. Tatsu, Daddy, Mother, Gan, the often-present aunts were all flying around with tight white looks on their faces. Makalii snatched me up, Tatsu took Gwen, an aunt carried Aina. . . .

The ground humped and shuddered; the island flung back and forth. Stock stampeded around the pastures, dogs howled, Mynah birds shrieked as they circled above jittering trees. *Paniolos'* wives, hampered by bug-eyed hordes of brown children, rushed from their little houses screaming, "Louis! Louis!"

After Daddy got them quieted, everyone collected in an open place in the garden which afforded an unobstructed view of Haleakala. Mother and her sisters, who were over from Honolulu for a visit, were crying and shaking. Tatsu clutched Gwen, her faithful yellow face white as dough. Portuguese called on their saints. Hawaiians looked uneasy. Ah Sin kept muttering Chinese swear words. Little Gan sat very still and collected, watching Daddy who had a new tense look in his eyes. Makalii squatted down, holding me between his knees, joking to make things seem less frightening.

As the night wore on, the earthquakes grew longer and more violent. Strange rushing noises, thumps and bumps, sounded deep in the earth as lava and gases thrust and pushed to get out. Finally, Daddy spoke to the *paniolos* in an undertone and they went off with lanterns and began hurriedly saddling horses. Makalii told me stories and let me play with his big bell-spurs.

Then slowly a dull red glare, very distant, very high in the heavens, began swelling upward. The Hawaiians shouted, "Mauna Loa! Mauna Loa!" in relieved voices. The Great Dome of Fire, a hundred and fifty miles away on the island of Hawaii, was erupting, and not Haleakala. The lava pressure against the earth's crust, which has one of its focal centers under the Islands, had found its usual vent. Makalii's eyes, which had been squinched up, began relaxing.

"See, Ummie," he said, smiling. "I tell to you no need be scare. Plenty time lava come out. Lava not so bad. It make Hawaii. Might-be you little sleepy?"

I nodded.

"Okay, I make good place for you to *moemoe.*"

He spread his slicker on the grass, removed his coat, though the night was chilly. I lay down and he carefully and lovingly tucked it about me. His eyes went up to the terrific red glare in the sky and rested on it thoughtfully.

"Might-be you like I sing you little song?" he suggested.

I nodded.

His eyes looked pleased. Seating himself on the grass beside me he laid his hand on me, then began chanting softly under his breath in Hawaiian:

Big Mountain, Mauna Loa!
Great Dome of Fire!
Grant us this—our heart's desire;
Spare us from the wrath within you,
Mauna Loa!

   Oh, hear our prayer!

For all the daytime
We'll spend in play-time,
With songs and laughter
We'll pass the golden hours away!
Oh, Mauna Loa!

   Hear our prayer!

3. I SEE A COLT BORN

LIKE most Island-born children I always woke early, sensing a vague, pleasurable stir in the atmosphere long before light welled into the sky. I knew as I lay in bed listening to wind prowling down from Haleakala that the stars outside the open windows were subtly changing. I knew grazing stock were raising their heads for an instant in their salute to the unending wonder of light being born out of darkness. Ah Sin was stealing into the kitchen, the lantern he carried making great shadows, like opening and shutting scissors, as his legs moved. Presently the smell of kerosene being poured on a wood fire and lighted drifted through the house, followed by the sound of coffee being ground and the swift rush of water in Dad's shower.

Then, mysteriously, from being just a small girl, I was transformed into an atom of the wide splendid life about me. Shivers of pleasure, mingled with anticipation for the royal new day being born, chased over me as I listened to whips cracking, the rush of horses' hoofs in the pastures and snatches of *hulas* being sung as men went about the great business of a sixty-thousand-acre ranch.

I always waited in a lather of impatience until I heard Tatsu coming toward my room. Often I couldn't control my impatience to go out and tried to dress myself.

When Tatsu appeared she'd begin: "Aloha, Ummie-san," then seeing that I was out of bed she would begin to scold. But she didn't fool me. While her lips reproved, her eyes were laughing at me and loving me. While she warmed her hands she listened to my chatter, then dressed my wriggling body, and the smell of her clean cotton kimono was cozy and comforting.

17

When my hair was brushed she took my hand and led me through the big still house, which always seemed larger when it was empty of people. Nishi and Adaji, the house-boys, moved about dusting objects carefully so Mother and other *haoles* who slept until seven-thirty or eight would not be disturbed.

Dad never seemed like a *haole*—a white person. He was the super-*paniolo* heading the goodly company of booted and spurred men who went out and came in like a vast tide at the beginning and end of each day. He was horses and trees, the blue mag' nificence of Haleakala. He was Hell, Damn, and By-Golly. He rode racehorses and roped wild bulls. He played polo, danced, and sang *hulas*. He sent ox-carts off for supplies, or up the mountain loaded with boxes of seedling trees and bags of grass seed to be planted on the ranch. He watched to see that young horses' training wasn't hurried or slurred over, and that old ones weren't worked too hard. When people were happy they came to celebrate with him. When they were in dilemmas they asked his advice. Every so often he had to "Give His Devil a Run" and went off for a couple of days with a few kindred-spirited males to celebrate and carouse, and when he came back his eyes were sorry and faraway.

As a rule he was gone long before I finished breakfast, but if something delayed him the day had an extra lift because he was so gay, strong, and eager about getting things under way. The Hawaiians looked on him as an *Alii*—a Chief—but called him by his first name. The Japanese addressed him as "Mr. Louis," but no one ever hailed him as Mr. von Tempsky. He didn't need a prefix to his name to command respect from those working for him.

Every morning when Tatsu and I entered the lofty kitchen, excitement trickled through me. A range the size of a grand piano filled one wall and the two-foot space behind it was usually jammed with straw-lined boxes filled with ailing, maimed, or motherless chicks, pups, ducklings, and kittens.

Forty people were fed out of the kitchen six days a week. Over Saturday and Sunday the thirty-odd *paniolos* and Japanese yard-men ate with their women to leave Ah Sin free to cope with guests.

Above the sink was a narrow shelf where he kept his personal treasures: a fat, amiable Kitchen God; a symbol of longevity; stacks of punks in long red envelopes. Little gaily-colored card-board boxes held Chinese cocoanut candy, like bits of starched tape. Green stone jars latticed with bamboo contained syrup-soaked ginger. An empty jam-jar held his toothbrush—a triply useful tool! One end was bristles, the opposite an ear-scratcher, and the middle widened into a flat blade to scrape his tongue.

I yearned to have one just like it and, once, unable to resist the unholy fascination it exerted over me, tried to steal it. Plac-ing a chair against the sink, I climbed on to the drainboard, missed my footing and fell against the dishpan. The clatter brought Ah Sin in on the run. Pouncing upon me, he spanked me until I howled, then soothed my sobs with ginger which both stung and delighted my tongue.

While Tatsu gave me my bread and milk I watched the old man dashing around lifting covers off bubbling cauldrons of salt pork, turkey, and mutton. Smaller pots filled with Oriental edi-bles sent up tantalizing odors and the capacious oven exhaled the smell of bread or cakes baking.

While I ate I listened for the bell in the little tower on the blacksmith shop to toll the *paniolos* in for their breakfast. Before it finished ringing, men began swarming into the kitchen: men with spurs at their heels, knives in their leggings, and flowers on their hats. Men who spoke with great outdoor voices which filled the kitchen with rolling Hawaiian words and booming Hawaiian laughter.

"Aloha, Ummie!"

"Aloha, Tatsu!"

"Aloha, Ah Sin! Too bad you so *makule* now. No cook good like before!"

"I no old! What-the-hell! I cook more better now than before!"

Fun, banter, crackled in the air. Ah Sin flew about muttering his pet swear word: "Sonna-pa-pitch!" which sounded like hot horseshoes being tossed into buckets of cold water.

Paniolos gathered up stacks of thick white dishes, collected steaming cauldrons of food and monster pots of coffee to take on the lawn. Through the windows I could see them seating themselves on the grass, under the spreading beauty of an *Inia* * tree, pouring tablespoonfuls of sugar into their cups, reaching for fat pieces of pork, dipping strong brown fingers into calabashes of *poi,* heaping smoking yellow sweet potatoes onto their plates.

I watched the garden gate feverishly for Makalii, and when he appeared rushed to the door to meet him. Swinging me onto his hip, he playfully lassoed my neck with the *lei* he made for me every morning, and the rich joyous hours we spent together leaped into reality. If Tatsu protested that I hadn't finished my bread and milk, I hid my face in my *paniolo's* neck, but my senses caught the flash of fun between this brown man and yellow woman I loved. Ah Sin chuckled, for he, too, knew that I always had a second secret breakfast of coffee, salt pork, and *poi* with Makalii and the *paniolos,* and Tatsu's protest was just a form. . . .

Astride of his hip, with flowers around my neck, in a dim childish way I felt as if the world was expanding to boundless proportions. The blue day went away to the bluer ocean, whispering its secrets to the Islands. Above swaying tree-tops, hills climbed toward the summit of Haleakala, which the sun was edging with quick gold. Beyond the nasturtium-smothered stone wall surrounding the garden, long lines of horses stamped at the

---

* The tree known elsewhere in the world as "Pride of India" is simply called "Inia" in Hawaii.

hitching rail. Dogs lay outside the circle of eating men waiting hopefully for bones, and flocks of pigeons strutted and bowed to each other on the roofs of the big house.

When Makalii set me down on the dewy grass, the naked bottoms of my feet tingled with secret messages that ran up my legs from the earth. Makalii put extra food on his plate for me, but I was so absorbed by everything going on about me that I kept forgetting to eat it. I didn't want to miss how Kimmo drank his coffee, with fine rushing noises, or how old Moku deftly caught up the grease running down his chin with swipes of the back of his hand. Everyone was gay, full of pranks and mischief.

These were the people I loved and felt close to. They always had time to joke and play with me. They never scolded. They brought me treasures from the vast mystery of Haleakala. Sometimes a parakeet's tail-feather, like a sliver of turquoise and jade. A polished adze from the stone quarry of Keonehaehae, on the summit of the mountain where in old times naked warriors had squatted on powerful hams shaping weapons of war. Once in a while, Hauki, the colt trainer, would bring me a wild peacock and somehow its dazzling presence seemed to crown the beauty of the garden with the final touch of splendor. Kodama, the yardboy, would tether the glittering-but-brief visitor by the leg with a long piece of cotton clothesline and I haunted the bird, hoping to tame it quickly. After a week Kodama would set it free. For a few days it would stalk haughtily and disgustedly among the flower beds dragging its jeweled tail and—if I came too close—screeching as if a demon had tweaked one of its trailing feathers. Then overnight it would vanish back to the blue wildness of Haleakala.

Once old Hu, who was the clown and buffoon of the ranch, gave me a curl off a wild bull's tail, as perfect as the shavings that Sonoda, the blacksmith, carpenter, and jack-of-all-trades, saved and tied into bunches for me to attach to my rear when

I played horse. In the thick skin I could see a trace of blood and the stiff curl had a strong wild smell which sent goose-prickles rushing over me. My high pride in possessing such a wonder made me smuggle it to bed. When Mother came to kiss me good night a rank odor betrayed the curl's presence under my pillow. I was spanked, and my treasure taken from me.

Often the pleasure of breakfast was sparked up by a brisk dog-fight, and one unforgettable morning a hen with a rooster pursuing her collided with a hitching post, causing a splendid uproar among the horses. Some reared, others lashed out with their heels, two pulled back, broke loose, and jumped the stone wall into the garden. *Paniolos* shouted, dogs barked. Enraged yard-boys protected carefully tended flower beds with their rakes. The lawn was torn up and garden furniture wrecked before the wild pair were lassoed and taken out.

The merry noisy breakfast always ended too soon but when the men rinsed off their cups and plates under a tap for Ah Sin to scald later, I followed suit without regret, for ahead was the adventure of making the rounds of the home-pastures with Makalii.

One morning for some disobedience, Mother told me for punishment I might not ride with Makalii until lunch was over. Screams, tears, and kickings were of no avail. Tatsu's efforts to comfort me were futile. When we went to the kitchen for a belated breakfast, Ah Sin did his bit to try and cheer me by slyly putting a hunk of fat pork into the bowl which should have held bread and milk. I pushed it aside. Pork only tasted good when it was eaten on the lawn with *paniolos*.

A sort of dull fury possessed me. The glittering morning was getting under way and I had to stay indoors. Soon Makalii would ride off to the brood-mare pasture to see if any little colts had been born. Beyond everything I loved colts, the newer the better.

Out of the kitchen windows I saw *paniolos* jogging away. Ox-wagons were bumping off to Kahului to fetch supplies, as it was steamer day. From the stable came the imperious whinny of thoroughbreds impatient to be led out for their morning gallop. It seemed as if everything I loved was going away and abandoning me to a gaunt impossible fate. For a while despair ate me, then I began plotting. I would sneak out, take a short-cut, and overtake Makalii! I knew all the trails leading to the brood-mare pasture.

But I realized it would be difficult to get away. Perhaps if I went back and did some plain-and-fancy begging Mother might relent and let me go out. Stimulated by the thought I slid from my chair and dashed for her room, Tatsu at my heels. I tore to Mother's bed. She looked so beautiful with her large blue eyes, reddish-brown hair, and big English body that my hopes soared. Anyone as lovely, and as loved by everyone, could not be cruel. Scrambling onto the huge *koa*-wood four-poster which Princess Ruth had presented to Major Wodehouse, I began arguing and pleading. Mother was adamant. It was only four hours until noon. I had been naughty and must accept my punishment.

"If you don't let me go with Makalii, I'll die!" I screamed. "And Daddy will kill you when he comes back and finds me dead!"

There was another brisk spanking and Tatsu carried me, limp and completely exhausted, back to bed.

"Ummie-san, Ummie-san," she murmured. "You torr much *kolohi*—naughty, today. I torr much sorry for you."

Aina and Gwen were being dressed by a Japanese woman who assisted Tatsu to care for us. They looked at me in amazement which, in my over-wrought state, seemed tinged with superiority. Pulling the bedcovers haughtily over my head, so I needn't see them, I lay still. Kama-san departed with Gwen and Aina; Tatsu moved quietly about the room, picking up scattered garments. A thought stabbed through my mind. If I pretended to be asleep she would leave. Then I could steal out and overtake Makalii.

He always rode slowly, listening to the voices of earth spirits talking in grass, trees, rocks, and wind.

Tatsu came to my bed. I did not open my eyes but I felt her love pouring over me as she pulled the covers closer. When she went out my heart beat so hard it felt like a bird inside me, opening and shutting its wings. I knew it was not seven yet because I could hear one of the house-boys setting the table. My ears, trained by Makalii, detected the tiny sounds of silver being carefully placed on linen and of salts and peppers being set at each place.

When I heard Nishi leave, I dressed quickly and stole through the house with its wonderful garden smells caught in curtains and corners. Breathing a prayer to the earth-*akuas* I tiptoed down the steps. Out-of-doors was my kingdom! In it unhappy things never touched me. It was only in houses that I ever felt sad.

Ducking under the garden fence I started running down the path leading to the brood-mare pasture. Dust squirted from under my bare feet, weeds snatched at me, my nostrils were filled with the scent of morning and freedom. I spied Makalii jogging through the hollow toward the magic pasture where sleek thoroughbred mares, with heavy *opus*—bellies—moved about grazing slowly while they waited for the little colts inside them to be born.

A flock of Mynah birds streamed across the sky. Above Haleakala the Cloud Warriors were assembling their forces for combat. I raced along hoping Makalii would stop to pull up a weed which had recently come in with hay from California. Dad had issued orders to everyone that it must be eradicated before it got a grip on the pastures he kept so proudly clean of pests. Makalii halted, dismounted. . . . He had seen a spear of the foreign intruder which must not take possession of our grasslands. Just as he was swinging back into the saddle, I tore up. The look of

mild astonishment and reproof in his eyes stung like a blow but
I flung myself at him.

"Naughty child," he reproved in Hawaiian, but his voice was
loving and gentle.

"Mother was sorry and said I might come," I panted.

"I tink *punipuni*," he announced.

"I'm *not* lying," I protested.

He gazed into my eyes.

"Well, I am," I admitted. "But I'll be spanked again anyhow
for running away, so take me to see the colts. You can tell
Mother you found me on the way home."

Smile wrinkles gathered up the outer corners of his eyes and I
knew I had won. Taking the slicker off the back of the saddle,
he improvised a pad, seated me upon it, and wiped my dust-
streaked, crimson face gently with a bandanna that smelled of
dust and horse-sweat. Its scent revived me. I was no longer just a
bad little girl, I was a *paniolo* riding about the great business of
green pastures and roving herds.

We jogged along slowly. Warm sky above us, feathered creatures darting through the blue overhead, creeping things moving in the grass, trees marching up the vast flanks of Haleakala.
The slow honey of complete happiness poured through me and
I relaxed against the faded blue shirt holding the old man I
loved.

Dismounting on the crest of a hill we sat down on the warm
fragrant earth. About us tall grasses waved in the wind. I knew
the names of most of the varieties Daddy had planted on the
ranch to make bone and muscle in growing creatures. The
Hawaiian grasses: *Kaakonokono, Lauki,* and *Kukai-puaa.* Clover
and bluegrass from Kentucky; *paspalum verbatum* and *paspalum
tillitatum;* Dantonia from New Zealand and the rest.

Feeling Makalii's wise tender eyes on me, all the rage and
frustration of the morning melted away and I was as happy as
young green leaves are when chilly dewdrops cling to their thin

edges. In an inarticulate way I wanted to repay the old fellow for the joy which was always mine when I was with him. Reaching into a bank of *palapalai* fern, I picked young fronds and began braiding them into a *lei*. Makalii watched my clumsy efforts, and when the garland got too disjointed he covered my hands with his old dry ones and guided my efforts.

Removing a *lei* of spicy red carnations, he placed his stained straw hat in my lap. I pressed down the fragrant green circle of ferns and surveyed it critically.

"This time you smart like enny-kind, Ummie," Makalii announced. His eyes were merry but I knew he was not laughing at my bungling *lei*, he was happy because we were together.

Fired by the praise, I suggested that I tell him all the things I could smell, see, and hear, which was a sort of game to me— then. Later I realized that his careful training of my senses made me wealthy in the ways of the earth and close to invisible forces in nature. He considered my blotched face and swollen eyes, then gently shook his head.

"No use make this kind today, Ummie," he said softly. *"When peoples sad, they not very smart.* Better us go look the mares. After by-and-by, maybe this afternoon us listen to the sea and sky and hear what the wind have to tell us."

Placing the gorgeous carnation *lei,* which he had discarded for my ferns, about my neck he got to his feet, lifted me on the horse, and swung up behind.

I rode in a trance reaching down occasionally to touch the horse Nani's reeking shoulder, then sniffed the nice salt smell of her sweat on my fingers. Light rained down on the island, wind flowed out of the east filled with the fragrance of forests growing out of wild wet earth. Green solitudes pulsing with life wrapped us in their magic. Flocks of white butterflies drifted past and the saddle creaked now and then like a lazy cricket.

I listened to the voice of the land, a great voice compounded out of lesser voices: doves cooing in groves of smoke-blue trees, plover whistling overhead, a cow lowing for her calf, the tiny rattle of shaken seedpods in the grass. Then from a swale below came the thin sweet whinny of a mare, followed by a colt's an· swering nicker. The blissful lassitude in my body changed to quick eagerness.

"Where are they?" Makalii asked in Hawaiian.

I studied the tree-filled hollow below, broken by grassy openings. Not a horse in sight. The whinny came again, like a clear bugle call. My trained ear caught the direction and I pointed at the third group of trees to our right.

"There!" I announced.

Makalii's eyes lighted and he nodded. He could not see the mares either, but I knew I was right. A warm tide flowed through me and the sorrows of the early morning were banished.

Makalii lifted Nani into an easy lope that dropped us down the hill and brought us to the grove where twenty brood mares were assembled, discussing horse affairs. They raised their heads as we approached, beautiful docile creatures with satiny coats, long springy limbs, and heavy *opus*. As we drew nearer, a dozen yearling colts streamed away, heads and tails held aloft, fluffy fore-tops lifting to the wind. Makalii halted and they circled back to inspect us, stepping high in the deep grass. He began counting the mares in Hawaiian. "Umph, Coquette no stop," he commented after a while. "Better us go find. Time for her to *haanau.*"

Coquette was Dad's prize thoroughbred. Three of her cups were on the piano and she was due to foal any day. We began scouring the pasture, dismounting once to put fresh salt in a licking-box and later to adjust the float in a water trough. While Makalii worked with it, I pulled off my clothes and dunked gleefully in the translucent oblong of clear water. He dried me off carefully with his bandanna, then held out my pants so I could step into them without getting dust on the little starched ruffles around the legs.

We finally found Coquette in a small opening surrounded by high guava bushes. She was standing with her hind legs on a slight rise, facing the cool wind. Her flanks heaved a little and her shoulders were dark with perspiration. Makalii dismounted hurriedly.

"Wait one minute, Ummie," he said.

Walking over to the mare he stroked her neck gently, then began feeling on each side of her tail. The hard muscles seemed strangely relaxed. Makalii talked to her while he considered her pelvis critically.

"Her baby is starting to come," he said after a minute. "It's her first one. No got time to take you home and come back."

"But I don't want to go away, I want to see the colt born," I protested eagerly.

Makalii looked unhappy. "This-kind hell!" he announced. "Sometimes young race-mare scare the first time she *haanau*— if colt no come easy. Then she run away and maybe lose the baby. Spose I stop with her okay. But might-be Mrs. Louis mad like hell if I let her small *haole* girl see a colt born. I no know what-kind to make."

"I must see it born," I insisted. "Little colts are so cute."

"Hawaiian peoples no care spose kids see this kind. This nature. But English peoples think different." Taking off his hat, he plucked nervously at a jutting fern-frond.

Coquette decided the matter. She began weaving from side to side. Her eyes dilated, her coral-lined nostrils flared. Then she lay down and got up. Makalii knotted his lasso about her neck, rubbing her and encouraging her. He knew exactly what to do and his kindness poured over her as he worked. Once Coquette groaned and I started.

"No scare, no *pilikea*—trouble," Makalii assured me. "First time colt come always little hard. Next time come easy."

While the awesome mystery of birth was in progress, my heart hammered so hard it almost choked me. Once Coquette showed signs of panic and Makalii tied her quickly to a tree so he could give her his entire attention and soothe her at the same time. But occupied as he was he didn't forget me. Every so often he glanced in my direction and made some pleased comment. "Coquette fine, she work swell. . . . Smart like enny-kind." And he would nod in a satisfied way which made the ordeal seem everyday.

When the colt lay on the grass, wet and inert, Coquette turned around. The baby's eyes were closed and it breathed unevenly. Coquette nosed it, shuddered with ecstasy and licked its face until its eyes opened. After a little it heaved clumsily to its feet. It was wet and weak, wobbly and beautiful. Tingling joy streamed through me.

"Oh, Makalii!" I squealed, sliding off Nani and running toward it.

"Wait," he said, catching me. The colt took a few awkward steps. Coquette watched it, then touched its nose with hers, as if she were kissing it. It gazed at her, then began hunting for its breakfast.

"Can I touch it, just once, while it's drinking?" I asked.

Makalii nodded and tousled my head with his kind old hand. I laid my fingers on the small damp rump and the colt gave a tiny kick. Makalii beamed.

"Sassy like enny-kind," he gloated, then slowly the joy ebbed from his face. "Better us go home now. May-be Mrs. Louis never let you ride with me again. But if I go and Coquette lose the baby or have bad-trouble I shame-my-eye because Louis tell to me, 'Never lose one colt since you taking care of the mares.'"

He swung me onto Nani and climbed up behind. By degrees the gravity of his plight penetrated my mind, diluting the wonder of seeing a colt come into the world.

"I won't tell Mother," I announced.

"I no like this lie-cheat kind, Ummie," he reproved. "Better us make some small prayers to the *haole* god Christ and the great

Akua for help us, so Mrs. Louis understand and no take you away from me."

We prayed to both gods and went on. Makalii was very quiet but something inside me kept singing:

> *I saw a colt born! I saw a colt born!*
> *It was little and wet and sweet.*
> *It touched its mother's nose with its nose.*
> *Then it drank from her!*

When we rode into the quadrangle between the Big House, Guest House, and Office, Dad's dripping horse was fastened to the ring in the big eucalyptus tree which no one else ever used.

"*Auwe*—woe is me!" Makalii moaned.

When he dismounted, he moved like a tired old man who has nothing more to live for. Horribly, I realized my running away was responsible for him being like this. Daddy came slashing out of the house, and when he saw us he rushed forward and snatched me into his arms. He burst into a stream of Hawaiian. When he finished Makalii talked to him, his face quivering. Daddy listened with a thoughtful expression in his eyes.

"First Born, I'm going to have to spank you," he informed me. "Mother is half crazy, the ranch is in an uproar and work's been at a standstill while everyone was hunting for you."

He placed a comforting hand on Makalii's shoulder and the old man covered his eyes for a moment. I knew what the gesture signified. To Makalii, Daddy was *Alii*. Then he kissed Dad's hand and held it to his forehead, pledging eternal allegiance. Dad's eyes misted, then he said with a kind of choke in his voice:

"Get about your work, *Ele-Makule*—Old One."

Makalii started for his horse and Daddy carried me into the Office and seated me in the Punishment Chair. His face was stern and sad. Then he began talking. Lumps kept pushing into my throat which I tried to swallow. All the bottles of medicine for men and animals on the long shelves were looking at me. The horse and cattle books, the books about grasses and trees seemed to turn their backs. Branding irons on the door hung their heads. I felt as if I were getting smaller and smaller and farther and farther away until I was only a dot. I wanted to get on Dad's lap but knew when I was in the Punishment Chair I must stay there. Patiently Daddy went over my transgressions until they were clear in my mind.

"It wasn't only running away that was so bad, Ummie. You cheated, pretended to be asleep so Tatsu would go away. Tatsu loves and trusts you, and you betrayed her. After deceiving her, you sneaked off. It got her in wrong with Mother. Makalii would have got in trouble too if he hadn't seen me first. Mother's prostrated with fright and nerve-shock. Ranch business has been held up and I had a bad moment when a *paniolo* on a lathered horse overtook me with Mother's message that you were missing."

I felt sunk and steeped in crime.

"Now do you understand why I must spank you?" Daddy asked.

I nodded. Daddy's spankings never hurt like Mother's because he was never angry when he punished.

"Yes," I choked. "Please spank me quickly and be *pau!*"

4. CIRCUS GIRLS

Long before I was five, I could sit a bareback horse securely but I did not consider myself a rider until Makalii finished the small saddle he had worked on so lovingly for months. It was his present to commemorate my fifth birthday. I had watched him shape the wood for the tree, helped him to prepare the leather from the hide of a wild bull he had roped, scraping the hair off it with a bit of broken bottle, working grease into it, stretching and re-stretching it until it was pliable. When he blew out the last hair-fine strip of leather from the carvings on the *tapaderos* covering the tiny stirrups, we surveyed our handiwork in awed silence. The beautiful creation of carefully shaped wood and hand-tooled leather sat on the grass between Makalii's spread legs. His eyes were moist and my throat ached.

"*Pau*—finished," he said.

"*Pau!*" I echoed.

The saddle symbolized an end—and a beginning, and the solemnity of the occasion grabbed us both. I had graduated from babyhood to childhood. I would no longer ride on a cushion before him but canter beside him on a small horse of my own.

Saturday afternoon excitement charged the atmosphere. Work on week-ends finished about three, and men were putting away gear while they planned the night's fun. Corrals were filled with horses rolling and grunting as they ground the itch of sweaty saddle blankets off their backs. Bullock wagons were trailing up from Kahului, piled with supplies. Dust smoked up from shuffling feet and heavy slow-turning wheels. Teamsters shouted and cracked their long whips. Oxen veered and backed the laden carts up to the warehouses, then stood still with long strings of moisture, like cobwebs, drifting from their mouths to the ground.

From the blacksmith shop came the sound of Sonoda hammering at the last horseshoe he would shape until Monday. Pili, who'd been a whaler and had abandoned the sea to become a *paniolo,* jigged away at his accordion, making the afternoon careless and gay.

The sound of Dad's horse jogging in brought me to my feet. How glad he would be to see my birthday saddle! The afternoon promised beautiful unknown things which left me slightly breathless. Trees stood proudly in the sunshine and their shadows looked holy. Dad swung into view. The flowers on his wide-brimmed straw hat were wilted, Champagne's gray hide caked with dry sweat. Tired dogs, with dust streaking from their eyes, ran ahead to sniff at the wheels of the ox-carts for scents of other dogs who lived at Kahului.

"My saddle is *pau!*" I squealed.

Dad signed that after he'd given the next week's orders to Holomalia, the foreman, he'd be with us. When he came over, Makalii held up the saddle proudly. Dad went over it carefully, felt the pliable latigos, praised the carvings of mangoes, bananas, and cocoanuts twining around the pommel, cantle, tapaderos, and sweat-guards. Makalii beamed, pushed his hat onto the back of his grizzled head and spoke to Daddy in an undertone. Dad bent down and swung me onto his hard arm, and imps played tag with each other in his gay blue eyes.

"Makalii says there's to be a circus in Paia tomorrow. How would you like to ride down on your birthday saddle and see it?"

I had no idea what a circus was and battered Daddy with questions. He explained.

"Can't we go now?" I begged. "Tomorrow is so far away."

Dad shook his head. "We have to go to the Office and pay off the men."

I brightened at once. I loved the Office, especially on Saturday afternoons when it was pay-day. The Office wasn't just a place where bookkeeping was done. It was as romantic and exciting as a Confessional. In the Office, heads were punched for brawling and praise was handed out for work well done. Here men and women confessed failure or achievement and plans were laid for shaping the future.

Dad carried me through the garden where flower beds flaunted their lawless symphonies of color. Makalii trailed at our heels with the precious new saddle. Setting me on the high desk in the center of the room Daddy opened the big black iron safe and took out canvas sacks filled with silver and gold coins which Makalii helped me to pile into neat stacks totaling the wages of each man.

Paniolos began drifting through the garden. They were never in a hurry and seated themselves on the steps in the sunshine waiting for their turns to be called. The whole world seemed to be overflowing with the song of big bell spurs and sumptuous Polynesian laughter. As Dad called out a name one of the men would rise and go into the Office. After receiving his pay, the *paniolo* drew out a medium-sized castor oil bottle and a pint of gin from his pockets and placed them side by side on the table. Then, as though moving through a solemn rite, he took the knife from his legging, beheaded each bottle with a neat tap, brushed the glass into the waste-basket, and with a flourish downed the contents of one after the other, the gin of course coming last.

When Hauki, the dashing young colt-breaker, came in he looked a trifle ill at ease. His black eyes were brilliant with excitement and his black hair seemed to go in laughing waves off his brown forehead.

"Sure I no get too *ona* tonight," he remarked into the air as he beheaded his bottles.

"If you get drunk again, I'll discharge you!" Dad announced.

"Sure, sure, I be good. Only letta-go-my-blouse a little."

"Damn little," Daddy warned.

"Tonight I make Missonary-style," Hauki promised, then gave a great "Ha!" of pleasure as the gin followed on the heels of the castor oil. Taking up his hat, he swaggered off as though he owned the world and intended to do exactly as he pleased with it.

Tatsu called me and I scampered off to be bathed. When Ah Sin brought supper to the "little dining room" where we children ate at night, I babbled about the circus I was going to see. His slant eyes squinched into laughing slits.

"After you come back you make slircus tlick for me," he said, patting my head, then scurried for the kitchen where pheasants and roasts were sending out splendid smells from the oven.

When we were tucked in bed, I was too excited to sleep and kept Gwen and Aina awake with descriptions of circuses which I'd never seen. Stars peeped through dark bending tree-tops and a cold lordly wind swept the sky. In the living room the grown-ups were making merry, for it was a week-end and the house was bursting with guests.

At times when the music stopped or conversations dropped to a lower key, I could hear Daddy and other horse-lovers chanting the pedigrees of racehorses. Mighty names that went into the making of English turf history . . . Isonomy, St. Simon, Flying Fox, Diamond Jubilee . . . the Fisherman, the Clown, Gallopin, Sceptre. . . . Back and back, until they reached the great ancestor of all thoroughbreds, the Godolphin Arab whose name is engraved in gold on the hearts of all real horse-lovers. . . .

From the laborers' camp came the sound of guitars and Pili's accordion. Hauki was shouting and singing. Soon he'd begin dancing *hulas,* then he'd start making love to the other men's wives and sweethearts. A fight would follow, and Daddy would have to rush out in his white flannels and scarlet cummerbund, knock Hauki out, and lock him into the Office until morning.

Gradually I got drowsy. Voices, laughter, and music grew fainter and farther away. When I fell asleep I dreamed of saddles with carved stirrups, of long-dead racehorses, of gin and castor-oil bottles being beheaded, and of girls jumping through paper hoops.

We left about eleven next day for the three-hour ride to Paia. To my delight most of the *paniolos,* their wives, and children went along. Fat Mele-Ann, Holomalia's wife, had a small child on the saddle behind her and her newest baby on a pillow in front. Makalii had decorated my bridle with flowers and had made an extra-special birthday *lei.* Daddy was riding his white fiery polo pony, Maluli, and the world was filled with the brave sound of hoofs, spurs, and laughter.

We set off forty-strong and rode through the tiny town of Makawao with its street-and-a-half of Chinese and Japanese stores. By the time we reached Paia my bare ankles were chafed raw but I scorned the pain. Was I not a *paniolo* riding my own saddle?

As we drew near the railroad track I saw a big brown tent with strong ropes stretching from it. Hundreds of Japanese plantation workers, Hawaiians, and Chinese were milling around it jabbering excitedly. Dad dismounted and lifted me off. Makalii tied the horses in the shade of some *kiawe* trees. Rank animal smells stung my nostrils, smells which seemed to make even the sunlight strange and powerful.

Paniolos swung off their horses. Fat *wahines* slid their children to the ground, then dismounted and shook out their voluminous *holokus*—Mother Hubbards—which had been transformed into a sort of riding costume by pulling the train up between their fat legs and tucking it into a belt. Kids yelled and scattered when weird beings in baggy clothes with dreadful white faces, daubed with red, gestured at them. I clung to Dad's and Makalii's hands. One of the clowns tweaked a lock of my hair. A scream leaped into my throat, but I thought about my saddle and choked it down.

At the tent door a man with a voice that was all hoarse and

worn out was shouting and talking. Daddy paid him money and got back small colored squares of paper with printing on them and we went in. The tent was crammed with people sitting on great benches that went up like steps. A band was playing in a roped-off space and overhead wires stretched like monster cobwebs and a man who looked as small as a bug was swinging among them.

The procession started, headed by the hateful fresh clowns. Tumblers followed them, then two sour-faced camels and a shuffling bear on a chain. Performing dogs walked stiffly by on their hind legs with sweet, jerking fore-paws. Ponies with monkeys on their backs, blinking and making faces, trotted past. Then I saw Them! Girls, in short ruffled skirts which looked like huge pink-and-white hibiscus flowers, sitting with daintily crossed pink legs on the round rumps of fat white horses with tied-down heads. They blew kisses off the tips of their fingers at the yelling crowd and smiled at everyone as they filed slowly past. Their low-cut dresses, sleek bobbing curls, held off their faces by gold bands topped off with a glittering star in the middle, sent blood tingling through my veins.

"When will they stand up and start jumping through hoops?" I asked, bouncing up and down between Dad and Makalii.

"Soon," Daddy promised.

Makalii smiled and held his hat happily between his hands, glad because the three of us were celebrating my birthday in such a splendid way.

Trapeze artists came out, dropped, caught ropes, swung from each other's feet. Trained dogs looking apologetic and foolish did their tricks. The bear went through some stunts. Then They came into the ring. The girls! I caught my breath at their loveliness. They rode bareback, stood upright, dropped off one side of their slowly galloping horses and popped up on the other. They cantered around the ring in pairs, holding hands, and the combed and waved tails of their horses floated out behind like silver threads.

Then the girls bent over, poised, taut, ready to spring. Men ran out and handed hoops to them. Their fluffy skirts looked like ruffly white blossoms. Their pink legs and tight pink behinds left me amazed and when they straightened up strange wrinkles showed in the flesh behind their knees and I concluded that their skin had stretched from bending over so much. . . .

After their act was done, Dad and Makalii took me behind the tent to look at the white horses and stocky little ponies. One of the circus girls passed by.

"A little white child," she said in an amazed way and squatted down in front of me.

Her skirts bent upwards until she looked like a big fairy in the center of a huge up-curving flower. Thick white powder covered her face and I felt as limp as wet macaroni with admiration. She and Daddy talked easily as people do whose lives are mixed up with horses. I heard her asking him about me but did not hear what she said because I kept thinking that, maybe, I'd never be so close to a circus girl again. When she straightened up to go, she drew a ring off her little finger and slid it on my middle one. "That's *my* birthday present to you," she announced, smiling and smoothing down her skirt.

I wanted to thank her, to tell her I'd keep it forever, but my throat wouldn't work so I reached up and hugged her neck tightly. When she kissed me back I was so happy that tears stung my eyes and bubbles rose up and burst inside me. The ring was too large, but Makalii pulled some string from his pocket and wound it around the gold band until it was small enough to stay on my finger.

I rode the long way home in a haze but the ring with three dull blue stones in it proved what I'd seen was real, not just a dream. I was so sleepy I bobbled in the saddle and thought how nice it would feel to be on my pillow in front of Makalii and have his arm hold me. But I was a big girl of five now, I reminded myself, riding my own saddle with the *paniolos.*

By the time we neared home long shadows stretched across the islands and twilight was gathering at the edge of the sea. The sun was sliding to its setting. Small fiery clouds floated above the island of Kahoolawe. Mystery was soaking into everything and stray gusts of wind, like swift-footed predatory animals, prowled down from the summit of Haleakala.

When I got home I rushed from person to person trying to tell them of the wonders I'd seen. Mother had gone to nurse a sick lady at Kaluanui, but Gan's old eyes grew bright and young when I gasped out details of the afternoon and showed her the circus girl's ring. She watched while Tatsu washed my chafed, bloody ankles with creolin and hot water. I felt important, like a racehorse being rubbed down after winning a big race.

Gan was especially mine, as Dad was. . . . When I was quiet long enough, she told me wonderful stories about Nicaragua where she had lived for five years while Granddad von Tempsky got mahogany out of the jungle. Uncle Stanley Bell, her twelve-year-old brother, had been the only other white person in the little settlement of Blewfields when the Major was gone for months up the great rivers felling timber with his Mosquito Indians and floating it down to the sea.

At other times she told me about New Zealand where she'd had a small house with Uncle Randal, Aunt Lina, and Daddy, her three children. When alarms were sent out that Maoris were going to attack she had to run two miles with her little ones through dark scary forests to take refuge with other white women and children in the stockade until the fighting was over. Between wars Granddad would come home for a few days. Then he sat at the piano playing Beethoven Sonatas, or painting at his easel. When his leave was up he went back to fight and was so wild and fearless that he was known to everyone as Terrible von Tempsky.

That night I felt that only Gan was equipped really to appreciate my adventures. After supper, she sat by my bed knitting and smiling while I talked. I knew I was her favorite grandchild and it made me feel rich. She wore little lace caps, shaped like horseshoes, with knotted bows of lavender ribbon tucked into the ruffles. Her wise merry eyes always had a far-off expression, as if behind the things she was saying and doing she was remembering wonderful adventures which had happened to her when she and her three young babies raced around the world trying to catch up with her wild Polish husband.

I told her I intended to be a circus girl when I grew up and she agreed it would be a fine career.

"I'm going to start tomorrow," I informed her. "I'll train Aina to be one, too. We can use Bella and Nigger, the plow-horses. Karamatsu doesn't use them in the vegetable garden on Mondays."

Next morning when I got up Gan had gone to help Mother with the sick lady but I determined to organize my circus anyway. Ah Sin's old face screwed into grinning wrinkles. Tatsu was dubious but I talked her down. When Makalii came for me, I launched into my plans and he said he would help me to stage the big show after lunch was over and his work was done.

About one, he caught Nigger and Bella. I told him to tie ropes around their tummies and to fasten in their heads. Tatsu and Gwen went to the camp to collect *wahines* and their children for the audience. I finally persuaded Aina to be a circus girl, too. The afternoon shook with excitement. Yardboys left their rakes. Ah Sin put on a clean apron in honor of the occasion and found a grandstand seat on the hitching-rail in the quadrangle. Tatsu was almost in tears.

"Maybe you fall off and broke head, then Mrs. Louis torr much mad with me."

"Mother'll be proud to know she has a circus girl for a daughter," I retorted.

Chuckling *wahines* with broods of wide-eyed brown children began trailing in and seating themselves on the outer edge of the quadrangle. Makalii had found two barrel hoops and was decorating them with flowers. I told him to stick flowers in the horses' bridles and around their tummies to improve on the circus we'd seen. Then grabbing Aina's hand I rushed indoors to dress. I scurried to Mother's room to find something which might do for ruffly skirts. My hair was wavy and wouldn't go into dark bobbing curls, but Aina's was just right. When I began emptying bureau drawers of their contents and scattering them on the floor, she watched with amazed eyes. Finally, I found what I wanted, four beautifully pleated organdie collars, edged with lace. Two for each would make a skirt. I began tearing off my clothes. Aina watched. *"Hemo* your *lole-waiwais,"* I directed.

"Mother'll be angry," Aina protested. "Only Japanese and Hawaiian kids go without pants."

"Haven't I seen circus girls' behinds with my own eyes?" I demanded. "It's okay in circuses or Dad and Makalii would have said something."

Large, slow tears spilled down her cheeks as I hauled off her dress and undershirt, but she squeezed her knees together so tightly and sobbed so hard when I tried to strip her bare that I snorted, "Well, wear your pants, coward!"

I tossed one pleated collar to her and wore the other three myself. The effect was breathtaking. We had no gold bands with diamonds on them for our heads; *leis* would have to do.

When we went out the horses were waiting, gorgeous with flowers. Aina's interest revived. *Wahines* sat cross-legged on the grass with their children clustered about them. Yardboys squatted on their hams and four or five *paniolos* home from work early perched on the stone wall.

Old Hu tossed Aina onto Nigger. Makalii set me on Bella's broad back. Grasping his hand I seated myself gingerly on her rump, crossed my legs, and signed to him to lead her around while I blew kisses and bowed to my audience.

Aina watched agog, then imitated me. When I got accustomed to Bella's large slow steps, I whispered to Makalii that I was going to stand up. After two or three unsuccessful attempts I got my balance and Makalii led Bella forward, keeping a wary eye on me. People yelled, cheered, and encouraged me. The afternoon got bigger and bigger, the sun brighter, the sea a deeper blue.

After making the circle without a mishap, Makalii put Bella into a trot, then a slow lope, running beside me and holding my hand. After one round I had to rest and get my breath. I looked at the barrel hoop wreathed with flowers that Ah Sin was holding, wondering if I could manage to jump through it. Whispering instructions to Makalii we started around the quadrangle again. While I assembled my energies, I wished that Gan and Mother would come home in time to see me perform. I signed at Ah Sin. Sliding off the hitching rail he handed up the gay circle of flowers.

"Now you make Number One big slircus tlick and I give you plenty ginger and maybe my toothbrush."

I stooped, balanced, bent over. Thrills ran up and down the bare backs of my legs. I was making a circus behind, tight, round and pink. When I straightened up I glanced at the backs of my knees. They were smooth and flat and I decided I hadn't stretched my skin enough to get creases. I resumed my position, took the hoop, leaped, struck the edge and would have fallen if Makalii hadn't been there to catch me.

Tatsu began crying and begging me to stop. Ah Sin shook with helpless laughter. Hawaiians flung their hats into the air and shouted, *"Welekahao!"* Japanese yelled *"Banzai!"* as if it were the Emperor's birthday.

"Start again, Makalii, I'll do it this time," I insisted.

I balanced, poised, got ready to spring. There was a sound of briskly trotting horses. Turning I saw Pili driving Gan and Mother home. My spirits hit a high. Their arrival was timed to the dot. Snatching the hoop from Makalii, I assumed the correct circus position. "Look at me!" I screamed, bending farther over. "I'm a circus girl!"

I held my pose triumphantly, expecting to see Mother, Gan, and the ex-whaler helpless with admiration. Mother snatched the reins out of Pili's big brown hands, stopped Briton and Banjo, and jumped over the wheel. Her face was scarlet, her eyes blazing. Snatching me off Bella, she turned me upside down and spanked me until she was breathless. The world flew into pieces.

"What have I done that's naughty?" I demanded, sobbing and fighting.

Mother couldn't speak. There were little dark marks along her lower lip where her teeth had dug. She spanked me some more. "You bad, bad little girl," she panted. "Exposing yourself to everyone. How *could* you?"

I tried to tear free to get to Makalii, Gan, Ah Sin, or Tatsu. People began sneaking off as if they'd done something bad. The afternoon which had been so rich and glistening became dark and heavy with Mother's anger, and when I tried sobbingly to tell her about circus girls she told me to be quiet. Without saying a word she carried me into the house. I fought, clawed, screamed until blood roared in my ears.

"I haven't done anything bad, I haven't done anything bad!" I insisted.

Mother kept telling me things, but I couldn't hear. The big house which always seemed to put its arms about you and gather you to its heart, was filled with menace. I was put to bed, fought my way out, got spanked again. The uproar brought Gan in. She spoke gently to Mother and I knew in a faraway manner that she was trying to explain about circus girls. When I was too exhausted to cry or move any more, Mother seated herself in a rocker and watched me in a strange white way that made me cold and shaky inside.

Gan left. I listened to hear Daddy ride in. He could explain because he'd seen a circus. Slow minutes went by. A lonely wind swayed the trees outside the windows. Even God and the earth *akuas* had got so far away that it was useless to pray to them for help. And still Mother sat on, a thinking look in her eyes. I began sinking into the deep place where sleep is. The tight aching knot inside me let go by degrees and the quick sobs jerking me got farther and farther apart.

Voices woke me. Night was outside and stars looked in. Daddy had come home. He and Mother were talking. Mother was crying and her voice was high and hysterical. Daddy waited until she finished speaking, then burst into shouts of laughter.

"But, Von—" Mother said, outraged.

"She thought the pink tights were *skin*," he said when he could speak through his mirth.

I let the sound pour through me; sunshine and wind were in it, hills, horses, and all the things I loved.

5. SHARKS

Most of the stock raised on the ranch was slaughtered locally, but four or five times a year surplus steers were sent to Honolulu to be marketed. Shortly after my fifth birthday Daddy announced that I was old enough to go with him when the next shipment of beeves was made, and not until I went on this expedition did I realize that Daddy and the *paniolos* often risked their lives when they jogged out of my secure world every morning.

For days after I knew I was to go I spent most of my time leaving offerings before *akua* stones, praying to Christ, burning incense before Tatsu's image of Buddha, and lighting candles before the shrines of Portuguese saints to make certain that all the Great Forces would be solidly ranged about me to prevent any possible disaster which might interfere with my going.

The afternoon the steers were due to come down the mountain Makalii took me out to meet them. We spotted the cattle and riders swooping down a green hill. The Herefords reminded me of a swift red river foaming at its edges where their white legs and faces showed. The afternoon shook as they bellowed their fury and bewilderment at being driven from the high grasslands they knew.

Makalii opened the gates into the holding pasture. Daddy galloped ahead of the herd, sitting his saddle in the straight-legged fashion of Hawaii—a beautiful, poised seat suggesting a winged centaur about to take flight and sail off into space. As he passed he brandished his coiled lasso and smiled. Owing to the steep pitch of the land it was impossible to prevent the wild mountain cattle from running. Daddy raced through the gates,

45

maneuvering so the stock would not collide with the posts and bruise themselves.

When they were safely through, he pulled out of their way. They surged across the pasture, belly-deep in grass, slowed up, wheeled around, and collected in a tight knot facing the riders. Holomalia followed Daddy into the pasture and they conferred for a few moments. The rest of the men halted at the gates which Makalii was closing, slacked girths, and shook saddles to cool their horses' hot backs.

Wind scurried down from Haleakala; the sharp sweet whistle of plover sounded overhead. Across the green isthmus joining the two halves of the island, the West Maui mountains stood out distinctly, golden mists hanging in their deep valleys. A sort of elemental excitement, brewed by animals, wind, grass, and drifting clouds, flowed toward me. Makalii had trained my ears to hear the minute sounds of rocks, soil, and vegetation worked on by changes in the atmosphere. I could listen in the dark, and by the sound of the wind name the point of the compass from which it was blowing. I could sense the imperceptible change of one season sliding into the other: a sort of vast, muted rustle in earth, sky, and sea—an instant of altered vibrations, then a great peace, like a sigh, when the transition was completed. In a dim instinctive way I was conscious now of the majestic rhythm of Nature's machinery moving behind tangible objects and, reaching out, I grabbed Makalii's hand.

"What is it?" he asked in Hawaiian.

I looked at Haleakala, at the men and cattle, listened to the majestic dissonances of the Pacific. How could I express even to my old Makalii what I was feeling? But with the amazing intuition of his race he knew. Wrinkles gathered up the outer corners of his eyes.

"Today you feel like an *akua* walking on earth," he said, smiling.

I nodded. He had it exactly. In that moment, I felt immortal,

I was a lesser god with a small niche in the huge swoop of living. During the forty-eight hours while the steers were resting I greased my saddle incessantly. At last the time came to go. I was fed supper and put to bed at four as we were to leave at one in the morning. The trip to Makena was always started at night when traveling was cool and the wild steers were less likely to take fright and stampede at strange sights and sounds.

Gan, Mother, and Tatsu dressed me but I was impatient to be rid of them and go. When Dad came I grabbed his hand and we started for the kitchen. The *paniolos* who were going along were eating at one of the tables. Daddy and I sat down at another and I felt enveloped by lusty manhood. When breakfast was over Ah Sin put a package in my hand. "Open after you stop at Makena," he instructed me.

Tatsu bundled me into a sweater and pulled one of Dad's old hats on my head. Mother and Gan came onto the back veranda, where the spurs and lassos always hung, to see us off. The night wind brought the lonely bellowing of uneasy steers scenting changes ahead and the sound lent the dark an awesome quality. Makalii appeared, put a *lei* on my hat, then, forgetting I was no longer a baby, swung me onto his hip. The night smelled of adventure. Horses humped and shivered when girths were drawn tight. Riders mounted warily. Daddy led off at a swinging trot and Ah Sin waved his lantern in a parting salute.

We stopped at the corrals while one of the *paniolos* drove out Keitchi and Pivela, two wise old oxen, used to escort beef cattle to market. Starlight shimmered on their long horns as they set off, businesslike and cool, knowing exactly what they had to do. Hu and Eole unfastened another gate and extra horses, used only for shipping cattle, followed on the heels of the two oxen. When we got clear of the trees the hugeness of the sky burst upon us. Myriads of stars blazed overhead, some winking and sparkling, others sending down a strong steady light. Spurting matches inside cupped hands threw dark faces into brief relief and the fragrance of cigarette smoke drifted back over men's shoulders.

The bawling of the apprehensive steers grew louder. While Daddy and Holomalia went into the pasture to drive them out, the rest of us lined along the road to head them in the right direction. The two old oxen watched and when the beeves raced out of the gate, like a dark tossing river, they slid into the herd. After a few minutes the steers slowed down to a trot, then to a walk. We moved between wire fences that caught gleams of starlight, and if a steer tried to break through them Keitchi or Pivela dug him with their long horns.

After a while we went through another gate and began moving across open pastures. Men rode taut in their saddles, coiled lassoes ready in their hands, watching every move of the cattle. *Wanaao,* the Ghost Dawn, stole into the sky. When it died down the darkness intensified. Stars enlarged to golden globes, faded to silver. In the direction of Kahoolawe, the Southern Cross burned above the dark sea.

We began working through cactus and *kiawe*-mesquite—covered wastes, and the fairy fragrance of *ilima* and *indigo* and warm animals filled our nostrils. A fresh chill breeze came out of the east and the pale morning sea girdled the islands with silver. Makalii pointed to a small rosy horseshoe of land lying in the channel between Maui and Kahoolawe. He told me the islet was Molokini, a cone that just got its head above water before the fires building it were extinguished.

The coast below us was covered with a dense growth of *kiawe* trees waving their lacy branches in the wind, and here and there cocoanut groves lifted their glittering green into the sunshine. A purple cone, like a boil, jutted into the sea at the southern end of Haleakala.

"That's Puuolai, the Hill of Earthquakes, where the last activity of the mountain took place," Daddy told me.

A little shiver ran over me. The cone looked so strong and

violent that it seemed as if at any minute it might begin spouting lava again. I asked about a three-storied house, miles away, standing on the shore without any other buildings about it.

"That's Kalepolepo, an abandoned store built in the Fifties when the Pacific whaling fleet used to anchor each winter off Maui," Daddy said. "It's a strange old place with tall rooms looking onto the sea. In one of them upstairs is a magnificent piano and below on the shelves of the store you still find bolts of calico and other things which have lain there through the years."

The steers were following the lead-oxen down the rough lava trail, but, every so often, one of the big wild fellows would halt to look back at Haleakala. A gaunt sow, grunting ill-humoredly at her piglets, appeared suddenly out of the cactus and crossed the trail. Without warning the cattle stampeded. Most of them headed upward, making a last mad dash to regain their lost mountain pastures. The still morning echoed with shouts, curses, and the sharp reports of running hoofs striking against loose fragments of lava.

I tore after Makalii. Cactus pads slapped savagely at my bare legs; I ducked my head to escape thorny *kiawe* branches. My horse dodged about to avoid spiny *indigo* bushes. Several times I was almost unseated and had to grab at the pommel, hoping that everyone was too occupied to see. Dad shouted commands, men dashed here and there trying to head the stock off and turn them back to the sea.

A big roan steer with spreading horns tore clear of his massed comrades and streaked away, Hauki racing in pursuit. Because of the high growth of cactus, ropes were useless except in infrequent openings. When the big steer realized that the horse was overtaking it, it swerved and charged. Hauki wrenched his mount onto its hind legs. One horn grazed Hauki's stirrup but the impetus of the beast took it past. With a deft turn of his wrist, Hauki threw his lasso over his shoulder, wheeled around, flung his horse to its haunches and braced back. The steer reached the end of the rope, turned head-over-heels and lay still, the wind partially knocked out of it.

After a furious ten minutes the herd was collected, hot-eyed, panting, with cobwebs of foam drifting from their mouths. Keitchi and Pivela, the old oxen, who had waited in the trail during the uproar, circled disgustedly among the beeves, quieting them, while we sat in a ring waiting until the animals cooled off enough to push on to the sea.

Finally, the herd was put in motion and we picked up a faint road winding under tall cocoanut trees which moved forlornly in the light air coming off the dancing blue water. The bulk of Haleakala above and behind us cut off the cool Trade-wind. Horses' hides were dark with sweat, men mopped their hot faces. My cheeks burned, my ankles were raw, and one bare knee ached dully from a broken-off cactus spine buried in it.

Daddy led the steers into a big stone corral and they crowded and jostled to get at a long dripping water trough. When they were all inside the enclosure, the old oxen came out and drifted off through the grove while two of the *paniolos* lashed a stout gate across the entrance. The spare horses nipped at tufts of *pualeli*—milkweed—growing at the bases of cocoanut trees and the morning seemed to exhale a sigh of relief and settle back into its peaceful warmness.

Paniolos unsaddled their horses, then went behind the stone wall to get out of their clothes and put on *malos*—breech-clouts. Makalii showed Dad the thorn in my knee and they knelt down to remove it. I shut my eyes. There was a sharp stab and it was out. Makalii took a small bottle of creolin out of his pocket, mixed it with water, and washed the small dark hole.

Eole, Pili, and Kahalewai were humping up long brown trunks, racing each other to reach clusters of green nuts hanging among feathery fronds. Eole got to the top of his tree first and shouted jibes at Pili and Kahalewai. Taking the knife out of his teeth he cut among the drooping leaves and great green nuts came bouncing down. The men on the ground ran to get them like big children on a lark. Makalii brought the finest one to Daddy and got the next best for me.

"Now you look close and I show you how to fix," he said, squatting on the ground. I edged up close. Turning the long green nut up in his hands so the end that grew on the tree faced the ground, he began bruising it against a stone until the fiber was pulverized. Bit by bit he stripped away the green outer covering, then went after the layers of tough white fibers underneath. When the last piece was off he began turning the nut around in his hand, striking it with short sharp taps on the stone, and suddenly the top cracked off like a neat cap.

"Drink," he said, placing the cool, fragrant chalice in my hands.

When I had all I could hold of the sweet fresh water, he broke the soft shell open and we scraped out the jello-like meat with our fingers.

The men fetched small canvas bags filled with salt meat and hard *poi* which, with the cocoanuts, make breakfast. Hauki saddled a fresh horse and went off to see if the steamer was in sight, and the rest of the men began working at a half-finished water trough. They uncovered concrete, mixing buckets, and some dynamite, stored under a tarpaulin.

"I'm going to blast out another well one of these days so there'll always be ample water for the cattle," Daddy told me.

I watched the men working and joking together but the warm morning made me drowsy and, in spite of my best efforts, people and trees began getting dimmer and farther away. When Hauki rode in I woke up.

"No more steamer," he announced.

Daddy swore, then lighted his pipe. "Last time the blasted boat was two days late and the cattle lost weight. But since nothing can be done about it we might as well have some fun while we're waiting."

The *paniolos'* eyes met his gaily. Dad knew that when Hawaiians have worked hard for a while they want to lay off for some fun. Dad and Holomalia volunteered to watch the cattle while the rest of us went to spear fish and gather *opihis* —edible limpets—for supper.

We drifted along the beach curving toward the Hill of Earthquakes. Through leaning brown cocoanut trunks, waves with crests of emerald and azure crisped toward the shore, or tore their blue into white lace against rough out-juttings of lava. The day had a breathless beauty that made me feel as though I were standing on tiptoe inside. When we reached the base of the big, angry-looking red hill I kept close to Makalii. Its name was frightening and the deep restless Pacific swelling against black lava ledges and falling back from them with sucking noises whispered about eerie things. Small eels hurtled through the air from warm brackish pools among the rocks where they'd been basking, and vanished into the safety of deep water.

Pili got a spear and a long pole out of a crevice where he kept them and went on ahead to look for squid and *ulua*— cavalla fish. The other men began searching among the rocks. Some gathered *wana,* a species of sea-urchin, and Makalii broke a hole in the top of one of the brittle shells and showed me how to suck out the meat which tasted like salty marrow. Other *paniolos* were gathering *limu*—a flat reddish seaweed that crunched crisply and pleasantly between my teeth.

Makalii gave me his legging knife and showed me how to gather *opihis*. I'd eaten them at *luaus* but never had the fun of collecting them. Watching for ones that weren't clamped down tightly, he slid the knife under them and pried them off quickly. After a few tries I got the knack of it and scooped them from their shells, eating them as we drifted along the shore.

Pili beckoned to us. *"He'i!*—squid!"—he shouted excitedly.

Makalii and I rushed up to him. In a clear pool at Pili's feet a waving tentacle showed. "You like see close-up?" he asked. I nodded.

Lowering the pole gently into the water, Pili touched the moving arm and it wrapped about the wood. He jiggled the pole, teasing the octopus, and another long slimy feeler came out and took hold. After a minute all the long arms were wrapped about the stick, then he drew the squid gently toward the edge of the pool so I might see it in detail. Its body, about the size of a small cocoanut, was like a dirty gray sack. Fiery round eyes gazed up hideously. Pili shook the pole; the squid retained its hold but began changing from a slate gray to red with black mottlings.

"He's *huhu*—mad," Pili chuckled, raising his right arm quickly. Feeling the menacing gesture the squid began to un-writhe, but Pili drove the spear into its body and the pool clouded with the sepia it ejected. With incredible swiftness long tentacles rushed up Pili's arm and wrapped tightly about it. I recoiled. Seizing the hideous squirming mass with his free hand, Pili bit the squid between the eyes and its hold began relaxing. Then, nonchalantly, he stripped the tentacles with their horrid sucking cups off his skin.

"In Kakiki and Samoa there are *he'i* with arms twenty and thirty feet long," he told me. "Once in their grip a man is lost. But if you can manage to spear them before they get hold of you you can hear them moan and cry until the hair stands up straight on your head."

Squatting down, he began cutting off the yard-long tentacles. "Tonight I stew in cocoanut milk," he smacked his lips. *"He'i* more good from lobster or crab but *haoles*—white fellas—no like eat because they so ugly."

Stuffing his catch into the bag tied about his brawny middle he straightened up. "Now us go look the place where the big *ulua* feed at half-tide." He measured the water with expert eyes and nodded in a satisfied manner. Securing his spear to his wrist with a long cord he began sneaking along, peering over the black lava ledges. Presently he pointed at a silver streak fathoms below. *"Ulua!"* he whispered excitedly.

The big fish was cruising back and forth, gradually working toward the surface. Peering down through translucent blue depths I saw *wana* like huge orange and vermilion cactus-dahlias blossoming on rough ledges and schools of small brightly-colored fish nibbling at invisible growths on the coral. Presently a flock of tiny black-and-white striped *maninis* came flitting through the water. Pili froze. The big *ulua* sighted the prized delicacy, flashed, and the flock of little fish exploded in all directions. Pili hurled his spear and braced back. The line tied to his wrist whanged taut and the water was thrown into terrific confusion as the yard-long *ulua* raced back and forth, diving and plunging to get free.

Makalii locked his arm through Pili's and they danced and teetered along the edges of the rocks. I was afraid that the *ulua* might pull them in, but after some breath-taking minutes it began losing strength and came to the surface. One moment it was electric blue, the next like a silver-white palm leaf flashing and turning from side to side. Finally it lay over limply and after a tussle Pili and Makalii landed it. It slapped at the rocks viciously with its tail until Pili struck it a blow on the back of its head. It arched over, stiffened, quivered, and the light went out of its scales.

When we rejoined the other *paniolos* who were prowling among the wet rocks, their eyes lighted. *"Ulua! Ulua!* Fine!" they shouted, crowding up to examine the yard-long fish hanging from the spear on Pili's shoulder.

When we got back to the corrals with our bags of plunder and the royal *ulua*, Holomalia had a fire going and Dad was smoking his pipe, a sort of lazy happiness wrapped around him. Some of the men began cooking, others spread a tablecloth of glittering young cocoanut fronds on the clean sand. I undid the package Ah Sin had given me and handed two brightly colored cardboard boxes of Chinese cocoanut candy and a green jar of ginger to Makalii.

"For the *luau*—feast," I said, and his kind face beamed because Hawaiians like to share everything with those around them.

"While supper cooks we'll go for a swim," Dad announced.

Makalii undressed me and made a sort of *malo*—breech-clout— out of his red bandanna. I felt quite grown up and like the brown *paniolos* heading for the sea. As they went into the water they struck it with their cupped hands, sending long hollow echoes traveling across it.

"Why are they doing that?" I asked.

"There's no reef here and the sound scares sharks away," Daddy said.

I drew back.

"No need scare," Makalii said, grinning.

Paniolos were swimming around, laughing and splashing. I hesitated and Daddy squatted down beside me. "First Born, if you want a rich full life you've got to gamble sometimes. As a whole, sharks in these waters are cowards. Now and then a school of *Niiuhis*—Tiger Sharks—cruise in from the South Pacific; then you've got to watch out."

I swallowed.

"*Niiuhis* are real man-eaters and will even attack canoes. At night their eyes are phosphorescent and when fishermen out laying nets see them they paddle like fury for land. I've only run into *Niiuhis* twice during all the years I've lived in Hawaii."

My stomach felt full of butterflies. I wanted to go into the water dancing in from the sky but fear glued my feet to the sand. Daddy looked at me in an odd way and dived in. The *paniolos* shouted, "*Hele mai*—Come, come!"

Shutting my eyes I dashed in, took a few strokes, then turned and swam frantically for shore. Everyone laughed, making my fright just a joke. Soon I was swimming between Daddy and Makalii, and the silken beauty of the ocean washed all other thoughts from my mind.

By the time we came out the afternoon was beginning to die. Clouds waited above the loneliness of the sea like great white birds with their heads hidden under folded wings. With lazy dignity and the unthinking grace of Polynesians, the *paniolos* went about getting supper. I was drugged with sunshine and my body had the fulfilled happy feeling of land after it has been soaked with rain. The grove was filled with shadows but the fire threw ruddy lights on the men crouching around it.

Pili got out his worn accordion, Kahalewai produced a ukulele. Everyone began singing the old cowboy *hula* about the *paniolos* living on the Great House of the Sun. The music had the swagger and swing of our wide careless life, a life with *akuas*—gods— moving in it to give it majesty, and lurking dangers to give it spice. I sat between Dad and Makalii while the song poured richly through me. When it was ended Hauki took the ukulele and sang *Wahine Ui,* Beautiful Woman. His eyes looked hot and wet, and I knew he was thinking about his newest sweetheart as his long slender hands moved lovingly across the small instrument he held to his breast. When he finished, Pili made a remark in Hawaiian, under his breath, that sent everyone into shouts of laughter. Hauki looked pleased and embarrassed, then returned the ukulele to Kahalewai. Moku shouted *"Kaukau!"* and everyone forgot about music and went after food.

I sucked *wana,* crunched seaweed and *opihis,* ate great golden-white flaky pieces of *ulua,* drank cocoanut milk, and last of all passed Ah Sin's ginger and candy around. My skin was hot from sunburn, my eyes heavy. Makalii spread his slicker on the sand.

"I don't want to go to sleep," I protested.

"No need *moemoe,* just lie down," he suggested, smiling.

The slicker felt nice and cool against my burned arms and

Makalii's fingers moved soothingly over my hot forehead. No one was anxious to end the fun. I heard Dad and the *paniolos* discussing work and talking about ancient times before white men invaded the scattered island groups of the Pacific. I wanted to share it all but despite my best efforts the thick dark curtain of sleep kept descending, shutting off firelight flickering on bulging muscles and flat backs, and on horses moving like shadows through the grove.

When I opened my eyes again light was stealing across the sea. The morning was as fragile and as sacredly beautiful as the first one of Creation. A pearl-and-silver dawn was lying in the sky and the mountains were steel blue and sharp. Pili was making coffee, Hauki riding off to see if the steamer was in sight. Men were coughing, clearing their throats, stretching and scratching. When the waking-up was over they lighted cigarettes. Moku rounded up the shipping horses and drove them into a rail-enclosure. Eole, Hu, and Kahalewai were coiling up ten-foot lengths of manila rope and placing them on the top of the stone corral where restless steers were shifting back and forth. By the time Hauki returned breakfast was ready.

"No more steamer," he announced.

"Blast it!" Dad said, then held out his cup for coffee.

After we'd eaten, Makalii saddled our two horses and took me to see an old *heiau*—temple—at the base of the Hill of Earthquakes, just beyond the point where Pili had speared the *ulua* the day before. Reverently we inspected the square heap of black stones. "In this temple *kahunas* prayed and offered sacrifices in old times," Makalii said in Hawaiian. "This was the temple of the Shark God where fishermen made offerings before putting out to sea."

Suddenly the mirror-like morning was split by wild shouts from the cocoanut grove. We wheeled and saw the whole herd of steers bolting for the sea. With great splashings they plunged into the water and began swimming off in the direction of

Kahoolawe. We raced to our horses, Makalii threw me into my saddle, vaulted onto his horse and we tore along the beach. *Paniolos* on saddleless horses were shooting out of the grove. Daddy's commands sounded like rifle-shots. Makalii's horse flattened into a run and my pony Haki laid back her ears trying to keep up.

"Stop here," Makalii ordered as we neared the grove. "I go *kokua*—help!" and he dashed into the blue water.

The steers were swimming steadily toward the distant red island. The black dots which were their heads had long ripples like V's running out from each side. Men were swimming their horses after them, Daddy on Champagne well in the lead.

A steer's head disappeared. "It's drowning," I thought, my heart pounding. Another head went under. The swimming men began striking the water with their cupped hands. Sharks! The quiet morning which had been so utterly lovely, became a chaos of horror. A third steer vanished. Panic seized the herd. They wheeled, milled, collided, tried to climb on each other's backs. *Paniolos* shouted to each other, striking the sea fiercely with their arched hands, sending long hollow sounds across it.

Breath jammed in my lungs. Daddy, Makalii, all these people and animals I loved, would be torn to pieces by sharks with cruel blunt snouts and wicked wedge-shaped mouths. I wanted to scream but my throat muscles were paralyzed. The panic in the water increased. Horses plunged, fought, reared, their eyes rolling wildly. Men cursed and yelled, steers shook their horns and sent dull unhappy bellows across the sea.

After milling and wheeling, the majority of the herd headed back for land. Makalii came splashing out of the water and raced along the beach, trying to head the cattle toward the corrals. A steer heaved onto the sand, followed by others. Streaming sides flashed in the sun, horns looked wild and strong. The animals collected in knots, debating which way to charge. Enemies in the water, enemies on land! They looked desperate and distracted, ferocious, and forsaken by all their gods.

Daddy raced out of the sea and Makalii galloped back and forth, swinging his lasso to turn the desperate beeves. Moku dashed for the cocoanut grove and reappeared with Keitchi and Pivela. The old oxen looked disgusted but slid among the frantic steers to quiet them.

Eight or ten of the cattle were still swimming around in the bay. Dark muddy spots stained the blue water around some of them. Two disappeared, came to the surface, and were pulled under again. The rangy steer who had started the stampede the previous morning came lurching up the sand. A great hole in his side poured blood and he kept looking at it in a bewildered manner as he ran to rejoin his mates.

Daddy and Holomalia dashed into the water to rescue the five steers whose white faces showed swimming in a circle a short distance from land. Striking the water, yelling in voices which sounded as loud and commanding as *akuas,* Daddy and Holomalia approached them. One steer was pulled under just as Dad got to it, but he and his foreman headed the rest to shore and they finally heaved onto the safety of the land.

I shook in my saddle. My bones felt like jelly and my stomach was empty and tight. The *paniolos* closed in on the animals moving in a restless ring on the trampled beach. I wanted to go to Daddy or Makalii but was afraid that if I moved the steers might stampede again. After what seemed hours, and which was probably only a few minutes, the men, with the old oxen's help, got the herd headed toward the corrals. The steers moved forward, taut and nervous, ready to bolt if a butterfly's shadow crossed their trail. When they were finally inside the stone fence and the gate was fastened, I started forward.

The sand was torn up and a long gory trail showed where the roan steer had been. I kept thinking of the cattle the sharks had eaten and I sobbed. When I rode up, Dad looked as if he didn't know who I was. His eyes were filled with man-thoughts: work and danger. All the other men's faces had the same expression. I felt like a person left out of the world and wailed like a puppy which has been tramped on. Daddy came to me, his strong arm swept me off my horse onto his and, all at once, I had him and everyone back again. When I stopped crying we were on the ground and Daddy held a wet handkerchief to my head.

"Steady, *paniolo*," he said.

The word jerked me back to my senses. "But the poor steers that got killed––" I said.

"They're with the Great *Akua* now."

"What made them stampede?"

"They were restless from waiting so long. A cocoanut frond fell with a rushing noise into the corral and they jumped the stone wall and bolted."

I held tightly to Dad and swallowed. He never talked to me as though I was a baby, but treated me like a grown-up and it made me want to be steady and brave, as he was.

"What about the roan steer?"

"The boys killed him, he's out of his misery."

Holomalia shouted, "*Hele mai*"—coming!—and pointed at the steamer, which was just pulling into sight beyond the Hill of Earthquakes.

"Will you and the boys have to go into the sea again?" I asked shakily.

"Of course, but those blasted sharks aren't going to get any more of my cattle," Daddy said, his jaw getting square. "Usually sharks cruise singly but that was a school of them this morning."

Calling the men together he talked to them in Hawaiian. They looked bothered and pleased and I knew they'd agreed to do something which, though it half scared them, made them glad at the same time. Pili hauled back the tarpaulin covering the dynamite. Daddy glanced at the rapidly approaching steamer, then at the corral full of steers.

"I'm going to risk it," he announced, and taking my hand headed for the beach. Pili went to the last rock jutting into the bay and hurled something far across the water. There was a dull explosion underneath.

"What was that?" I asked.

"Dynamite to stun the sharks and scare them away." Dad's mouth shut into a hard line.

"Why don't you always use it?"

"It's illegal to dynamite fish. Sharks are fish but in this instance dynamiting is justifiable."

Pili hurled in another charge, then we walked back to the corrals and I knew as dogs know such things that Daddy didn't want to talk about it any more. When we reached the corrals the boys were in short dungarees and had their stripped shipping saddles on their horses. The steamer dropped anchor about half a mile offshore and the morning got underway once more.

A whaleboat was lowered and began coming in. Dad went into the corrals and maneuvered among the steers. The boat anchored about fifty feet from the beach and the sailors called out greetings. Holomalia and Eole guarded the open gate of the corral. When everything was ready Dad roped a steer about the horns and dashed out, Hauki galloping beside the captive. They rushed across the beach at full speed and hit the sea. A great splash went up into the air, then they began swimming for the boat. Flinging the manila rope, which was about the steer's horns, to one of the men in the boat, Daddy wheeled. The man threw a fresh rope to him and he swam back to the beach.

The men worked in pairs, perfectly and without mishap. Dad and Hauki, Pili and Moku, Hu and Kahalewai. Makalii explained details which I didn't understand. The boat had to anchor far enough out so the struggling cattle couldn't get their feet on the bottom and tear free. Eight animals on each side constituted a boatload. When it had its quota it was drawn back to the ship by a long rope as oars could not be used with the animals floating on each side. When it reached the ship the cattle would have a sling put around them and be hoisted aboard.

The work was rhythmic. Rope, rush, splash, throw, catch, tie . . . then the swim back. Men's shoulder muscles flashed, showers of spray winked in the sunshine, horses came out of the water like wet, sleek seals. As each loaded boat was drawn back to the ship, another took its place. While sailors and *paniolos* worked they held a shouted conversation, punctuated by quick orders when some steer proved troublesome and unruly. There were good-natured insults about the invariable unpunctuality of the steamer. There were explanations . . . A big surf had been running at Kawaihae and the Parker Ranch had shipped a hundred and fifteen head. Regrets were expressed for the steers which the sharks had got. And so forth. . . .

Finally, the last steer was lashed by its horns to the boat. Farewells sounded across the widening strip of water. The steamer blew its whistle. Tired men spilled off tired horses, pulled off their saddles and the horses rolled luxuriously in the moist sand while the men slaked their thirst from green cocoanuts. Sunlight poured down on sparkling blue water. Clouds drifted overhead like white squadrons of ships cruising forever southward to islands lying below the curve of the earth.

Makalii came to me and looked into my eyes. "You like go inside water on a horse like a *paniolo?*" he asked.

I wanted to, it looked beautiful, the horses breasting waves with their tails floating out behind like spreading fans. But I thought of the sharks and hesitated.

"I take you behind me on Nani, if you like to go," Makalii said.

I was torn between doubt and desire, then I remembered what

Daddy had said, that if a person wanted a rich full life they had to take risks sometimes.

"Yes," I said finally.

Makalii's eyes lighted. "Good girl!" he announced, and reaching down pulled me up behind him.

6. I MEET A MAGDALENE

ONE AFTERNOON as I sat on the warm grass helping Makalii to prepare rawhide for a new lasso, Gan came slowly and heavily across the vivid lawn and halted beside us. "Ummie, you're a very small girl, just a little over five, but you've got to learn to read and write quickly."

"Why?" I asked.

She did not reply for an instant, but gazed thoughtfully across the highly colored reaches of the island. Then she said in a dry voice, "I'm leaving for New Zealand in six months. You've got to learn to write letters to me and read mine."

"Why do you have to go?" I asked indignantly.

"I have a daughter and four grandchildren there. It's their turn to have me."

"Daddy and I love you more than they do."

She smiled. "I know it, but I'm getting old and—" breaking off, she gazed at cloud-shadows lying like sunken islands on the blue breast of the Pacific. Something vaguely frightening brushed me. What was she thinking about that kept her so still?

"I don't want you to go away, Gan," I insisted. "I'll have nobody to tell me about Granddad."

"After you learn to read I'll send his book 'Mitla' to you," she promised. "It's full of drawings and paintings he did, of Indians, fighting, Aztec ruins and"—she smiled faintly—"of beautiful Señoritas."

Every afternoon, after that, Makalii brought me home early and Gan taught me at a small table under the Pride of India tree. She told me first about the *paniolos* of other lands; the *gauchos* of South America, who used bolas—two round balls on each end of a rawhide—which they whirled around their heads and threw at the feet of animals they wanted to catch; about Mexican *vaqueros* who had taught Hawaiians the art of horsemanship, whose bits and saddles were inlaid with silver; of the stock-riders of Australia and New Zealand who rode on flat saddles after cattle and used long, echoing whips; of the cowboys of the American West who had guns strapped to their hips instead of wearing knives in their leggings as *paniolos* did. . . .

After a few days I'd pounce on colored spots on the map, my imagination afire with her word-pictures. "There's South America where *gauchos* are swinging *bolas;* that's Australia where whips are cracking; this is the West where American cowboys are shooting; and this dot is Hawaii."

Gan had the ability to make even dry tasks an adventure. I speedily mastered the alphabet, learned to scrawl my name, then Aloha. Makalii would be speechless with admiration when I traced the letters I knew in the dust of the corrals while he saddled Nani for himself and Haki for me. "You smart like hell, Ummie," he'd tell me. "After by and by you write hot-style letters to Gan."

That was the rub behind the thrill of my new accomplishment, knowing that someone I loved was going to be taken from me. When I attempted to think of life without Makalii, Ah Sin, Gan, Daddy, or Tatsu a sort of panic filled me but Gan, like Daddy, had the power to steady me.

"You mustn't cry," she insisted, when I occasionally verged on tears. "When you're older I'll come around the world and meet you."

"Where?"

Gan thought for a moment. "Red's your pet color. How'd you like to meet me at the Red Sea?"

Was there really a red sea, I wanted to know? Gan showed it to me on the map. "The water isn't red but looks that way sometimes because red seaweed floats on it." I was intrigued. Okay, that was a promise, I agreed, we'd meet at the Red Sea. . . .

Then swiftly, as such things happen, the six months before she sailed slid toward their finish. I was informed that Mother and my sisters and Tatsu were leaving for Honolulu in two weeks. Daddy and I were to stay at the ranch and accompany Gan while she paid farewell visits to Maui friends.

The first morning I woke up without Tatsu there to dress me, I felt as though one of the main props of my immediate world had been rudely removed. I missed the cozy smell of her clean cotton kimono and her smile, but Gan called me to her room and I had tea in bed with her.

"Now you can help *me* to dress," she told me. "You see it's difficult for me to put on my stockings and shoes. Tatsu always helped me, but you can be my little handmaid while we're visiting. I've got friends at Waikapu, Wailuku, and other places whom I must see."

"Who're we going to see first?" I asked.

"Old Billy and Young Billy."

I knew they lived at Waikapu and had even more racehorses than we had and I could hardly wait to get started. Daddy arranged ranch work so he could be free to accompany Gan on her round of farewells.

We left for Waikapu at the foot of the West Maui mountains early one morning. Waikapu means Forbidden Waters and the name thrilled me. Makalii drove Gan in the dog-cart, Daddy and I rode on each side. The long hot trek across the cane-covered isthmus, which joined together the two halves of the island, took hours. Afternoon lights were creeping into the deep-cleft valleys of the West Maui mountains when the sweating horses started climbing their lower slopes. Gan was as gay as a girl. Daddy joked. There seemed a tacit conspiracy between them that no sorrow of parting must mar their last jaunts together.

We drove through the small town of Wailuku. Spreading *kamani* trees leaned over shrubbery-smothered cottages. Rustling rivulets banked with fragrant ginger blossoms and four-o'clocks flashed on each side of the streets. A straggling cemetery with Japanese writing on the graves climbed up the sandhills and Dad said on Ghost-Night the place was beautiful with paper lanterns and filled with food and flowers for the spirits of the departed who were privileged to return to earth on that night. Fat old Chinamen, watching their littlest grandsons crawling around on the ground, sat outside their stores which sent spicy odors into the street. A sugar mill filled the air with vast vibrations and the heavy, sweet odor of molasses being boiled weighted the afternoon. In the yards about the mill with its great smoking stacks and rumbling machinery, teams of mules, driven by blue-clad Japanese, strained at cars loaded with ruddy-stalked cane. . . .

Daddy told me the name Wailuku meant Bloody Water. When Kamehameha set out to conquer the Islands he started with Maui and after terrific fighting drove the Maui chieftain, Kahikili, and his valiant warriors back from Hana toward the West Maui mountains. The Maui men made a last desperate stand against the overwhelming masses of Kamehameha's army at the mouth of Iao Valley, just back of the town through which we were riding. The Maui men resisted so savagely that the river was dammed with corpses and flowed red for several days. Hence the name, Wailuku.

Leaving the town behind, the road skirted savage ranges that cut at low drifting clouds. Dark valleys, swathed with a thousand shades of green, retreated into mysterious mazes of ridges, eroded by the winds and rains of time. Vivid green cane fields wedged back into the foothills and sparkling water poured along wooden flumes and ditches.

Finally, the road ducked toward a dark valley whose walls rushed up into the clouds. It looked forbidding despite its breathtaking beauty. Daddy told me that when people went to the head of Waikapu they must not speak above a whisper. Echoes traveling upward through the narrowing walls frightened bands of wild goats that lived on the cliffs and they went rushing away, sending boulders crashing down into the stream that wound its way along the bottom.

A short distance from the sheer walls of rock which made a sort of awesome portal, a sprawling house sat on a low hilltop surrounded by Norfolk Island pines. Purple mango trees and dark pointing fingers of Italian cypresses flanked brick walks which leaped down through terraces of gay flowers in wide steps to meet the road. A feeling of excitement poured from the house though no people were visible. Curtains moving in and out of open windows with the Trade-wind created an impression that the structure was breathing. Then a laugh like the chime of golden bells poured through the afternoon, making it spill over with richness.

"Helen!" Dad and Gan exclaimed, looking at each other delightedly.

Helen . . . as long as I live I'll always feel that Helen is the most beautiful name a woman can wear. A tall girl in a vermilion kimono flashed out of a door and came running down the path between the flowers. Before she reached us I knew she was part Hawaiian, although her skin was creamy white as a gardenia. There was a soft bloom to it and her laughter held cadences that only come from Polynesian throats. Long black hair, curling at the edges, spilled over her shoulders as she darted like a bright flame through the afternoon.

Makalii helped Gan out of the dog-cart and the girl swept her into her arms, kissed her, then wiped her brimming brown eyes.

"It's silly to cry, but I'm so happy to see you, Gan," she said. "Uncle Bill Calhoun wrote saying you were leaving soon for New Zealand, so I came over. We'll have fun, all of us together again."

Tears winked on her long curling lashes, and her hair, moving in the wind, caught the sun. Then she said, "Von," in a voice that made me feel as if a thin silver wire had pierced me. Coming over to where he sat on his horse, she laid her hand on his knee and looked up. He bent and kissed her gently. She kissed him back, then came to me in her quick fluid way. "Ummie," she said, her voice getting warm and indulgent as Hawaiian voices always do when addressing children. I gazed at her spellbound.

"Now come on in. I'll wake everyone." Laughter rippled from her throat. "We played poker all night. And drank. Dick and his new *haole* wife came over from Hana." Her eyes shuttled from Gan to Dad, and she laughed again. "And dear Uncle Bill Calhoun celebrated seeing you, Gan, ahead of time, and—" She gestured expressively.

When we got in the house a big booming voice called from a room, "Who's there, Helen?"

She led the way into a spacious room filled with pictures of racehorses and women. A jowled man lay in the four-poster, propped up on a quantity of pillows. Going over, Helen laced her fingers warmly through his thick purple ones. He greeted Gan and Daddy vociferously, pinched my cheek, and shouted for drinks. While the grown-ups sipped from tall glasses filled with clinking ice, I sat in a chair sucking sweet soda from a bottle which Helen instructed a Japanese house-boy to fetch me. When I could get my eyes off her I watched the old man.

He was lavender and worn-out but I sensed he was a great figure. His conversation was punctuated with damns, shouts, and "Let's hoist another!" Open-armed, open-hearted, he seemed to embrace life as it came toward him. From laughing remarks which made the atmosphere of the bedroom as heady as a party, I absorbed the fact that thoroughbreds' hoofs had beaten a tattoo on his heart and women's perfume gladdened his nostrils.

After a while, Helen rose. Whenever she moved, even slightly, invisible fires seemed to accompany her. "These dear people must want baths, Uncle Bill," she reminded him.

"Demmit, of course! But hurry back, Helen, when you're around life's a fine song. And get the rest of the household up. We got to begin celebratin'." The tired look went out of his old brown eyes and he seemed like a huge, merry boy thinking of pranks. Helen kissed his jowled cheek and touched his head with her rosy palm.

Footsteps sounded in the hall. "Dick and Di," Helen said. Uncle Bill grimaced roguishly at the last name but when a tall handsome man walked in, his eyes were fond.

"Hi, son, sleepin' when friends arrive. What's this generation comin' to? Only Helen, she's always on deck."

The woman with Dick looked as if she were locked inside herself and distrusted everyone. Her high cheekbones were sprayed with fine color and her eyes seemed not to see Helen where she stood by Uncle Bill. Then noticing the highball in Uncle Bill's hand she bustled forward.

"Your heart—" she said, indicating the glass in his hand.

"Haven't got one, I lost it years ago—to Helen," and the room shook with his laughter. "And don't go foolin' yourself, Di. Good whisky never hurt anyone. It's all that keeps an old fellow young. You're a good gel, Di. Too demmed good. Letta-go-your-blouse—chuck restraint to the winds once in a while as we Islanders do and you'll feel better." He chuckled. "You and Dicky haven't been married a year and you're out to reform the lot of us. Can't teach old dogs new tricks, Di. We *like* the way we live. Give up and get into the swim." He patted her hand kindly.

The woman's face tightened. Dick and Helen were gazing at each other as if they were thinking about something which only the two of them knew. It lasted for only an instant but it seemed as if the room might explode.

Then Helen took us to our rooms down the long hall, rapping

on closed doors as she passed, calling out, laughing, and life seemed to trail behind her.

After I was bathed and clean, Makalii took me to see the long stable full of racehorses. But I couldn't get Helen out of my mind. When Makalii took me in to bed, Gan was ready for dinner, looking as if she'd forgotten that she was old, had dropsy, and was going away. "Be a good little girl," she cautioned as she kissed me, then tucked in the mosquito net.

"Can I say good night to Helen?" I asked.

Gan nodded, went to the door and called out. An exciting silken rustle came along the hall and my heart gave a queer half-stifled beat as Helen entered. Her dress, actually white, seemed to glow as if it had absorbed the fire in her. Her eyes were so brilliant that they looked polished, but a sort of warm melting softness swam in them.

Lifting the net, she seated herself on the edge of the bed. Her long fingers closed on my arms with a touch that was electrical. Her skin had a mysterious fragrance and her hair held the scent of strong sunshine on a hot still day. Bending over, she kissed me. "I had a baby—once," she murmured.

Gan stood quiet, as if she were giving life her entire attention, while a blue twilight, sifted with silver, sank down on the Island outside the open windows.

"I didn't know that, Helen," she remarked, after an instant.

"No one does—except Uncle Bill. It died. I was fourteen."

7. HELEN OF HONOLULU

IT TOOK me years to fit the fragments of her fabulous history together, and probably some of the most poignant passages nobody will ever know. She was a blueblood to the ends of her curling black hair. Her father was an English lord. Her young part-Hawaiian mother, the daughter of chiefs, died giving Helen birth. The crazed young father rushed to the Sisters of the Sacred Heart Convent and dumped the new-born baby into their arms, leaving sufficient money to educate her, then fled from the Islands, as men are apt to do, leaving his offspring to an unknown fate.

The Sisters of the Sacred Heart Convent devoted their time to raising homeless young half-white girls, educating them and placing them in respectable homes when, at the age of fourteen, they graduated. The good women deluded themselves with the old adage, "Give me a child to shape until the age of seven, and I'll not worry about the rest of its life." But in their innocence, and ignorance, of the volatile Polynesian disposition they could not foresee that in the majority of cases their careful training of the lustrous young creatures left to their care was just so much wasted time and effort.

As the girls graduated, they were assigned to First Matrons of Honolulu who wanted well-reared girls to work in their homes. Sacred Heart girls spoke perfect English, were neat, knew how to cook, sew, embroider, and housekeep, and the First Matrons visited the Convent periodically to select new girls for their ménages when their other girls married, or as was more often the case, went wrong. These First Matrons had none of the gentle sweetness of the Sisters who, while they quelled the kittenish pranks of their charges, smiled with understanding and tolerance at the same time.

"Polynesians are such children," the Sisters would explain if visiting matrons tightened their lips and looked disapproving. "They can only be handled through the heart."

"Is Maile reliable and efficient?" one of the visitors might enquire.

A roguish glance from the dark eyes of the girl in question, a ducked head, cascades of giggles.

The Sister: "Maile, Mrs. Crank thinks that possibly she'll take you when you graduate. Won't that be nice?"

Maile (in a whisper): "Sister, I don't like her sour face!" Then more smothered laughter.

The quiet of the convent, the example of the low-voiced steady sisters, could not entirely quench the up-well of life in these exuberant children of the tropics. Cool rooms where they bent industriously over embroidery hoops, scrubbed kitchens where they busied themselves learning to cook, bubbled with gaiety. Classes over, passers-by on Fort Street heard squeals of glee coming over the high white wall of the Sacred Heart. Girls were romping and playing with each other under the hot sun in a courtyard where magenta bougainvilleas swarmed up the white bricks and leaped into ancient *kiawe* trees and embraced them.

Once or twice a year the girls emerged from the tall gates to attend some special Mass. Two by two, with Sisters spaced at close intervals between, the girls walked along the streets to the Cathedral, their eyes avidly drinking in glimpses of the world which waited to engulf them when they emerged at last from the high walls.

How were the Sisters, who never took their eyes off the ground, to know that the male population of Honolulu was always on hand at such occasions? By word of mouth, by telephone, by cocoanut radio the news would be broadcast: "The Sacred Heart girls are coming out today."

Men who were pillars of churches, banks, mercantile houses, would be walking and driving up and down Fort Street when the long procession of virgins emerged. And others—sailors off rusty freighters, roisterers, wastrels, young bloods of a dozen nationalities lurked on street corners, idled in doorways. Lusty young Hawaiians strolled on the opposite side of the street making the day careless with softly strummed music.

"That one, number t'ree in line, pretty like hibiscus flower," some young blade would comment to his crony.

"Bet-you-my-life she never smile if you Give The Eye!"

The wager taken. A daring message flashed across the street to the girl in question. A quick flush, a sparkle, then hastily lowered lashes.

"I lose, but I win!" the young fellow would comment and later, probably, prove it.

Because of her chief's blood, Helen was as tall as a girl of seventeen when she was twelve years old and her quick mind and intelligence made her graduate a year sooner than her mates. In private, the Sisters confided to each other their inability to teach her very much. She seemed to know it all before she was born.

When she walked out of the gates of the Sacred Heart and got into the surrey of the Matron who had elected to take her, she had barely turned thirteen. Her smile of unexpected loveliness would have melted a glacier. Her body was delicate as April rain. The male populace gasped and over drinks at the Union Bar laid wagers as to who would succeed in possessing her.

In a few days she learned that the gentle constraint of the Sisters was quite different from the rigid restrictions imposed on her in the household to which she had been assigned. She could not realize that her beauty and electric presence were resented by the dull virtuous woman who was housing her. She missed the ripply laughter of her mates. When, through sheer exuberance, she overstepped, or forgot, the restrictions imposed on her activities, she was stunned by the tide of female anger that swamped her. High-spirited, inherently imperious, she flashed back, then was instantly repentant. This white woman was kind, in her own fashion. She had given her a home, a nice room, a few dresses. Beautiful things were about her, rich rugs, paintings, books. . . .

Each time she tried, to the best of her ability, to make amends and be a credit to the Sisters whom she adored. The grudging forgiveness of her patron bewildered her. She was too young to realize that her outrageous loveliness, the royal dignity she displayed even in making a bed or scrubbing a bathtub, was an affront to a woman less lavishly endowed by nature.

She had the instinct of her race to adorn herself with flowers and, after she felt sufficiently at home, she went into the garden and made a *lei* to wear while she did her housework. When she was ordered to remove it and was informed that such heathen practices led to sin and destruction, she closed her proud lips and blinked back the tears stinging her eyes. After one particularly sharp dressing down she threatened to go back to the Sisters. *"They're* kind, they love me!" she sobbed. Stampeded at the thought of appearing at a disadvantage before Honolulu, the Matron made amends and temporary peace was restored.

Then one afternoon when Helen carried in a tray of mild drinks to half a dozen First Ladies, assembled to sew and gossip, she overheard herself being discussed. Blood flamed into her face. "You think I'm like that!" she demanded, setting down the tray. Silence paralyzed the gathering. "I'm going back to the Sisters, I won't stay in this dirty house!" she cried, and rushed out.

The house was high up Nuuanu Valley, miles from the Sacred Heart. Blinded by tears, distracted by such grief as only the early 'teens know, she ran along the dusty highway leading toward Honolulu. Proud homes sitting importantly in tropical gardens, the golden-green walls of the valley blurred in her tears.

The sound of carriage wheels behind her sent her leaping into a thicket of ginger, scattering its sweetness on the wind. *She* was coming to take her back! But she would not subject herself to more of that brand of vilification!

Crouching deep in the greenery she watched. But it was not the fringed surrey with its cruelly checked horses that was approaching. It was a dilapidated hack driven by an oldish, lounging Hawaiian. The horse slopped along happily, its check dangling. The driver's large bare feet were propped on the dashboard, and he was singing snatches of some sort of music which she had never heard, but to which her blood responded.

Maybe, she thought with a rush of hope, this man of her mother's race would give her a lift into town. Darting from the shiny green leaves and white flowers which had concealed her, she called out. The Hawaiian stopped, she went forward. When she saw there was a passenger in the back seat she hung her head.

"Hey, demmit, you're crying," the portly white man began explosively. "This won't do. You're too young and lovely to be unhappy. Get in, and tell me what's troubling you."

Helen hesitated, then with the impulsiveness of her race, spilled her troubles into his ample lap. "Will you, who are so old and so kind, take me back to my beloved Sister Bueneventura at the Sacred Heart?" she finished.

"Hell, why bury yourself in a Convent and cheat the world and yourself?" the old man wanted to know. "I've a fine place on Maui. Lots of racehorses. I've an eye for horses. And gels." He chuckled. "You're well born, it sticks out all over you. I'm sailing on the *Claudine* tonight. Come along. I've a boy about your age."

"I'm thirteen and three months," Helen told him shyly.

"Demmit, you look sixteen! But it don't matter. When you are you'll knock the eight islands into a cocked hat. I'll dress you in

style, see you meet the right people and give you a sportin'
chance to make something of your life."

Helen hesitated. She felt magically wrapped in fun, approval,
and laughter, but her Convent training held her back.

"We live and love a little time in the sun, then we die," the
driver remarked lazily. "If you go back and live with a lot of
old women you're crazy!"

Helen looked at clouds holding spectacular conferences above
the proud Pacific, inhaled the fragrance of white ginger, saw
golden sunlight lying warmly against the green earth. Drawing
a deep breath she ducked her beautiful head and got in beside
the portly old man.

There are localities in Hawaii beautiful as Eden, isolated from
the bulk of the island by lava-flows and mighty ravines, which
constitute complete worlds of their own. In them people live
as they please, conscious that they're beyond the censorship of
onlookers. Hana, on the island of Maui, is such a place. Mighty
headlands face the unbroken sweep of the Pacific. Mountain
streams fall thunderously through the jade and amber of forest
shadow and sunlight. Rain showers move along the horizon
like ghosts. Cane fields flutter beneath a guava-scented, brine-
impregnated wind. The majestic music of the Pacific, bursting
at the base of thousand-foot cliffs, sounds like the deep voices of
forgotten gods. And from every fold of the land a sort of heady
freedom injects itself into the atmosphere.

Into such an environment Helen was taken and enthroned
like a queen. Probably the impulse that originally prompted old
Bill Calhoun to make her part of his prodigal household was
carnal enough, but by some unexpected sensitivity and strength
of character, for which the world gave him no credit, he denied
her to himself.

He pensioned the hack driver to silence him in case a hue and
cry should be raised about her disappearance. There was some

talk, but in those days communication between the Islands was sketchy and old Bill's friends, roisterers like himself, abetted him gleefully. Just another half-white girl lost in the shuffle, gone on her destined way—with a sea captain probably. So talk went in Honolulu and Bill's friends chuckled over their drinks at bars and in clubs whenever the subject was under discussion.

Helen was essentially a product of the tropics where women mate early. Dick Calhoun, Bill's son, turning seventeen, took one look at her. She at him—

Some obscure fragment of conscience, implanted by the Sisters, gripped her when she realized she was going to have a baby. She must not bring disgrace on this royal household which had been so generous and so loving. To whom should she go for help and advice?

With instinctive intelligence she went to the one person she should have, to old Bill Calhoun with his merry twinkling eyes which had never looked on anyone unkindly. Old Bill, a spendthrift, a gambler, a drunkard, a lover of blueblooded horses and beautiful women. Rushing to him, Helen wept at his knee.

"Tut, tut, don't break your heart over it, my dear," Old Calhoun advised, wiping tears from her cheeks with a strand of her brown hair. "All mankind has gone this way. I don't blame Dicky, or you. I've handled such situations before. It'll all work out. If I'd been thirty years younger it might have been me."

"Then, dear Uncle Bill, you're not angry?"

"Hell, why should I be? Let him who is without sin cast the first stone, the Bible advises."

"Don't tell Dicky, it was my fault."

Old Calhoun chuckled. "I know my own flesh and blood! If Dicky had missed you he'd have been a blockhead. But I understand. We'll decide what's to be done, after the baby is born."

With easy tact, before her condition became evident, Old Calhoun announced he was sending her to the Convent in Wailuku for a few months' further education. If any of his cronies sus-

pected complications they did not pry. Life among the Missionaries might be a serious matter, but among the Outsiders it was
a colorful pageant going on its careless, rackety way.

To Helen's delight she discovered that Sister Bueneventura,
her idol, had been temporarily transferred to Maui to superintend
improvements in the hospital which had recently been added to
the Convent. The good Sister's feelings can be imagined. Mercifully, the baby died at birth, sparing from censure the household which had taken Helen in. But the child of fourteen who
had screamed her way through premature motherhood, emerged
from the ordeal a woman whose duplicate the Pacific has never
known.

Her beauty, her essential goodness beneath her passionate nature, made her a loved and honored guest in many prominent
Island households. Wrapped in her magical beauty she moved
on her way, an acknowledged Magdalene whose lovers ranged
from frigid missionaries to visiting potentates, and only the
dullest failed to realize that she was simply a child of joy and
not a wicked woman.

She emphasized and crystallized her environment and era. She
was Hawaii in the flesh. She helped to bring laughter to life,
taught people to forget mildewed creeds and fusty ways of thinking. She could make prudish persons take excursions into the
forbidden country of joy, love, wine, and laughter, without feeling steeped in sin. She splashed color over drab lives, sent people
away feeling better and richer simply by remembering her. The
repressed, she released; the reckless, she controlled and coun-
seled. In emergencies she acted swiftly and with effect. She had
a curious genius for life, divining its hidden workings where less
gifted persons had to learn from years of painful experience.

She saved Honolulu when Boat-House Maggie, best known
of all the harlots in Iwilei, "got religion." Boat-House had fallen
under the spell of a religious reformer who was shouting nightly
in Aaala Park. Honolulu, he declaimed, was an abscess in the

clean heart of the Pacific! God would destroy it as He had destroyed Babylon! Behind its smug white front it was all slimy corruption. Pillars of Banks, Pillars of Churches, the Governor, the Police Department, the City Fathers were all parts of the great cancer—Iwilei! Let them come forth, declare their sins and ask God's forgiveness! Or else—!

Each night Boat-House edged closer and hung more breathlessly on the fanatic's words. Rumors began spreading like fire running through dry grass. Boat-House was getting religion. Had got it! Boat-House was going to confess all and save her soul. . . .

Sleek cars driven by uniformed chauffeurs, carrying men of prominence, scooted to Iwilei. Broken-down cars sagging under the weight of portly Hawaiian policemen halted steaming at Boat-House Maggie's door. But Boat-House was impervious to bribes, pleadings, or threats. Before her black soul could be redeemed, it must be purged of its years of sinning by confession. Several of the other residents of Iwilei argued with her—after their own fashion. But Boat-House blackened one's eye, knocked another's teeth down her throat, and the one nearest her match in size and brawn came out of the tussle minus an ear and eye.

Then Helen stepped into the breech. She visited Boat-House and agreed with her that a white soul was more important than a big brown body. With tears, shed as only Hawaiians can shed them, Helen told Boat-House her own story.

"We scarlet women of shame can destroy or sustain our Hawaii. We, not persons of power, hold the whip. Shall we, to save ourselves, destroy those who've loved us, trusted us, and come to us for comfort? Did not the greatest Christian of all, out of love for His fellows, allow Himself to be destroyed to save them?"

Hawaiians are swayed by eloquence. Boat-House wept large tears over the sorrows and responsibilities of women, and Helen saw to it that she was promptly established in luxury and given sufficient gin. Boat-House had the satisfaction of feeling herself elevated to the galaxy of the great martyrs, and Honolulu was saved.

If Hawaii had loved Helen before this, it worshiped her afterward. In Polynesian fashion each lover retained a particular shrine in Helen's heart. The gifts they showered on her ran through her fingers like quicksilver, but she never forgot the Sisters. When she visited them, with the strange deep wisdom of their kind, they accepted the largesse she showered upon them without questioning its source, and used it for those needing assistance.

No one took greater pride in her career and conquests than Old Man Calhoun. Her devotion to him through the decline of his grandiose household won her everyone's respect. She sat by his bedside as he was dying, while grooms led thoroughbred horses, which he could no longer see, up and down under his bedroom windows, in order that he could hear their proud eager feet crunching the gravel of the driveway. When he died and the Calhoun estate crashed into splinters she rushed to Dick. Distracted with remorse, crazed with alcohol because his wife had left him and his young sister was going to the devil, Dick went out and shot the stableful of thoroughbreds which had ruined him—then died in Helen's arms.

Bad? Weak? Loose? She walked her destined road with superb, unfaltering tread. She comforted those whose lives were barren. She warmed those who felt left out in the cold. She gave of herself, with both hands, never counting the cost. She was gay when people were happy, laughed when moments were dark, spilled the sparkling, inexhaustible wealth of herself through three-and-a-half splendid decades. And she had enough wisdom, knowing her nature, not to marry the one man whom she had always loved—Dick Calhoun.

Mercifully she burned out before her beauty faded, succumbing to tuberculosis in her thirty-sixth year. Her shroud probably has no duplicate in history. A white satin bedspread on whose lustrous folds her hordes of lovers had signed their names as the years rolled along. With childlike naïveté and pride, in spare moments she sat, huddled over, dreaming the wickedly gorgeous dreams of the flesh, while she embroidered each name in scarlet silk with careful, Convent-trained stitches. At her death the roll, as honorable as the names upon it, was complete.

8. FEAST OF THE FLYING FISH

A**N UNEXPECTED** hitch in ranch affairs prevented Daddy from taking the same boat to Honolulu with Gan, Makalii, and myself, but I knew he would follow as soon as possible to be with Gan before she sailed for New Zealand.

Like all inter-Island steamers, the *Claudine* was to dock in Honolulu before dawn, but the spicy fragrance of a tropic morning filled the air and the excitement of landings permeated everything. Despite the increasing feeling of oppression that weighted me because Gan was going away, my spirits picked up when a Chinese steward popped his head in our cabin and said: "Honolulu, fifteen minute more."

Outside, the deck was wet and slippery from high seas in the channel between Molokai and Oahu. Hawaiian sailors were scurrying about attending to last-minute details. As they worked, they sang a rollicking tune.

> *Diamond A-head*
> *Is now inna view!*
> *Johnny Kanaka-naka*
> *Tu lai e.*
>
> *Ten minutes more*
> *Us all be-a-shore*
> *Johnny Kanaka-naka*
> *Tu lai e!*

When we were dressed and the bags closed, Gan and I went out. Makalii was waiting for us, and a steward hurried up with cups of coffee. The deck was thickly spread with single mattresses, placed side by side. Hawaiian, Japanese, and Chinese women, woebegone children who had been abundantly ill in the rough channel were beginning to gather themselves together. While the mothers combed out their long hair, re-coiled it and gossiped, little ones compared notes about their individual agonies and bragged over them.

An old *Tutu*—grandmother—of sumptuous proportions with a threatening mane of iron-gray hair spilling down her broad back, was methodically assembling her belongings: a huge *lauhala* hat with a peacock feather *lei* about the crown; a gay Japanese paper parasol; a moist bag of *poi;* a string container filled with rosy Lahaina mangoes; and an *ipu*—chamber pot—of imposing dimensions with gaudy flowers painted on its curved sides and handle.

Makalii took me toward the bow to look down at the forward deck, filled with restless steers, tied by their horns to stanchions. Crates of pigs and chickens added their smell to that of the cattle and the heavy reek of brown sugar, coming from the ship's hold.

When the gangway was lowered, old *Tutu* took the lead, rolling along like a heavily laden freighter. A bevy of relatives was waiting to greet her. After the customary hugging and crying, they escorted her to the street where a sorry-looking horse was waiting, held by a thin boy. Handing her possessions to admiring relatives—in-laws and out-of-laws—she shouted at the two most stalwart males of the clan and with grunts, shoves, and boosts they got her into the saddle.

With the dignity of an empress she settled herself, made sure her hat was at the right angle, adjusted her *holoku* about her big body, fitted her bare feet into the stirrups. Then taking the paper parasol, she opened it and held it above her head, although dawn was just showing behind the dark, moist ranges. Twisting the reins about her wrist, she slung the bag of *poi* and string hamper of mangoes over the pommel. Last, she grasped the precious chamber pot in her right hand so everyone could gaze admiringly at its full curves and gay flowers. Settling herself, she cocked the parasol over her shoulder, drummed a mighty tattoo on the horse's ribs with her bare heels and streamed off through the sleeping town at full gallop.

Our departure was more humdrum. A friend of Gan's, who was away, had lent her his Waikiki house and sent his surrey to fetch us. A thin Chinaman assisted Makalii to stow the luggage under the seats, then took up the reins.

The Honolulu of that first visit was a far cry from the publicized Honolulu of today. There were some automobiles, but hacks, surreys, and mule-drawn street cars were the chief means of transportation. The horses' hoofs made a nice clopping sound on freshly-watered asphalt streets. I was agog over four- and five-story buildings and fascinated by windows with huge, colored bottles in them, which Gan explained were drug stores. The drive to Waikiki, then separated from the town proper by a gap of several miles, took perhaps two hours.

Waikiki, now the Mecca of spinsters, divorcees, hussies, and debutantes in search of romance, was a spot loved for its peace, beauty, and magnificent swimming. Robert Louis Stevenson, Mark Twain, Charles Warren Stoddard had succumbed to its leisurely gracious atmosphere. It was the spot *par excellence,* as it still is, for the ancient Polynesian sport of surf-riding. Most of the ground now occupied by enormous up-to-date hotels, shoppes, and flimsy bungalows to accommodate visitors whose purses cannot meet the cost of fashionable hostelries, was privately owned by prominent white families and members of the Hawaiian royalty.

After driving through the business section of town we began passing lovely homes set back in gracious gardens. Gradually the houses became farther apart, and finally the road started across a marshy tract of ground paralleled by a solitary street-car track. On either side of the dike were vivid green rice paddies and taro patches. Thin-legged Chinamen in coolie hats were wading around, tending the crops. Each paddy was surrounded by raised ground planted with stocky banana trees bending under huge bunches of fruit. Shanties on high poles showed here and there and imposing flects of ducks paddled through the reed ponds quacking, shaking their tails and up-ending to dive for minnows and frogs.

Groves of cocoanut trees lifted their casual beauty to the sky and the scent of forests, which swathed the knife-edged ranges forming the backbone of the island, drifted by. Diamond Head loomed up, recalling the song the sailors had sung as we docked.

The road left the duck ponds and swerved into *Kiawe* and cocoanut groves. Through the dark trunks there were glimpses of the sea broken by a smoking line of surf. Houses began appearing again and presently we swung into spacious grounds filled with tall thickets of yellow-stemmed bamboo, hedges of autumn-hued crotons and hibiscus and oleander bushes ablaze with ruffly blossoms.

The carriage halted before a big white house that stood about where the Moana Hotel now rears above the beach. Half-a-dozen Chinese servants in starched duck uniforms greeted us. The head-boy led us into a *lanai*—living-room—with a balcony running around it and glass doors opening onto the beach. Chinese rugs covered the polished floor, carved teakwood furniture, an opium bed, embroidered and carved screens, brass-bound chests, and four-sided glass and teakwood lamps, decorated with dangling silk tassels, made the place seem like a Chinese palace.

We were taken upstairs to a bedroom which must have been forty feet square. It opened onto a wide balcony overlooking the white coral beach and dancing blue water. Twin four-posters, sitting majestically side by side, loomed up like islands. Beautifully woven *lauhala* mats covered the floor and the wardrobes and bureaus were made of richly polished black *koa* wood. I was impressed by the elegance of everything and slightly awed.

After a few minutes the breakfast gong sounded. We went

down and were seated at an expanse of polished table. Handsomely woven pandanus mats, set with heavy silver and fragile china, were in front of us. Two crystal peacocks, with dragging tails, minced toward a large crystal platter in the center heaped with monstrous Indian mangoes which, Gan informed me, came from the sacred Valley of Moanalua.

While I rapturously ate fragrant crescents of chilled *papaia,* Gan read a letter from her host which the serving boy handed her. When she finished it her eyes were wet. I wish I could recall his name and what he said but matters of much more pressing interest to a child crowded out the memory during the magic ten days I spent alone with Gan in Honolulu.

People called or we drove around seeing places which Gan wanted to revisit. I was rather bumptious and impossible, very aware of my elevated position as Gan's chosen companion before she sailed. We saw Mother, Gwen, and Aina every other day or so but it was of minor importance to me. Tatsu hugged me, and I was happy to see her but not the least interested in what my sisters and Mother were doing.

When Gwen or Aina attempted to recount their puny adventures, I silenced them with descriptions of Gan and my house at Waikiki, or strutted about the high-stepping carriage horses, exhibiting their points. But behind all the glow there was a dull increasing ache. As the days slid by, shortening the time before Gan sailed, I began waking up in the dark crying and scrambling about the vast bed searching for her. She tried to comfort me, explaining that parting only separated people's bodies, not their hearts or minds, but I couldn't comprehend. All I knew was that this wonderful person whom I loved, who was part of my life, who told me enchanting stories and laughed at my antics, was going to be torn from me.

During the first few days I had been content to play on the beach with Makalii during the forenoons, leaving Gan free to visit with friends or sit alone, as she loved to do, looking back on her wealth of memories. I began haunting her like a puppy sensing pending separation from an idolized master. I made her re-tell all the stories I loved, re-promise to meet me by the Red Sea, and still I could not be comforted. Why must she go, when would she come back? I asked weepily.

In an effort to distract my mind, she contrived expeditions to interest me. One morning she said she had a splendid surprise in store. Nakamura, the head-gardener, who had been a house-boy years before in the family where she had been governess as a young woman, had invited us to his son's house for the Feast of the Flying Fish. Would I like to go?

As usual I was agog for anything new.

"That's settled, then," Gan smiled though I doubt if a woman of her age, suffering from dropsy, could really have relished such a jaunt.

Next morning Nakamura, dressed in a new store suit and looking inflated with importance, squeezed into the front seat of the carriage between Makalii and the Chinese driver, while Gan and I sat behind. As we drove Nakamura explained that his boy Nakagowa was very smart. He was studying to be a dentist and was the father of four small boy-sans.

We drove beyond the Fish Market to the Oriental quarter where queer buildings with overhanging balconies lined both sides of the street. Behind them were jumbles of rickety houses, threaded by narrow alleys which smelt of salt fish, incense, and *shoyu*—soy bean sauce. Half-naked babies swarmed about the doorstep like fat little brown dolls gazing at the world with astonished eyes. Peddlers trotted by with wicker baskets loaded with all manner of merchandise swinging from poles balanced on their shoulders.

Above most of the houses great colored-paper fish, ten or more feet in length, were dipping and ducking in the wind, filling the sky with movement. Children, mostly boys, were racing about making a terrible racket, playing games and chasing each other.

Gan told Makalii to go into a store and he returned with a big crackling paper bundle.

Nakamura directed Ching where to go and we made our slow way among the crawling babies, racing boys, and jogging peddlers. Finally, we stopped in front of a small neat house set back in a tiny garden. Shiny black pebbles made a walk up to the door and on either side were wee Japanese water-gardens with china temples, bridges, and stunted trees. Nakagowa hurried out, bowing and smiling, proud and happy with four boy-sans, one a mere toddler, at his heels.

"My household is indeed honored," he said, bowing and inhaling, "to shelter such distinguished guests on Boy Day."

At the door we all took off our shoes, and Nakagowa's wife, in a lustrous silk kimono, gave us slippers. The instant the door closed behind us the whole world seemed to become Japanese. The exquisite simplicity of the interior with its sliding rice-paper walls and matted floors was restful. A lacquered table, not more than six inches high, occupied the center of the floor and around it cushions were placed to sit on. Nakagowa had borrowed a chair for Gan as her dropsy made it difficult for her to sit on the matting. I knew from Tatsu's teaching that in Japan the correct way for a person to seat himself was to sink to the knees, then drop back to the heels.

We met the rest of the family, two oldish aunts and their husbands and a girl of sixteen in a colorful kimono and elaborate headdress. After much bowing and inhaling, Gan and I expressed our admiration for the room, displaying our familiarity with Japanese etiquette. Then the women, except Nakagowa's wife who was to serve tea, withdrew to continue preparations for the feast which was to follow.

When my bowl of tea was passed, I took it in both hands, turned it around three times and took a small swallow.

"You are indeed conversant with Japanese etiquette," Nakagowa praised me and I wished that Tatsu could have heard.

While we sipped from tiny bowls and nibbled rice-cakes, Nakagowa seized his chance to tell us about the Feast of the Flying Fish. I knew about it sketchily, but being a very educated man Nakagowa went into details.

"May Fifth, Boy Day," he explained, "is known among Japanese as Shobu-no-Sakku, and the occasion has many of the elements of Christmas among Occidentals. However, this celebration is not limited to honoring an individual male child. It includes all boys, although the first-born of a family is apt to be slightly favored."

Nakagowa watched his sons proudly and I was awed by his fine English.

"In keeping with the spirit of the festivity," he went on, "the occasion calls for hanging paper banners as well as flying paper fish. Some houses have more banners and carp than others but there is no hard-and-fast rule. Sometimes the number of fish announces the number of male children in a household. But it also tells of the number of kind friends who remembered the family." He smiled at us benignly.

Gan signed to Makalii and he presented the big paper parcel to Nakagowa. The four boys seated like squat brown idols on small cushions beside their father, looked interested and eager. Nakagowa undid the string and inhaled with pleasure when he saw an immense purple fish. After polite exclamations about its beauty old Nakamura went off with his four grandsons to run up the new fish for all the neighbors to see.

The little house had almost the feeling of Christmas in it. This was the Japanese time of year to be merry, to spread cheer and call down blessings on everyone, but mostly on the boys. Incense burned slowly before a small shrine at the end of the room and prominently displayed in cloisonné vases was a variety of iris, the Shobu, a blossom dedicated exclusively to Boy Day. Gan remarked the flowers and Nakagowa brightened at another chance to show off his English.

"Shobu means 'win,'" he said. "Hence a lesson of victory for male youngsters is in the very decorations of the house."

While Nakagowa entertained us, his wife had slipped off to join her woman relatives who were trotting between the kitchen and the inner room where the feast was to be held. Finally, the paper walls were slid back and bowing women with smiling faces urged everyone to come and partake.

With elaborate ceremonies we were all seated about the low table. As well as all the more usual delicacies, special foods, served only on Boy Day, had been prepared. *Chimaki,* made of beans and red rice wrapped in lily leaves was handed around. *Haskiwa mochi,* a rice cake wrapped with oak leaves, symbolizing strength, simply melted in my mouth and as soon as I finished one, another was handed to me. The food was served in special bowls and plates, never used on ordinary occasions and when nobody could eat any more toasts were drunk in hot sake.

The feast over, the usual formalities, dear to Japanese hearts, were discarded as far as the boys were concerned. They raced off to play with their comrades and add to the racket coming from the street.

"On this one day," Nakagowa explained, "boys are free to call on their friends without asking permission and to shout and play to their hearts' content." He smiled. "Would it interest you to see their toys?"

Gan nodded politely and he led us into another room. Tiny manikins in suits and trappings of old Japan were arranged on a long low shelf in front of an exquisitely carved screen. Nakagowa approached them reverently.

"This," he took up the center figure, "is Jimmu Tenno, the first mortal Emperor of Japan, a direct descendant of the Sun Goddess. During his long and fabulous career, Jimmu Tenno was often aided by divine powers, but as a rule he relied on himself. He is remembered as a noble warrior because he showed mercy to those he conquered, something unheard of in ancient times."

Setting the wee image of the warrior back in position, he picked up another toy. "The second most valued toy is Benkei, a priest as well as a fighter. This superb character lived about the twelfth century. He was born near Shungu, but became famous all over Japan." He inhaled respectfully. "Benkei collected 999 swords from less able warriors by the simple method of demand and take. So fierce were his demands that taking was simple. But when he set out to get his 1000th sword he met his match."

I waited eagerly.

"On the Gojo bridge he met Yoshitune of the Miamoto feudal clan. Yoshitune proved the David of the Japanese Goliath. The warrior-priest was heavily armed, the youth had one puny weapon which resembled a fan—as long as it remained open. When it snapped shut it was transformed into a two-edged sword. Yoshitune knocked the halberd out of Benkei's hands. The giant wept over his defeat but publicly acknowledged Yoshitune as the better man and served him faithfully through triumphs as well as setbacks."

I gazed at the likeness of Benkei, impatient for Nakagowa to go on.

"After some years Yoshitune ran into a long streak of bad luck and committed *hari-kari*. Benkei refused to surrender. A great battle took place in one of the swift rivers of Japan. Benkei guarded the ford singlehanded. His body was shot so full of arrows that he looked more like a pin cushion than a man. He continued to stand erect though his arm swung no more. So firmly had his feet been planted that the muscles held the dead man rigid, dauntless in death as he had been in life."

"May I hold Benkei for an instant?" I asked.

Nakagowa smiled. "You are impressed. You had a grandfather

who was also a great warrior who died in battle." And he handed me the toy which commemorated valor.

After examining it, I thanked Nakagowa and handed it back.

"Kato Kiyomasa," Nakagowa indicated a small figure in stiff brocaded robes, "is the third most popular toy. Kato was born a blacksmith but rose to command the second army to invade Korea in 1592. But," Nakagowa smiled, "the fourth toy is the one dearest to boys' hearts."

He paused dramatically.

"Kintaro, a fabled strong boy, lived in the mountains. His origin no one knows. Kintaro never grew up but possessed powerful muscles. He liked horses and rode them bareback—"

I settled myself to listen.

"Kintaro was a mighty hunter and a great fisherman but he only caught destructive beasts and the gamest of fish. He had Robin Hood qualities and shared what he had with less fortunate folks. The swiftest hare could not outrun him and he liked to wrestle with bears and throw them."

Picking up a manikin which vaguely suggested a chubby cherub, Nakagowa displayed it. I felt rather let down but, to be polite, asked:

"What happened next?"

"That is the most delightful part, nobody knows." Nakagowa's smiles were getting wider and wider. "Kintaro may be immortal and still living in his cave, but it is certain that his brave spirit lives on in all boys as they live on in him."

Outside the windows the sky was beginning to have the clean-washed texture that announces the sun is getting low. Great fish were rolling, dipping, and twisting impressively on their slender bamboo poles. Gan said we must be going. Everyone looked sorry, except old Nakamura who was still in a happy haze, though most of the fun was over. Gan had bought a purple fish for his grandson and met his dentist-son who spoke such good English!

Ching went for the carriage which he'd left at a nearby stable. When the sound of wheels announced his return, the entire family accompanied us to the garden gate. Nakagowa seized his last chance to tell about things he hadn't yet got around to.

"You see, Mrs. von Tempsky," he said, as he proudly escorted her, "Japanese make Boy Day an occasion in which to teach youth lessons of character, utilizing toys with legends, house-decorations with morals, and even serving food with meaning, like *Haskiwa mochi,* which symbolizes strength. Even the carp," he gestured at twenty great fish floating over his house, "has a specific significance."

Gan became attentive.

"In Japan, rivers are swift and narrow with many rapids and waterfalls. Of all the fish in our streams only carp ever reach headwaters. They are powerful enough to breast the strong current, fight raging rapids, and leap waterfalls. That is why we fly carp on Boy Day, so youngsters may see them and remember to be steady, strong, and courageous as they swim the river of life."

9. UNLAID GHOSTS AND FAREWELL

NEXT morning before it was light I was awakened from dreams of Kintaro, Jimmu Tenno, and Benkei by the thin silvery whistle of a plover, followed by the sound of carriage wheels going away. Daddy!

"He's come a boat earlier than he planned!" Gan exclaimed, her face lighting. I leaped out of bed, dashed along the balcony, and slid down the bannister.

Before I reached the bottom, the door opened. There he was! In his fresh riding breeches and red carnation *lei* he seemed to bring the ranch in with him. I was so glad I could hardly speak. He asked if I'd taken good care of Gan, then we hurried upstairs.

One of the Chinese boys appeared shortly with a tray of coffee. The French doors opened on the balcony, green branches moved softly against the railing and because of Dad's blithe presence it seemed as if we were all having fun together in the tree-tops. Waikiki mornings were always lovely but this one was nicer than the others, because Daddy was with us. The curved domes of monkey-pod trees leaning over blossoming oleanders and hibiscus, looked bigger and greener than they had been yesterday and the ocean was a more dazzling blue.

I went out on the balcony. Old Nakamura was making the round of the lawns with a sharpened bamboo pole, harpooning red and brown *kamani* leaves which had dropped off the trees. He looked like a slightly bored fisherman, impossibly plying his trade on land. I called out and he brandished his pole and shouted, *"Banzai!"* his face still glowing with recollections of Boy Day.

I overheard Gan telling Dad that Mr. Cleghorn had invited her and the whole family to take tea with him that afternoon at Ainahau, and I raced in. To Island-born children of this generation the word Ainahau probably means just—Land of the Hau Trees. When I was small the word was sheer magic. Ainahau had more glamor and mystery than even Washington Place where dethroned Queen Liliuokalani lived. The gates of Ainahau were always locked. No one except specially invited guests ever went through them. Mr. Cleghorn, dead Princess Likiliki's husband, lived there with memories of his royal wife and daughter Princess Kaiulani, who had died before she was eighteen.

After breakfast Dad went to fetch Mother, Aina, and Gwen. While Makalii took me for my morning swim, Gan sat on the wide flagged veranda, reveling in her contentment at having two extra days with Daddy.

After lunch she put on a dark silk frock and her most frivolous lace cap. Then she got out a dress Grandmother Wodehouse had sent me from London. When I had on my white kid shoes, silk socks, and fancy little pants, Gan buttoned up the back of the short ruffly dress with a smocked yolk and sleeves. I felt like somebody else, but rushed down to show Makalii. He was in clean dungarees and a starched shirt, waiting for me.

He had made me a white jasmine *lei*, like carved ivory and pearls, and when he put it around my neck it added the last touch of splendor to my finery. Carriage wheels announced the arrival of the rest of the family. Aina was bristling with importance. *She* was going to spend the week-end with Mr. Cleghorn, her grandfather—at Ainahau.

Because I'd heard so much about Ainahau I'd imagined it would be miles away but it proved to be quite close to where we were staying. There was the locked gate with high strong fences going away on both sides; and a tangle of trees and shrubs so dense that passers-by could get no idea of what was inside. When our carriages stopped, a Chinaman appeared, unlocked the gates, and, after we were through, vanished like a silent spirit into the undergrowth.

A dusty road wound through greenery: spreading banyan trees, *haus,* bamboos, oleanders, and hibiscus made a tangle on all sides. Tall cocoanuts, singly and in rustling groves, lifted their feathery heads high into the sky. Water gurgled pleasantly as we passed hidden streams. I almost fell off Makalii's lap trying to see what lay ahead. Gardens opened out suddenly in the jungle. Old taro patches had been transformed into lily-pools with azure, rose-madder, and pink flowers starring them. Peacocks dozed in the sun, light flashing off their jeweled feathers. Banyan trees with their thousands of branches and spreading roots stood proudly in the clear afternoon, and tall cocoanuts moved like solemn *kahilis,* the feather ceremonial emblems used on state occasions in Hawaii.

The horses' hoofs were muffled by deep spicy dust, and the voice of the locality murmuring in its sleep awed everything into silence, as if the garden had secret tragic memories hugged to its heart. The warm air was heavy with the fragrance of earth, fruit and flowers. Even the sunlight looked unreal, as if ghosts, which the years could not lay, paced here incessantly.

The carriages stopped before a group of houses half-hidden by tangled growth. A China boy came out and said he'd tell Mr. Cleghorn we'd arrived. I wondered what Aina's grandfather was like and which of the houses he lived in. A tall man with a loping sort of walk appeared. He was wearing a starched white suit and a pith helmet. His eyes were dark and burning, set under bristling brows, and as he walked he kept slashing at invisible enemies with a malacca cane.

After greeting the grown-ups, he looked at Aina.

"She's grown, Amy, and looks well," he commented in his stiff way. "I hope she's not too much trouble."

Mother told him Aina was a good child.

Mr. Cleghorn glanced at us. "Armine and Gwen can play in

the garden until tea-time," he announced. "Aina, go with Chong." He gestured at the China-boy. "Your brother Hay has just waked up. His nurse, Mary O'Donnel, is with him."

The older people went into the nearest house. Chong picked up Aina's week-end bag. Tears began spilling down her cheeks and her chin got flat and shaky. Tatsu took her hand. "S'pose you like I go with you," she suggested in her kind way. Aina grabbed her, and hoisting Gwen higher on her arm, Tatsu followed Chong.

Makalii took me through the gardens, telling me in a low voice about Ainahau. Mr. Cleghorn was an *Alii* from Scotland. He had come to Hawaii years ago and married Princess Likiliki, who had large estates. Here in Ainahau, Kaiulani, most deeply loved of all Island Princesses, had been born. Princess Likiliki died and several years later Mr. Cleghorn had married another Hawaiian connected with the royal family. She had adored Kaiulani as much as her own daughter, Annie Leialoha—Aina's mother. Kaiulani was sent to England to be educated and presented at court. Her charm and beauty caused a furore in London. But after she came back to Hawaii she contracted some mysterious malady and before she was eighteen she died.

"There's a bad *kahuna* on Ainahau," Makalii said in low tones, glancing uneasily around as though he feared some malignant entity might overhear. "Someone connected with the family broke a *tabu,* maybe without knowing it. Ainahau will be wiped out, too, in time." The awesome prediction, spoken in Hawaiian, made me shiver.

A delicate breeze rustled the foliage. The voices of hidden things whispered about us. The afternoon was so quiet that it shouted for attention but behind the beauty surrounding us there was a strange impression of impending decay. Did Ainahau know, on that afternoon so long ago, that someday its jealously guarded, inviolate acres would be covered with little shoppes filled with trashy hula-skirts, paper *leis,* and cheap ukuleles to attract tourists? That the shoddy bungalows of Flappers Acre, with their rowdy "oke" parties and tawdry love-affairs, would supplant lily-ponds and winding-walks where Princess Kaiulani had played as a child?

In spite of the thrill of being at Ainahau a foreboding of doom weighted the afternoon. I was glad when Tatsu, Gwen, Aina, and her sturdy little brother came along the walk. We played quietly, climbing through the great banyans and watching peacocks sliding about. Finally, Mary O'Donnel called out that we were wanted for tea.

Separate from the main dwelling was a one-story structure where Mr. Cleghorn had entertained during the days of the Monarchy. The immense room was crowded with brocaded love-seats, gilt chairs, huge satin hassocks, and tall lamps. Across one end, wide steps covered with Chinese rugs went up to a sort of stage where important personages had stood during receptions while less important people came to pay them homage. An atmosphere distilled from the stately past of Hawaii lingered over everything. Here Princesses had held court. Here jovial kings had carelessly gambled away their substance as they avalanched toward their doom. Here brilliant statesmen, representing the leading nations of the earth, and naval officers in glittering uniforms had gathered to dance, talk, and discuss world affairs.

While I sat nibbling plum cake, eating wafer-thin sandwiches, and sipping my weak tea, my eyes wandered over gold and glass cabinets filled with medals, orders, and jewelry which had belonged to Mr. Cleghorn's royal wives.

When tea was over and we climbed into the surrey, Aina began crying. "Don't be a baby," Mother said gently. "I'll be back to get you in three days. Have a nice time with your little brother and don't trouble your grandfather."

Aina let out a wail. Mr. Cleghorn glared from under his bristling eyebrows. "Mary, take her," he ordered, and the Irish woman carried her away. Mother started to apologize but Mr.

Cleghorn lashed at one of his invisible enemies with his cane. "There's no need to explain, Amy. Aina's reluctance to be parted from you proves how kind you've been. She's soft. Steel must be injected into her."

I no longer envied Aina staying at Ainahau. It was a place of menace and shadows even if Princesses had once lived there. When the iron gates clanged shut behind us and the lock clicked in place, my muscles relaxed. I had seen Ainahau and my spirit had heard the restless pacing of the great dead who haunted it. I snuggled thankfully against Makalii and asked him to sing me the Haleakala Hula to shake off the lingering spell of the place.

A day or so later, my first real sorrow was upon me. In the afternoon Daddy drove in to announce he was spending the night with us, that Gan's ship was ahead of schedule and would dock about ten next morning and sail for New Zealand at three. The bright afternoon came to a standstill and my insides felt quivery and soft, like the meat of a young cocoanut. I tried to swallow but my throat closed up. Inside my head little hammers kept tapping: Gan's going . . . Gan's going.

Daddy and Gan were looking at each other in a deep still way that hurt more than if they had broken down completely. Suddenly I knew that there was something I hadn't been told. For Gan, there would be no coming back. It was in their eyes, in their faces, in the way that they looked at each other. All the experiences they had shared were quivering in the room. The seven-month voyage that Gan had made around the Horn with her children. The years in Australia and New Zealand. . . . Their happy days at the ranch. Only a few hours more and it would be *pau* forever!

The afternoon seemed a terrible dream from which I couldn't wake. I have hazy memories of lying half-asleep in Gan's lap after dinner. People kept coming in to pay last calls. There were lights and voices. Someone said, "Her eyes are glassy, she's feverish, but children soon forget."

"Sometimes children's memories reach back into eternity," Gan's quiet voice said.

When morning came I went around in a blur. Daddy and Gan sat on the *lanai* looking at the sea. They held hands but said little. About noon a hack called for Gan's luggage and I watched it being put in.

"Where's your little camphor chest?" I asked, not seeing it among her belongings. I loved it. It was part of Gan. In it she kept her "Desert Island Bag" that contained everything a person needed in an emergency and couldn't find.

"I left it behind for you to remember me by," she told me.

All the tears jammed inside me tried to get out at once and after the convulsive sobs were over I felt weak and spent. "You must be brave and take care of Daddy for me," Gan said. "We three belong to each other. We're the same breed. Don't forget. I'll write to you every mail and you must write to me. Daddy will read this letter to you"—she took a folded note out of her pocket—"after I'm gone. There are things in it that I want you to remember. Always."

My fingers closed on the precious paper. My first letter!

"Wait, I must give you one too," I cried.

Dashing indoors I went to a desk, found paper and a pencil, and scrawled, "Aloha . . . Ummie." When I gave it to Gan, she slipped it into her handbag and patted it in a pleased way.

Then all at once we were on the hot crowded wharf. People were scurrying about, their arms loaded with *leis*. The band was playing. Mother kept wiping her eyes. Mr. Cleghorn, looking fiercer than ever, arrived and stood beside Gan. People we'd called on, people I'd never seen, made a deepening ring around her loading her with presents and *leis*. So many people came that Makalii had to pick me up and set me on his shoulder so I could see her.

The captain in a white gold-braided uniform came down the gangway of a ship bigger than any I'd ever seen. He pushed his way through the jam until he reached Gan. "Mrs. von Tempsky?" he asked.

The whistle blew hoarsely, tearing the bright afternoon into shreds. Vague female relatives of Mother's, big Englishmen who were my uncles, blew their noses resoundingly. The day seemed to be getting out of control and running away like a crazed horse. Makalii was crying, Tatsu too, but Daddy stood like a soldier waiting for the last kiss of all. His eyes had a funny distant expression as if they were made of blue ice that ached in his head.

When all the good-bying was done, Dad took Gan's arm and started toward the gangway, Makalii carrying me at their heels. I felt frightened. There was a great stiff hole inside me. Makalii held me so Gan could kiss me. "Don't cry," she said. "Hold fast to your letter."

There was a ring in her voice which made me feel as if I, too, had been one of her children in far-off times when alarms were sent out that Maoris were attacking and she had had to run through dark scary forests with Aunt Lina, Uncle Randal, and Daddy at her heels. "Don't be frightened, we'll make the stockade," she always told them when they had to hurry from their little house.

The whistle blew again. The band began playing "Aloha Oe!" Daddy and Gan went silently and tightly into each other's arms. Daddy watched Gan go up the gangway with the captain. Then Makalii, in the wonderful way of Hawaiians, knew what to do. He put me into Daddy's arms. Daddy looked as he had the day that the sharks attacked the steers, as if he didn't know who I was, then he smiled his valiant heart-lifting smile.

"Wave to her, First Born, there she is!"

I found her face, finally, among the many hanging over the rail. Gan was going . . . Gan was going.

10. I MEET A GOD AND ATTEND HAWAIIAN CHURCH

SHORTLY after Gan sailed, Great-Aunt Jane arrived from England. Every morning for two hours after breakfast she taught Aina and me lessons under the Pride of India tree. She was a large woman who wore her thin hair parted in the middle but it was not finished with gay lace caps as Gan's had been. However, her peculiarities intrigued me and made me fond of her in an unemotional way.

She always had to have a slug of cold boiled bacon handy on the sideboard to nibble at if she grew hungry. Three times a week she planted mustard and cress seeds on a strip of wet white flannel laid on a sunny shelf outside the kitchen window. When they sprouted, about every forty-eight hours she scraped the tiny green shoots into a bowl and gave them to Ah Sin to make into paper-thin sandwiches for afternoon tea. No matter how warm the weather might be, when she occupied herself with household duties she pinned back her *holoku,* displaying a colorful expanse of red-flannel petticoat.

She was strict about the way we held our pencils and if Mother called her away from school for a minute and I drew horses on my slate or scribbled a few lines on a bit of paper to Gan, she rapped my fingers with a small ruler. But she was a likeable person and my determination to master reading and writing had her entire support.

If New Zealand mail arrived and Dad wasn't around, Great-Aunt Jane patiently helped me to read my letter over half-a-dozen times. When longing for Gan overtook me I'd go to the little camphor chest and sit down beside it for comfort. Presently

103

Great-Aunt would come trotting through the house. "What would your Gan think of you if she could see you crying?" she'd ask. "Be off like a good child and play in the garden, or find Makalii." I always sensed that behind her abrupt manner only her English upbringing prevented her from showing her affection.

About this time Dad determined to provide the ranch with an adequate water system. The previous manager had not been an expert stockman and overlooked the fact that an insufficiency of water troughs compelled the cattle to walk miles a day, working off the fat they accumulated from grazing.

Making Ukulele Dairy his headquarters, Daddy explored the watershed on the eastern shoulder of Haleakala and surveyed a pipeline to tap a succession of gulches where streams ran the year around. The Dairy was maintained solely to keep the mountain cattle fairly tame. Herefords are not milking stock, but eight per cent of the cows that calved in the vicinity were driven in and milked for three or four months to accustom the new crops of calves to human beings.

Being practical, Daddy had the milk separated and churned into butter, and the surplus was fed to hogs and chickens kept for the larder. The Japanese in charge of the place, being an ex-gardener, took it upon himself to plant flowers, in addition to his other duties. Twice a week he came down to the ranch with pack-animals covered with panniers bursting with roses, violets, calla lilies, and heliotrope bobbing above butter, eggs, poultry, and suckling pigs.

The Dairy was at the edge of the forest, about seven thousand feet up Haleakala. Night and morning cold mists drifted in. The house was roughly built but boasted a fireplace, and old Shobu always kept the rooms decorated with bouquets in case Dad might drop in unexpectedly. For six months Dad and a gang of men worked there, going up late Sunday night and returning on Saturday around noon to spend the week-end at home. At the

end of seven or eight months the new water system was completed and a network of pipelines and water troughs, the right
distance apart, was laid out in the pastures. Daddy was justly
proud of his work, but after these months of being soaked to
the skin at a high chill altitude he contracted a severe case of
bronchitis.

Ah Sin appointed himself Dad's nurse and trotted between the
kitchen and the bedroom with containers of hot water to which
he added eucalyptus oil or tincture of benzoin for Dad to inhale
if his paroxysms of coughing grew too violent. Mother was up
half-a-dozen times a night and I would fly in to see if I could
help.

After several weeks of night sessions, my lessons began to suffer and I was ordered to stay in bed. But I could not do it and
sat outside his door shivering with anxiety. One night, when a
spasm was over, Mother came out and stumbled against me. At
first she was angry.

"But Gan told me to take care of Dad for her," I protested.
"She said we three belonged to each other, because we're the
same breed."

Mother looked at me oddly, then concluded that as long as I
wasn't going to stay put I might as well be installed as Dad's
nurse until he was better. I was elated and in spite of my concern over Dad's health, there was a flavor of adventure to the
night watches. To see Ah Sin sitting in a corner, his slant eyes
smiling as he watched me rub Dad's chest with eucalyptus oil,
kept me from feeling frightened or lonely. Usually around three
the paroxysms grew less violent, then old Ah Sin concocted a
light supper of milk and crackers which sent me off to sleep on
the foot of Dad's bed until five when he got up and went to
work. For a while during this siege, Dad was unable to retain
any solid food on his stomach and lived entirely on whisky and
milk. How he ever managed to cover his forty or fifty miles a
day on horseback remains a miracle. . . .

He was markedly better when the time came to shift steers to Waiopai ranch for fattening. Mother was nervous about horses and riding and decided I'd better go with him even if it meant missing ten days of school. I was just seven but felt quite adult with the notion that Dad's health depended on my care.

The trek to Waiopai, on the opposite side of the mountain, was about fifty miles and took two days. The four or five hundred head of cattle to be fattened there annually were prize stock and had to be moved with care. The first night's stop was always at Ulupalakua Ranch. It was the most talked-about place on Maui and had a history which read like a Greek tragedy set in tropic latitudes. In the Polynesian language the name had enormous significance; Ulupalakua means Ripe Breadfruit of the Gods, and it was so-called because wealth and profusion bordering on the supernatural were in the district. Its lush acres lay in a protected pocket where the gusty Trade-winds, which blow for nine months of the year in Hawaii, never reached. When the Equinox roared overhead, harrying the rest of Maui, Ulupalakua lay in a miraculous pool of peace. Special rain showers, generated by its position on the mountainside, below the air currents of the Cloud Warriors, fell on Ulupalakua when the rest of the island was dry. Strange happenings had befallen the families who'd successively lived at Ulupalakua. The Hawaiians held that when the Moon was in Ku, and supernatural forces had ascendency on earth, gods walked boldly about the locality which was set aside expressly for them. But behind Island gossip and conjectures no person who ever spent a day at Ulupalakua denied the curious spell of the atmosphere hovering over it. . . .

As we crossed the boundary of the 90,000 acre ranch, my perceptions, developed by Makalii, sensed the prodigal abundance in the deep, damp soil.

About three o'clock we entered a long avenue of eucalyptus and Pride of India trees. The slowly moving herd of steers raised a cloud of golden dust with their feet and off in the southwest red Kahoolawe lay in the path of the falling sun. Half an hour's ride brought us to majestic gardens. A long concrete walk led back to a many-winged house sitting under towering camphor, breadfruit, and *kukui* trees.

Ulupalakua *paniolos* coming in from work greeted our men delightedly, and opened gates into a green pasture where the tired cattle could graze and drink their fill before going on next morning.

A handsome laughing man who was part Hawaiian came from the house and took us in. As usual on Island ranches the place was overflowing with people, young and old, all having a good time. After I'd been fed a bowl of cool *poi* and some *upihis* I went out, eager to explore my surroundings. Makalii was waiting for me.

"First, us go look the *akua*," he announced, taking my hand.

"The god of Ulupalakua?" I asked.

He nodded and headed for a *kukui* grove. My eyes drank in the loveliness of the gardens. Great urns filled with fantastic Century plants were set here and there against the trees. Violets, forget-me-nots, and pansies crowded against concrete walks and great reservoirs. The air was heavy and sweet with the smell of Easter lilies, gardenias, orange trees in bloom, and plumaria. Wild peacocks shrieked in tree-massed slopes that marched up Haleakala. The old house in its stately setting of pools and walks seemed to thrust back against the mountain as if trying to get a longer perspective on everything before it.

We followed a walk between ancient, silvery-trunked *kukui* trees, draped with staghorn ferns, then came on a circular opening in the garden. Makalii removed his hat. "The Shark God," he said in a low whisper. A rock idol two feet high was set on a pedestal in the center of the clearing. It was a double-faced image with cruel eyes that squinted at the past and future, mocking both.

Makalii took the *lei* off his hat and advancing warily laid it on the grass at the base of the god. I saw other offerings of food and flowers tied up in green *ti* leaves. Hastily snatching a crimson rose off a nearby bush I tiptoed forward and dropped it before the Shark God. Makalii prayed, under his breath in Hawaiian, some ancient propitiatory chant that sent shivers over me, then he made a quick sign to avert evil.

It made my footsteps cautious as Makalii led me along a path winding up a steep hill. After a scramble we came upon the brink of a great shining reservoir reflecting tall Italian cypresses planted about it. Dragon flies skimmed over the water and tall urns grouped against fern banks cast trembling reflections across the pool.

While we sat in the sun soaking in the beauty of the spot Makalii told me the story of how the reservoir came to be built. The original owner of Ulupalakua decided one morning that he wanted a half-million gallon reservoir on the hill behind the gardens which he so passionately loved. By noon he had eight hundred Chinamen digging. In a week the vast undertaking was completed, pit dug, concrete work finished, but the men worked so hard that two of them died.

"And because the Shark God had its human sacrifices, rain fell immediately filling the reservoir to the brim," Makalii finished solemnly, in Hawaiian.

A thrill followed swiftly by a tinge of panic made me grab for his hand.

Next morning when the somber groves of trees fell behind us, the stifled sensation which had filled me from the instant we'd ridden into Ulupalakua faded away. A narrow trail, winding through lava wastes and poking among cinder cones, led around the southern shoulder of Haleakala.

About an hour's riding brought us to the small village of Kanaio. A dozen-or-so houses flanked the trail, enclosed by well-built stone walls. Pale-eyed dogs wandered around, fowls scratched at flower beds and a dejected-looking peacock, with a plucked neck, sat on a log. The bird seemed aggrieved and uncomfortably conscious of its bare neck. With a hostile expression it eyed a woman sitting in a doorway painstakingly stitching its iridescent feathers into a hatband such as Hawaiian men like to wear on gala occasions.

As the cattle began pouring through the village the peacock became alarmed. With a shriek it flapped its wings and sailed over the wall, upsetting a row of glistening chamber pots.

During the early 1900's the social standing of Hawaiian families living in isolated districts was daily announced to the world at large by the number of *ipus* they possessed. Poor families only rated a couple. Rich ones boasted a dozen: papa's monster one with flamboyant flowers adorning its swelling sides; mother's slightly more modest one; then others in diminishing sizes to accommodate smaller and smaller members of the family. Religiously each morning they were set out to sun along stone walls or placed like China hats on fenceposts, adding a raffish flavor to any scene.

After pausing to chat with the villagers we pushed on. Hour by hour the country grew wilder and lonelier. Not a house showed along the faint trail winding through the barren land, naked with the newness of recent birth. The slope of the island on this side was twice as precipitous as on the Makawao side and a feeling of violence hung over it. Here, in the last eruption from Haleakala, cones had spouted their final fury and molten masses of rock had poured into the ocean, filling the world with shattering explosions.

About noon we picked up the twin blow-holes of Lua-lai-lua, and as we rode through the swale between them the wild land of Waiopai burst into view. Mighty headlands rushed down from the summit of Haleakala to meet the sea. Deep ravines opened their foaming white jaws to the blue Pacific. The lava trail had merged into a narrow cobblestone path that wound up and down the sides of sheer gorges and leveled away through grassy reaches.

"This old trail was for the King's Runners," Daddy told me. "It was in use for hundreds of years before white men came to the Islands."

In places, freshets had cut it through; in other spots, lava had poured over it. But it went on and on like a glittering serpent whose scales were pebbles worn shiny and smooth by sprinting brown feet carrying royal messages and ultimatums.

After climbing out of a shadowy canyon, Daddy said we'd left the district of Kehekenui behind and crossed the Waiopai boundary. The land was clothed with thick tawny pili grass that shivered under the Trade-wind like the fur of a living beast. Cresting a rise we sighted the Waiopai stallion with his harem of sleek brood-mares and colts. Whinnying imperiously he rounded up his herd, gave them horse-orders, then with head-shakings, stampings, and whistlings he came forward to see who was daring to invade his kingdom. Daddy dismounted, gave me his reins to hold, and went forward.

"Here, Maui, you can't bluff me," he said.

The stallion stretched out his slender red neck, sniffed Dad's hand, and allowed himself to be petted. His Arab ancestry was plain: tiny ears, prominent eyes, a slightly dished face finished by a sweeping jaw and tiny muzzle. When he and Dad finished talking he went back to his waiting flock.

The Waiopai horse-herd was bred expressly for long hard trips. The steep pitch of the land developed lungs and muscles, the rocky ground made hoofs as hard as obsidian. Waiopai horses never wore shoes and the roughest lava could not grind down their feet or lame them.

Wild lights were hitting the headlands as we dropped down Manuwainui gulch. The thirsty stock crowded up to a long water trough and drank their fill. There was no beach, but shiny black boulders like cannon balls rolled back and forth with each wave, filling the canyon with dull thunder that echoed up the walls.

When the footsore steers had drunk their fill they began filing up the narrow trail. We followed in their wake. I felt drugged with the happy tiredness of a long day on horseback and wondered when we would reach the ranch of Waiopai. Then I sighted a cluster of weather-worn houses a short distance away, a water tank, and hitching rails enclosed by neat stone walls.

We spent several days rounding up and branding stock, inspecting water troughs and checking the condition of the feed. Each evening after supper Dad and I sat on the veranda steps playing cribbage while tropic birds with long red tail feathers soared about the cliffs or sailed like silver dots far out to sea. Dad's bronchitis was not troublesome but I insisted on rubbing his chest every night with camphor oil and dosing him with some dark evil-looking Chinese medicine which Ah Sin had sneaked to me.

"You're trying to make yourself indispensable, aren't you," Dad teased, "so I'll take you with me whenever I leave home?"

I nodded.

One evening when we returned from the mountain a strange mule was tied to the hitching rail. A jolly Hawaiian was waiting on the veranda. He rushed to meet us bursting with great news. The preacher who visited the district of Kaupo two or three times a year had written that he was unable to come. Kane, our merry caller, had decided to preach in his stead and had a fine sermon prepared. Wouldn't we all ride over and hear him Sunday?

The following afternoon the lot of us, including the Hawaiian who was in charge of Waiopai, set off to spend the week-end in Kaupo. A village of small wooden houses and a few grass shacks straggled along a mile or so of road, outlined by stone walls. *Papaia* and orange trees, clumps of red-stalked native cane, neat small fields of sweet potatoes and stands of dry-land taro grew about each house. Kane's was the best built and biggest in the village. Dad, Makalii, and I were to be his guests. The other *paniolos* went to stay with relatives and friends.

Kane's wife rushed out and we were swept indoors on a cloud of affection. Big-eyed children peeped at us from behind pieces of furniture. The house boasted several bedrooms, a living room, and a wide cool *lanai*, facing the spectacular shore-line. Well-woven mats covered the floor and the beds were covered with finely stitched quilts of gay colors. The sideboard, placed in a prominent position in the living room, compelled attention. Two kerosene lamps with brightly-painted china shades stood upon it, and between them, in the place of honor, was a pair of number twelve boots, with white tops finished with pearl buttons. I wanted to ask why shoes were kept on the sideboard but thought it mightn't be etiquette to inquire.

While Dad and Kane yarned and smoked, the rest of the household busied themselves with the pleasant task of assembling supper. As we had ridden in I'd heard that most hospitable of all Island sounds, the squealing of a pig being killed. I knew it would be hours before it was ready to be eaten and suggested to Makalii that we visit around a bit.

It was ten before we sat down to supper. I'd fallen asleep and waked up in several houses before we were called to the feast. Everyone was in holiday spirits and excited at the prospect of Kane's preaching. Lanterns spilled orange light on shiny green banana leaves spread on the ground for our tablecloth. I ate my fill of perfectly roasted pig, gorged *opihis*, stuffed myself with *poi*, chewed sections of sugar cane which Makalii peeled for me, and sucked juicy oranges.

No one was in a hurry to retire, even with the excitement of the next day looming ahead. Wind poured out of the gap thousands of feet above us where some mighty explosion in Haleakala had blown out the towering crater walls. The sea crooned to the islands. Hauki, Eole, and other *paniolos* drifted in with relatives and friends to join our group. Pili produced his accordion, Daddy borrowed a guitar, and they began playing "Nancy, Letta-Go-Your-Blouse!"

Tutus with gray hair, holding limp sleeping grandchildren on their capacious laps, brightened. Mothers suckling their newest babies laid them on the grass. Young bloods sat erect, girls preened themselves and waited while Dad and Pili eyed the gathering, debating who to call out to perform while they sang the opening verse.

> *Nancy, Letta-go-your-blouse!*
> *Hemo la! Hemo La!*
> *Letta-go-your-blouse!*
> *If you want a jolly good time,*
> *Down on the beach at Waikiki,*
> *Nancy, Letta-go-your-blouse!*

In turn Dad and Pili substituted a person's name for Nancy and he or she got up to do a stunt. Some sang, others danced *hulas,* the wags clowned. One *tutu* who looked too ancient and obese to do more than sit, amazed everyone by doing a *hula* that put younger fry to shame. Greedily, I drank it all up and when I could not keep my eyes open any longer comforted myself that the fun wasn't over. There was church tomorrow.

The entire village was up before dawn. Freshly starched *holokus* crackled as women brushed out the glossy lengths of their hair. Kids were stuck into fresh breeches and shirts, young girls hurried around with fresh *leis* for everyone to wear.

But getting Kane ready was the chief thrill. His wife, four daughters, his old mother and small son Willie scuttled about fetching this and that. A dark suit and stiff white shirt, originally intended to be worn with a wing-collar, were taken out of a tall *koa* wardrobe. Kane substituted a red rose *lei* for the restricting collar and surveyed himself in the mirror. Then he went to the sideboard and picked up the button-top boots.

Carrying them in his hand he started out of the house, his family following behind. Other groups added themselves to the procession. We started down a narrow trail winding across lava beds and I spied the church some distance ahead.

Churches in isolated districts in Hawaii always have a melancholy air. Whether they are built of lava-rock, coral, or wood they look forsaken. During the early days of the missionaries, when religion was the rage and fashion, church was a weekly event. But, as preachers drifted off to more profitable professions, attendance dropped away. The desolate little church in Kaupo, facing wind-swept bluffs and ragged lava headlands, seemed to brighten a little as our laughing procession approached.

Kane halted at the sagging gate set into a stone wall. Dragging a key out of his pocket he unlocked the church door, and half-a-dozen girls carrying extra *leis* went inside, humming love songs and *hulas* as they brightened the bare interior with flowers. When the pulpit and altar were decorated to their satisfaction they came out and perched on the stone wall, or sat cross-legged on the grass.

With great throat-clearings, Kane pulled on his number twelves and with huge clumpings walked down the aisle. Seating himself in the front pew beside an open window, he removed the boots and handed them out to his wife. Donning them, she walked in, seated herself beside her portly husband and passed the boots out to the eldest daughter to wear. One by one each member of the family used them until, last of all, small Willie skipped up the aisle looking like a lively brownie in oversize boots.

When the family was seated, the rest of the congregation filed in. Dad, Makalii, and I, being Kane's guests, occupied what was left of his pew. The pitifully bare and shabby interior of the church looked quite cheery when it was filled. Bright, eager-faced Hawaiians turned over the leaves of worn prayer books, which the majority of them couldn't read; flowers sent up their perfume.

Abundant mothers settled what they could of themselves on the narrow pews. Round-eyed children gazed interestedly at everything. Girls eyed their swains. An old man with a noble face meditatively plucked red-hot chili peppers off a spray of the bush which he held in his hand. I watched him munching steadily and asked Makalii in a whisper why he ate *niiois* in church. Makalii whispered back that old Kekei was firing himself up for prayer.

While the shoeless (with the exception of Dad and the *paniolos*) congregation gazed in mute admiration at Kane's boots, placed in a conspicuous position on the windowsill, a middle-aged woman went to a small wheezy organ and began playing a hymn. Then, as one man, the congregation began singing with the passion and abandon of the children of the lonely Pacific. The voices rising, falling, swelled into organ harmonies.

After perhaps twenty minutes of singing Kane walked dramatically to the pulpit and, beginning with a short prayer, started the sermon. His booming voice, flashing eyes, eloquent gestures, and passionate exhortations held the congregation spellbound. The longer he preached the more worked-up he became. He wiped perspiration off his face, shifted the *lei* about his throat to give himself more air, and finally unbuttoned his shirt. Children lounged contentedly against their mothers' soft sides, old men nodded approvingly, lovers held hands, women wiped their eyes.

I, too, sat spellbound. Kane was enjoying his own oratory which filled the building and flowed out of the windows in the gold and sapphire day. The noble roll of Hawaiian words pouring from his mouth had the sound of rivers in them and the deep resounding notes of the sea. No white preacher could have moved a congregation as profoundly as he did. I could not follow everything he said but was hypnotized by his gestures, earnestness, and by the deep cadences in his voice.

When he, reluctantly, brought the sermon to an end everyone sighed with admiration. Another hymn was sung. There was no collection. Kekei ate his last chili pepper and smacked his lips. Kane returned to his pew, pulled on his boots, and led the way out of doors. Church in Kaupo was over.

11. CHRISTMAS

LIKE cadenced *meles*—chants—which put an everlasting spell upon you, memories of Christmases on the ranch persist with undying vividness. Contrary to the common belief that seasons in the sub-tropics are much alike, each season is invested with distinct characteristics. In autumn, days are so utterly beautiful that you scarcely dare to breathe for fear of shattering the fragile loveliness of earth, water, and sky. In winter, mountains look stronger and more saturated with mystery. Periods of slashing silver rain alternate with days of brilliant sunshine while the atmosphere is impregnated with an electric quality that defies description. Trees look sacred and rocks seem on the verge of giving up the spirits lurking in them. *Kona* storms roar up from the equator, convulsing the land for forty-eight to seventy-two hours. First comes a louder note in the surf, then a shouting hurricane followed by clouds black with thunder and heavy with savage rain. When the atmospheric convulsion is over, the ten-thousand-foot volcano of Haleakala is covered with a glittering cape of snow, in contrast to sun-soaked, palm-fringed beaches at its feet.

We children used to watch the sea and sky for days before Christmas, praying to God and propitiating *akuas* with *leis* to send a *kona* gale to crown Haleakala with silver. If our prayers and offerings were rewarded by the white beauty of snow on the summit it seemed as if God, the *akuas*, and the mountains were all celebrating the holiday season with us.

With the white cap safely established, we dived wholeheartedly into the exciting preparations which took place on the ranch for a week before Christmas. Days weren't long enough to hold all

117

that there was to do and our activities spilled far over into the nights.

First came the ride up Haleakala with Daddy and two cow-boys to choose a sandalwood log to burn Christmas Eve. A short distance below the summit, but miles above the last outposts of common trees, was a small grove overlooked by the men who raped the Hawaiian forests of the precious fragrant wood in the early 1800's. Daddy cherished this grove. It was the last on Maui. Logs were cut only from fallen trees. When a section sufficient to fill the fireplace had been measured and sawed through, it was placed on the pack-horse, then we rode back to the forests below our mountain dairy and wove wreaths of green fragrant *maile* and draped the log with them.

When we got home at sunset, with our garland-draped trophy, the Yule season was formally ushered in. Next morning the ranch had a new bustle, a new activity. The usual work of herds and pastures continued but became of secondary importance. Two heifers, the fattest and best on the place, were slaughtered and divided equally among the workmen and their families. Pack-trains of horses and mules were dispatched to distant val-leys for additional supplies of *poi* and sweet potatoes. Each family must have all it could possibly eat between Christmas and New Year's to make a good *kahuna* and ensure abundance during the coming year. Next came expeditions to the forests and up the mountain for wild hogs, turkeys, and sheep.

While these happenings were going on, matters of breathless interest were in progress about the house. Japanese were con-cocting *mochi,* a species of rice-cake made only at that time of year. Portuguese were baking great yellow loaves of bread a yard in diameter with whole hard-boiled eggs in them. Ah Sin was mixing plum puddings and Christmas cakes made from rec-ipes three hundred years old which had been handed down in Mother's family. Hawaiians were making *kulolo* and *haupia.*

I used to wish I were half a dozen persons instead of one so

I could divide myself equally among the enchanting activities going on around me. Should I watch the Japanese working about a hollowed tree-trunk beating rice-grains to powder-fineness with great flails, smashing up *shoyu* beans and mixing them into a black, smooth paste? It was an adventure to watch them working with white cloths bound about their foreheads to catch the sweat, men and women working in turns, thrashing at glistening white kernels which they kneaded with water into flat cakes like pale, round pieces of soap. When they had been patted into shape, a finger was deftly inserted into the center of each one and a wad of slightly sweet, slightly salty bean paste was poked in and covered over. Great tubs were filled with layers upon layers of the dainties, covered with clean cloths and set away until Christmas and New Year's morning when they would be heated and eaten. After they had been in the oven fifteen minutes they puffed into huge round balls slightly crisp on the outside, like a persimmon, and inside like chewy white rubber.

Or should I go across the gulch, to the Portuguese Camp? There old Marias were boiling dozens of eggs hard, pounding at mountains of dough, into which they broke other dozens of eggs, while younger and less expert women stoked the white cone-shaped ovens behind the houses until they reached the right heat to bake the bread to proper brownness.

If I lingered among the Portuguese, snatches of music and laughter would tempt me to the Hawaiian Camp where large good-natured *wahines* were seated cross-legged on the ground kneading *kulolo* and *haupia*. *Kulolo,* made from sweet potatoes and taro and shredded cocoanut and baked for hours underground, looked like great yellowish-brown plum puddings and was chewy and stiff like caramels. *Haupia,* made from a starchy root mixed with sweetened cocoanut cream, had the consistency of soft jello and tasted like divinity fudge crossed with arrowroot pudding.

If I lingered too long among the Hawaiians, I might miss being allowed to lick the great basin in which Ah Sin was mixing Christmas cake, or might not see him frosting it with almond-flavored icing, squeezed through a twisted piece of brown paper with a hole in it.

Enticing smells filled the air. Spurred men rode out and returned with the plunder of forests and mountains. Great gunny sacks, sprouting *maile* vines, which would be twisted into fragrant wreaths, were brought in. Turkeys, hogs, sheep dangled against the heated flanks of pack-animals.

The day before Christmas a small light cart drawn by six yoke of sturdy oxen, was dispatched up the mountain for the trees. Real pine or spruce. At the seven-thousand-foot level, where frost broke the ground and occasional snow fell, Daddy had planted a grove of evergreens to supply the ranch and special friends with Christmas trees. He called the spot Little America and had a great pride and affection for these strange green friends from colder lands. New seedlings were always taken up to replace the trees which were cut down.

When the wagon was loaded it started home, escorted by riders on horseback. Decorating the family tree, set up in the living room, was a ceremony. Mother supervised proceedings but Dad always mounted the ladder, placed the silver star on the tip with three white angels beneath it, then arranged the Savior in his Manger on the right and the Three Wise Men Bringing Gifts on the left. Then, his part over, he went off and Ah Sin, Mother, and the house-servants took over the rest of the decorating. Glittering ornaments, yards of tinsel, transparent bags of hard candy were hung among the branches. Gifts were stacked around the base; toys for little boy-sans and girl-sans, yards of material for kimonos, yards of calico for *holokus,* bolts of sturdy dungaree for *paniolos'* riding breeches, shawls to cover Portuguese heads. Bangles for young girls, neckerchiefs for young bloods. Silly gifts to make Hawaiians yell with mirth, funny gifts to make Japanese chuckle.

The day of Christmas Eve was always unending. The instant breakfast was cleared away, Hawaiians began arriving carrying yards and yards of *maile* wreaths to drape doors and windows, rafters and fireplace. Bowls of fruit and candy were set out, the fire laid and the sandalwood log placed carefully upon it. Suddenly the house, the ranch, the whole world smelled of Christmas.

All afternoon the ranch hands came and went, adding their presents to those already stacked for yards about the base of the tree: bunches of bananas swathed in garlands; lengths of black Portuguese sausage, like policemen's clubs; brown paper packages tied with red string and decked with flowers. We knew the light packages were egg-bread, the heavy ones *mochi* or *kulolo*.

Then *leis* which Hawaiian girls had been weaving for the past twenty-four hours began arriving. *Leis* for each member of the family, for noted visitors, for old friends. Special red carnation *leis*, like fluffy red feather boas, were hung in the trees, giving the already heady Christmas smell which filled the house its final fillip.

As the afternoon waned, wonderful odors began emanating from the kitchen: plum puddings boiling rowdily, turkeys and pheasants roasting. Behind the Beef House, hidden by clumps of oleanders and graceful bamboos, men were preparing an earth oven for the hogs which would be roasted for the *luau* held on Christmas Day.

As evening drew closer I could hardly stay inside my skin. All the joy, excitement, and beauty of the world seemed centered in our house. Distant islands, pastures, and cane fields seemed to inch closer, as if the soil under our house was a magnetized spot drawing the rest of the earth toward it.

Steadily the atmosphere of wonder-in-waiting mounted toward its climax. Dinner, set for thirty or more people, was only another rung up the ladder of thrills when Christmas would really begin. The gleam of fine damask, light shed from heavy silver candle-sticks, mammoth turkeys, flanked by pheasants, blazing plum-puddings, goblets of wine hurried the evening toward the moment my soul craved.

My ears strained toward the dark waiting garden. On Maui and other outlying islands, Christmas was carried in on horseback and the jingle of *paniolos'* spurs replaced the imagined tinkle of Santa's sleighbells, as cowboy serenaders rode from ranch to ranch filling an already overflowing occasion with more beauty and glamor.

Behind the merriment of guests seated around our table my ears strained for the sound of horses' hoofs, and men's joyous voices singing. Yes . . . no . . . there they were. Off in the distance, coming down the road.

Then came the moment I loved beyond everything, that brought Christmas to life in a leap: the shouting *Kilo-kilo o Haleakala hula* bursting from strong brown throats and big brown guitars, blending into a joyful symphony that seemed to well up from the depths of the earth. Our *paniolos* had come, mounted on their best horses, decked with *leis,* to serenade us with the great *hula,* telling of their love and allegiance to the mountain of Haleakala and to the island of Maui, on which we all lived and which blended our lives into a whole. Behind them, on foot, came their wives, children, and relatives. We were one: a great funny family made up of all nationalities.

Daddy went out to greet them. Chairs were thrust back, guests, men in formal black and white, women in evening dress, swarmed onto the eighty foot veranda fronting the lawn. When the last stirring line of the *hula* died away, Daddy shouted "Aloha—my love to you! Merry Christmas." And was answered with the same words.

Men dismounted, tied their horses to the trees, and came in hugging musical instruments to their broad breasts. Sitting on *puunes*—couches—in corners of the room they struck up a new song. Their women, carrying the newest, littlest babies, came up the steps. Japanese mama-sans hoisting sons or daughters into more comfortable positions on their backs. Hawaiian *wahines* cuddling infants against their ample breasts. Hordes of children. Portuguese Marias looking out from under shawls wrapped about their heads. Scrubbed Japanese men holding their first-born sons by the hand.

Every available chair was filled, couches were jammed, and the overflow sat cross-legged on the floor. Ah Sin, his mummy-face cracked by a grin, lighted the tree with a candle tied to the end of a slender bamboo pole. When the tree was a blaze of quivering light, Dad went to the piano and struck the opening chords of "Little Town of Bethlehem." With the simultaneous singing of the words by all nationalities, light brighter and stronger than that shed by candles, or sent up by the sandalwood fire, filled the room and stayed there until dawn.

When the last verse was finished the distribution of presents began, interspersed by jokes, speeches, *hulas,* and ancient chants sung by the *paniolos.* Babies too small to participate actively in the gaiety were parked on beds, children played with new toys or rolled oranges and apples across the floor. Busy mothers abandoned themselves to the fun. Staid Japanese women and their stolid husbands danced Japanese dances. Portuguese gave jerky imitations of *hulas* which evoked shouts of glee from the Hawaiians.

Daddy went onto the floor, his erect, military figure suddenly fluid as a Polynesian's while he went through intricate *hula* steps learned when he was a gay young blade in the days of the Monarchy. Shy young girls, sumptuous *wahines* uttering cascades of smothered chuckles, danced with American and English ranch owners or sugar planters. Visiting celebrities became infected with the spirit of the evening. *Paniolos* gravely asked lovely white ladies for the "honor of a dance."

House-servants made unending rounds with cups of claret

punch, cake, fruit, and candy, eating as they went. The evening mounted and mounted. . . . Then once again the night caught its breath. More hoofs approaching, more ringing spurs and singing voices. The first group of visiting screnaders from another ranch were coming in to swell the ever-increasing richness of the evening. Our men determined not to be outdone. Daddy out to welcome the newcomers. Horses being tied up. Men stamping in. More shouts of "Aloha—Merry Christmas!" Then competitive singing.

Supposedly these wandering troupes of Christmas musicians, mounted on their top horses, spent the night riding from estate to estate. But the ones who came to serenade Dad, either made the rounds early, or did not bother to go on. Why move when the ultimate in fun had been attained?

Wild with happiness I dashed around, spoke briefly to people, went to the door to gaze on the glittering snow-cap of Haleakala looming against legions of stars. The night mounted steadily to a peak. Children dozed and played alternately. Adults sang, ate, chatted, or paused to nurse a child. Gifts were re-examined and gloated over. More troupes of singers arrived, contributing their particular numbers, then joining in the songs being sung by erstwhile rival bands of serenaders. All differences of race, sex, age, and station were obliterated. Something radiant and tangible had come to earth.

When dawn began breaking, slowly and sacredly, behind the vast blue dome of Haleakala, everyone began dispersing, calling over their shoulders, "Aloha—my love to you!—Merry Christmas!" then adding, as an afterthought, "See you at the *luau!*"

And the Day of Days, the Birthday of Birthdays, was ushered in by singing horsemen riding off into the light pouring its splendor out of the east.

12. KAHUNA

SOME months after my first trip to Waiopai, Daddy arranged a deal which enabled him to lease a tract of Government land lying along the eastern boundary of the ranch. The two pastures known as Ohia Nui and Ohia Lili were lightly forested and well grassed. Dad bought more cattle, building the herd up to five thousand head.

To take care of the extra territory and stock, more *paniolos* were needed. Hawaiians from all over the island applied for the job. After looking the applicants over, Daddy decided that the three Hopu brothers, from the district of Kula, were best fitted for the work. Before hiring them he consulted with Holomalia. The foreman agreed that the Hopu boys were honest, dependable, and fine horsemen and they were taken on. Three new houses were added to the Hawaiian Camp and the men and their families moved in.

For a while everything went smoothly and Daddy was satisfied with his choice. Then gradually it became apparent that the other *paniolos* were giving the Hopus a wide berth. Dad attempted to question the old hands to find out what was wrong, but they became silent and evasive as Hawaiians will when they do not wish to commit themselves. Everything was okay, they insisted, the Hopus were fine *paniolos* and likeable fellows. . . . But despite their assertions to the contrary, an intangible tension crept into the atmosphere.

Hopu Kane, the oldest of the three brothers was something of a wit in his quiet way. He became more and more silent and his large dark eyes had a haunted expression as if he were listening and waiting apprehensively for a far-off bell to toll. By one means or another the other Hawaiians on the place, excepting his two brothers, avoided being long in his company, as though he were the carrier of some insidious malevolent disease.

Daddy watched developments. Something out of the ordinary was afoot. As the days went by, Hopu Kane's face grew more and more strained and his eyes more haunted. His two husky brothers Kealoha and Keiki almost jumped out of their skins if someone made a sudden movement or spoke to them unexpectedly.

"Blast it!" Daddy said one Sunday when he was discussing the situation with Mother and some guests. "I'm going to get at the bottom of this. There's no reason why the Hopus should be sent to Coventry." He mulled the matter over for some moments. "I've got it! The Hopus are crackerjacks with horses. The Maui team needs extra ponies for the Inter-Island tournament this summer. I'll take the Hopus off stock work for the present and instruct them in stick work and riding off. That'll give me a logical excuse to be with them every afternoon. Given a chance, they may break down after a bit and tell me what the matter is."

As a rule when Dad figured a thing out, it worked along the lines he expected. Next morning when the men assembled for the day's orders he told the Hopus they were to assist him to train extra mounts needed to augment the Maui string.

There was an almost level field inside the ranch racetrack and Dad had goal posts set up and every afternoon worked with the three brothers. They proved such fine polo material that, after a few weeks, he played a match with them against the No. 1 Maui team and almost beat it. Under normal circumstances such an event would have established the Hopus as persons of consequence on the ranch. The rest of the Hawaiians, however, continued to avoid them adroitly and with the exception of the two hours while Dad was with them, the Hopu boys' tail feathers dragged in the dirt.

Knowing Hawaiians, Dad made no attempt to cross-question

them, but in indirect subtle ways he made it clear that he was ready for any confidences they might choose to spill into his private ear. It netted nothing.

Dad had been told secrets entrusted to no other white man because the Hawaiians knew he respected their customs and beliefs. They had showed him the secret leper settlement in a lost valley between Kaupo and Kipahulu where unfortunates, who did not wish to be parted forever from their families and exiled to Molokai, had isolated themselves in order not to spread the dread disease. The victims never came down off the cliff, but their relatives visited them at regular intervals, leaving food at the bottom of the bluff, and they were able to see their loved ones and talk to them from a reasonable distance.

Kaupo Hawaiians had taken Daddy into a cave at Nuu, filled with the pomp and splendor of ancient Polynesia. On a certain extra low tide, during a certain phase of the moon, when the great oily swells preceding a *kona* gale minimized danger from heavy seas, old-timers, of their own volition, had paddled him through the low, usually submerged cave-mouth into the secret burial chambers of the great chiefs of Maui. On ledges chopped out of rock in the lofty cavern were canoes filled with feather cloaks, spears, and bones, and on a smooth wall of stone an amazing carving of an Indian with a headdress of turkey feathers. But even those who trusted him completely would not talk to him about the Hopus.

Baffled and checkmated, Daddy pondered the matter. Possibly the boycotting of the three brothers might be of a religious nature. Before Christianity was introduced, religion had been as much a part of a Hawaiian's daily life as eating and drinking, as real to him as the stones with which he built house-foundations or as the wood from which he shaped canoes. Everything in life, birth, work, and death had a spiritual as well as a physical significance, and in order to undertake anything successfully it was necessary to perform appropriate religious rites.

Dad knew that Polynesians recognized the regularity of nature, day following night, stars moving in their orbits, rain, tides, wind, seasons, the growth of vegetation, and explained it all by the belief that every living thing possessed its particular variety of intelligence and worked in harmony with the rest for the benefit of the whole.

They believed that every animate and inanimate object differed slightly from every other of its class and kind because it was endowed with a different sort of *mana*—spirit substance. The *mana* of an orator, poet, fisherman, or canoe-builder was evidenced by his skill in his chosen profession. A dishonest person or unskillful workman was believed to have lost or mislaid his *mana*. If a canoe was not seaworthy, or fishhooks unlucky, they were rated as having weak *mana* and discarded. Certain localities had transcendent *mana* enabling them to bring luck to those living under their spell.

To Polynesians everything from gods to stones was interrelated, having descended from a Sky-Father and Earth-Mother. They worshiped a Supreme Being above all images, chiefs, and lesser gods, and some branches of the race held the Creator's name to be so sacred that it must only be uttered in a whisper in sacred localities where no human ear could hear. Breaking certain laws relating to this Diety was punishable by death but Dad knew such *tabus* were a thing of the past, and in spite of his intimate knowledge of things Hawaiian he could find no clue to explain the mystery enveloping the Hopus.

Then one morning Hopu Kane did not turn up for work. With pale averted faces his brothers told Daddy that Kane was ill. Dad went to see him, then called up old Dr. MacKonkey. He arrived a couple of hours later in his rattly old trap drawn by a fat white mare. Dad took him to Hopu Kane's house and the *paniolo's* big haunted eyes hung on their faces while they examined him. There was nothing physically wrong MacKonkey insisted, no temperature, no organic disturbances. . . .

Dad questioned Kane but he only looked up hopelessly, his eyes wet with tears. Nothing could break his silence or compel his wife and members of the family to reveal what was wrong. Dr. MacKonkey made repeated calls in an effort to diagnose what was causing Kane to waste away. Finally, in desperation, he sum. moned another physician from Wailuku for consultation. They went over Kane thoroughly while his weeping wife and tense-faced brothers looked on. But the new doctor could not discover any physical ailment to account for his condition.

From a hundred and eighty pounds he dropped to a hundred and fifty, a hundred and thirty-five, a hundred and sixteen. His huge frame which three weeks previously had been powerfully muscled was simply bones and skin.

A pall of gloom hung over the usually gay noisy ranch. Weekends of singing and drinking were abandoned. Hawaiians moved about in an awed way. Japanese and Portuguese went silently about their tasks. Mystery and menace filled the atmosphere. We children pussyfooted around and did not venture into the garden after twilight. Every mind on the place was in the small wooden house where Hopu Kane lay, getting weaker and weaker.

One afternoon a wild burst of wailing from the Camp announced that the big *paniolo* had gone to his Creator. It was the first time I'd heard the terrible crying of Hawaiians for their dead. The sound seemed to rise from the depths of the earth and float off to spaces beyond the stars. I fled to Ah Sin.

The warm kitchen with its food-smells and boxes of puppies, kittens, and chickens behind the stove slowed down the pounding of my heart. Ah Sin produced a box of cocoanut candy and said philosophically, "No can help if Kane dead. That life." And went on with his work.

When Dad rode in, he went to comfort the widow and brothers. Now Kane was dead, Dad was further puzzled to find the other Hawaiians went to see him and help with the wailing.

All evening, all night the sound continued, with intervals of rest while *leis* were made for the departed. I was so profoundly affected that I couldn't sleep and lay shaking in bed. Finally, I crept to Dad's room, snuggled against him and dozed off. About three, Mother came in and said in a jumpy voice, "Von, *can't* you stop them?"

"It's impossible," he replied gently. "That's their way of show-ing respect for the dead."

Next morning ranch work, except for absolute necessities such as milking the cows, feeding racehorses and polo ponies, was at a standstill. Sonoda hammered a coffin together in the black-smith shop. Four *paniolos* went to dig a grave on a nearby hill where other Hawaiians had been buried. The Japanese gardeners took time off to gather quantities of flowers and carried them to *wahines* who were making *leis*. A small ox-cart was prepared to take the coffin to the grave.

Hawaiians from outlying districts who had known Hopu Kane kept arriving, and as each new contingent arrived the wailing was redoubled for a while, then dropped to a lower key. The veranda and garden of Kane's house were crowded with knots of solemn-faced men and women, while skittering children played tag or collapsed suddenly into sleep.

About noon Dad started to take over *leis* which Makalii had made for him to give. "May I go with you?" I asked. "I've never seen a dead person but I won't be scared if you hold my hand."

Dad thought, then said: "You might as well. There's nothing dreadful about death. Often it's a release." Giving me one of the *leis* off his arm, we started for the gate.

Mother saw us and called out, and I knew from the tone of her voice she intended to stop Dad from taking me to see Kane. While Mother talked I kept tight hold of Dad's hand. I didn't want to listen to Mother's arguments, but couldn't help hearing snatches of what she said. "It's absurd to allow a high-strung child like Armine to see a dead person . . . She'll be unhinged for days . . . At best she's always in a lather about something."

Daddy waited until Mother finished talking, then said quietly, "Those are the very reasons, Amy, why I want her to see that there's nothing frightful about death."

The feeling of panic which had had me in its grip since the previous afternoon when the wailing started, ebbed away. Dad's voice was as normal as if he were talking about ranch work.

"Well, I shan't permit Aina and Gwen to go in," Mother announced, walking away.

As we neared Kane's house, women seated on the veranda rocked back and forth, beating their breasts and wiping tears off their cheeks with their unbound hair. Daddy spoke to Kane's father and mother, who were mute with grief, then went indoors. In the center of the room, set on four chairs, was the huge new coffin of pine boards, draped solidly with *leis*.

I swallowed lumps that kept pushing into my throat. I'd been to see Kane with Daddy, while he was ill, but everything felt different and I was afraid that, if I cried and acted like a baby, next time Dad did something out of the common he would leave me behind.

"Give Kane your *lei*," Daddy ordered, leading me up to the coffin. Kane lay inside, dressed in his best riding clothes, looking as if he were asleep, only stiller. Aside from the fact that he was dreadfully thin, there was nothing frightening about him. I placed my *lei* among the masses draped over the sides of the coffin and waited.

Daddy looked at the big man who had worked for him, then with a sort of regret laid his *lei* over the *paniolo's* folded hands. The Hawaiians looking on burst into an abandonment of grief that subsided when we started out of the room. In some funny way I felt better because I'd seen Kane with the dreadful frightened look off his face, which had been there for so long.

Some women relatives of Kane's asked Dad if he wouldn't

have something to eat and drink. There was plenty; Kane had had many, many friends. Of course Dad said yes. We went into the kitchen which smelled like a *luau* from all the fine food piled around.

When we came away Daddy remarked in puzzled tones, as if he were thinking aloud: "What gets me is, there's none of the gaiety between rounds of wailing usual to such occasions. Behind everything, that solid wall of silence persists!"

Daddy vetoed my bright suggestion that I go to see Kane buried. "You're too young and soft yet for an ordeal like that. I'll tell you about it when I come back."

About two, the coffin was placed in the forward part of the bullock-wagon and the immediate members of the family piled in, filling what space was left. The oxen started and *paniolos,* on their best horses, rode like an escort on each side. The rest of the ranch people followed on foot. The graveyard was only half a mile away and in an hour I heard Daddy ride in. Before he had tied Champagne to the iron ring in the big tree, I was panting for details.

Sitting down on the mounting block he lighted his pipe. Kane had been lowered into his grave with lassoes while women wailed and men sung. After the hole had been filled with earth it had been covered with *leis* which looked like a royal robe.

When Daddy talked to me alone I always felt grown-up, and when he finished speaking I asked why he hadn't wanted me to go.

"Hawaiian singing gets under a person's skin on occasions such as this. I didn't want you to get all stirred up. Kane's been frightened and unhappy about some matter for a long time. He's at rest now and that's the way I want you to think about him. And death."

Dad tapped out his pipe and we went to the Office. Studying the Alexander and Baldwin calendar which hung on the wall, he said after a little: "It's exactly twenty-eight days since Kane was taken ill. Maybe life'll go on normally now. Let's have tea."

We went to the lawn where Mother and Great-Aunt Jane were seated at the table. Great-Aunt was munching the mustard-and-cress sandwiches she loved, her old mouth working with quick, pleased little chews. Gwen and Aina had already had their cups of weak tea and as soon as I'd downed mine I joined them in the deep cool grass under the peach trees where they were playing. They wanted to hear about Kane and I described the funeral as if I'd been to it. That night, for the first time for weeks, we went into the garden after supper and the *akua* feeling seemed to have gone from it.

But next day it hit the ranch with redoubled violence. Kealoha had taken to his bed! His illness was a repetition of Kane's. As the days marched along he grew weaker and thinner and his eyes had the same horrible frightened expression which had been in Kane's. And still Dad couldn't get a word out of any Hawaiian. One by one he took them into the Office and battered them with questions. They simply stood and looked at him like respectful but stubborn children.

In exactly twenty-eight days Kealoha was buried and next day Keiki was down.

"By God, I'll get at the bottom of this!" Daddy said.

For twenty-four hours he went around with a reflective look in his eyes. Next evening while Mother was seeing if Ah Sin had given us the supper she had ordered, Dad came slashing in. "I've got it! It's a case of *Ananaa!*" he announced explosively.

We froze in our seats. There was a sound of doom and terror in the sinister syllables. *Ananaa* . . . Praying to Death! I knew from Makalii that when the moon was in its last quarter super-natural forces had ascendency on earth. Often when I woke extra early and saw the yellow dying quarter hanging in the sky I hid my head under the covers and prayed quickly to Christ, Buddha, and the Great *Akua* to protect that ranch and its people from possible disaster.

"Look," Dad went on in a tense, indignant way, "the moon was in *Ku* when Kane took ill—"

"Von, remember the children!" Mother cautioned, but he was so intent he did not even hear her.

"Twenty-eight days from the time Kane took ill he was buried. Kealoha's illness duplicated his. Now Keiki's down. Some *kahuna*—sorcerer—has a grudge against the Hopu family and is killing off the males to wipe out the line!"

Mother was Island-born and did not pooh-pooh matters of this nature. Her face was concerned.

"This explains why the other Hawaiians avoided the Hopus," Daddy went on. "They were doomed and no one dared to tell me what was afoot for fear the *kahuna* would turn his evil powers on them, too. At any rate, now, I know what's going on."

"But what'll you do about it?" Mother asked.

"I haven't figured out exactly, but I've got to do something at once or Keiki will die too. I'm damned if I'll stand for any more of my men being killed off by that son-of-a-gun of a *kahuna*. I'll find him and—"

Terror melted my bones. Dad mustn't risk his life by acquiring the enmity of the worker in dark magic. I opened my lips to protest but he looked so resolute and strong that some of the black flavor in the evening retreated, as if he were a good *akua* fighting evil.

"Go on with your supper, children," Mother ordered, then added, "Poor Keiki, he has the idea firmly fixed in his head that he's got to die—"

"I'll dynamite it out—somehow," Dad declared, as he and Mother went out of the room.

When Tatsu put us to bed, my mind was seething. Somewhere, in a place of concealment, a wicked *kahuna* was making spells and evoking the aid of evil forces to squeeze the life out of Keiki. Could Daddy save him? I tried, unsuccessfully, to overhear the running conversation going on at the dinner table, but knew from its tone that everyone was thoroughly worked up.

I knew Dad would take immediate action and when I heard him go off in the direction of the Office, I wanted to steal out, hide in the ginger bushes under the windows, and see what was going to happen. But I dared not attempt it until Mother had been in to see if we had been properly covered.

I listened to her voice in the parlor. Why did she waste time trying to convince Great-Aunt Jane that even if there were no *akuas* and *kahunas* in England, there were in Hawaii. The Great Ancient Dead and Mighty Invisible Ones hadn't withdrawn from the Pacific as they had from other lands where doubting scoffing folk let their limited consciousness shut them off from realms and forces they could not touch or see. They didn't feel the Great *Akua's* breath in the wind, sense his Presence in the ebb and flow of tides, and in the pulse of growing vegetation. Their dull ears could not vibrate to messages whispering their subtle language as nature moved along its appointed way.

Finally, unable to endure the suspense of not knowing what was happening in the Office, I slid out of bed and stole to the *lanai*. The darkness daunted me momentarily. Somewhere, hidden by the black night wrapping the world, a wicked *kahuna* was working. I hesitated, rushed down the steps, collided with a flowerpot set slightly out of line—and with horrible, noisy bumpings it went down the steps and landed on the lawn. Mother's smothered scream came from the living room, followed by flying steps bringing her to the *lanai*. She swooped on me and her nerves, ragged from the strain of the past two months, flew to pieces.

"I'm going to lock her in her room," she panted to Great-Aunt Jane, when she finished spanking me. "She's twice as much trouble as both the other children put together."

I knew the futility of trying to explain that I only wanted to be near Daddy, lending him my support in his battle to save

Keiki. Mother wasn't like Dad and Gan who understood the impulses behind my clumsy bungling actions.

I was dumped in bed and left in disgrace.

Next morning when I woke light was stealing into the sky over Haleakala. The thrill that always poured through me at dawn was replaced by a dull heaviness which reminded me that I'd been bad. I wanted to get out of the house but remembered that the door was locked and the drop under the windows was too high to risk a jump.

After what seemed eons Great-Aunt Jane came to dress me and I knew there wasn't to be any freedom that day. She didn't warm her hands before touching me, as Tatsu did, and they felt cold, bony, and clumsy. While she brushed my hair she kept telling me what a naughty girl I was, scaring people out of their wits instead of behaving like a well-brought-up English child.

By the time lessons and lunch were over I was frantic. Where was Dad? How was Keiki? Knowing that the afternoon was a total loss as far as freedom was concerned, I asked if I might write to Gan. I could, Mother said, providing I did it in Great-Aunt Jane's room while she rested. The old lady went with me to the camphor chest where I kept a pencil and paper that I used only for writing to Gan. Then she made a place at her desk for me in her bedroom and as she napped I tried to tell Gan about Kane, Kealoha, and Keiki, while I listened for Dad to come home.

"Where is he?" I burst out finally, unable to stand the suspense any longer.

"Your father didn't tell anyone where he was going, he just said he might be away for a day or so," Great-Aunt Jane retorted.

The following morning before breakfast I heard his strong light steps crossing the small veranda where spurs and lassoes hung. I tore to meet him. People seemed to burst out of every door.

"Keiki's off to work with the other boys," he announced, not attempting to conceal the triumph in his eyes and voice.

The *hi-yahs* of relief from the house-servants and exclamations of astonishment from Mother and Great-Aunt Jane filled the air for a few moments, then Mother asked, "What did you do?"

"There wasn't much to it," Dad replied. "I succeeded in convincing Holomalia night before last that if he'd tell me the name of the *kahuna* who was praying the Hopus to death I was sure I could make him stop the *ananaa*-ing. He finally told me it was Puhi but he shook like a leaf." Dad grinned. "After I had the information I needed I set off to hunt for Puhi. I finally located him and after a little convinced him it would be best for him to go back to the ranch with me and tell Hopu Keiki he'd decided, after all, not to pray him to death."

"Then what?" I gasped.

"We got back here about three this morning. When I came to Keiki's bed with Puhi I was scared for a moment that he might die of heart failure. However, Puhi lost no time in convincing him the praying to death was ended. For good. Then I told Keiki that Puhi was leaving Maui and going to Lanai to live. I told Keiki to get up and go to work. He was into his breeches and boots in nothing flat!"

Dad chuckled.

Great-Aunt Jane fixed Daddy with her eyes. "And how, if I may ask, did you succeed in persuading the necromancer to discontinue his sinister activities?" she demanded in an amused and slightly superior manner.

Imps played tag with each other in Dad's eyes, then he said as innocently as a cherub, "My dear Jane, it was as simple as taking candy from a baby. I roped the beggar and dragged him behind Champagne until he promised to do exactly as I wanted."

Great-Aunt Jane gasped, Mother looked aghast, but the servants and we children gazed at Daddy as if he were a god.

13. "MORE THINGS IN HEAVEN AND EARTH"

FOR A while the affair of the Hopu brothers haunted me to the exclusion of everything else. The deep mystery of it had cried itself into my blood. Beyond the objects about me were other worlds, other forces, half-tones of which overlapped into everyday life and wound through it. Tiny happenings assumed immense proportions and the unknown seemed to blink at me like a sly cat. Shadowy forms crept along the edges of my sleep or sat in the middle of bright afternoons staring at me. I attempted to question Makalii.

"Better no tink too much this kind things, Ummie," he advised. "All *pau*—finish—now, and better you forget."

But I was not to be put off and one afternoon while Daddy was braiding a lasso, I went to the Office steps and sat down beside him.

"I want to talk to you," I said.

"Fire away, First Born."

"I want to talk to you about *kahunas* and things like that—" I hesitated.

Dad's busy fingers stopped moving for an instant.

"That's rather a large order, First Born, and you're a bit young to bother your head about matters of this sort," he suggested.

"But I want to, I have to know," I insisted. "I keep thinking and thinking about it, even when I'm asleep. Great-Aunt Jane says that *kahunas,* and praying to death and superstitions, are just twaddle, but Kane and Kealoha are dead, and Keiki would be too if you hadn't made Puhi stop his *ananaa*-ing."

"Yes," Daddy agreed. His eyes weighed me thoughtfully and he coiled up the lasso he was working on. "Suppose you run and tell Ah Sin to make some tea to take under the pepper trees, where we won't be disturbed, and we'll see if we can't sift this matter over and clarify it a bit in your mind."

Pleasure surged through me. I loved having Dad to myself and the prospect of a long session with him discussing the thing uppermost in my mind branded the afternoon with distinction. I scampered off joyously. I knew I'd find Ah Sin under the bamboos smoking his short, three-sided pipe with its wee brass bowl halfway up the stem. He always sat there between three and four concocting new dishes or thinking about China—which he hadn't seen for forty years.

"All right, I make tea *wikiwiki,*" he agreed good-naturedly, though tea-hour was far away.

When he appeared with the neatly-appointed tray, Dad rose and led the way to the pepper trees in the corner of the garden by the horse-corral. The drooping branches made a cool tent that shut out the rest of the world. When we were settled in the grass with the pack of fox terriers lying around us, I poured out two cups and we sipped them in silence.

"The human mind is a wonderful thing, Ummie," Dad remarked after a while, "but most people use only a tenth of their brains. The world of such people is as limited as they are themselves. If a thing is outside their personal experience, they immediately discredit it, or brush it aside. A hundred years ago if a person had announced that the human voice could travel over a wire, as it does in a telephone, he would have been called crazy."

I nodded.

"The average person is like a blind man tapping his way forward with a cane, believing only in what he touches at the moment—which alone exists for him. But it would be a bold materialist who would dare to assert that the universe has been revealed to us in all its dimensions." He gazed off into space, and I waited.

"The average white person is prone to look on the superstitions and beliefs of primitive people as so much rot, but"—Dad gestured as expressively as a Hawaiian—"anyone with an open mind has got to admit that, occasionally, there are happenings which defy analysis and challenge thought and investigation. I'll illustrate what I mean by telling you a story which is famous all over Hawaii.

"I met David Gore soon after I landed in Hawaii," Dad began. "He was an ex-Annapolis man, over six feet tall with ice-blue eyes. He had graduated at the top of his class, had a mind like a sword and an education like nobody's business. As a youngster, Gore sailed past the southern end of Hawaii and saw the grassy reaches of Kau from the bridge of his warship, and he fell in love with the place. When he retired from the Navy he came back to the Islands. Land was dirt cheap during the days of the Monarchy and he bought 180,000 acres of grazing range in Kau. His herd increased and after some fifteen years he was regarded as a sort of king in the district."

Dad stuffed tobacco into his pipe. "Like all sailors Gore was nutty about his garden. He laid out flower beds, walks, and fountains, and roared like a bo'sun if his workmen laid a stone the fraction of an inch out of line. His house wasn't much to look at, but his garden became famous for he imported rare flowers from all over the world and collected every variety indigenous to the Islands.

"Behind the beautifully laid-out walks and pools Mauna Loa towered into the sky. One night when I was staying with Gore the mountain erupted. We sat up all night watching the show. The flow was some forty miles east of Gore's ranch but from the back porch we could hear the terrific thrashing of lava at white heat falling on streams and making its slow way down the mountain. . . .

"During the twenty years Gore lived in Kau, Mauna Loa erupted five times. Hundreds of thousands of acres of the sur-

rounding country were wiped out, but Gore's land remained unharmed. Talk had it that because of Gore's many secret kind-
nesses to the natives, his land was *tabu* ground which even the
Goddess of Volcanoes dared not violate.

"The superstitions and strange happenings which you're always bumping into in Hawaii, in spite of a hundred years of
occupation by Whites, set you thinking at times. I tried to discuss
them with Gore on a couple of occasions, figuring with his
unusual education he might be able to analyze and explain them.
Instead he snorted with contempt and insisted they were so much
rot and twaddle.

"In time, Gore's garden got so beautiful that he decided to
build a house to match it. While the Hawaiians were excavating
for foundations they unearthed an idol. Gore ordered it set up
in the garden. The Hawaiians protested. The idol was a likeness
of Kamapuaa, sea-lover of Pele, Goddess of Volcanos. She would
take offense if Kamapuaa's likeness was made into an accessory
for a white man's garden. The idol must be placed in a *heiau*—
temple—with ceremonies and offerings or disaster would result.
Gore flew into a passion. As though anyone could be such a
blasted jackass as to imagine that a piece of rock had any power
over humans!

"The house was finished, the idol placed among tall irises
growing around the fountain. Three months later Mauna Loa
erupted and the flow went over a part of Gore's land. The Hawaiians made no comment. Gore was amused. Just a coincidence."

"Go on," I begged.

"During the next five years two more flows wiped out 50,000
acres of Gore's original 180,000. The Hawaiians intimated that
if the idol was put into a *heiau* there would be no recurrence.
Gore was adamant.

"But the atmosphere of his place had changed. It no longer
radiated two-handed hospitality, it was grim and forbidding.
Whenever business called me to Hawaii, I dropped in to see

him and I got the impression that Gore was pitting his education, intelligence, and the force of his will against the convictions of the people living about him and against the volcano that shadowed and menaced his land. When a lot of people get to thinking in the same direction, Ummie, it charges the atmosphere with dynamite and, seemingly, impossible things result.

"When a fourth flow engulfed another 30,000 acres of the ranch, Gore's foreman, Kanepololei, staged a battle. The idol must be removed, or—

" 'By Heaven I'll show you!' Gore bellowed.

"On the island of Hawaii the affair had become an absorbing topic for conversation and conjecture. Gore was getting on in years and, except for occasional visitors, lived alone. Once when I dropped in without warning I saw him standing in front of the idol studying it. Before I was halfway up the driveway he saw me and began prowling among the flower beds like an old lion.

"Instead of discussing the matter which occupied all his thoughts and those of everyone on Hawaii, Gore pointedly avoided it. But you couldn't help thinking about it when you saw his lava-spoiled pastures, his lined face, and the contemptuous image sitting complacently among the flowers. I noticed that the attitude of the Hawaiians toward him had changed. They gave him the respect which was his due, but looked on him as a doomed man whose reign was land-sliding toward its finish.

"When earthquakes announced that Mauna Loa was preparing to erupt again, Kanepololei had another set-to with Gore. The details of the explosion leaked out, as such things will in small communities. Because of his kindness to the natives, Kane declared, the Hawaiians all loved Gore, but because of his stubborn refusal to acknowledge the power of the Fiery Goddess to avenge the insult to her lover, which had been proved by the behavior of Mauna Loa, the Hawaiians would have to leave the place before the new flow came down. Even a Goddess's patience with a human being had its limits. No one could fly in the face of an *akua* forever. Gore shouted Kane down. The old man looked at him regretfully, listened to his vitriolic comments, and shrugged his shoulders.

" 'Very well, the matter now rests between you and Pele,' Kane told him. 'As you will not heed the advice of those who know more about these matters than white folk, you will have to take the consequences.'

"As the earthquakes increased in violence and frequency, the mind of every person on the island centered on Gore. An old man fighting the concentrated thought-force of a primitive people plus a mammoth volcano.

"When the light-cloud above the summit of Mauna Loa showed that the mountain was preparing to overwhelm the district of Kau again, the entire population of the island, including most of the Whites, held its breath. It was just coincidence, it would have happened as it had anyhow, but it would have done Gore no harm to consider how Hawaiians felt about such matters. Being bull-headed was all right, to a point. . . . So talk went.

"With the exception of Kane, all the Hawaiians working for Gore pulled out. The foreman lingered after the others had gone, imploring Gore not to continue to pit himself against Pele. It does not take much imagination to figure out what Gore said. . . .

"When the direction of the flow was established, every white person on Hawaii was indignant with Gore. A contingent of leading men hurried over. No will on earth, they told him, could halt the advance of millions of tons of lava. It was sheer insanity to remain where he was. What the hell were convictions when your life was at stake? But no arguments could budge him. . . .

"The matter had got beyond merely being a question of reason against superstition. Gore seemed to feel that he was personally responsible to defend the white man's way of thinking.

"When the first red trickle of lava, heading directly for Gore's house, showed high on the dark shoulder of the mountain the committee prepared hurriedly to leave. Kanepololei, who had lingered on in the hope that Gore might be persuaded to give in when his own people took a hand in the matter, cast a despairing glance at the stubborn, magnificent, white-headed figure sitting in the house, and then vanished.

"For three days dense smoke clouds unrolled over land and sea. The air was dry and hot, filled with cindery powder that caught in your throat and choked you. When dark fell the glare in the sky showed that the lava was heading for Gore's house. Steadily, the flow pushed its fiery snout toward the sea and when it hit the water the night seemed to split and stagger backwards.

"On the fifth day the flow ceased. In thirty-six hours the crust had cooled sufficiently to make it possible for a rescue party to cross it and investigate. As if a magic circle had been drawn about Gore's house, it stood intact. A slight rise in the ground had freakishly split the advancing mass of lava into two streams which encircled gardens and buildings, leaving them singed but unharmed.

"I had gone to Hawaii to see the eruption and with others, who were Gore's friends, went to see what had become of the old man. He was seated in the living room with an extraordinary expression on his face. He had experienced something too terrific to put into words and his eyes had a strange glittering brilliance. He glanced up as we entered, then seeing Kanepololei began laughing like a man who has triumphed over the forces of the universe. What he said I can't recall. My brain couldn't digest it. When he stopped tongue-lashing his foreman, the old fellow looked at him in a strange way.

"As if his glance were annihilation, Gore got to his feet and struggled to speak. The Hawaiian regarded him regretfully. 'But I had no choice,' he insisted. 'To save your life, when I left, I took Kamapuaa's image with me and placed it in the *heiau* with correct ceremonies and offerings.' "

Daddy ceased talking and I looked at the proud blue Pacific wearing green islands like jewels on its breast.

"What became of Gore?" I asked finally.

"He left Hawaii a licked man. About a year after he returned to New England, I got word of his death."

I glanced at Daddy and waited.

"Remember the lines of that poem Gan used to say, I'm not absolutely sure I'm quoting them correctly:

> *'There are more things in heaven and earth,*
> *Than we can understand,*
> *Or are dreamed of in our philosophy.'*

"Well, *kahunas* and things of that kind are like that." Dad's steady eyes held mine. "Never close your mind against things which you don't understand. Never be intolerant, for that is the sign of a limited person."

14. THE ROAD TURNS

THERE are days full of mystery and power when you sense the presence of the Angel of Great Happenings hovering overhead and wait, holding your breath, to find out what is on its way toward you. One hot noon when Makalii and I were seated in the shade of some trees on a hilltop mending a broken stirrup leather, the atmosphere tingled with secret messages. Blue shadows seemed to be holding mysterious consultations with the valleys they crouched in. Mountains conferred majestically with clouds piled above their summits. Little breezes came from beyond the horizon, whispering of the future.

"Today gods are walking on earth," Makalii remarked, his wise gentle eyes meeting mine.

A delicious chill ran up my spine. "What is coming?" I asked in awed tones.

Makalii sat still while his veined old hands continued to work expertly with the leather thong. "I can't get it, child," he said at length, "but I sense the approach of something coming from a great distance."

I inched closer. In an inarticulate way I realized how closely my life had been bound up with that of my *paniolo*. He had taught me to ride and swim, braided the first tiny lasso for my fingers to hold, shaped my first saddle. He had taught me how to make *leis,* screened me from punishment when I deserved it, and passed on to me, with both hands, all the knowledge of the visible and invisible he had gathered from sixty years of living.

"Makalii," I begged. "See if you can't find out what the *akuas* are trying to tell us."

He stopped working and listened with his spirit. "I'm old now

146

and no longer very keen," he told me in Hawaiian, "but I know the road has turned in a new direction."

In a smothered way I sensed it too and all the time we were riding home I wondered what hidden happenings were waiting for us. But when the familiar things of the busy ranch closed in about us the mood passed. Sunlight slanted through the trees and the bustle of approaching evening seethed about stables and corrals.

Dad called out as I passed the Office. I ran in and saw a package with the New Zealand Kiwi bird stamps on it and began tugging at the string binding the bundle. What had Gan sent me! Daddy's eyes reminded me that Gan never wasted string. Painstakingly I undid each knot and it made me feel closer to her. When I hauled off the paper I went into dithers. Plus a long letter there was the promised copy of Grandfather's book "Mitla," telling of his two-year ride through Mexico, and with it was Uncle Stanley Bell's book "Tangwiera" about his boyhood spent with the Mosquito Indians in Nicaragua.

Daddy and I pored over the illustrations done by Grandfather in both the volumes—delicate pencil drawings and exquisite detail-perfect water colors. There were paintings of *vaqueros* lassoing bulls, Indians clamped like crabs against the sides of their horses, shooting arrows from under their mounts' necks. Views of waterfalls, valleys, mountains, Señoritas, caballeros, and, of course, the famed ruins from which the book had taken its name.

"Tangwiera" was not illustrated in color but had fine pencil pictures of Central American jungles, interiors of Mosquito Indians' huts, views of the village where Gan had lived for so long with her fourteen-year-old brother while the Major was absent floating mahogany down the rivers.

I rushed off with the books to show Makalii. I was glad I'd applied myself to my studies. "I can read these aloud to you," I told him.

He nodded. "I was right. The road has turned. Before I was the wise-one, now my *keiki* is the *akamai.*"

We devoted every spare moment during the afternoons to reading the two volumes, absorbing every detail of Grandfather's long ride on his beloved white stallion Shimmel. It was almost like having Gan back, telling me stories. When I ran into words I could not pronounce, or did not understand, I raced to the nearest grown-up, found out their meanings and hurried back to where Makalii waited patiently for me to go on.

After reading "Mitla" aloud four times I could quote pages of it by heart as Makalii and I rode about the pastures. Then we plunged into "Tangwiera" with equal zest, for little Gan figured in it largely. "This time you smart like hell, Ummie," Makalii would comment, as I read at full speed, stumbling over long words as I panted for the next adventure. We shivered with Gan and her young brother when pythons or jaguars raided the goat-pen under their high-legged house. We battled squalls with Uncle Stanley when he and the twelve-year-old Mosquito King sailed their dugout on jungle-girt rivers down to where they met the Gulf of Mexico, and waited anxiously when the Major was weeks overdue to return.

When we had absorbed every word of the two volumes my mind was on fire with the wonders of faraway and when I was not at lessons or on horseback I devoured the hundreds of books filling our home. Aina and I had been moved into an upstairs bedroom adjoining Great-Aunt Jane's, while Gwen continued to occupy our old quarters next to Mother. Long before I knew how to read, the book cupboard at the head of the stairs had exerted a spell over me. Now the moment I knew from her snoring that Great-Aunt was asleep, I stole out of bed, pirated the lantern, grabbed whatever book was nearest and crept back to bed to read.

The cupboard was a clearing-house for outdated literature and for worth-while books whose worn covers necessitated buying newer editions. I devoured "A Romance of Two Worlds" by Corelli, "Trilby," "Peter Ibbetson," and other novels which had been the rage in the just past gay nineties. "A Blameless Woman," by God-knows-whom, held me spellbound. I fought and bled through Prescott's "Rise and Fall of the Dutch Republic," and his "Conquest of Mexico." I was boiled in oil, poisoned with mushrooms, torn to shreds by wild beasts in "Quo Vadis," and buried under the ashes of Vesuvius (with of course a faithful dog at my feet) in the "Last Days of Pompeii."

Heretofore Makalii had been the Teller of Tales. Now I was the spinner of magic and he listened as avidly as I had done in the past to legends of *akuas* and *kahunas*. The change in our status intensified the tie binding us together. Often as we sat on the grass under the trees with the fragrant island spread out before us I was conscious of the old man's soul watching me through his brown eyes.

"Do you really think I'm smart?" I'd ask occasionally.

"The sandcrab is small but digs a deep hole," he would reply in Hawaiian, tousling my head fondly, then sign to me to go on with whatever story was occupying my mind.

Mysterious headaches which Mother could not account for in a seven-year-old child began laying me up, but even the pain shooting through my head, low fevers, and occasional nausea would not make me confess to my nocturnal prowlings in faroff enchanted places. Lessons and health began to suffer, but the marvelous constitution I'd inherited from Gan and Daddy survived somehow. Often when I was lost in some book I'd realize suddenly from the stars outside the open windows that it was getting on toward three. Then I'd hurriedly return the book to the cupboard, the lantern to the landing, and fall asleep.

Dad divined that I was going through some sort of transition and if Mother reprimanded me at meals for not replying to some question, he would say, "Leave her alone, her mind is in Mars.

She'll come back to us presently." And my love would rush to him.

Then destiny took a hand in affairs and my night-prowlings in literature were stopped until I got a sort of mental second-breath. One day when Mother and Great-Aunt Jane were at a tea I went to the Office for a bottle of creolin to wash a cut in my horse's leg. Dad was seated at his desk and the rigidity of his figure frightened me. He made a jerky gesture at an open letter lying before him.

"Gan is dead," he said.

I clutched him, feeling hollow.

"You know she was ill," Dad said, staring into space. "Aunt Lina wheeled her into the garden, as she did every morning, leaving her with her knitting, facing the Pacific, as she loved to be. When Aunt Lina went to get her for lunch, she was sitting with her work in her hands, serene and peaceful as always . . . but she was dead. She went quietly and without pain, thank God, as such a great woman should have—"

Makalii patted Dad with gentle awkwardness, his seamed face screwing up as he fought tears.

For a while afterwards I slept with Dad, and Mother even let me off lessons for a time so I could ride with him. Mother, too, had loved Gan but she seemed to realize that there had been some strange bond binding the three of us together in a different way.

And then, in life's way, the old order which had existed for as long as I could remember, began breaking up. One day Tatsu came in crying, with a letter. Her old mother was *byoki* and wanted her to go back to Japan. I was aghast.

"Maybe she'll get better," I suggested.

Tatsu shook her head. "Oka-san too old."

"When are you going?" I asked, when I could manage my voice.

"No got boat for one month," she told me, and I felt temporarily comforted.

A week later when Dad was paying off the men on a Saturday afternoon and I was proudly helping him and Makalii to stack up silver dollars, Ah Sin came in and leaned against the door jamb with an odd expression in his eyes. After he had received his wages, he said, "Mr. Louis, I like talk-talk."

"Fire away," Daddy said.

"You know China-style, when fellas die always he like bones go back to China. Sometimes family pay for it, sometimes the Tong. My bones velly old now. I got plenty silver dollar save up. I tink better I go China when Tatsu and Karamatsu go Japan. If I wait till I die, never I see old flens again."

"Who will cook for us?" I wailed.

Ah Sin grinned and patted my head with his skinny saffron-colored hand. "Got plenty cook fellas more smart from me," he announced cheerily. "I like go with Tatsu and Karamatsu. All fella can talk-talk about Mr. Louis and Haleakala Lanch and time on boat go fast."

"Very well, *makule*—Old One," Daddy agreed. "You've cooked for me almost eighteen years, and been a loyal friend to me. I'll miss you like hell, but if you must leave—" Going to the safe, he counted out two extra months' pay and put the money into Ah Sin's hands. "For Aloha," he explained, but there was a choke in his voice.

"Velly good," Ah Sin said, in an offhand manner, but a suspicion of moisture showed in his eyes. "Go-time I steal one suit and one shirt from you. I got tailor-flen in China and order one fine pongee suit and some silk shirts for you and make Aloha, too. . . . And mebb-so I send one China-style toothbrush so you no steal my old one when I go," he added, glancing at me.

In the way of Chinese cooks, Ah Sin wanted to train a young China-boy to fill his place but Mother decided she'd try a Japanese. Feeding the *paniolos* from the house was a growing problem as the increasing herd kept necessitating taking on more men. She persuaded Dad to inform the ranch that after Ah Sin left, the ranch-hands must eat with their families in order to simplify the machinery of household and kitchen.

Dull indignation filled me when I learned of the change. I couldn't imagine the garden in the early morning without brawny flower-decked men eating on the lawn and filling the new day with noisy fun and laughter. When I told Makalii about it, he remarked with the quiet wisdom of age, "To be happy, a person must adjust to things as they change." The words, spoken in Hawaiian, were solemn and made me think. Yesterday was *pau*—finished, tomorrow hadn't come; only today was actually yours.

Of course, the family was smothered with presents by the departing Orientals. For mornings before Tatsu left she broke down whenever she came to help me to dress. She loved us all but I had been the first white child entrusted to her care. When we wept together she insisted she would come back. But I wasn't to be fooled. People who went away never came back, I told her. Gan hadn't. . . .

When the desolate day came for the three old servants to leave and catch the Inter-Island steamer connecting with the liner for Japan, instead of sending them to Kahului on horseback or in an ox-wagon, Dad ordered Briton and Banjo put in their best harness and hitched to the new surrey.

I avoided the kitchen. It seemed a place of echoing sadness with a new strange cook in it. Just before Ah Sin left he went into it for an instant, as if he were taking a silent farewell of every cup, dish, and implement.

Standing with my hand locked in Dad's, watching the smart bays waiting to take away these three people I loved, a sort of panic filled me at the swiftly changing face of life. My earliest and fondest memories centered about them, and about Makalii, who stood on my other side, his hands looking strangely empty of the *leis* he had held, now piled about Tatsu's, Ah Sin's, and Karamatsu's necks.

Tatsu knelt down and took me into her arms. I tried to speak but could not utter that saddest of all farewells: *"Sayonara—Since It Must Be So."*

As the carriage vanished around a turn in the avenue, I tore free and raced after it. Dad overtook me, picked me up, and carried me to the Office, Makalii at his heels.

"Look here, First Born, if you're a brave warrior and won't go to pieces in this wholesale way, I'll give you the most wonderful present in the world at Christmas, but you've got to *earn* it."

"What is it?" I asked, when I could speak.

"Bedouin."

Bedouin! I could not credit my ears. He was one of the most beautiful horses on the ranch. A fiery four-year-old, mahogany brown and dappled on shoulders and quarters. Bedouin who was always standing on his hindlegs and prancing. Bedouin whom Dad had only ridden for a few months, who could sail over a stone wall, who, with Champagne, had won the relay race at the Fourth of July just a little while before. Bedouin! My eyes rushed to Makalii and he smiled confirmingly.

"Bedouin'll be yours in five months, *if* you're a good soldier," Daddy went on. "In the meantime, you've got to learn to ride and manage him properly."

Surges of bliss made me wobbly. What a world! It tore precious things from you and, in the next instant, gave you something as beautiful to fill the aching void. "Oh, *Daddy!*" I gasped.

"Don't say a word to anyone. This is our secret." His eyes included Makalii. "Mother's nervous about horses and would have a fit if she knew I was going to let you ride Bedouin. When you can sit him, she'll be proud. By Christmas you should do a first-class job of riding that young bunch of dynamite. He's high-spirited, but has a perfect mouth and disposition. If you keep your head and do exactly as I tell you, there'll be no risk to it."

"When can I have my first ride?" I asked excitedly.

"After lunch."

Makalii's old hooded eyes beamed with approval. Dad didn't dull the edge of joy by withholding it until it was stale, he let you have it on the flood tide. No days of waiting. In a few hours I'd be astride Bedouin's royal back. And he would be mine, providing I earned him by learning courage and self-control.

I wandered around holding Makalii's hand, my mind hazed with happiness. After lunch Dad pretended he needed a fresh horse. Makalii saddled Bedouin for him and put me up on one of Dad's other mounts.

After some furious galloping to take the edge off Bedouin, we halted. Makalii transferred my saddle to Bedouin's back and held him while Dad lifted me aboard. "Sit tight," he cautioned. "He can almost jump out of his skin. Today we'll only go at a walk."

We started, the two men I loved riding on each side. I felt like an ant. Bedouin was fifteen hands high and weighed eleven hundred pounds. The spring in his stride, the way his mane divided evenly down the middle of his neck and flowed back like water, his dark prominent eyes, the quick way his ears moved, like little birds changing positions on a clothesline, transported me to such heights of bliss that I could only look dumbly at Dad and Makalii. All the words in the dictionary were inadequate to express what I felt.

When we reached the top of the long steep hill, I was taken off.

"Nice job," Dad said, and Makalii's eyes praised me. "When we get home I expect you to go into the kitchen, and to Tatsu's room, and come out with a smile—even if it's only a circus one."

During the months before Christmas my horsemanship progressed steadily. Three or four times a week Dad managed to take me for secret rides. From a walk I graduated to a trot, then to a canter. After I'd sat a canter several times without Bedouin getting out of control, we tried a gallop, and with Dad and Makalii racing on each side I surrendered myself to the blissful stream of Bedouin's body under me. One day he threw me but I scrambled up and could hardly wait to get back into the saddle. The magic between a horse and its rider had taken place, our spirits had fused into a unit which no mishap or accident could jar apart. Then one joyous afternoon Dad told me to jump him over a log.

"Bully!" he shouted when I landed safely on the far side.

"May I do it again?" I asked.

Dad grinned and nodded. During the early 1900's it wasn't considered proper for white children to learn to speak Hawaiian, but I knew the language badly, and many of the proverbs by heart. When I made my second jump correctly I galloped back to where Dad and Makalii waited.

"He ulu iki no au, kakaa nae i ke kahua loa!—I'm a small bowling stone but can roll the full length of the course!" I chanted and Dad and Makalii slapped their sides with mirth.

When Christmas finally came, I waited for Daddy to announce to the world that I was the lucky owner of Bedouin. Present after present came off the tree. My impatience mounted. Finally, I was handed a long, official-looking envelope, with Dad's hand-writing on it. I tore it open. It was a Bill of Sale, announcing: "Bedouin, mahogany-brown, four-year-old gelding, is from Dec. 25th the property of Armine von Tempsky. Paid for by valor on the field of battle. Louis von Tempsky."

I tried to get up but my legs were as useless as melted butter. When I finally got to Dad I was crying as Polynesians cry, because my body wasn't big enough to hold the joy filling it. Dad whispered, "Paid for by valor on the field of battle means—Gan, Tatsu, and Ah Sin."

Everyone crowded around to see what the fuss was over and

Dad handed the Bill of Sale to someone to read aloud. They couldn't credit their ears.

"That's absurd. Armine can't ride Bedouin!" someone said.

"The hell she can't!" Dad retorted. "She's been riding him for five months."

15. I RIDE MY FIRST HORSE RACE

D URING the early days of racing on Maui the white residents
were roughly divided into two factions, not at enmity with
each other, but widely separated in spirit. The descendants of the
New England Missionaries formed one clique, the Outsiders the
other. The Outsiders were mostly sporty young Britons, Ger-
mans, and a sprinkling of Americans. The Missionaries raised
sugar cane. The Outsiders raised cattle and—Cain of another variety. On the Fourth of July the Missionaries staged what the
Outsiders termed "A Sunday School Picnic" at Sunnyside, while
the Outsiders rode horse races at Kahului.

In its infancy, the Maui Racing Association which Daddy organized and kept going, boasted only a one-day meet on the
Fourth of July but the entire horse-loving population of the island
looked forward to the event for six months and backward at it
for another six. The Corporation Dad worked for was made up
of Missionaries, and when Dad accepted the management of the
Haleakala Ranch he informed his employer that he intended to
continue to ride his thoroughbreds at Kahului. He pointed out
the fact that since the racehorses were owned by well-to-do families and purses were small, none of the corruption characteristic
of big tracks would creep into racing on Maui. It was purely for
sport. Horse racing gave impetus to breeding better quality stock
and he hoped that in time he could convince all concerned that
it would be to the profit of the Haleakala Ranch to buy thoroughbred stallions and raise racehorses and polo ponies of its
own.

When I was about nine, Dad told me he was going to let me
ride a small but extremely fast thoroughbred called "Don" at the

157

next race meet. By dint of his enthusiasm and effort, he rounded up half a dozen girls in their 'teens and a couple of young women and sold them the idea of riding a half-mile race. I was delirious with joy.

For a month before the meet I took Don out at dawn and galloped him on the ranch race track. Dew in the grass, birds singing, the spring of elastic muscles beneath me, glossy neck reaching for the bit, mutter of wind in my ears, the fun and gamble of staying aboard a saddle about the size of a postage stamp.

When I came in with some of the *paniolos* who were working out other animals which were to participate in the meet, I cooled Don off and spent hours polishing him with a silk handkerchief and the palms of my hands until his Burgundy-colored coat flashed in the sun.

Dad bought me a small pair of English riding boots, white gabardine breeches, and a silk shirt. Makalii carved me a narrow leather belt. As the Fourth of July drew nearer, every minute of every day was a sharp-flavored adventure.

The night before the race meet Dad called me into his room.

"Listen, First Born. Thinking about riding a race and doing it are two very different matters. Often a perfectly schooled horse, who behaves well in work-outs, will get out of hand when he lines up for a real race. Tomorrow when you ride remember to do exactly as I tell you. Don's fast and if you obey orders you'll probably win."

I gripped his hand.

"Mother isn't keen about you doing this, but riding horse races is an excellent training for life. In a horse race you've got to obey rules, do your damnedest to be first without fouling, take bumps without crying, and win or lose with a smile! That formula applies to life, too, especially the smiling part. A smile is the most heroic front man can present to God."

I'd sensed that from watching him. Often when things seemed

tough and tangled, the flash of his eyes and teeth caught me up like a lifting wave and flung me forward.

"I'll do my very best, Daddy," I promised, "so you can be proud of me."

The entire ranch had breakfasted and was mounted by dawn. The Kahului track was about twenty-five miles away and in order to rest animals taking part in the day's program it was necessary to get there early. Daddy on Champagne headed the cavalcade, boots gleaming, spicy red carnations around his hat. Bedouin was in hard training for the Cowboy Relay Race and it took all the horsemanship I had to keep him between my legs.

Japanese mama-sans balanced insecurely on sober old work horses, repeatedly rearranged their kimonos which kept flapping back in the wind, exposing their bare legs, or put up dainty hands to steady their elaborately polished and puffed headdresses. Japanese gardeners who had become infected by the racing bug which infested the ranch argued with nervous, overwrought "dace-horses" which they'd bought. Hawaiian women uttered fat merry chuckles when their nags pranced. Wrinkled *tutus* tenderly balanced wee sleeping grandchildren on pillows strapped in front of their saddles. *Paniolos* guarded ukuleles and guitars slung over their shoulders when their mounts shied or reared. Don, Jubilee, and other thoroughbreds in smart blankets with flowers tucked in their halters snuffed the breeze.

As we journeyed down the mountain, groups of riders and a small sprinkling of carriages joined us. Every so often we ran into a contingent of Missionaries.

"Right about face—the races are at Kahului!" Daddy would say laughingly.

"Turn around, the picnic's at Sunnyside," they joked back.

The closer we got to the track the more colorful it all became. Sunlight flashing off my boots blinded me, wind fluttering the silk shirt tickled my back. More riders, more racehorses came out of side roads leading into the main highway to Kahului.

Paniolos swung guitars into position and sung as they rode. Thoroughbreds sidestepped and blew dust disdainfully out of their coral-lined nostrils or squealed with indignation when some strange horse jostled them. Badinage in five tongues, the universal language of laughter, and the brave sound of hoofs filled the world.

Although we arrived early, crowds had already gathered. Swarms of laborers from sugar plantations, cowboys from other ranches leading their thoroughbreds, called out challenges as they passed. Carriages filled with flower-decked visitors who had arrived that morning from Honolulu on the flag-decked steamer rolled up to the grandstand. Hawaiian *wahines* grabbed their hats when the wind tried to snatch them off. Japanese mamasans hoisted the babies strapped to their backs into more comfortable positions. Venders of foodstuffs called out their wares. *Poi* for Hawaiians; garlic sausage and bread for Portuguese; rice balls and fishy-smelling things for Japanese; chop suey for Chinese. Watermelons, pop, and ice-cream for everyone.

The Royal Hawaiian Band, imported from Honolulu for the occasion, tossed noisy music into the air. In grandstand and bleachers people were laying bets, chatting, and laughing. Friends arriving from outlying islands greeted each other with back-clappings, whoops of glee, and shouted Alohas.

Our ranch was famed for its fleet horses, and a Fourth seldom passed without at least one new silver trophy to take home. I hoped frantically that I might supply an extra one from this meet. Bedouin was half-crazed with excitement. He stood on his hind legs, leaped sideways, tossed his head, but I felt secure on the familiar throne of his back.

Mother, Aina, Gwen, and some white women who were visiting us had left ahead in the surrey. After Dad and I saw our horses established in loose boxes we headed for the grandstand. As we made our way toward the family box, I watched the famous of the Islands visiting with each other and laying bets.

The noisy Calhouns were present in force, passing flasks around. Helen had a crowd of men about her, and other people whose faces I knew but whose names did not register, made the day sparkle with fun. Everyone had *leis* on and the ranked bleachers and crammed grandstand were as fragrant as a garden and as colorful.

Then a hush fell on the crowd. The parade was starting. A strapping Hawaiian on a fancy black horse, with flowers woven into its mane, came on the track. Standing in his stirrups he carried the Stars and Stripes. Behind him in twos came the Paa'u riders: lovely young Hawaiian girls, representing the different islands. Each wore identifying *leis* on her head and about her neck. Short capes floated from their shoulders and from the waist down they were wrapped in yards and yards of bright green, red, yellow, blue, purple, and other colored silk. The material was caught in their stirrups and flowed back on each side of their proudly stepping horses. Thoroughbreds, which were to have part in the program, followed, led by grooms and trainers. *Paniolos* came on their heels, then Japanese jockeys, and, as a sort of half-comical, half-touching windup, bevies of laughing children of all nationalities mounted on donkeys and old nags trailed in the rear.

The band struck up the "Star-Spangled Banner." Something soul-stirring gripped the day. The track, and the island, seemed to be following the flag and move forward with the parade. The dark blue field with its white stars, the long red and white strips, like carnation *leis* floating in the wind, went slowly around the brown oval of track, beckoning to the polyglot nationalities to fall in behind and unite.

The first race on the program was the Japanese race. The Japanese method of training racehorses was unique. For weeks before the Fourth they fed their animals barley mixed with dozens of raw eggs, and gave them weak tea to drink instead of water. The day before the race all liquid was withheld and half an hour before the race, the "dace-horses" were given half a pint of *sake* in a scant bucket of water.

When the horses lined up, nerves on edge with tea-drinking, half tipsy from *sake,* the starters had a problem to get them off fairly. Tense little jockeys, very professional as to caps and colors, crouched over the animals' withers, watching for the flag to fall. Spectators yelled advice.

"Look out, Yamaichi, sit in your saddle, not on your horse's neck! Kitchi's off. . . . Taka's horse is going over backwards. . . . Hang on, Japan-boy-san, I've got five bucks on you."

At last they got away. Oriental laborers, swept away by the derring-do of their compatriots, surged against the rail, Oriental calm forgotten in the excitement. Yells and shouted commands filled the day. "Hi-yah! Taka front-side now. What-for Sera try jomp fence? Kasaki dronk. I think he *kaukau sake* and no give to dace-horse. . . . Hi-yah! Sonna-pa-pitch! *Bakatari!"*

While jingled horses and inexpert jockeys streamed around the track, onlookers rocked with mirth, threw their hats into the air, shouted with delight as rider after rider parted company with his mount. Sorry apologies for what had been dapper jockeys in silk shirts resplendent with various aspects of the Rising Sun scrambled out of the dust and ducked under the rail to avoid thundering hoofs. Some horses balked, others wheeled, others jumped the fence. And the race was won by a solitary horseman busily running his horse in the opposite direction to that in which he had been started!

Relay races between rival ranches came next. *Paniolos* in teams of two, using two or three horses, took their places on the track. One man held the horses, the other rode. Saddle and bridle were placed on the ground at the rider's feet. At the signal, the first rider snatched up his gear, flung the saddle onto the horse's back, slipped on the bridle, leaped up and smoked off.

Coming down the home stretch they began uncinching, and as they came abreast of their team-mates, waiting with the next horses, they whipped off the bridles and leaped down. The riding *paniolo* slapped his leather onto his new mount while his partner seized the flying neck-rope of the one he had just used.

Three times around the half-mile track they raced, hoofs ringing, dust flying, people yelling. Hauki using Champagne and my Bedouin won by half-a-length. Another cup for our mantel!

Between noon and one there was an hour's intermission but realization that my time to ride was drawing near made me too nervous to eat.

"Wind up, First Born?" Daddy teased.

"A little," I admitted.

"Barge around with Makalii, you'll ride better empty," he said.

I found my old man waiting at the grandstand steps. Suspecting how I felt he wandered through the crowd and his kindly presence let go some of the tension inside me. He bought a few *opihis* and I munched a half-dozen. We peeped into tents and watched monstrous oiled Japanese wrestlers leaping with squatting frog-jumps, slapping their fat thighs, and taunting each other. Children squealed and raced through the crowd playing tag, their legs looking mischievous and gay.

When the gong sounded announcing the Gentleman's Race, which was the main event of the meet, we hurried back to the grandstand. Ranchers and sugar-planters rode their own mounts. At Maui race meets, jockeys and horses weren't just names printed on programs, they were people and animals you knew and loved.

When they came on the track to warm up, every cell of my body was quivering. Would Daddy win? He had to! Young Billy Cornwall had imported a powerful black stallion from America expressly to beat Jubilee, who had won cups two Fourths of July in succession. Jubilee was Island-bred, but her dam had a fine strain of English racing blood. A round dozen glossy beauties were competing for the big trophy, but the real struggle, barring accidents, lay between Jubilee and Young Billy's horse, Defender.

While the animals were lining up, I held Makalii's hand so tight that my finger-tips felt as if they would burst. The horses were mad with excitement: bucking, lunging, crashing into each other. At last the starters got them into position and the flag fell. Bunched together they swept around the first curve. A poor start left Jubilee behind but, presently, she got into her stride. Defender stretched out. The pace was terrific. Horses struggled to the front, dropped back, positions changed, then the majority of the field fell to the rear. By masterly riding Dad managed to overtake Young Billy on his black stallion. Neck to neck, flank to flank the two horses raced. Roars of excitement jarred the day as the spectators rose to their feet while black and golden-sorrel streaked down the home stretch to a thunderous finish.

Maui shouted itself hoarse, for Island-bred Jubilee, half the size of her imported rival, won by a nose. *Paniolos* rushed onto the track, tearing *leis* off their hats and loading them alike on victorious and vanquished horses and riders. The grandstand overflowed. Young Billy and Dad pounded each other's backs. What's defeat among friends? was their attitude. That *was* a race!

When the tremendous excitement subsided, panic began stealing through me. Panic, and a sort of wild hope. Two cups for the ranch. Things went by threes. It seemed predestined that I should bring in the magic third.

Two more races before my time to go out; the Bareback Race and Mule Race.

Makalii pushed through the crowd to the paddock where Dad would meet us when the Girls' Race was called. The Haleakala Ranch *paniolos* were rushing around collecting bets they'd won on Jubilee. The girls who were going to ride, young part-Hawaiians, a Portuguese, and two white girls from San Francisco visiting on one of the plantations, were loafing around the paddock waiting. They were all in their 'teens. I was a sprout. My confidence began ebbing.

Hauki and Pili were saddling Don. He looked so beautiful, so fleet, that it seemed impossible that anything could beat him. I tried to remind myself that there was no difference taking him around the Kahului track or the track at the ranch.

"Ha, Ummie!" Hauki said as Makalii and I came up. "Letta-go-your-blouse when you go out. Don hot-style horse. Run like hell. You only sit tight."

My heart was thumping so hard that I felt seasick. Presently I saw Dad coming through the crowd. The day swayed and seemed to get out of focus. But the instant he put his hand on my shoulder I felt steadier. If he thought I could ride a race, I could. Hadn't he bought me real racing boots, breeches, and a fine silk shirt? Given me a horse which had won two races already?

The minutes rushed with indecent haste toward the time I must go out.

"Remember, First Born," Dad said. "Do exactly as I tell you. Sit tight and well forward, cross your reins like this." He showed me the correct hold. "When the flag goes down, Don'll leap from under you like a bolt. He's trained to 'break.' If you're not careful you'll land behind the saddle. And remember, keep your head and don't foul. Don't cut in for the rail unless there are two full lengths behind you and the nearest horse. And whether you win or lose, come in with a smile!"

Makalii held Don, Dad gave me a leg up. Quivers of excitement were transmitted into me from the body of the eager animal between my knees. I didn't feel like me. I was just a dot in a universe which seemed too big to endure. *Paniolos* ran beside me as I started for the track, cheering me.

Something inside me was running around laughing, crying, jumping, and wringing its hands. There were odd muffled noises in my ears. I kept swallowing my heart which had got stuck in my throat, but some section of my mind was clear. I knew what I must do, and how I must do it. Don would see to the rest.

The older girls were laughing and joking, a race was just a lark to them. Probably they'd never ride another. But horses were in my blood, Dad had started and upheld racing on Maui. I was the first of his children to ride a race on the track and I wanted to distinguish myself.

We were lining up. Suddenly the girls settled down to business. They jockeyed for position, thrust, and shoved. Don was almost unmanageable. Once he almost flung me over his head and I only recovered myself by a miracle. Panic made my limbs weak. I mustn't fall off and disgrace Dad in front of the whole island of Maui.

"Get your horse around, kid!" one of the starters shouted, as Don leaped out sideways.

With a tussle I dragged him around. I began to wonder if I would be able to handle him once he got going. From what seemed to be half across the world I saw Daddy and Makalii standing at the rail looking on. I knew Dad would not call out advice. I was up and on my own. I felt lost in a sea of darkness, surrounded by legions of immortal invisible enemies. Don was fighting to get away, impatient and irritated at the delay in lining up caused by inexperienced jockeys. We broke once, a girl was left at the post, and we were called back.

Already I was dizzy and exhausted. Before I was quite in position the flag fell. A hot iron of agony rushed down my back. The grandstand roared: *"Let them go!"*

Don shot forward like a catapult, my hold on the reins slipped, and with a bang I landed behind the saddle! And stayed there the whole half-mile! My weight was wrong, my position hampered Don and in spite of his speed we were left behind. The track was damp. Earth pellets, hurled from flying hoofs, stung me like bullets. Before we had run a sixteenth of a mile I knew I could never get back into the saddle and there was a question as to whether or not I could stay on to the finish. But that I determined to do. I knew the absurd and ridiculous figure I was cutting—like a Japanese jockey. Tears scalded my cheeks and I tasted their salt bitterness in my mouth.

On the home stretch I made up two lengths and the barrage of earth-clods became almost unbearable. I could see nothing but felt the horses thundering ahead of me. A roar struck me like a blow. We were over the finish line and—I was the donkey's tail!

I got Don stopped finally, scrambled back into the saddle and rode back. The world was a gray mist through my tears, then something jerked me to my senses. Dad's words echoed in my ears. "Whether you win or lose, come in with a smile." I'd have one for him, even if it was a bleary one! Then strong hands pulled me off: Daddy's, Makalii's.

"Good girl, swell girl, *you stuck on.*" Daddy was shaking with laughter. He wasn't disgusted or disgraced. Suddenly instead of a tragedy it was sport. Just fun among friends. I forgot that I looked like a leopard, my fine white breeches and shirt all spotted with mud. Makalii piled me with *leis, paniolos* beat me on the back.

"Circus-girl, circus-girl, like before when you ride Bella and catch hell! Next time you ride again and sure you win. *Wela-kahao!*"

The band struck up "America," the steamer blew its whistle. The crowd began dispersing. Slowly, reluctantly, I left the track with everyone else and headed back for Haleakala. Strummed guitars lulled babies to rest and soothed tired horses as we made our slow way up the long slopes of the mountain.

When the late dinner was over, Dad, after riding fifty miles and a horse race, danced *hulas* with his *paniolos* on the lawn.

Two new silver cups, draped with *leis* and filled with fizzing champagne, passed among the Whites. There was *sake* for Japanese, *samshu* for the Chinese, wine for Portuguese, *okolehao* for Hawaiians. Races were verbally re-ridden, victories re-enjoyed, defeats laughed over. Letta-go-your-blouse! The Fourth of July!

16. MY PANIOLO

SHORTLY after my ninth birthday Great-Aunt Jane was offered a position as governess in a family living on Hawaii. The salary was good and she accepted it when Mother found another woman to teach us. New governess Number One was a pleasant plump young woman who speedily married a man from Honolulu.

Number Two came from a fine old Virginia family. She was tall and had clouds of red hair which fell like a glittering cloak to her knees when she washed it. The sheer beauty of it hypnotized us and often if we were restless at lessons we'd promise to be good if she'd take it down while she taught us. Because her family owned hunters in Warrenton and rode to hounds we respected her, but after she was with us for a while, illness in her family compelled her to go home.

A young German ex-officer filled her shoes. From the start we despised Tutor. He shouted at us and rapped us on the knuckles with a ruler if we missed a note while we practiced the piano. He boasted about his horsemanship and when Cigarette, the mare Dad assigned to him, threw him over the stone wall one Saturday afternoon, when all the *paniolos* were there to see, we were delighted. He stayed about eight months, then got a Hawaiian girl into trouble, and was hustled off overnight.

Governess Number Three was a starched woman who wore high-boned collars and a frightening pompadour. As I walked around the table one morning handing out papers, I brushed it. Something inside moved slightly and I shied away like a scared horse. I asked about it and Number Three informed me coldly that all pompadours were built over rats. "Do you keep rats in

169

your hair?" I asked, horrified. Her face grew scarlet. Pompadour rats were made of wire, she explained. We begged her to show us the marvel but she refused.

When I told Makalii about it, he was as curious as I was. I tried to devise some way to steal it but Number Three always locked her door and as her room was upstairs there was no way of climbing in the window. However, a week or so later she washed her hair, and she placed the rat on the window sill to dry. A gust of wind blew it off. Makalii and I were sitting below in the shade and I pounced upon it. It compressed and expanded like Pili's accordion. I showed it to Gwen and Aina and when I returned it I asked Number Three to let me see how it went on, but she snatched it and flounced off.

Her reign was brief. She spoke of horses "lapping" water and we told her only dogs did that. On another occasion she told Dad one morning at breakfast that the mushroom spawn he had imported from New Zealand and planted in the fern house had sprouted. "I saw the green shoots," she finished. Our contempt for her was complete. Anyone who thought horses lapped water and mushrooms had green sprouts was beyond the pale.

Great-Aunt Jane was written for. She commanded respect and could handle us. What I didn't know at the time was that Mother expected a baby in a few months and wanted one of her own family around. With the exception of two uncles, living on other islands, all the Wodehouses had gone back to England.

It was cheery having Great-Aunt back, munching mustard-and-cress sandwiches and nibbling cold boiled bacon at breakfast. Her old bedroom was now the schoolroom and she occupied one of the guest-rooms off the Office. The arrangement suited me as I'd resumed my night reading and did not want her too near.

One day Makalii showed me a lump on his leg which he said was very painful. I told Dad and he ordered the old man to take a month off and rest. Like most of the Hawaiians working on the ranch, Makalii had a small *kuleana* of his own, cultivated by other members of his family. Dad asked him how the leg had been injured and he said a horse shied him into a gate post a few weeks previously.

Every few days we rode over to see him but instead of improving his leg got rapidly worse. Dr. MacKonkey went to look at it. When he came back he went to the Office and when Dad came out his eyes were troubled. I wanted to know what was wrong but Dad seemed unwilling to go into details. I did not press the matter as I knew we'd be going to see Makalii again shortly and felt sure I could worm the truth out of him.

Three or four days passed, then Mahiai, Makalii's fifteen-year-old son, rode in from Kula and asked Dad to take me to see Makalii at once. We reached his hot little house in the cactus around two. Dad told me to wait outside for a few minutes and when he called me I felt apprehensive and upset.

My dear old *paniolo* was seated on the floor, his back against the wall. The smile-wrinkles at the outer corners of his eyes and the seams in his forehead and cheeks were deeper, and pain had carved terrible new lines around his mouth. His sore leg was stretched out in front of him, packed in *laukahi* leaves and wrapped with layers of newspapers.

When he saw me he began crying without any sound. I rushed to him. Something grim and horrible was in the room, which even Dad's presence could not dispel. After Makalii got hold of himself he began asking me about Bedouin. I told him he'd have to make me a bigger saddle as soon as he got well as my old one was getting too small to use much longer. He gazed at Dad as if someone had struck him a staggering blow over the heart.

"I'll order leather and wood," Dad said, then quickly changed the subject.

After a while the atmosphere seemed more normal. Flies buzzed against the windowpanes and, outside, pigs grunted and rooted in the cactus. I heard Bedouin stamping and the sweet sound of wind pouring over the island. But when the time drew near to go home, terror and sadness crept into the house again.

Makalii began kneading my hands in a distressed way, his eyes riveted on my face. All our beautiful years together, all the fun we had shared, all he taught me rushed over us like a flood which strangled and drowned us, making words useless. I began crying wildly, "Are you going to die, Makalii?"

He gestured at his leg. "Yes, *pau, wikiki,*" he said, and began kissing my hands. "My *keiki,*" he kept saying under his breath in Hawaiian, "my *keiki,* who I carried on a pillow before she could walk, whose golden head has rested on my heart . . . who I taught to ride and swim . . . my *keiki.*"

I felt all control slipping from me, and Dad said in a quick reminding voice, "Valor on the field of battle." It gave me strength.

Makalii held my hands to his forehead, pledging eternal fidelity. Flinging my arms about him I clung close. It seemed to comfort him in a deep wordless way. He knew, as I did, that he would always mean something to me that no one else in life ever could. His wistful eyes followed us as we went slowly toward the door.

"*Me ke aloha pau ole!*" he called to me.

He didn't need to tell me. My love for him would never end, either. Dad gripped my hand and my voice, jammed achingly in my throat, did its duty. "*Me ke aloha pau ole—my paniolo!*" I said shakily.

Two nights later, just after dinner, Dad came to where I sat with an open book on my knee. "Word's come that Makalii's dying. I need Bedouin; no other horse will get me there in time."

While Dad changed out of flannels into riding togs I went upstairs for a plumaria *lei* I'd made to wear next day. After Dad's spurs were buckled on I gave it to him. He took it and I went out to see him mount.

"Thanks, First Born, for the loan of your horse—and your steadiness," he said, kissing me and vaulting into the saddle.

I listened to the swift thud of Bedouin's hoofs getting fainter and farther away. The stars looked lonely and remote, and slowly swaying trees were full of disaster, but I knew I was behaving as Daddy wanted me to. I had crossed some invisible boundary into a new country, the country where Dad and Gan had lived all the crowded colorful years of their lives.

The knowledge made me feel closer to them and better able to bear the thought that Makalii was dying without my being beside him. If I had insisted on going on a slower horse, Daddy might not reach him in time. Makalii would know from my *lei* that I was with him in spirit, as Daddy would be in the flesh.

I looked at the lighted windows of the big house. I didn't want to go indoors and have my sorrow pressed in on me, making me feel more bereft and cut off from the things Makalii and I had shared: wind, stars, growing green things, and the mysterious forces behind them. I strained my ears to see if I could hear Bedouin's flying hoofbeats, but they had died away. Each passing instant took Daddy closer to the bedside of the dying man who had served him faithfully for a quarter of a century. Yes, I thought as I sat on the mounting block, Dad would be the most fortifying person to have near when a spirit slid out of its envelope of flesh to go on its mysterious, unseeable way back to the source from which it had sprung. . . .

Hawaiians from all over the island attended Makalii's funeral. In his humble quiet way he had been a great personage, loved by everyone who knew him. At his own request, instead of being buried in the family plot adjoining his small homestead, his grave was dug in ranch soil on the hilltop where the Hopu boys lay.

All the Japanese women on the place blackened their front teeth with *ahaguro* and powdered gall nuts, as was the custom in the past to show they were mourning a dear one. Mother cried until her face was swollen. When she had come to Maui as a bride, Makalii had met her and Dad at Makena with horses and when they finally reached the little house in Kula, where Daddy lived then, Makalii had it decorated with *leis* and made it beautiful to receive her.

Shortly before the funeral cortege was ready to start, Dad called me into the Office. "I haven't given you details of what was wrong with Makalii. He died of the most swift-moving and painful form of cancer. You must be glad his agony is over and he is free. It's like the old horses on the ranch. When they're too crippled with age to live in comfort I shoot them to spare them needless suffering. Makalii's death was a blessed release."

My insides were quivery, but the feeling of steadiness which had been born in me when my horse's fleet legs enabled Dad to get to my *paniolo* before he went, overrode my emotion and kept it in control. In a fumbling way, I tried to tell Dad about it and his eyes, which had been filled with pain, grew a bit glad.

"Bully. From now on you're my First Lieutenant. Funerals are harrowing affairs. I don't believe, as a rule, that children should go to them. But under the circumstances you should be present. He was your *paniolo*."

When I stood beside Dad and the crowd of people around Makalii's open grave, sobs rose inside me and I had to lean my forehead against Dad's arm to stop my body shaking. "From now on you're my First Lieutenant," I kept saying to myself, and behind my sorrow there was a glow. It was like, "And you shall stand on my right hand and keep the bridge with me!" in the Horatius poem.

My memory recalls, across all the years, every detail of the occasion. Japanese yardboys and nurserymen with dogged, almost angry, expressions on their faces as they fought their emotion. Japanese mama-sans with blackened teeth. Hawaiian women with loosened hair, wailing. *Paniolos* singing in voices

like echoing organs. The six best oxen with *leis* twined around
their horns, waiting in the small wagon. Tied horses stamping
at flies and the tawny-blue shape of Haleakala stretching across
the sky.

Daddy's other arm was around Mahiai, Makalii's orphan son—
whom Makalii had entrusted to Dad. Hawaiian men aren't
ashamed to cry and when Holomalia, Pili, and the other older
men began lowering the coffin with *lei*-covered lassos into the
grave slow tears spilled down their cheeks. Big, gentle, and strong
they reverently went through the last services they could render
to a comrade of the saddle who would ride with them no more.

Dad flung me a silent command to give him his arm so that
he could put it about Mother who was crying with the abandon
of a Hawaiian *wahine*. Instinctively I glanced about for Tatsu,
Gan, or Ah Sin. They were all gone. But I would not fail Dad,
the last of my very-loved ones. Pushing back, I sat down in a
huddle on the grass.

Nothing seemed real: the slowly moving figures working about
the grave, the thud of spadefuls of earth falling on the coffin
Sonoda had made. I mustn't think that Makalii was inside it,
that I'd never see him again, I reminded myself frantically. I
must do something to get my mind off in a safe place. Then, in
the queer way of times of stress, a merry little Hawaiian verse
Makalii had taught me to say when I rode my single-footing
pony flashed into my mind.

> *Kau lana mai nei*
> *O Aala lai*
> *O ka lio holo peki*
> *O ka lei aloha la.*

> (*Gallantly famous*
> *Is Aala Lai*
> *The single-footing horse*
> *Of our Child of Love.*)

As I repeated it over and over, it seemed as though Makalii and I were riding together with wind in our faces and flowers on our hats. The rhythm of the words created the illusion that a horse was under me, and when I repeated the verse for the fifteenth time, I realized men were swinging onto their horses and women and children piling into the empty bullock wagon, or starting off on foot for the dark groves of trees hiding the ranch and camp.

When Pili had driven off in the surrey with Mother and the rest of the household, Dad came to where I was sitting.

"Nice job, First Lieutenant. *Mahalo nui*—thanks a lot," was all he said, but no man kneeling before a king to be decorated for some outstanding achievement felt more exalted than I did.

17. A BABY AND A WRITER ARE BORN

SHORTLY after Makalii's death, a letter came from Major Wode-house in England saying that three distinguished Britishers, en route to New Zealand and Australia to fill official positions, would stop off for a week at the ranch. Mother and Great-Aunt Jane were in their element.

Guests were no novelty. We had permanent guests, semi-permanent guests, week-end guests, drop-in guests—guests for dinner, wild-cattle hunting, Christmas, polo, and the Fourth of July. There were social guests, business guests, and all the in-betweens. Sometimes it was like a wheel spinning so fast you couldn't see the spokes, and on other occasions we were briefly alone, but—these three gentlemen were *England!*

Bachelors' Roost, the big guest house separate from the main house, was cleared of local males of more-or-less English extraction who haunted it over week-ends, holidays, and between jobs. A charming, raffish, and often worthless crew: young scions of great families, remittance men, cashiered officers who, while they contributed nothing of lasting good to life, added to the gaiety of nations.

One or two of them were rather disgruntled at being ousted from their comfortable quarters into a set of smaller rooms ad-joining the Office, where wandering priests of various religions were housed when they drifted through the ranch on their way to obscure parishes. Dad chuckled and told the grumblers:

"This is Amy's turn to howl, her particular show. If you don't want to occupy beds which Mormon, Catholic, and Shinto priests have slept in, shove off somewhere until the show's over. Personally, I don't think a little religion, even if it's absorbed through a mattress, will do you any harm."

One shoved off, the others went cheerfully to temporary quarters. Hemstitched, hand-woven sheets of Irish linen were laid out; embroidered pillow cases; the biggest, fluffiest towels. The house-boys arranged bouquets which were masterpieces of Japanese art. The new cook concocted special dishes in honor of the visiting Great Men. Hawaiian girls wove *leis* to hang around their noble necks. I was burning to see the important personages whose advent had thrown our household into such a lather.

Whisky and Soda, the new carriage horses, were put in the hand-stitched, brass-mounted London harness and sent to meet the steamer. An elaborate afternoon tea was prepared. About three, the rumble of wheels sounded in the avenue and I hurried into the garden for a peep at the visiting Archangels.

I was prepared for uniforms covered with glittering medals, helmets with sweeping plumes, swords, and was completely let down when three tall, angular, bleak-faced men, in ordinary clothes, got out of the surrey. Mother in a foaming white *holoku* with a flower in her hair, Great-Aunt Jane in crackling black taffeta, and Dad in smart riding clothes welcomed them.

Sir Hugh, the most important one, was over six feet tall and his loosely made but extremely well-cut tweed suit gave him an air of distinction. Captain Bailey was shorter. He had merry blue eyes, a tomato-colored face, and his close-cropped military mustache was so white that it looked like a dab of soapsuds he'd omitted to wipe off his upper lip after shaving. Viscount Ashley was handsome in a weak way. He had never been out of England, wore a monocle, and his one comment for everything new was " 'Pon my word!" in half-shocked, half-amazed tones.

But Mother was happy. These were her people, the kind of people who had foregathered at Major Wodehouse's residence on Beretania Avenue in Honolulu when he had been British Ambassador to the Court of Kalakaua. They talked her talk, thought her thoughts. They commented on the excellence of her tea; praised the mustard-and-cress sandwiches of unbelievable thinness that Great-Aunt Jane had made; came back for second servings of Scotch short-bread made from Gan's receipt; and finished the plate of plum cake.

While Mother and Aunt Jane sat with them talking of England and things English, I watched the house-boys setting the dinner table. Glossy damask, huge hemstitched napkins, heavy silver, sparkling crystal, massive candlesticks, which had been handed down through generations of Wodehouses, gave the long table a flavor of bygone days when knights and princesses had been seated above the salt. When the last heavy silver salt cellar was in place, *paniolos* came in and hung fluffy carnation *leis* on the back of each chair.

Saturday night the ranch was on tiptoe with excitement, as usual, but the tingly atmosphere was stepped up notches by the arrival of the important *Pelekanes*—Britishers—who were honoring the place with their presence. Over week-ends the Camp where the workmen lived was always noisy and gay. Portuguese celebrated whatever Saint's day was nearest; Japanese celebrated events of importance on their calendar; Hawaiians celebrated— everything.

As a special concession, we children were informed that we were to come in and meet the notable personages for a few moments when after-dinner coffee was served in the living room. Mary, a lovable Hawaiian from Kona, who had replaced Tatsu, dressed us in our ruffly best.

When the party assembled in the *lanai* for canapés, cocktails, or Scotch and soda, we flitted around the garden watching the show. The three Britishers were in formal evening dress; Mother in a new frock ordered from Honolulu, Great-Aunt Jane in heavy black satin with an old-fashioned coral brooch at her throat. Dad wore white flannels, a maroon cummerbund, silk shirt, and white coat. A few hand-picked Maui people had been invited and when everyone went into the dining room, the most important women of the party took up the red carnation *leis* and decorated the visitors.

" 'Pon my word! Quaint—what?" Viscount Ashley stuttered.

Captain Bailey gave a short bark of laughter: "I must look like a positive jackass, but the flowers smell nice."

And Sir Hugh, "It's the custom of the country, I presume." And he resigned himself to his fate with as much grace as he could summon.

"We're, ah, going to sample, ah, native foods, I presume," Viscount Ashley observed, making polite conversation.

Mother shook her head. "No, the Roast Beef of Old England," she assured him, "and Yorkshire pudding."

"Upon my word, how perfectly topping," Sir Hugh exclaimed, "after weeks of American food—" He could get no further.

I had never seen Mother so happy, so animated. Through the window curtains she looked like a girl. She was back in her proper English atmosphere, which the Major had faithfully preserved in Hawaii. Nothing can match the treasure of shared memories and Mother was sharing them with these, her own people. They brought her first-hand news of the net of Wodehouse relatives: the Earl of Errol, Lord Wodehouse, the Duke of Kimberly. . . . She loved Dad, loved Hawaii, but she had never merged into it completely. Part of her clung to the Rock-of-Gibraltar atmosphere which had surrounded her early years— the level ordered path trodden by English feet in far-flung lands forming the British Empire and all its over-lappings the world over. For once she had the atmosphere she craved in her own home, to the exclusion of everything else. Hawaii was pushed out into the purple night. England was enthroned in the house. Noble roast, men and women in formal evening clothes. Lowered voices, pleasant conversation. Candlelight, silver, knives and forks moving precisely on Crown Derby china.

Daddy kept watching her in a happy way. "Your night to howl, Amy," his eyes seemed to say. "Your night to howl." And his gladness for her was a delight to watch.

Suddenly the side-door of the dining room flew open as though it had been blown inwards by the blast of a volcano. A frantic scramble of bare brown limbs, naked brown body, flying black hair propelled itself across the room into Dad's arms.

"Louis, Louis, *kokua*—help me, save me!"

Sobbing, hysterical, Moku's wife, Lehua, tried to scramble into Dad's lap. Terrified brown eyes rolled apprehensively over her bare shoulder, and her big brown body shook like bamboos in a high wind. In the candlelight, against the white tablecloth she showed absolutely, and shockingly, naked!

Aunt Jane made a smothered sound, Mother went white as chalk. Captain Bailey's soapsud mustache froze on his lip. Viscount Ashley gagged. The monocle dropped out of Sir Hugh's eyes, and a visiting Island woman burst into high hysterical laughter, as, terribly and suddenly, the elegant dinner party smashed into a million screaming fragments.

"What in blazes is the matter?" Daddy demanded, hurriedly draping his big napkin over what it would cover of Lehua's ample form.

"Moku like kill me," Lehua shrieked, burrowing her head into Dad's neck. "Moku too much *huhu*—mad. I dance hot-style *hula* with Hauki, but only for make some little fun. Hauki, you know Hauki, you know how he make Saturday-night style. *Ona*—crock to the gills!"

She was crying with the abandon of a child, wiping tears away with her long black hair, eyeing the paralyzed, scandalized guests. Then with Polynesian aplomb she tried to make amends and inject an everyday flavor into the occasion.

"I too sorry, too shame, this kind things happen when swell *Pelekanes* come here." Her glance included the three Britishers. "But no can help. That Hauki, he bad rascal." A rather admiring note crept into her voice. "Always he raise hell with girls. Moku, he get mad and tear off my clothes so he can lick me. Then Hauki get mad and pick up lasso—" She was warming to her story, then the tempo of her voice changed. "Oh, better you go quick, Louis. Maybe this time Hauki rope Moku and kill him."

Suddenly she was the loyal wife, rushing to the defense of her man.

"Go *wikiwiki*, Louis. That damn-blasted Hauki like crazy fella when he drunk. Knock him out, Louis. I scare for go back. Moku, maybe, he no finish mad with me yet. You lock me inside Office till tomorrow—"

Dad slid Lehua off his lap, ripped off his coat, put it around her bare abundant form and hustled her from the dining room. But the dinner party was left in ruins. Lawless, pagan, prodigal Hawaii had triumphed over England.

Locking Lehua in the Office, Dad dashed for the Camp. Hauki was running amok, swinging a lasso and pursuing Moku who was dodging around trees trying to escape from the fury of his wife's admirer. I climbed shakily onto the stone wall when I saw Dad charge into the Camp filled with shouting Hawaiians, Portuguese, and Japanese milling around like cattle.

Then I saw a white wedge of shirt-front hurrying through the garden—Captain Bailey. He flashed through the gate and vanished into the crowd surging among the little houses. After four or five minutes, he and Daddy came back.

"It was no trick to knock Hauki out, he was blind drunk," Dad said. "But this has happened once too often. He gets the sack tomorrow. Blast his eyes. It's his fault that Amy's nice party was spoiled."

Captain Bailey gave his usual short bark of mirth. "But upon my word it was topping! I'll never forget that naked brown woman bursting in like an explosion! It was worth the whole trip from England."

Next morning Hauki was waiting on the Office steps with his usual *lei* of repentance.

"You're *pau,* for good," Dad told him sternly. "You scandalized high-born guests. Amy had hysterics, which is bad for her because she's going to have a baby."

Hauki wept and pleaded. Dad was adamant. Suddenly Hauki realized that this *was* the end. Tears poured down his cheeks, he dumped his handsome head on the desk, then flung it up. Grabbing Dad he burst into impassioned Hawaiian.

If he could be *paniolo* to the new baby he'd quit drinking. Forever! He would become a dyed-in-the-wool Missionary. More than he craved *okolehao*—spirits—or *paanini*—beer—he wanted the honor of having charge of one of Dad's children. He would be a second Makalii!

Dad listened, then debated for a few moments. "Well, Hauki, I was no angel when I was young. I'll give you one more chance. That's every man's right. If you stop drinking, you can stay on. When the new baby's born, I'll decide whether or not you can be its *paniolo.*"

We children and the ranch were informed, officially, a few weeks later that a new baby was in the offing. Mother was a highly strung, nervous woman and the solicitude of everyone on the place was a wonderful example to us children who, otherwise, might not have shown any particular consideration for her condition. But *paniolos* coming home after twelve hours in the saddle rode miles out of their way for some delicacy of food that some specific district had to offer. Japanese houseboys held her head tenderly when nausea overtook her and every *wahine* on the place waited on her hand and foot.

As time drew near for her to *hanao,* baby presents poured in: kimonos, tiny straw sandals, gaily embroidered little caps from Orientals. Hand-stitched quilts, *lauhala* mats from the Hawaiians. Dainty dresses, bibs, and bonnets from white people.

With a sort of awe I saw that on all sides still newer designs were being woven into the pattern of our lives. Hauki had turned Missionary. Kasaki, the Japanese cook, whom I had resented, had become a close friend. When letters from Tatsu came from Japan, he gave me her news and her messages. And a new von Tempsky was shortly to be born.

When a mail brought Dad the promised pongee suit and silk shirts, plus a Chinese toothbrush for me, it took all the self-control I possessed to go near the kitchen. I missed old Ah Sin, missed seeing the *paniolos* eating on the lawn, but remembered what Makalii had said, that if a person wanted to be happy he must adjust to things as they changed.

Mary, the Hawaiian woman who filled Tatsu's shoes, had been educated in the Sacred Heart Convent, and took over the running of the house. She taught us to sew and embroider, to weave *lauhala* mats, and make imitation feather *leis* out of frayed silk ribbon, and *lomilomi*-ed Mother to make her supple and ready for the arrival of the new baby.

While she worked over her, Mary instructed us in the art of massage. Her brown hands and sensitive fingertips knew the location of each nerve and muscle and the proper way to manipulate it to refresh and re-energize the body. While she went over Mother inch by inch she explained that the *lomilomi* of Hawaii, the *omiomi* of the Marquesas Islands, the *taurumi* of Tahiti, and the *momi-ryoji* practiced in Japan were all fundamentally related.

After some instruction I tried out my skill on Dad when he came in tired from an extra hard day in the saddle. Working over his back and legs I learned the truth of what Mary had told us—that to *lomilomi* successfully, the life energy in your body must be released through the fingertips so the magnetism flows into the person under your hands. As a patient's body revived, the force in it began flowing back into the operator, enabling anyone with skill to work for hours without becoming fatigued.

One Sunday morning after breakfast, Mary told us to get our books, the current litter of puppies, and go and play quietly under the pepper trees, away from the house. Mother was starting to have her baby and mustn't be disturbed. Just as we were starting off Great-Aunt Jane bustled out looking as scattered as a hen in a high wind.

"Your mother wants to see you before you go off," she told us.

Mother was seated on the couch in the living room, holding Dad's hand. Her eyes were full of tears. The door leading into her bedroom was open and Princess Ruth's four-poster was draped with a big Union Jack which Major Wodehouse had left her. "My new baby will be born under the English flag—as you all were," she said, and Dad pressed her hand. She kissed us each, tremulously, in turn, Gwen last.

When Mary brought us lunch we saw Dr. MacKonkey driving in.

"Is Mother ill?" we asked anxiously.

Mary explained that white women always had a doctor when they had a baby, unlike Japanese mama-sans and Hawaiian *wahines* who had children with only a husband or some female relative to assist.

The day melted into evening. *Paniolos* and their wives gathered in the garden to learn how matters were progressing. Hauki looked hopeful and apprehensive, wondering if his long period of sobriety was to be rewarded in the way he craved.

About eight Mary rushed out to tell us we had a new sister. Hauki locked his arms tightly across his chest, and waited like a sentry at his post to learn Dad's decision. The other men joshed him about his ambition and his dark eyes blazed.

"Never mind, you laugh on me," he flashed. "Eleven weeks now I make Missionary-style and sure Louis take notice!"

But when Dad came out Hauki didn't look so cocky and moved closer to make sure Daddy saw him. "Amy's fine," Dad said happily. "Tomorrow, after work, you can all go in and see her and the new baby. As you're Lorna's *paniolo,* Hauki, you can see her in the morning before breakfast."

Hauki made a happy lunge at Dad and threw his arms about him.

"*Mahalo, mahalo*—thank you, thank you," he choked. "My happy too big for me to hold." And he wiped his brimming eyes.

Dad called for drinks to toast Lorna's health. Hauki asked for sweet soda and everyone whooped with delight.

At dawn he was waiting on the Office steps in clean riding clothes holding a long white carnation *lei* he had made. We were as eager to see Lorna as he was. When Dad called us, we followed him through the house, Hauki bursting with importance. Mother was awake and smiled as we filed in. Hauki kissed her hand, then we all peered over the crib and looked at the fuzzy little head and glimpse of pink baby-cheek not hidden by the blue blanket.

"My *keiki*, my *keiki*," Hauki kept murmuring rapturously, wiping tears off his cheeks. Hanging the *lei* on the corner of the crib nearest Lorna's head, he kissed the edge of her blanket, then tiptoed out of the room as if he were going through a church.

Each morning he came to gaze adoringly at her and left *leis*. When she was three months old he took her for her first ride on a pillow before his saddle. As time went on, her face would light up when he appeared. She was a roly-poly, adorable baby with a curly smile and eyes like blue stars. Hauki was clay in her hands.

The immediate life of our household was revolutionized by the new sister. Mother was always hushing and shushing if we made a noise and maneuvered so that week-end guests came less often. Mary continued to run the house so Mother could spend all her time with her new treasure, and Aina didn't want to play or even ride any more. She haunted Lorna and proved to be a baby wizard, helping to bathe, feed, and wash her as well as a grown-up.

Mother and I had never been close to each other, and, after Lorna came, in indefinite ways I felt pushed further into the background. Finally, after weeks of pestering, Mother consented to let me bathe Lorna. It was getting near Christmas and, being chilly, there was a lamp on the floor near the small, portable bathtub. Somehow or other, while I was washing Lorna, I knocked it over and the matting caught fire.

For punishment, Mother said I couldn't ride Bedouin for two weeks. I was outraged, feeling I was being unjustly robbed of my horse for a mishap which hadn't been deliberate badness. When Dad came home I hurried to him with my trouble.

"Don't break your heart over this," he advised. "You and Mother are cut from two different pieces of cloth. You'll never be the sort of daughter she wants, Ummie."

I felt small and faraway.

"Don't look so sunk. You suit me, just the way you are. You'll get into lots of trouble, but you'll get a hell of a lot out of life. Do your best where Mother's concerned and call it a day. I have to back her up when she punishes you, or I wouldn't be a loyal husband. But when you fumble some job, or fall down on something, remember *I* understand. *Mea culpa*—I'm guilty too. Often."

That was all I needed, or wanted. Dad understood. I became his shadow, absenting myself as much as possible from the house —where I always seemed to get into trouble. I rode with him after school, assisted with the horse-hospital, helped him to dress *paniolos'* wounds when they sustained the injuries which occur on even the most efficiently run ranches. He taught me about grasses and trees, interested me in crops and seasons, discussed Kipling, Jack London, and Shakespeare as I read them.

Then Mother suddenly decided I must assume my share of responsibility where Lorna was concerned. It wasn't fair for Aina to sacrifice all her playtime. I was deputized to push Lorna's pram around the garden for an hour every day after lunch. For a couple of weeks I acquitted myself creditably, but growing over-confident I figured I could kill two birds with one stone, read whatever book was the current thrill, and push the baby buggy at the same time.

Deep in "King Solomon's Mines," I forgot I had any responsibility other than to find out if Sir Hugh, Good, and Allan Quartermain would find the diamonds they were after. Glancing up as I turned a page I saw to my horror that the pram was rolling with gathering speed down the sloping lawn toward a three-foot drop into the horse pasture. I tore after it but before I could grab the handle it charged through the ginger bushes and crashed over the bank into the deep grass. Instinct urged me to flee but Lorna's frantic squalls deterred me. Had she been fatally injured? Terror swamped me. Mother would never forgive this. Leaping down I picked Lorna up, dusted her off, and her cries subsided. But the pram was too heavy to boost up the bank. I looked for some yardboy, but the lawn had been raked the previous day and they were all working in the tree nursery or vegetable garden.

Lorna's cries had been louder than I, in my panic, realized. While I debated what to do, Mother, Great-Aunt Jane, and Mary came rushing out of the house. In my overwrought state "King Solomon's Mines' " red cover looked like a pool of blood in the grass. The explanation for the accident was there for everyone to see. Mother boxed my ears, scolded me, and sent me to the Office to wait until Daddy returned. When he appeared his eyes were sad.

No riding of any sort for a month, and I wasn't to touch a book, except during school, for the same period. "It's tough to have to do this to you, First Lieutenant," Dad said. "But Amy's nerves get the best of her and if I don't back her up, they'll get worse."

I clutched him. He wasn't angry. That was all that mattered.

But night after night I lay awake in bed, my mind on fire trying to figure out the end of the story which had precipitated this double disaster. Finally, I made up my own end—and boomed into a new world. I would be a writer, like Grandfather and Uncle Stanley! Making up stories of my own would be more fun than slavishly following someone else's.

The next day was Sunday. Aina was busy with Lorna, Gwen was with Mother. I couldn't ride, or read, or even play out of doors with the dogs, for rain was slashing down, sputtering along choked gutters which were emptying their loads into hollow-sounding cisterns. Drenched vines flopped against the house.

Going into the silent schoolroom I got an empty notebook and began scribbling, "Firebrand: The Story of a Horse." It was half completed when the lunch gong sounded. I ate in a haze and hurried back upstairs. By tea time the "book" was done, including half-a-dozen fiery illustrations.

Racing downstairs I gave it to Dad. He didn't laugh, much as he must have wanted to. Mother, Great-Aunt Jane, and a few week-end guests were present. "Firebrand" was passed around and I forgot I was in disgrace and felt swollen with pride. When everyone had seen the "book," Dad took it back.

"I'll read it tonight," he promised.

Next morning he came to me. "It's got a spark," he said. "Stick to your guns, work like blazes, and in time you'll make the grade. But remember, Rome wasn't built in a day."

Fired by his encouragement, I produced other atrocities. "Constance, or the Uncle's Niece," was laid in feudal times. The clash of battle, noble chargers and floating ostrich plumes filled every page. Next came a tale about a dissolute Roman Senator's efforts to win the love of a pure Christian slave. It was followed by "Madam de Courcey," which had a decidedly French flavor, acquired probably from too much reading of De Maupassant translations.

One afternoon while I was scribbling at the newest masterpiece, Great-Aunt Jane bustled up and looked over my shoulder. She had a secret pride in my ambition to become a literary figure, but she gave a startled gasp. "What—*what* is that last sentence?"

I read it aloud with an author's pride. "He laid her bare gleaming body on the black velvet couch and gazed admiringly at her little pink stomach."

Great-Aunt Jane recoiled as if I'd lashed her with a serpent, snatched the manuscript from me and rushed away. The rest can be imagined, but it ended with Mother's ultimatum that I wasn't to write another word until I was old enough to know what I was saying.

18. I MEET A PRINCESS

WHEN Lorna was about two years old, persons in power brought pressure on outstanding men in Hawaii to run for the Legislature. Among others, Daddy was informed that he must be among the Whites representing Maui. He insisted that he couldn't make political speeches, but his protests were brushed aside and his name listed among the candidates for various offices.

Elections in Hawaii have the flavor and color of Roman holidays, and during campaigns work on the Islands is, practically, at a standstill, for each ranch and plantation prepares mighty *luaus,* and laborers are let off work so they can listen to the speeches.

On this occasion Prince Jonah Kuhio Kalanianiole and his brother Prince David Kawananakoa, with their two beautiful wives, were touring the group, taking troupes of singers and *hula* dancers along in their retinues. No expense for entertainment was spared at our ranch, or on any other estate where the Royal party was to visit.

For a week before the date when they were to come, pack trains of mules went off to distant parts of the island for delicacies. Hawaiians love feasting and oratory, and although everyone worked full blast all day, at night the Camp echoed with jollity. *Hulas* to commemorate the great event were composed by the song-makers among the *paniolos* and Sonoda was kept busy hammering long, low, portable tables to set out under the trees where the feast was to be held. Three prime heifers, twelve of the fattest hogs, and a hundred chickens were set aside to provide the main course of the *luau.*

191

The day before the electioneering party was due at the ranch, half a dozen *paniolos,* their wives, sweethearts, and we children went to the forests to get *maile* vines for *leis,* and *palapalai* fern to cover the tables. Brisk fresh wind blew from the east. Clouds crossed the face of the sun and the periods of light, alternating with shadows, made it seem as if the day was constantly re‐ settling its bright plumage as it went on its way. The sweet secret peace that fills Hawaiian forests lay over everything. When we were deep among the crowding trees we dismounted and began stripping fragrant *maile* creepers off the brown tree-trunks. After enough had been gathered we sat in the warm greenery and pulled the stems out of the vines, packing the fragrant coils in gunnysacks. Then we gathered ferns and when we had all the decorations that could possibly be needed we gathered purple *lilikois*—passion fruit—and sucked the black seeds and sherbet-like pulp out of them. Then everyone made *leis* to wear home.

We raced back to the ranch, snatching ripe guavas off bushes as we passed and pelted each other with them until we were spattered with pink meat and yellow seeds. As we rode into the ranch, the dusk was rent by the squealing of hogs being slaugh‐ tered. All night the tumult and bustle continued. Women braided garlands and laid them on cool dewy grass to keep fresh. Men prepared earth ovens. Young folk supplied music while stars looked on and the Pacific sang to its islands.

Next morning Japanese men in fresh clothes hurried around placing tables in the right places, while Hawaiians worked around blazing fires heating porous rocks to line the sides of the pits which waited to be filled with food. When everything was packed in and covered with layers of green banana and *ti* leaves, earth was mounded on top and the edibles were left to steam. Mother came out to see if the tables were perfect and if enough *leis* had been twined around the trunks of the trees in the garden.

All morning, Hawaiians kept arriving from surrounding districts: *wahines* in their best *holokus; tutus* with beaming, wrinkled faces; men with peacock-and-pheasant-feather *leis* around their hats. Japanese and Portuguese drifted around, for etiquette demanded that everyone must be on hand to greet the Royal guests when they arrived with their retinues.

The electioneering party usually had to ride on horseback from district to district, but whenever it was possible, carriages were used. Long before I heard the roll of approaching wheels I slipped off and hid among the tall nasturtiums crowding against the stone wall. I wanted to see the Princes and Princesses at close range.

About one o'clock, Mother appeared in her best *holoku*. Hauki, his eyes clear from twenty months of sobriety, followed her, carrying Lorna. His white breeches and shirt, topped off by a red *lei*, fairly bristled with purity and virtue. Mary had Aina and Gwen in tow, and, suspecting that they were hunting for me, I kept very still.

So many people had poured in since morning that I was afraid I mightn't get a chance to get near the Royal party. Their carriage would stop at the front gate and they would have to pass within a few feet of my hiding place.

At last I heard wheels coming along the avenue. Grizzled Hawaiians with tears streaming down their cheeks crowded forward, eager to pay homage to their *Aliis*. Younger folk waited expectantly. Two hacks rolled up and stopped. Daddy, *paniolos,* and members of the electioneering party who had escorted the Princes and their wives, dismounted. The Princes were gay laughing fellows with flashing dark eyes and vital hair. Behind their imperious carriage I sensed they were warm, friendly, and simple. After the hubbub of greetings subsided, the Princesses got out of the carriage, smiling graciously at the excited throng. Princess Kalanianiole was lovely, but I forgot her when I saw Princess Abbie Kawananakoa.

She was six feet tall, but as delicately boned as a gazelle. Her eyes were enormous, sparkling, and fringed by outrageously long lashes. Richness enveloped her as if she had been born at high noon in golden sunlight. She was a princess in any language, in any age. I'd read about Cleopatra, Circe, and Aspasia and suspected she was the three of them rolled into one. People standing near her looked as if their blood had been diluted with water. If only I could touch her *holoku!* But it wasn't likely with so many important people present that she'd even be aware of my existence. However, I'd forgotten that the Royal quartette were Hawaiians, to whom children are always of prime importance.

After the tumultuous greetings subsided they pounced on Lorna with cries of delight, then transferred their attention to Gwen and Aina. I wished I'd stayed with them instead of hiding and trying to be smart.

"Isn't there a fourth little girl?" one of the Princesses asked.

I knew that the back of my dress was streaked with green stains from crushed nasturtium stems, but I scrambled out of my juicy hiding place.

"This is my First Born," Dad said, then added, "What the hell were you doing in the flowers?"

I explained, and the Princesses laughed delightedly. I shook hands with each of the Royal four but had eyes only for Princess Abbie. The way she spoke, moved, held her head; her tiny feet and tapering, expressive fingers had me spellbound. Like Daddy, even when she was in repose, an invisible spotlight seemed to be focused on her, setting her apart from everyone else.

Speech-making started. Impassioned words in Hawaiian and English were flung into the air. Prince Kuhio, Delegate to Washington and recently returned from the mainland, spoke of his efforts in behalf of Hawaii. His brother, Prince David, took the stump and when he finished, the Reverend Stephen Desha, from Hilo, got up. He spoke in the almost-lost language of the

Chiefs of old times. Even some of the Hawaiians could not follow all he said, but his flashing eyes and eloquent gestures fired his listeners. He made them laugh, he made them cry. He tore them to ribbons, made them indignant, then in a swoop fused them into a whole. It wasn't the individual, it was Hawaii that mattered! Hawaii, the land of Aloha, where all nationalities worked together like one. Hawaii, where life-term prisoners were granted the privilege of week-ending with their families! Hawaii, which obeyed God's command that people love one another! In a remote way he reminded me of Kane preaching in Kaupo. He had no white-topped, pearl-buttoned boots sitting on a church window sill to impress his listeners, but he had the same fire, the same spirit that swept people out of themselves.

About three, the speech-making ended and people began drifting toward the tables. The fragrance characteristic of *luaus,* a mingling of hot food, *palapalai* fern, garlands wilting about warm human necks, drifted through the afternoon. Bronzed hogs steamed on each table, calabashes of pink *poi,* beautifully kneaded fragments of tomato, onion, and salmon, chickens stewed in cocoanut milk, butter-yellow *opihis,* dried garnet-colored shrimps waited temptingly in polished wooden bowls and cocoanut-shell containers. Dark slices of *kulolo,* like rich brown plum pudding, semi-transparent slices of *haupia,* like cocoanut-flavored arrowroot pudding, heaped mangoes, pineapples, freckled hands of bananas, polished ruby-colored mountain apples crowded every available inch of the fern-spread, flower-decked tables.

The feast got under way. Music throbbed in the background, voices merged into a low roar like a long lazy surf breaking with undisturbed majesty against barrier reefs. Guests called for favorite songs, glasses were emptied and refilled, platters and bowls whisked away to be heaped with fresh food.

Then the Princes clapped their hands sharply. Silence fell on the garden and there was a tenseness of anticipation. I snapped to attention. I'd seen informal *hulas* danced hundreds of times, but never one of the ceremonial *hulas,* belonging to ancient times and danced only on great occasions. Mythology, genealogy, history, and poetry were the stuff from which *hulas* originally sprung. The record of the ages which have passed over the islands of the Pacific is written in songs and dances.

Hidden drums began beating. Without haste they swelled deliberately toward a sustained crescendo which seemed to summon up the life-force in the soil to meet sun and rain. Behind the sonorous reverberation, men and women, seated cross-legged on the grass, began a cadenced chanting. Gradually their voices rose to a higher pitch, as if evoking ancient gods to come out of sacred fastnesses to which they'd retreated. On and on the steady pounding went, like an endless procession of invisible feet passing majestically through the garden. Individuals seemed to merge into one solemn push toward some distant goal.

Then from behind the bamboo grove a dancer appeared, followed by another and another until ten girls with unbound hair and flowers about heads, necks, wrists, and ankles were swaying in unison on the lawn. The slow undulations of their bodies, the liquid grace of gesturing hands and arms, deftly, proudly moving feet spoke of wind, water, flowers, hills, trees, and the unseen spirits animating them. The swishing of glossy *ti*-leaf skirts was the sound of warm rain falling, the song of streams making their way to the sea, the whisper of lovers in the dark. Nature in all her majesty was filing past. Behind the men and women's chanting, behind supple, swaying dancers the drums spoke an older, fiercer tongue summoning spirits and ancient withdrawn forces to return to earth.

Then gradually, imperceptibly, the drum-beat slowed down. Dancers began vanishing like spirits retreating into inviolate citadels from which they'd emerged to counsel mortals for a while. I felt as if I were being carried forward by a mighty tide. Past, present, future formed an intricate design woven into the pattern of the whole.

After an instant of silence a roar of applause broke out for the magic of the dancers and chanters, then gradually subsided. Cries of "Aloha, Aloha—my love to you!" sounded as tables began breaking up and parties assembled to go on their way. Another *luau* was being held at one of the big plantations that night and Daddy had to go along with the electioneering party. The ranch seemed strangely silent when the last visitor had gone, but the garden looked wild and strong as if it were still vibrating to the message of the old *hula*.

Weeks later, election returns came in. Groups of interested persons met at the ranch and sat up all night while Central phoned in the poll of each district. I was eager to find out if Dad had got in.

It was his first fling at politics and he had used his own method to get votes. Knowing Hawaiians are passionate lovers of music and fine horsemanship, he went on tour with Champagne and Bedouin and a guitar slung over his shoulder. In localities where stone walls were high and plentiful, he jumped his horses over them, ad-libbing for the entertainment of voters gathered to listen to campaign talks. In districts where there were no stone walls he swung his guitar into position and sang *hulas* in which Hawaiians, and everyone, joyfully joined. When the last count was in, he found he had won by a large margin in every precinct!

19. I MEET A GREAT WRITER AND DEATH KNOCKS AT OUR DOOR

A WHILE after Dad returned from the session of the Legislature in Honolulu, Lorrin Thurston, Editor of the *Advertiser,* and a lawyer of distinction in Hawaii, wrote saying that he was bringing Jack London and his seagoing wife, Charmian, over to the ranch for ten days.

Lorrin Thurston had been one of Dad's first friends in the Islands. As young men they had hunted wild cattle together on Mauna Kea. Kakina, as Dad called him, came from Missionary stock. He didn't smoke, swear, or drink. Dad did all three, but their affection was unshakable. Kakina was a tall, heavy-set, noble man with burning dark eyes, who moved and gestured in the large sweeping way of Hawaiians. The fact that he was Dad's closest friend, and an Editor, made me admire him greatly. Of course his stock, where I was concerned, went to an all-time high when I found he was bringing one of the most famous writers of the day to the ranch.

I was going to see Jack London, whose books I'd read avidly. It seemed too good to be possible. Dad took me to meet them. Because they were such notables they were breakfasted and lunched en route to the ranch and a special plantation train brought them from Kahului to Paia.

I was prepared for an awe-inspiring person. Kakina jumped off the train followed by a sort of breezy, boyish-looking man with brilliant blue eyes and a mop of rather untidy hair. Intelligence, vigor, and a gusto for life emanated from him. He and Dad looked at each other, laughed, hooked their fingers in their own shirt collars and shook them with a sort of delight, signifying they were one breed. In a day when men wore stiff detachable collars, they both wore soft-collared shirts. It was an immediate bond of outlawry.

Tall Aunt Hattie, Kakina's wife, got off the train and Jack's wife, Charmian, followed. She was a small vivid person whom I loved instantly.

It was a memorable ten days. The August round-up was going full blast. From dawn until dark the bawling of cattle being drafted, counted, and branded filled the air. Jack rode all over his horse, like a sailor. Charmian was such a finished performer that I lent her Bedouin, who had never carried another woman on his back—and she managed him perfectly. She was out with us at daybreak; Jack joined us around noon, after he'd written the thousand words which were his daily output.

I was in heaven. All day we did the things I loved best, riding, working with cattle. In the evenings I listened to flashing conversation. Jack had a mind like a sword and when he grew eloquent about some subject which was close to his heart the air crackled. Of course, I shyly showed him a couple of my manuscripts. He was honest and straight from the shoulder. "Writing's the hardest work in the world," he told me. "The stuff you're producing at present is clumsy incoherent tripe, but every so often there's a streak of fire on your pages. You're only a kid, but everything registers with you and you've a zest for life. If you're game enough to take all the lickings that will come to you, and keep on writing and writing, you'll make out."

That was enough for me. I determined I would keep on, until I was ninety, if necessary.

Shortly after the Londons resumed their trans-Pacific cruise on the *Snark,* Mother told us she was going to have another baby. All the ranch hoped for a son. Eole, the assistant colt-breaker, put in a bid to be *paniolo* to the new von Tempsky who was on the way. Eole was a rascal, as his name, Rat, implied. But Dad, with his gift of sensing a man's real worth, said if he'd trim his sails and steer a straight course, it was a go.

At eight o'clock of another Sunday night, our brother Errol was born. Japanese *banzaied,* Hawaiians went crazy. Eole couldn't be touched with a ten-foot pole. After the hubbub subsided, the *paniolos* serenaded Mother and the new little son under her bedroom windows.

Shortly after, Lorna, who had been health personified, developed asthma. I assembled my courage and suggested to Mother that I could take care of her at night. I was twelve now and eager to assume my share of the family load. She was skeptical of my trustworthiness, but exhaustion compelled her to give me a trial.

At first she slept in the same room with Lorna and me, but no matter how active I'd been during the day, the first wheeze from my small sister snapped me to my feet and I administered the succession of medicines and powders vainly bought in the hope of easing Lorna's spasms. As I proved my efficiency Mother began sleeping through the tussles and after a few weeks she moved back to her room and I was left in complete charge. Mother was going to pieces before my eyes, killing herself with worry, not only about Lorna but for fear Errol would catch it too. The babies were never allowed out of doors if a breath of wind was stirring and when they were taken from one room to another blankets were laid before every door to keep out possible drafts. The household was haggard. The joyous stream of people who had poured through the ranch over week-ends had once again been largely diverted, for Mother was too tired and too preoccupied with the babies' health to enjoy company or bother with jollity.

I saw, as Dad did, what was happening to the babies and to our home, but we were both powerless to do anything about it. He ventured to suggest to Mother that possibly keeping the babies bundled up all the time and away from sunshine and fresh air would not improve their stamina. But her phobia about drafts had grown into a sort of mental hysteria which nothing could combat.

Errol had become delicate from too much coddling and, at the slightest provocation, contracted chest colds with bronchial complications, and when both babies were sick at once poor Mother was like a distracted creature.

For almost two years neither of them had been allowed to ride or even play with animals for fear excitement might precipitate asthma spasms. They were kept quiet with toys and books. If they started to laugh or play violently, they were hushed. Hilarity, leaping around, tended to make breathing more difficult, Mother insisted. Sometimes when I saw the two pallid little creatures in a tightly closed room I thought of my joyous years with Makalii. They were missing their Island heritage of sunshine, horses, swimming, and the comradeship of their *paniolos* who would have made their days bright with laughter and their minds rich with the lore of the Pacific.

Lorna was old enough to remember that life had not always been a monotone punctuated with periods of choking. She begged constantly to go to the stables, to see Hauki. In addition to the family passion for horseflesh, she had a gift for animals, evident from the time she could toddle. Horses and dogs accepted her immediately. Once when she was about eighteen months old Hauki saw her seated on the ground hugging the hind leg of a half-broken colt. Hauki was terror-stricken. If he moved, the snorty young beast might go on the rampage and trample the baby. Wiping sweat off his face, he called Lorna softly. She gave the colt's leg a parting hug, got up and walked away without disturbing the animal or precipitating a disaster.

During her two years of imprisonment she begged daily to see Kolea, a four-year-old stallion on whose back she had sat when he was a small colt. Couldn't he be brought into the house so she could pet him? Couldn't she go outside and sit on his back if she kept quiet? Finally, Mother told Dad to bring Kolea into the garden where Lorna could see him through the windows. When Dad led the proud glossy creature up to the house Lorna forgot her promise not to get excited and fought and screamed to get to him until she was purple in the face. A frightful asthma spasm resulted, so that finished that.

The end came with unexpected suddenness. The entire family and most of the ranch, with the exception of Dad and myself, succumbed to an epidemic of influenza. For a week we were nursing practically twenty-four hours a day, with brief snatches of sleep in the afternoon when friends came in to relieve us. Just as Mother got back on her feet, Lorna's influenza developed into pneumonia.

In her delirium Lorna begged incessantly for Kolea and Hauki. At the end of six days Mother collapsed. Two days later Lorna passed the crisis successfully. In her relief Mother, without consulting the doctor who'd given her a nerve sedative, took a large dose of a sleeping medicine she was in the habit of using. The two formed a poison and in five hours she was dead.

20. THE LONE EAGLE AND HIS NESTLINGS

For days everything felt hollow and empty. Life seemed to have come to a dead stop before starting off across a perilous uncharted country. Shadows stretching across the garden looked treacherous and the distant boom of surf sounded like a voice murmuring some warning in a language I could not understand.

I had been fond of Mother in an unemotional way, for we were diametrically opposed in spirit, but the disaster of her loss where Dad was concerned appalled me. She had been his wife, mistress of his household, mother of his children, and with her death he was left to rear a family of five, two of them mere tots and invalids. Added to ranch responsibilities, it was a Herculean task.

He had nominated me his First Lieutenant and I realized it was my duty to try and hold the fort with him. But how could a girl in her first 'teens hope to run a lavish household, be hostess at a table where the world was entertained, not to mention all the other responsibilities connected with rearing a family? Like all children of English parents, we had been kept largely in the background and now, overnight, I was jerked out of the nursery to find myself faced with the knowledge that I must be Dad's hostess and partner.

Aina, my adopted sister, was capable, devoted, and less than a year my junior, but I was Dad's eldest child and must accept most of the responsibility. I wished Gan or Makalii had been alive. I could have confided my misgivings to them, but my own troubles must not be heaped on Dad's already overburdened shoulders. And I must not fail him for he had never failed me.

Being a man of action, a few days after Mother's funeral he

called a family council in the Office. The relatives and friends who had jammed the house for ten days had dispersed, but Kakina stayed on. He had left his family, law-practice, and newspaper to stay with Dad and help him to get his household reorganized and under way.

Dad's mind was steady and direct even in the midst of tragedy. I was slated with Mary and the servants' help to run the house and manage it to the best of my ability. The current governess would stay to teach us, for Great-Aunt Jane had passed away in Honolulu some months previously. Aina was to have entire charge of Lorna during the day and, unless the baby had asthma, at night. Then I must pinch-hit. Gwen, when she recovered from Mother's loss, must contribute her bit where she could. But in the final analysis I was to be Mother, hostess, and head of the household.

I tried not to see how Dad's jaw muscles bunched into knots as he talked. Dominating his sorrow he was obeying the silent ultimatum in all nature—to go on. He was walking in step with autumn which spread over the land. The island, soaked and rich with rain, was generating new power, assembling itself for new growth.

After thrashing out his plans in detail, Dad said with an effort at gaiety, "Well, school is dismissed." He held me back by the hand. Everyone began filing out of the Office but when Kakina rose to go Daddy signed at him to remain. "You're in on the next round, old man."

Taking up his pipe, Daddy filled it. "This is a show-down and all the cards are going on the table." He glanced at Kakina, then looked at me. "I'm going to talk to you as if you were a man too, Ummie."

I felt proud at being included in the council. In their different ways Dad and Kakina were prominent personalities in Hawaii. An odd faraway expression crept into Dad's eyes and when he lighted his pipe his hands were slightly unsteady. "I've tried my damnedest to be a good husband and father, but I'm no saint," he said, finally. "I enjoy raising Cain once in a while, and at intervals I have to give my devil a run. I work like a mule and play like a Hawaiian. Between the two, without a good woman like Amy to consider, there's a possibility I may smash up and take the lot of you down with me—" He broke off and stared at some distance of his own.

Kakina's dark eyes had never swerved from Dad's face while he had been talking. Leaning forward he laid his heavy hand on Dad's shoulder.

"I know your caliber, Von, but I know sometimes that the very force in a person may be his undoing. However, I'm betting you won't go down. You may take a few spills, get a bit off the track sometimes, but you'll do a hundred per cent job of raising your kids, or I don't know men."

Dad's face got all broken and funny, then the tide of power which had been temporarily shocked out of him began flowing back. "Damnation, I won't fail you," he announced with quiet violence. "I won't rush hurdles, or cross bridges before I get to them. We'll go ahead a step at a time. The first problem is the babies. Are they to continue to be coddled and kept indoors, or shall I risk a complete right-about-face, turn them out to pasture, and see what results?"

Relief poured through me. Here were concrete problems that were part of my experience. Echoes of Dad's rollicking youth had drifted to me, enhancing the glamor of his personality, but they did not seem an actual part of the man I knew. The escapades of his young manhood, part of the colorful tapestry of Hawaii, were in no way personally associated with the man I worshiped.

Kakina smoothed his mustache between his first and second fingers with a familiar gesture while he gave the matter under consideration his entire thought. "It doesn't seem possible in a climate like this that any child could be hurt by living out of doors. My youngsters and your first batch of kids ran wild, and a sturdier lot would be hard to find."

"That's exactly how I figure," Dad said. "I'm not criticizing Amy's methods. She was a devoted mother, sacrificing herself for her children at every turn—and killed herself in the process."

The Office seemed to wait impatiently for him to continue.

"If we turn Lorna and Errol loose and they can't take it, they won't be any worse off than they are now, living the way they do."

"Let's take off their woolen clothes, shingle their hair, give them cold baths every morning, and let them ride with their *paniolos* and see if it won't make men of them," I suggested eagerly.

Kakina chuckled and faint amusement showed in Dad's sad eyes.

"Are you willing to take your share of the responsibility if we follow this course?" he asked. "If the kids can't stand the gaff—" he hesitated, "even if they do, a certain percentage of people will criticize us. 'Poor Amy, the instant she's gone her methods go into the discard' will be their song. You're my right hand now, and you may have to take a hell of a beating if we set off on this course."

I thought of the wretched nights Lorna had spent, of dreary days in tightly closed rooms. If a person couldn't snatch fun, joy, and beauty as he went, what was the good of living? I tried to put my thought into words.

"Okay, we'll burn our bridges and make a new start," Dad agreed. "I've a hunch the kids can take it; they come from tough stock."

"Let's start now," I suggested. "Lorna's still in bed and weak as a rat, but we can take Kolea into the nursery so she can pet him and that'll give her a boost."

For the first time in days Dad smiled a real smile. "Tell her she's going to have a caller. Kakina and I'll fetch the horse."

I rushed to the nursery. Aina was showing Lorna pictures. Her wan little face and patient eyes hurt me. Since passing her pneumonia crisis, no asthma had tortured her but her face had the old lack-luster expression. I whispered the exciting news to Aina and we hugged each other with glee.

While Aina brushed Lorna's hair and put on a fresh ribbon I rounded up the rest of the household to share the fun. In a few minutes, hoofs sounded on the cement walk. Lorna sat up, her eyes like blue stars. The hoofs crossed the wooden veranda, then Kolea put his wise, beautiful head through the door. Lorna's pallid face lighted, as if a great lamp had been turned up inside her. *"Kolea!"* she squeaked, holding out her arms.

Dad and Hauki, each holding to the cheek strap of the halter, made a careful entry. The stallion snuffed suspiciously at pieces of furniture, then got a whiff of Lorna and his nostrils ceased dilating. Dad and Hauki led him to the side of the bed.

Lorna hugged his velvety muzzle, making soft loving noises as she hungrily inhaled the fragrance of his clean skin. Ever since they had met as yearlings, two-legged and four, one of those mystic bonds binding certain people and animals together had existed between them. Any real lover of horses has, at some time or another, experienced the miracle of finding a horse which is in perfect accord with him. Often the animal may belong to another person, but the flash of recognition, the I-belong-to-you and You-belong-to-me, as spirits rush together, is as real as a message flashed between radio stations on the same wavelength.

As the life-force in the horse met the life-force in the wan little girl and fused, making them a unit, the onlookers were silent. Mary, holding Errol astride of her hip, wiped her eyes, Daddy smiled, Japanese faces became wooden as they fought against emotion, and Kakina blew his nose.

Lorna's stick-like fingers, starved for contact with the splendid animal she loved, went over the lean contours of Kolea's perfect head while he sighed blissfully and dropped a hip, signifying complete relaxation.

News had flashed over the ranch by cocoanut radio that from now on the kids were to share the fun we all had. The tidings tingled in the atmosphere and the old house seemed to stir as it roused itself from its long torpor to move forward with life again.

Our mutual efforts at baby-wrangling helped to get Dad over the first reaches of his grief. Lorna's bout with pneumonia had, at least, knocked her asthma into a cocked hat. She was pitifully weak and looked like a wet bedraggled kitten. But Kolea's daily visits and presently the thrill of being in the garden for a while every morning lent impetus to recovery. Life was no longer a deadly round of choking and being shut away from all the things she loved. While she lay on a mat under the trees with wind blowing over her and sun soaking into her skin, Hauki, her *paniolo,* hovered over her, and her four-legged friend, Kolea, cropped the lawn near-by.

Errol, having no cold at the moment, came in for more drastic treatment. We cut off his curls and took him out of dresses. He strutted proudly about in short breeches and shirts of the same cut worn by Japanese boy-sans. We plunged him yelling into a cold bath every morning and after he'd eaten breakfast Eole took him riding until noon. During the afternoon, while Eole trained colts, we parked him on an old mare without a bridle, who grazed about the garden as she pleased. Once in a while a bleat would send someone speeding out to pick him up off the grass and put him back into the saddle. The accident could always be traced to one of two sources: either the little fellow had fallen asleep and toppled off, or the old mare in feeding had gone under a low-hanging limb which scraped him off her back. Of course, Mother's women friends were scandalized at our methods, but he got tanned and the colds got farther and farther apart.

As soon as Lorna was more or less on her feet we "hogged her mane." No more silly curls which had to be rolled up on rags every night. No more being bundled up in woolen dresses and sweaters. While Dad ran the horse-clippers over her head, leaving only a stubble of hair, she sat as still as a mouse. When she saw herself in the mirror she danced up and down. "I'm a boy now, Daddy! Can I wear pants?" she squealed.

One of the house-boys was sent off to the Camp to borrow a clean pair of trousers about the right size from some Japanese or Hawaiian lad. When she was dressed she glanced down at her feet, flashed an excited smile at Dad and tore off the shoes and stockings Mother had made her wear for so long. "I'm going to show Hauki!" she cried. "I'm not a weak *haole* any more!"

Her bare flying feet pressed against the grass they had not felt for so long as she went speeding off toward the corrals and stables, and her soul seemed to be chanting a saga of freedom.

But cutting off Lorna's hair precipitated a disaster. Her ears, which had not been exposed to sunlight for two years, became badly sunburnt and swelled up into vast bat-like affairs. She was a ludicrous object and whenever she appeared people laughed. In a few days, however, it became a serious matter. Great blisters swelled and burst and she began to run a fever. Dad and I invented a sort of head-gear of tape which we named the Bridle. Because it made Lorna feel close to her beloved four-legged friends she was happy to wear it. We soaked gauze pads in a solution of creolin and water, placed them over her ears, and fastened the throat-latch, and after a few days of the treatment her ears shrank back to normal size and healed.

Shortly after the bat-ears episode, Governess Number Five was obliged, by a death in her family, to return to San Francisco. Daddy called a family council and told us that, after weighing the pros and cons of this new development, he'd arrived at the conclusion that a year without school, for us older girls, would not be out of line, provided we occupied the time usefully.

"I need you all around me," he went on. "When we're home I expect you to buckle down and learn everything you can about housekeeping. When work calls me to Waiopai, or into the crater, I'll take the lot of you along with me. In the evenings, after the babies are bedded down, no matter where we are I'll read aloud to you, adding to your education as I can. As problems come up, we'll thrash them out together. If you give me your word to try and get the ultimate from being turned out to pasture for a while—"

Would we! We milled around like a joyous pack of pups loosed from their kennels. No more school. Going everywhere with him and taking the babies along. Learning housekeeping from servants we loved. What a harvest of fun!

The council had started, as usual, in the Office but no mere house could hold such a tempest of delight. After the first froth of glee subsided a little, we sat down on the Office steps to plan and gloat.

The evening was laden with the incense of vegetation growing in valleys, spiked with the stronger smell of warm horses, the reek of well-greased leather and flowers fading about sweat-stained straw hats. Men were joking and calling to each other as they wound up the day's work. Trees rearranged their foliage and the garden gave little secret rustles as it settled itself for sleep. Daddy sat still, wrestling with the responsibility which would be his in the years unrolling ahead.

I sensed the solemnity of the moment. We were launched on a new phase of living. A new era had begun. Heretofore our lives had been largely patterned along the lines of Mother's English upbringing. Now we were to plunge into Dad's man-existence. I knew from the fluttering of a muscle in Dad's lean cheek that he was wondering if he could steer us all to happy landings.

The garden gate clicked. Kakina, who had returned to Honolulu some weeks previously, had dropped in unexpectedly to spend a day or so with us before proceeding to Hawaii on business. As we sat in a happy huddle on the steps, he came strolling back from a tour of the corrals and stables. His big, leonine head was thrust slightly forward from the hands clasped behind his strong back. Coming toward us in his deliberate way he came to a dead halt a short distance from us. After watching us intently for a moment, he gave an odd laugh.

"You're a wild-looking crew, even the babies, sitting there in your big straw hats and spurs. The Lone Eagle and his nestlings —poised for flight!"

21. TIED TO DEATH

E VER since Makalii had given me my first curl off a wild bull's tail, I'd longed to see them roped. Riding along I stared at the vast shape of Haleakala looming blackly against the stars. The eager thud of hoofs, men's laughing voices about me, horses blowing out their nostrils, and the electrical *kiu* wind swooping down from the crater rim sent a queer surf running through my heart.

The beasts we were going after were longhorns gone wild, descendants of the stock landed in Hawaii in 1793 by Lord Vancouver. Weighing up to 1,600 pounds, savage, nimble as cats, they were ready to charge riders on sight. Roping them was as dangerous as lion- or tiger-hunting and required more precision from man and mount than pig-sticking in India. Yet whenever ranch work was slack Dad and the boys went up the mountain after wild bulls, for they raised havoc with the purity of registered bulls and wasted pasturage. After they were secured, they were tied to old oxen and dragged home to be castrated and trained for ox-wagons. Those that would not tame were slaughtered to supply extra beef for the ranch larder.

Watching the jaunty figures about me I knew I mustn't make mental pictures of what might occur on the rough slopes of Haleakala when dawn came. If I was going to lead a man's life with Dad, I must think man-thoughts and keep a grip on my emotions. But it was a difficult thing to do under the circumstances. I knew that Dad, and every self-respecting *paniolo,* rode —to translate an old Spanish term—"tied to death." To lose a lasso, or cast off from an animal once it had been roped was a

212

paniolo's ultimate disgrace, even though failure to do so had cost many a man's and horse's life.

It didn't seem fantastic to me that necks and lives were risked unnecessarily by adherence to this code. It had produced the finest roper in the world. In 1908, Ikuwa Purdy, a part-Hawaiian *paniolo* from the Parker ranch, had gone to Cheyenne and defeated Angus MacPhee, who had been champion roper of the world for five years in succession. Angus came to Hawaii the following year to get back his title, but Ikuwa beat him again and the big Wyoming man stayed on in the Islands. As well as being champion roper of the world for five years, Angus had been top bronc-buster in Buffalo Bill's Wild West show, but the first time he went out to rope wild cattle on Maui he declared that only the insane rode like *paniolos*.

I thought of the biggest wild-bull horns ever roped on Maui, which adorned the mantel at home. Over four inches in diameter at the base, the span from needle-tip to needle-tip was five feet three inches. Swipes from those horns had cost three valiant horses their lives and injured two men before Dad roped and killed the outlaw.

I knew from the contours of the cones and ridges we were passing that we were nearing the lava beds below the summit. There we would wait until the wild cattle returned from their night maraudings to seek the safety of wastelands which were too rough for men and horses to ride through. Getting to a commanding hilltop, Dad halted and studied the sky.

"About an hour to dawn," he announced. "Get a fire going, someone."

Eole touched a match to a *kawao* bush. Little tongues of flame licked greedily through the tiny leaves, sending up dense clouds of white smoke. The men secured the spare horses, brought along in case of accidents, to trees. I thawed out my stiff fingers before slacking Bedouin's girths. Men began squatting down and went carefully over their lassos, tossing them out coil by coil, hunting for possible kinks which under terrific strain might snap the stout rawhides which they painstakingly braided in slack moments. Then with equal care they coiled up two fathom-lengths of thick manila rope, finished with heavy metal swivels, and tied them to their saddles. Each man carried three with which to tie up wild bulls after they had snubbed the animals to trees with lassos.

The wind coming from the summit had an eerie quality, as if it were blowing from black spaces between the stars. Gradually the Ghost Dawn welled into the sky and subsided. Stars enlarged and faded. A pale daffodil light crept up behind the cold blue shoulder of Haleakala. The world seemed big, empty, and awesome in the morning light. Above us, some five miles away, naked, deluged by old lava flows, the summit of the dead volcano towered.

Men began getting to their feet, watching the country below. Shortly the wild cattle would begin working back from the pastures and forests. To bolster up my spirits for what was ahead I whispered an old verse Dad had taught me.

> *I trust my sword,*
> *I trust my steed,*
> *But most I trust*
> *Myself—in need!*

Daddy grinned. "Right," he agreed. "And get this thoroughly into your head. Once we start roping we won't have time to look out for you. Keep a sharp watch out for lava pits. Some are easy to see, others are hidden by brush. The horses are sure-footed and know their business but that doesn't excuse you from not being on the job every instant. Remember old John Paris whom I visited in Kona last summer?"

I nodded.

"One day he went up Hualalai to rope wild cattle and didn't come back. For three days search parties scoured the mountain for him. Finally, a *paniolo* picked up his trail, which ended in a patch of scrub. The *paniolo* went forward cautiously on foot. There at the bottom of a forty-foot pit was old John, still alive but weak from lack of food and water. His horse, and luckily for old John, the bull he had been tied to, were killed by the fall. The *paniolo* hauled him out with a lasso, but it was a close call."

I looked at Dad, swallowed, and managed a smile. I was not at all sure, now, that I wanted to see him and the *paniolos* lassoing wild bulls. I thought of the babies asleep at home, of my two sisters. What would become of us if anything happened to Dad?

The *kawao* bush had burned to a heap of white ashes. Men had ridden off and posted themselves on commanding ridges. Only Dad, Holomalia the foreman, and I were left with the tied-up extra horses. With a sort of restrained eagerness, Dad and Holomalia began cinching up their saddles. Holomalia was riding Tradewind, a gray gelding about eleven years old, in the height of his vigor and strength, as beautiful and courageous as Champagne. While Holomalia worked about him the horse kept his eyes fixed on the country below, alert for the first sound or smell of wild cattle emerging from the woods. He looked like a charger scenting battle as he waited with lifted head and pricked ears, ready to spring away at the first signal.

Dad swung onto Champagne. "Remember, keep *above* the cattle, First Born," he cautioned. "When a bull charges uphill he hasn't enough momentum to knock a horse over or hurt him badly. If he charges and *you're* below, the weight of his body, added to the pitch of the land, will knock you galley west. You're an expert enough horsewoman to handle yourself properly in tight spots or I wouldn't have let you come out with us."

I scrambled into my saddle, my heart hammering, as I wondered how expert I *would* be in this new field. Clean wind rushed down from the mountain. Live, feel, dare, it taunted me.

Tradewind froze to attention and I clamped into the saddle. A moment later Hauki, posted on the next ridge, called out, "Wild cattle below."

Bedouin began dancing about in circles, keyed up by the excitement which had suddenly charged the fragile blue morning. Holomalia watched critically, then satisfied that I could handle him, grinned. "Wait, swell-fun rope wild cattle. You see!" Then he became all business.

A herd of about forty wild cattle were standing at the edge of the forest. An enormous brindled bull leading the herd, left the shelter of the trees, and stood with lifted head, scenting the air. His huge up-sweeping horns looked like arms lifted for a wicked embrace. Harsh black curls grew in his forehead and crested his heavy shoulders. Evil and magnificent, reluctant to abandon cover, he stood, the Monarch of the Mountain, then as if he had made his decision he began to cross the stretch of open grassy ground lying between him and the safety of the lava beds. When he had advanced about fifty feet he snuffed danger, paused, and began lashing his sides with his tail while he pawed up dust and threw it over his shoulders. Behind him a dozen lesser bulls, which he had awed into submission, watched him, waiting for orders. He gave a low warning bellow and cows, heifers, and a few small calves gathered in a close knot behind their males. The truculent leader started forward again, stopping now and then to stamp and shake his great horns.

After a few tense minutes the Monarch began streaking up the long slope at a fast trot which broke into a running canter, his herd at his heels. When they were a couple of hundred yards from the trees Dad gave a shout and *paniolos* swooped in from right and left. With wild cries they urged the herd toward a more-or-less level space where ropes could be used to best advantage. For an instant the brindled outlaw and his mates were startled and raced in the direction wanted, then they scattered and began charging. The mountaintop echoed with the whine of swinging lassos, dull bellows, shouts, and the fiery run of hoofs.

Jamming my heels into Bedouin's ribs I headed him for a small hill where I could watch without getting in the way. Brave and beautiful Dad and the *paniolos* looked, leaning forward over their pommels, swinging their great loops with rhythmic precision. The brindled bull that everyone wanted to get streaked out sideways. Eole, yelling like a maniac, raced to head him off. A tawny three-year-old crossed Dad's bows and with a deft twist of his wrist his noose whizzed out, closed about the bull's horns, snapped taut and the animal went head over heels. It struck the earth with a hollow thud but was on its feet instantly charging for Champagne. Dad dodged its rushes and after a little maneuvering he got into position, feinting for the bull to attack Champagne from the rear. Before its horns could graze the glossy gray quarters, Dad was racing off, flipping his lasso from side to side over his head as he dashed for a *koa* tree. Before I could see how he managed it he had dodged around and snubbed the bull's horns against the stout trunk. Champagne braced back, while the rest of the wild cattle went streaming on toward the mountain.

Eole, riding like a madman, was racing to head off the outlaw while the rest of the *paniolos* tore among the charging cattle, swinging for the bulls. A mahogany-colored five-year-old charged Pili and one long wicked horn grazed his stirrup but the impetus of the attack took the animal by and Pili roped it. Hauki was racing in pursuit of a steel-gray bull with long white horns that flashed off the early sunlight. The rest of the herd, realizing too late that they could never regain their wastelands, wheeled back for the comparative safety of the scattered forests below, *paniolos* who had not already secured animals tearing in pursuit.

I tried to hold Bedouin and wait for Dad but with a sideways wrench at the bit he took off down the mountain after the herd and racing riders. Swooping through a hollow I nearly ran over Holomalia tying up a rangy strawberry roan which must have weighed 1,500 pounds. Bedouin gave a convulsive sideways leap to avoid bowling over Tradewind, braced on his haunches while his master tied one of the heavy manila swivel-ropes about the great neck thrashing savagely against the tree trunk. "Wait one minute," Holomalia called, his white teeth flashing in a grin; "maybe I catch the big bull for you."

In less than a minute the strawberry roan was fastened solidly to the tree. Holomalia leaped into the saddle and Tradewind flattened out, trying to overtake the Mountain King which Eole had succeeded in turning back from the lava wastes. We could see the mammoth beast tearing down a ridge some distance away intent on regaining the forests.

Leaping and plunging, our horses went up the steep side of the gulch and tore away. Below us fleeing cattle were crashing through the scrub bordering the forest. Neck and neck Tradewind and Bedouin sailed over logs, swerved to avoid lava holes too wide to leap, and splashed through boggy hollows. The rush of wind in our ears and the thud of flying hoofs and the bellowing of cattle filled the morning.

We slid down the steep side of a small gulch, leaped across the deep wash at the bottom, and scrambled up the farther side. Tradewind's small ears were pricked up, his dark eyes wild with excitement. While part of his superbly functioning horse-mind was busy with his footing, the rest was focused on the animal we were after. He knew his work and loved it—the dash, danger, and risk of it were ingrained in his soul. Faint shouts and thuds below told us other men were bringing cattle down, but Holomalia was bent on roping the old bull which had flouted capture for ten years. Reaching the crest of a hill we halted for a split second. The brindle bull was nowhere in sight.

"He's hiding," Holomalia announced in Hawaiian, sweeping

the scrubby ridges ahead of us with expert eyes. Our lathered horses sniffed the wind, then Tradewind darted away like a silver javelin. Sure enough, the *kawao* bushes ahead of us whipped into motion and with an enraged bellow the Ancient One wheeled and charged. Just as his appalling horns were lowered for Tradewind he sprang aside, evading the charge. Holomalia threw and his noose snapped fast about the massive up-sweeping horns.

For a few minutes there was a wicked tangle of horse, bull, and man as the Ancient One lunged and swung his heavy head with side-tosses which, had they landed right, would have disemboweled Tradewind. But expert from years of handling wild stock, the magnificent gray made inspired backward leaps, turns, and stops. A dozen times I thought the bull's horns would reach their goal but Tradewind managed to keep clear. Finally he offered his haunches invitingly to the lowered horns. The bull roared and charged, but Tradewind sprang away and tore for some trees. With knotted tail, lowered head, bellowing and blowing great puffs of spray from his nostrils, the bull took after his retreating enemy. But Tradewind had maneuvered into position and deftly put a tree between himself and the wild bull. The lasso whined taut. Tradewind wheeled, propped, and darted back around the tree, whanging the huge curly head with its death-dealing horns against the trunk.

When the bull's raging rushes and plunges to get free subsided a little, Holomalia dismounted. Tradewind braced back on his haunches, keeping the rope taut and the bull's head against the tree, eyes and ears alert for possible mishaps which might imperil Holomalia's life. Edging forward cautiously with the manila tie-rope, Holomalia succeeded, after repeated tries, in getting it about the bull's massive neck and tied him fast. Signing to Tradewind that everything was finished, he stepped back and the gray eased up on the lasso. Holomalia flashed in, snatched off his rawhide and stepped back grinning as only a *paniolo* can grin when he's succeeded in roping a famous outlaw. Then with a quick grateful movement he pressed his hand on Tradewind's reeking shoulder. "Fine," he said to his partner.

Swinging into the saddle, Holomalia started down the ridge in the direction of the forests below where faint shouts told us the other men were still busy. We tore along the rough hogback and a great bull leaped out of his hiding place in the scrub. His lowered horns seemed to expand to twice their size as he came for me. Our horses shied out in opposite directions, but the huge beast passed so close I could feel the heat of his body. Bedouin swerved, the bull vanished, and I felt my horse give a convulsive leap in the air as he sailed over the corner of a lava pit which had engulfed the bull.

"Never mind, us get him tomorrow," Holomalia yelled and we tore on. This was life, this was living and glory, I thought. We sped on down the rough shoulder of the mountain. Far ahead we saw racing specks, then a wild cry from the left stopped us. In an opening Eole was racing for a tree with a bull pursuing him. His horse, which had come a cropper, was off in the distance. Holomalia yelled and I shut my eyes. He was racing to Eole's rescue—from *below*. Tradewind would be knocked off his feet if the bull charged him.

I jerked Bedouin to a trembling standstill and against my will my eyes opened. Eole, his face blanched with terror, sprang for the limb of the tree, missed it, and dodged behind the trunk. The bull roared, charged, and swept past. When it wheeled to attack a second time it spied Tradewind. Tradewind flung up his head protestingly when Holomalia jammed in the spurs, knowing it was a wrong maneuver, then submitted to his master's order. With flattened ears he rushed in. Holomalia threw, caught the bull as it was charging, wrenched Tradewind out sideways and tried to brace against the weight of the bull when it reached the end of the lasso. But Tradewind was on a side-hill. . . . There was a sickening thud and horse and rider went down.

Holomalia was on his feet instantly but Tradewind had the wind partially knocked out of him. The bull, which had pitched head over heels, scrambled up, mad to destroy. Tradewind gave a leap to his feet and wavered on wide-straddled legs. Snatching out his legging-knife, Holomalia slashed through his lasso, free-ing his horse, then swung into the tree, shouting to distract the bull's attention to himself. But blind with fury the bull struck Tradewind a terrific blow. One long horn disappeared into the gray flank. The bull tossed his head and ripped the horse open. Entrails dropped.

Dad and Hauki, attracted by the commotion, rushed in and from above this time they re-roped the bull. Tradewind stood braced, his magnificent muscles quivering, his noble head held high. Then his legs collapsed. Holomalia rushed to him. Muscles all over the horse's body were cramping and bunching as he kicked on the grass. Holomalia swooped for the knife he had dropped when he cut Tradewind free, then pressed his hand fiercely against the gray's shoulder. With a smothered oath he slipped the sharp blade in just behind the horse's ears, severing the spinal cord. A shiver passed through the silver-gray body and it was still.

Straightening up Holomalia stared at the slow drops of blood falling from his knife point and frowned at his severed lasso as though he did not recognize it. Then like a boy who is hurt he scraped his arm across his wet eyes.

Paniolos crowded up. When Dad and Hauki finished tying the bull they came forward. Dad laid his hand on Holomalia's rigid shoulder. "Don't grieve," he said in Hawaiian. "Trade-wind has gone like a god—on the flood tide! To outlive your usefulness, to feel life passing you by, to sense your hold is slipping—that's tragedy. But to leap from Here to There while life's still a rich song, is a blessing!"

Holomalia nodded, wiped his wet eyes on his wrist and began mechanically unstrapping the saddle from the gray body it still girdled, lying limply on the jewel-green grass.

22. HELL'S HOLIDAY

WHILE Tradewind's death was still vivid in my mind, violent earthquakes began shaking the Islands announcing that a major eruption of Mauna Loa was imminent. On several occasions when the great volcano on Hawaii had been active Dad had taken us to the top of Haleakala to watch the awesome dome, a hundred miles away, spilling lava into the sea, and, although I'd never seen a flow close by, even at a distance the Long Mountain in action was an appalling sight.

Geologically, Mauna Loa is the largest individual mountain mass in the world. Rising 18,000 feet from ocean bottom to sealevel, it towers an additional 14,000 feet into the sky, a conical monster of 32,000 feet, built up from layers upon layers of lava. The vast dome has two outlets: Kilauea, about four thousand feet up its slope; and Mokuaweoweo, the main vent, at the summit.

To my consternation, Dad became furiously active, hurriedly arranging ranch business so he and *I* could dash to Hawaii if there was an eruption. A second cousin of his who lived on Maui was summoned to take over my duties teaching the babies and running the house. I had a horror of earthquakes and volcanoes which, being an Islander, I was ashamed to voice. The fear had been born in me by a coincidence. I had been deep in "The Last Days of Pompeii," far too mature a book for a child of eight, when a series of violent shocks hit Maui. Stimulated by the account of that disaster, my imagination had painted monstrous pictures of what might possibly happen at any moment in my own Paradise, and the maturity of the 'teens had not dulled my horror of volcanoes in the slightest.

223

The temporary regime at home had hardly been installed before Central phoned saying word had been radioed from Hawaii that the outbreak had started and those wishing to see the eruption must be at Lahaina by midnight to catch the sight-seeing steamers taking people to the Big Island. Daddy was jubilant over the prospect of the exciting holiday.

We packed hastily and started on the sixty-mile trip to Lahaina. Before we were halfway there, smoke began to obscure the sky and through the tawny-blue haze the sun shone red and angry, dim and diminished. In the east, Haleakala was exaggerated to twice its size and the West Maui mountains, whose bases we were skirting, seemed like sheer chiffon folds disappearing into the dun smoke-canopy overhead. The sea had a curious stillness, which made me reluctant to board the steamer and trust myself to it. Tidal waves and volcanoes went hand in hand and Heaven only knew what convulsions were brewing on ocean bottom.

When we picked up the lights of the steamer in the channel between Lanai and Molokai my skin got cold and clammy. I would have given everything I possessed, except Bedouin, to turn back. But I recalled Dad's bitter disappointment on another occasion when he had persuaded Mother to leave the babies and go to Hawaii with him to see an eruption, and at the last minute she had turned back. He looked so gay that I choked down my fear and pretended an eagerness I did not feel.

With dozens of other excited Maui people, we boarded the already-crowded ship and sat up all night. Everyone was in a dither. Where was the flow heading? Would it do as much damage as the last? Whose ranch was menaced?

The oily unnatural stillness of the sea was horrible. A dank smell rose from it. The whole ocean-bottom must be atilt somewhere. I sat as close to Daddy as possible. About three in the morning a long shudder passed through the ship and the rank smell of slime from the uttermost depths filled the night. Presently a grating sound mingled with the ripple of water passing along the ship's hull. Everyone rushed to the railing and looked over. We were sailing through seas of floating pumice that some undersea volcano had spewed up.

Shortly before dawn we anchored off Kailua, chief port of the district of Kona. The red light overhead had subsided and the mammoth island was half obscured by a choking smoke pall which made everything appear troubled and menacing. When we piled with other passengers into the small boats I could hardly swallow and thought longingly of my own beloved Maui.

"We're going to see a real show, this time," Dad exulted. "The old mountain is Letta-going-its-blouse with a vengeance."

Ashore everything was a turmoil. Seven new cones had broken out and were spouting liquid lava hundreds of feet into the air. The flow was traveling at the rate of almost thirty miles an hour and had reached the sea long ago. Guides were beyond price but Dad had wired ahead to secure the services of Charlie Kaa, who had seen Mauna Loa erupt over forty times.

Pushing through the mob we found him waiting with three horses in addition to his own. After greetings, Dad asked who the extra horse was for. Charlie's aquiline features broke into a grin and he gestured at a small Chinese restaurant, looking mysterious and important. "Wait, you see," he said.

Kakina came out. "Hello, you old duffer!" Dad shouted delightedly.

Kakina told him he had been running down a story for his paper. "When Charlie phoned me in Hilo, saying you both would be over, I decided instead of seeing the flow from the Kau side I'd join you here. Charlie and I decided that before seeing the flow from the road we'd go up Mauna Loa and get as near to the source of the outbreak as it's safe to go."

"Bully!" Dad exclaimed.

I was stunned. It was well enough to watch a lava flow from a so-called grandstand seat, but I had no wish to go behind scenes. Why hadn't I had sense enough to fake illness before we set off? Dad didn't know my secret horror of volcanoes and would have taken one of my sisters. The brief delight I'd felt when Kakina appeared, at the thought of seeing my first eruption with the two men I loved best, faded away. Let people who enjoyed flirting with destruction do it, I thought indignantly. I preferred other forms of extinction to being blown up or boiled in lava. But Dad's delight and the eagerness in Kakina's eyes made me choke back the words.

A struggling crowd of automobiles, carriages, and riders was pouring along the main highway, paralleling the shore. Friends cried out as they recognized each other, or passed on the latest bulletins of the outbreak. As we rode up the steep slopes through dense forests of glossy coffee, the road became more and more congested with traffic. Every so often, smothered explosions deep in the earth jarred the four thousand square miles of the island and everyone became tense and still. But after an instant the gala spirit reasserted itself and the long procession went on. Some parties which had come from distant portions of Hawaii were picnicking hurriedly on the roadside; others stopped off to rest in friends' houses, sitting back in bright careless gardens.

The smell of blossoming gardenias, coffee, and guavas in bloom mingled incongruously with the taint of sulphur in the atmosphere. Under the dense smoke pall the vividly green vegetation, marred in places by black lava outpourings from previous eruptions, looked eerie and disturbing. Even when the earth underfoot was quiet, a person sensed that the mightiest forces in the universe were working secretly in the vitals of the island.

Dad and Kakina rode together most of the time, and Charlie Kaa chatted pridefully about his home district. Kona, he told me, was known in ancient times as the Land of Hanging Rain and the Land of the Setting Sun. It had been loved by the chiefs of old. In Kona, people were gayer and kinder, flowers brighter, and fruit grew to greater sizes than on any of the other islands. If you were very still at night you could hear landshells singing in the forests and the whisper of gods' feet on the beaches. The blue bay below was Kealakekua, The Highway of the Gods, where Captain Cook had been killed. In the frowning cliffs overhanging the blue water were caves filled with the bones of chiefs, war canoes, feather cloaks, and polished *koa* spears, hidden forever from white men. Beyond, on the dark lava promontory, was Honaunau, the City of Refuge. In olden times if a man was falsely accused of a crime and his life was at stake, if he could outrun his enemies, plunge into the sea and swim across the shark-infested strip of water and reach the walled City of Refuge without mishap he was automatically exonerated. He had survived the Gauntlet of the Gods who would have destroyed him if he had broken a *tabu*.

About noon we halted to rest the horses and secure provisions from a Chinese store which was all but bought out of foodstuffs. My misgivings were mounting with each instant that passed. Even if the direction of the flow had been established I had no wish to go up Mauna Loa. It didn't make sense. As a rule once an eruption gets under way, easing the pressure of gases against the earth's crust, the earthquakes stop. But during the fifteen minutes we'd been in the store, half-a-dozen violent jolts had shaken the island. My outlaw imagination pictured new fissures opening the sides of Mauna Loa, or the entire top might blow off, as Karakatoa had. . . .

I could hardly swallow the bowl of rice and *pake* stew the proprietor of the store-restaurant served while he assembled the provisions we needed. His voice was quite unreal as he jabbered to Dad and Kakina.

"Velly fine business wen wolokano blow off. I catchem plenty dollars yesterday and today. Tonight I go Kailua in tluck and buy more supplies. I like fine spose lava come out five-six times every year."

A savage shake joggled the store, and I prayed that Kakina and

Dad would reconsider their plan of getting as close as possible to the source of the outbreak. But no such luck.

Shortly I found myself riding along a thin trail up the shaking slopes of Mauna Loa, obscured by heavy drifting smoke. The insides of my legs itched and hair prickled on my scalp. The forest looked eerie and the hot stillness of the day made the horses lather with sweat. As we got higher I caught ghostly glimpses of wild cattle flitting past as they headed for the safety of lower regions. Their hatred of men-with-ropes was forgotten in the greater terror of the cataclysm which had their wastelands in its grip. Herds of wild jackasses and goats lolloped by, and the grunting of wild hogs crashing in the underbrush told me that they, too, were leaving. Still Charlie Kaa, wise with fifty-odd years of intimate acquaintance with Mauna Loa in all its destructive moods, pressed on.

My uneasiness began to verge on anger. Wild animals' instincts urged them to flee. Who wanted to get practically into bed with a volcano? The roaring of the mountain, which had been dulled by distance, was growing noticeably louder. With each passing instant my panic mounted but rather than show the white feather before men, or spoil Dad's fun by turning back, I followed doggedly.

After hours of climbing we halted on a hill and Charlie told Dad and Kakina that the original plan of going to within a mile or so of the spouting cones would have to be abandoned as the continued shaking of the earth hinted that a fresh outbreak might occur lower on the flank of Mauna Loa. We could camp overnight in safety where we were and watch the new cones spouting and the river of red molten slag pouring into the sea.

Relief made me weak. The air was hot and dry, filled with fine cindery particles that caught in my throat and made even the horses cough. We made camp and waited for darkness.

When night came Mauna Loa looked like the funeral pyre

of the world. Even from a distance of thirty miles we could plainly see the continuous jets of lava spouting from the new cones, like miniature firehoses playing against dark, rolling smoke columns. From the white-hot throat of an aperture just below them, vermilion and dull-red lava shot out with deep unearthly roarings alternating with shattering explosions.

The horses were uneasy and shifted on their tether ropes, sniffing the acrid air and starting when some extra loud noise came from the distant summit of Mauna Loa. I gripped Daddy's hand and stood close, watching the fiery flood pouring down the slopes of the mountain.

"Wind up, First Lieutenant?" he asked.

"A bit," I admitted.

"We're safe here, Charlie knows his business. Get an eyeful of this, there's no show on earth to equal it. Seeing the lava pouring across the road is well enough, but—" He gestured at the terrific spectacle.

About two we rolled up in our blankets, but about three-thirty a Behemoth of a roar brought us all leaping to our feet. Across the gulf between our hilltop and the summit of the volcano, explosions shook the night and we could hear the terrific thrashing of lava at white heat. Three more cones had opened up.

The lava flow, which was about two miles wide, was swelling to gigantic proportions and filling a great swale on the mountainside. After a little, the vast depression was transformed into a lake of fire miles in breadth that illuminated the sky overhead until it glowed like a red-hot oven. The new flow was pouring over the first with thudding explosions, spilling livid trickles through the forests high on the slopes of Mauna Loa. Dark smoke was pouring with redoubled violence from the summit, and we could hear the colossal roaring of masses of liquid rock falling back on the cones which were spouting it out. They retaliated by discharging it with fresh fury, flinging it over the monster dome, and the incessant rattling of a hail of cooling fragments falling back on the flows of other ages sounded like metallic rain through the greater noises of the night.

Kakina estimated that the smoke pillar must be about twenty thousand feet high. At intervals the ominous darkness was torn by vile lightings, then became dense again. It seemed as if the whole island was going upwards in one vast, steady conflagration.

When dawn broke, the smoke cloud shut off the spectacle. Nothing seemed real. The coffee Charlie made for us, the bacon and eggs were all tainted with the foul, sulphurous breath of the volcano. When we started down I wanted to jam my spurs into my horse's side and race back to safety. As long as I lived, the sights and sounds of that night would be engraved on my brain.

When we got back to Kona proper I was amazed to find that nothing had changed. People were still hurrying toward the flow, gay, eager and excited. We stopped at the Chinaman's store for iced pop, which I drank avidly.

"Well, First Born, you've seen something!" Dad exulted.

I had to admit that. Like Dad I loved nature on a rampage but such a one as we'd just witnessed had to be digested slowly. "But suppose," I ventured, "something entirely unexpected happened, like the side of Mauna Loa blowing out."

Dad smiled. "We'd make the leap from Here to There in a splash of splendor."

We started on, then, to see the flow crossing the road, and I tried to fortify myself with the thought that watching lava flows at close range must be more or less safe or Island people would not rush to see them every time they poured out of Mauna Loa. When we got to within a mile of where the river of fire was thundering down the slope of the island we could only move at a snail's pace. People were everywhere, camping on the roadsides, among the guava bushes, or sitting on the narrow verandas of natives' houses while they waited for night to come and intensify the spectacle.

Shortly after dark we neared the main flow, and the world, which had been blotted out by low-lying smoke, opened up to unbelievable proportions. Where the two-mile-wide fiery Niagara dumped its billions of tons of molten matter into the sea, a steam jet 18,000 feet high stood up like a gigantic ostrich plume and the water was boiling for miles off the shore. Whenever a fresh mass of slag came into the ocean, the night seemed to stagger and recoil. Shattering, splitting noises, roars, muffled detonations came from the seashore, jarring the atmosphere.

Kulilna looked on, his hands clasped behind him, making no comment. Despite his Aryan ancestry he was Hawaiian to the core. He had the leisurely dignity, the directness and simplicity, characteristic of Polynesians. His black eyes were blazing with pride as he watched the spectacle.

Dad gripped my shoulder. In his face was the strange happiness that Islanders show when their volcano goes off. I recognized the same expression on the faces of all the old-timers. It was reminiscent of a decent family's secret delight and interest in the Black Sheep of the clan whose escapades and outlaw acts make history.

Every so often the heat from the shifting mass of rock crossing the road grew so intense that everyone retreated hastily. When the flow humped or jarred, Charlie and the other Hawaiian guides shepherded the press of humanity to a safe distance in case of a minor explosion within the flow. When the river of horror grew temporarily sluggish, people chatted, ate sandwiches, and the musically-inclined took out guitars and ukuleles. Some joked about the fury of the Supervisors who'd have to rebuild the road after the lava cooled. It had only been three-and-a-half years since the last flow wrecked it. Their budget would be shot to hell. No chance of graft there. . . . Children romped, older folk recalled eruptions of their youth.

Suddenly I felt myself swing into the mood of the crowd. It was a thrilling, magnificent occasion—completely mad, completely gorgeous, and utterly characteristic of Hawaii. Hell's Holiday—in the middle of the Pacific!

23. DEEP HAWAII

IN DADDY's young manhood it had been his fortunate lot to know most of the outstanding personalities of Hawaii. He had known King Kalakaua who, as a ruler, was a failure but who, as a personality, was a triumph. He had gone with Major Wodehouse, while he was British Ambassador, to call on Princess Ruth whose four hundred pounds of flesh, ferocious features, and mastodon bellows brought trembling retainers crawling to her on their stomachs. He had seen Helen skyrocket to fame as the Magdalene of the Pacific, and he knew scores of other personalities who made the days of the Monarchy as rich in sweep and detail as any era in history.

I envied him his contacts with a vanished Hawaii which I could never know and prodded him for details about it.

"How would you like to meet the head *hula*-dancer of Kalakaua's court?" he asked me one evening. " 'Lively,' as Hinano was nicknamed by the King's courtiers, left Honolulu when Kalakaua died and retired to Honamanu Valley where she'e lived ever since."

My pulses leaped. Honomanu Valley. We had skirted the head of the monster gorge when we took the Jack Londons around the eastern end of Maui, following the more-or-less new Ditch Trail. Constructed by the Hawaiian Commercial Sugar Company, the "Ditch" was a stately aqueduct which gathered up the surplus water of East Maui and brought it around the island to irrigate the once-arid isthmus between Haleakala and the West Maui mountains, now covered with luxuriant fields of cane.

"I didn't know you knew anyone in Honomanu," I said.

"Until the Ditch Trail was finished I stayed with Lively every time I made trips round the island by the old King's Runners road. I've been intending to check up on some water-rights in Pohakumoa gulch. We'll all take a week off, attend to the job, and sandwich in a visit with Lively."

A few days later we started for the splendid section of Maui loosely classed as the Ditch Country. After leaving the ranches and plantations of Central Maui behind, the trail began winding up and down spray-filled gorges filled with rainbows, choked with bananas, thickets of bamboo, mighty *koa* trees, tangled creepers, and wet banks of fern. Blossoming ginger, indigenous begonias, and *ape-ape* leaves six feet in diameter fringed the forest pools. Dad told us that in ages past this plant grew on all the continents, but today was only to be found in the humid rain-forests of Hawaii. The name *ape-ape* meant "The Flying Away of the Fowls."

Deeper and deeper we pushed into the wild tangled country, too steep for either cattle or cultivation, which constituted the last stand of Old Hawaii on Maui. The ground oozed water, ferns and trees dripped it, secret rills gurgled, gulches and canyons thundered their silvery burdens to the sea. Hot forests steamed and rain squalls marched like ghosts above us on the huge shoulder of Haleakala. Ravines thousands of feet deep, gouged out of solid rock, gave evidence of the torrential downpours of centuries.

After a few miles Dad abandoned the Ditch Trail to follow the old trail of the King's Runners, in order to let us enjoy some extra-fine scenery. When we reached Pohakumoa, the river, pouring along the bottom of the gulch, was swollen and muddy from a cloudburst high on the slopes of Haleakala. A hundred yards below the ford where we were to cross, the foaming torrent disappeared over a cliff and the roar of the water hitting boulders hundreds of feet below filled the day with hollow thunder.

Dad, Hauki, then Eole studied a long groove chipped in the face of a sheer rock at the edge of the rushing water. The mark had been put there in olden times to gauge the volume of the river. If it was hidden, it was not safe to cross. The churning flood was still four inches below the danger line. Dad tied the end of his lasso solidly to his pommel and gave the other end to Hauki who fastened it to his own saddle-horn. After a few instructions, Dad spurred Champagne into the angry water, letting out slack as he went. Hauki gathered his horse together and braced back in case Champagne should lose his footing and be swept toward the falls. We watched tensely.

When the water got deep Champagne began half-swimming across the tossing floor, losing a foot every yard, but about a hundred feet above the lip of the falls he gave a violent plunge and scrambled up the far bank. One by one we swam our horses across with the stout rawhide guarding us from the menace of the cataract whose threatening voice filled the rocky walls.

When we began descending the narrow cobblestone path into Honomanu, long slanting rays of sunlight were filling the valley below with moonstone colors. Checkerboards of taro patches showed, and a long lazy surf was breaking on the black shingle beach fronting the sea. Dad explained that the trail we were descending ended at the bottom of the bluff and we would have to swim our horses across a narrow treacherous arm of the sea on a timed wave-count, the secret of which had been handed down in one family for generations.

When we were about halfway down he gave a long hail and after a minute or so an answering shout came from below. "Old Kamanawa's on the job," Dad said in relieved tones, glancing at the tired babies. "Sometimes when he's up the valley working in his taro patches you have to wait hours."

We finally emerged from the overgrown trail onto a small sandspit. Across the tossing arm of water a tall Hawaiian, naked except for a scarlet *malo,* waited, his eyes intent upon waves running past up a deep narrow lagoon paralleling the cliff on the eastern side of the valley. Hauki took Lorna in front of him,

Eole took Errol. Kamanawa shouted *"Hele—go!"* and Daddy plunged in. After a couple of minutes of furious swimming, Champagne lunged up the shingle beach, his gray coat flashing like quicksilver in the rays of the sinking sun.

When the waves were right again, Hauki and Lorna went across, swimming her pony beside them. In turn we all crossed without mishap and were enthusiastically greeted by Hawaiians who had collected on the beach. Since the building of the Ditch Trail, few Whites ever entered the valley. The villagers escorted us toward a doubledecker frame-house set in a tangle of plumaria, gardenias, hibiscus, and ginger flowers whose fragrance mingled with the clean salty smell of waves tumbling up the black pebble beach.

As we approached the house a majestic woman emerged from the doorway, and, seeing Daddy, held out her arms as a person does to a hurt child. "Louis, Louis, swell you and your *keikis* come my house. I too sorry when I hearing Amy die on you!"

After a brief tribute of tears to the dead, her eyes sparkled and it seemed as if all the fun and laughter of the world was housed in her two hundred pounds of golden flesh. Although she carried herself imperiously, she was as unaware of herself as a child and, despite her bulk, moved with the sure, easy grace of a cat. A voluminous red-and-white-flowered *holoku* failed to conceal the noble curves of her body. She had heavily lashed, curiously young eyes, a proud merry mouth, and her voice held all the warmth of the wide lazy evening.

"Get down your horse, you kids. Aunt Lively happy you come. Us all have jolly fun. Tomorrow night we have fine *luau*. Maybe"—imps danced behind her fringing lashes—"if I drink nuff *okolehao* and feel sassy, I tell you about when I young girl and every peoples saying I the best dancer in Kalakaua's Court."

She embraced us each in turn, shouted a few orders to the Hawaiians loafing about the garden chatting with Eole and Hauki, then took us into a cool lofty room. Vast couches filled two corners, covered with priceless Niihau mats. Tall *kahilis* standing in great Canton vases were grouped against one wall, their feathery heads close together as if they were whispering about state scandals of the past.

That night after supper everyone congregated on the wide grassy bank of the limpid river to swim. Babies, grandmothers, lovers, husbands, and wives romped and shrieked together, seemingly of one age, while a young moon sailed above the sheer cliffs, enameling the water with gold. Beyond the hump of the shingle beach a great surf roared dully, and, every so often, a long white arm of spray sprang up for a brief instant like an envious ghost forbidden by a *tabu* to mingle with human beings.

As I lolled on the fine black sand of the river bank, my mind reverted to descriptions of Polynesians by explorers who visited the Pacific long ago. No people in ancient or modern times rated beauty higher among life's gifts than did the people who inhabited the star-scattered archipelagos of the tropics. They brought the culture of beauty, the rhythm of motion, to unequaled perfection; the adornment of their bodies and the development of natural attractions to a pitch of artistry that struck every early navigator as nothing short of miraculous. In their use of flowers for personal adornment, unguents, and lotions to intensify the charm of their persons, in their singular and astounding art of pantomime, in dancing and story-telling, in their simple garb and unaffected natural manners, they showed a delicacy of feeling and understanding of elegance unsurpassed in the records of any nation on earth.

When we retraced our steps to the old friendly frame-house, I spoke to Aunt Lively about it. Seating herself on the floor she tossed back an armful of hair. Yes, she agreed, speaking in Hawaiian, the old-time Polynesians were like that. Pausing, she let her mind drift back into the shrouded past of her people. Before Whites came, she went on, we had no words like barter or sell.

Everyone, individuals and tribes, shared bumper crops and large catches of fish.

The hour was late but Islanders are not time-conscious. While constellations glittered overhead and sea and river sung to each other, Aunt Lively talked on in stately Hawaiian. When she spoke of the trans-Pacific voyages of centuries ago, her fine intelligent eyes misted. While Europeans were still creeping cautiously along their coasts, or venturing to cross the Mediterranean only within the threatening Pillars of Hercules, Polynesians in frail canoes were fearlessly making trips between Hawaii and New Zealand. During the daytime they guided themselves by the sun, trend of waves, wind, and the flight of sea-birds, but in long voyages between island groups stars were used as guides.

The Polynesian outposts in the Carolines and Easter Island were nearly nine thousand miles apart, and three thousand eight hundred miles of water lie between Hawaii and New Zealand. Without chart, compass, or sextant the Vikings of the Pacific explored every island in their vast domain. Even uninhabited atolls give up stone or shell implements proving that they had been visited at some time by the hardy navigators of long ago.

A youth studying navigation was taught to view the heavens as a cylinder on which were marked the highways of navigation. An invisible line bisected the sky leading from Noholoa, the North Star, to Newa, the Southern Cross. The portions of the heavens east of this line was known as the "Bright Road of Kane." That to the west was called the "Highway of Kanaloa."

For trans-Pacific voyages large twin canoes were often used, fastened together by a canopied platform which shielded the voyagers from sun and rain. Such craft were remarkably seaworthy and could accommodate as many as sixty or eighty persons, in addition to water, food, domestic animals, and other supplies necessary for a long voyage. Some of the vessels had as many as three masts. The sails were made of braided pandanus sewed in triangular form with wooden booms and yards to strengthen them. As the Vikings of the Atlantic were equipped with oars, so the mariners of the Pacific were fitted with paddles. The Norsemen looked at the wake lying behind, Polynesians faced the waves and horizons ahead. A steering-paddle took the place of a rudder and was so important that it always had a personal name. Polynesian legends of old-time voyages give not only the name of the canoe, the hero who discovered the new island, but also the name of the steering-paddle he used.

Building a big seaworthy canoe with nothing but stone chisels and adzes and cocoanut-fiber lashing was the work of trained craftsmen. Canoes played such a major role in the life of Islanders that each one was constructed with chants and ceremonies. When the tree was felled, when the wood was shaped, and when launching-time came the entire population assembled for the event. By the time Columbus ventured with his fearful crew across the Atlantic, the great voyages of Polynesia were over, and most of the island groups had been discovered and inhabited. . . .

While Aunt Lively talked there was an immortal quality about her. She was the soul of Polynesia; proud, poised, adventurous, drinking a deeper draught of life than the average person has courage for.

Light was showing above the wild cliffs when she ceased talking. With child-like amazement she looked out of the open door. There was a pearl-like luster to the ocean and a wave, fresh with the flow of the incoming tide, broke in quicksilver on the black pebble beach.

"Sha, all night us fellas talk!" she exclaimed, lapsing back into English. "Better us catch some coffee, then go sleep for little time. Then us fresh for all the fun us making today and tonight."

After a nap, when the tide was right, she led us to the beach. "Look, you kids, all this kind black stones. No seem like they got plenty good food inside them. Wait, I show you."

Squatting down she scooped a hole in the loose pebbles, deep enough so each in-washing wave, without spilling into it, oozed in from below. Taking a flat black crab from the bag tied about her opulent waist, she smashed it to pulp with a stone, placed the fragments in her cupped palm, then with partially spread fingers lowered her hand into the frothing pool. Little black eels, she explained, lived in the loose shingle. When they smelt the crab, they poked their heads between her fingers to nibble it and —with a shriek of glee she jerked her hand out. Between her clenched fingers, three small eels dangled. "Go ahead, you make like me, easy like anykind."

Before long we each had a hole and were snatching out eels about ten inches long as fast as Aunt Lively. When the cloth bag, resting on her stomach, was filled to capacity with a writhing mass we started for the house. Dumping the eels into a large tin washtub she sprinkled them liberally with native salt crystals and shook with laughter as they lashed about. "Make hot-style *hula,* eh?" she demanded. When the eels became still they had emptied themselves of all refuse and were clean and ready to eat. After washing them carefully she fried them in oil, and when they were cooked we picked them up in our fingers and stripped off the delicate silver meat with our teeth.

After lunch she collected a merry throng and we went up the valley to do some tropical tobogganing. Stopping in a moist glade we snapped off heads of glossy *ti* leaves and scrambled to the top of the slide. The long grass was as slippery as ice and while we panted and fought up the incline Aunt Lively told us that, beside special slides constructed for chiefs, stones were placed forming a stairway to enable them to enjoy themselves with the minimum of effort. When we came to the top we sat down to regain our breath, then seated ourselves on the bunches of *ti* leaves. Holding the stalk between our legs, we shot with yells and shrieks to the bottom.

We lingered for two days in the valley, swimming, fishing, feasting, and soaking in the atmosphere of by-gone days which Dad and Aunt Lively had enjoyed before we were born. With

the gusto characteristic of her race, Aunt Lively relived her joy
ous youth when she had been royal favorite, sitting beside Kala·
kaua on his *Makaloa* mat, eating *poi* out of the monster calabash,
and dancing for the royal pleasure when the King and his merry
court toured the islands.

Whenever she spoke of the past she relapsed into Hawaiian
and, magically, her voice and words conjured up pictures of the
merry careless rout when King, courtiers, wives, sweethearts, and
troupes of singers and dancers circled each island, feasting and
celebrating as they went. Commoners and nobles assembled to
pay tribute to their Monarch in each district, then with pride and
delight brought out their young daughters to dance.

"Before Whites came to the Pacific," she explained, "orators
and dancers of note were supported by the state to enable them
to devote all their time to their art, for the pleasure and education of the tribe, and even in my day every girl dreamed of
becoming a Court dancer.

"I was not yet fifteen when I was selected as the most likely
girl in my district to dance for Kalakaua. When the time came
for me to dance I was shaking like a leaf. To bolster up my
courage I gazed repeatedly into a little mirror my mother held
up for me behind the bushes where we were concealed. I saw my
body, round, silken, slender as a young bamboo. My skin shone
from ceaseless care. My curling hair had a red-gold glint linking
me in ancestry to the Spanish aristocrat and his sister from Anda-
lusia who were wrecked on the coast of Kona in the sixteenth
century.

"The King and his Court were feasting in a grove out of doors
and from the place where I was hiding I could see Kalakaua's
strong back as he lolled on his elbow watching the Court favorite, Lehua, doing a special *hula* for the assemblage. Watching
her, I wondered how I, a mere child, could hope to compete
with such a performer. I prayed passionately to the Goddess

Laka, patron of the *hula,* to aid me. I had to be a credit to my family and clan gathered to watch me dance.

"When my turn came to go out, I advanced like the slow waters of a winding brook. As I passed each man or woman I caught their eyes and challenged them, as a fighting man his enemy. Only I looked love and not hate. Then I slid into the story of the dance. If I could move the hearts of the King and his courtiers, so their breaths quickened and their limbs jerked and their eyes fell before me, my fame would be assured and my existence as a woman justified.

"I listened for applause to break out, but everyone remained silent. The music went into a faster tempo and fear began weakening my limbs, then I realized that everyone was mute and helpless under my spell. I began dancing for the King only. My body became a flame. He signed to the musicians to go into an old intricate *hula,* without ever taking his eyes off me. When at last the music stopped, Kalakaua raised up off his elbow. Looking at his courtiers he said, 'A new enchantress has come into our midst to torment us,' and reaching out his hand drew me down beside him on his *Makaloa* mat."

The atmosphere of old Hawaii seemed to fill the house as Aunt Lively sat with regal memories wrapped lavishly about her. Kalakaua's generosity had built this house for her. He had conferred grants of land on her in far-off valleys on other islands. Delving into the bottom of a handsomely carved chest she dragged out a heavy album fastened with metal clasps and showed us intimate snapshots of Kalakaua, as well as formal ones of him in uniform with medals and regalia. Reverently she unwrapped layers of tissue paper and displayed two yellow feather *leis.* One had been given to her by Kalakaua, the other she had inherited. "In old times," she told us in Hawaiian, "noble families kept retainers who spent their lives in the forest smearing a sticky substance on flowering trees where *Mamo* and *O-o* birds sucked honey. When they were caught the men robbed them of the few tiny yellow feathers under each wing, then set them free to grow more. It took years to assemble enough to make a neck-*lei* and generations to collect sufficient to fashion the cloaks and helmets worn by the warriors of long ago."

On the last night, while we lolled in the moonlight on the turf sloping down to the placid river, she recounted episodes in Kalakaua's life which have been repeated with gusto from Shanghai to London. Kalakaua's passion for gambling was such that his subjects allotted him an annual sum so that he might play poker, but his bad luck was notorious. However, on one occasion he won a pot sufficient to satisfy even his extravagant soul.

A game was started with four men with whom he habitually played. It continued without cessation for seventy-two hours. Then, after a deal, an excited light showed in the King's eyes. Through narrowed lids he watched the sugar baron who openly boasted that the wide lands he had planted in cane had been won from Kalakaua in poker.

The baron smiled, raised the ante, and waited. The King raised in turn. The pot assumed vaster and vaster proportions and one by one the other players dropped out. Finally, the baron called for a showdown. Kalakaua gave him a quick look and placed four Kings on the table. The baron triumphantly laid down four aces. Kalakaua reached out and jovially swept the mountain of gold pieces, greenbacks, and I.O.U.'s toward him.

"Hold on, four aces take four kings," the baron protested.

"But five kings beat four aces," Kalakaua announced, laughing uproariously, striking the cards before him with one hand while he thumped his magnificent chest with the other. There was no questioning his kingship. He took the pot, but from that day the baron never spoke to him again.

Then with misted eyes Aunt Lively told us of his true royalty. He was the first crowned head ever to circumnavigate the globe and his advent everywhere was triumphal. Queen Victoria entertained him and was impressed by his charm, polished manners, and regal bearing. Wilhelm of Prussia, Leopold of Belgium, the King and Queen of Italy were proud to count him a personal friend. In Japan he was greeted with a royal salute from a dozen warships. The Mikado outdid himself by coming to escort Kalakaua personally in the royal coach.

For an instant Aunt Lively's eyes grew mischievous, as she paused briefly and dramatically before going on with her story. Kalakaua loved the good things of life and amply sampled the vintages of all the lands he visited. Having breakfasted heavily and washed down his food with good wine, he dozed off for a few moments while driving with the Mikado from his ship to the palace. Just as the royal equipage approached the Imperial Palace, another salvo of guns saluted Kalakaua. The King opened his eyes, looked about him, then remarked in the tones of polite conversation, "How sweetly the birds sing in Japan!"

Aunt Lively shook with mirth, then wiped her eyes on a fold of her *holoku.* "But Kalakaua was no buffoon," she insisted, in the rich words of her own language. "In China, Siam, India, and Egypt he was received with as much honor as though he had been the most powerful monarch on earth. Returning home by way of the United States, he completed the first journey ever made around the world by royalty. His homecoming was celebrated with triumphal arches and commemorative *hulas* for he had, by the sheer charm of his personality, brought Hawaii to the attention of the world."

Breaking off, she watched waves tumbling up the shingle beach set between shadowy cliffs two thousand feet high. She looked rich and proud as she let her memory rest on the man whose royal favorite she had been. With the wisdom of her race she had drunk the cup of youth to the last drop, then relinquished it without regret to wear the luxurious mantle of Polynesian maturity. Observing her serene eyes I knew that no person who had lived with so much laughter, zest, and love in her soul could ever be lonely, or ever grow old. Her golden body housed a heart as richly full as autumn—when the harvest has been safely gathered in.

24. UGLY DUSTLING

ONE SUNDAY night when we were at dinner the telephone rang shrilly and insistently. Dad went to answer it. When he returned I knew from his expression that some damned thing had happened.

"Central phoned that Angus MacPhee blew off his hand accidentally and is bleeding to death. The doctor can't be located. There's no time to waste. Saddle Bedouin. I've got to change."

I rushed out, snatched up the lantern which always stood in the Office in case of emergencies, and ran through the dark garden to the stables. I went into Bedouin's loose box. He snorted until he realized it was I inside the fluffs and ruffles.

Because Angus MacPhee had been champion roper of the world for five years until Ikuwa had beaten him, he was a hero to me. Bedouin sensed that something unusual was afoot for though he was in hard training to run a match race, full of oats and ginger, he stood quite still while I saddled him. As soon as the girth was fast, I swung to his back and galloped into the quadrangle. Dad appeared just as I was tying him to the ring in the eucalyptus tree. He kissed me hurriedly. "Carry on while I'm gone. I'll phone as soon as I've seen Mac. I'll have to ride like hell."

He dashed off into the night. I went back to our guests but my mind was rushing with Daddy and Bedouin along the rough flank of Haleakala. Once more my beautiful horse was racing with Dad to beat death. About midnight Dad phoned. Mac was barely alive. Kinau, Aina, and the other Hawaiians who worked for Mac had been helpless through panic. "I've stopped the flow of blood," he went on, "and Dr. Osmers has finally been located, but Mac's so weak there's a chance he won't live. I didn't spare Bedouin, but he's in fine shape."

It was eight days before the doctor dared to move Mac to the hospital in Wailuku, forty miles away. Dad went along and stayed a few days with him. When Mac was well enough to leave he found out that his employer had installed another man as manager of Ulupalakua. Mac was sunk at the ingratitude, for he had just pulled the ranch through the longest toughest drought that ever hit the Islands. Dad went down and brought him home. We girls dressed his poor stump of an arm daily and, gradually, he regained his strength and driving power and learned how to rope, shoot, and dress himself all over again.

He and Dad talked the same talk, loved the same things, horses, cattle, trees and grasses, and dreamed the same dreams of steadily building up the land for posterity. When Mac got on his feet sufficiently he rustled other jobs and by degrees became one of the outstanding figures of Maui, as well as being practically a member of our family.

One night when we got in from a wild-cattle hunt we found him waiting for us, his hazel eyes shining with some great idea.

"Well, what card have you up your sleeve now?" Dad asked, grinning, as he swung off Champagne.

"I'll tell you after dinner," Mac said in an eager secret way.

When the babies were bedded down, Dad and Mac settled themselves in the living room. "Maybe you'll think I'm crazy," Mac began, "but I'm convinced that with intelligent handling, and sufficient time, the island of Kahoolawe can be reclaimed."

I thought of the desolate island whose red dust, for as far back as I could remember, had been blowing away toward the southwest like a funeral pyre. An eerie sensation went through me. In island parlance, Kahoolawe was *pau*—finished. Mac might just as well have announced that he could raise the dead!

"When did this idea first occur to you?" Daddy asked after a silence.

"When I took over the management of Ulupalakua ranch, shortly after I came here, I couldn't figure out, being a new-comer, why Kahoolawe was barren and all the other islands green. I asked the Kanakas about it and learned that it used to have trees and grass on it." Mac paused, as if he were sifting something around in his mind. "During the three years I man-aged Ulupalakua, Kahoolawe put a sort of spell on me. I hunted up all the information I could about it by checking Government records and learned that it had been leased from the Crown by two men whose names are best forgotten. They took over fifteen hundred head of cattle, a hundred horses, and ten thousand sheep. Later they added a thousand goats, more stock than the forty thousand acres of the island could possibly carry."

"I know its history," Dad said. "I was here when it all hap-pened."

Mac leaned forward eagerly.

"First the top, then the sides of the island began to go," Dad went on. "The owners made no efforts to check what was hap-pening. In three years they had to take the cattle and horses off because there wasn't enough pasturage to support them. With no vegetation to conserve moisture the water supply dwindled until there wasn't enough left even for sheep. They were taken off, too, but the goats, not worth the time or money to collect, were left behind to multiply and complete Kahoolawe's ruin."

Mac looked at Dad. "But while I managed Ulupalakua, I no-ticed that every winter after the rains the island was tinged with green for a few weeks, which proves, or makes it look as if, the island has a come-back in it. Last week I rented a sampan and sneaked over for a close look at it." Mac's eyes were getting warmer and brighter. "I spent five days there and covered the entire island on foot. Wherever the goats can't get, there's some sort of vegetation."

While the two men talked I thought about Kahoolawe, blown by wind, trampled down to the hard-pan. A victim of man's greed. Occasionally hunters went over it for a day to shoot some of the thousands of goats swarming there, and rumor had it that opium smugglers took advantage of its isolation to ply their unlawful trade.

Before the evening ended, Dad had promised to go with Mac to look the island over.

A few days later Mac, Jackie—Mac's young daughter who had recently come from Cheyenne and was living with us—Dad, and I put off from Kekei to visit the forsaken island. The awesome pre-dawn hush of the tropics lay on the sea as the blue sampan nosed its way through the satiny water, heading for the low red streak in the southwest.

When we got into the channel, Yamaichi, the big knotty Japanese captain who had a truculent swagger, gave the tiller to a listless youth and busied himself about a charcoal brazier. He helped himself to some cooked rice and fish, and with his eyes fastened on the island ahead, poured a liberal measure of *shoyu* over the contents of his bowl, then filled another bowl with pale fragrant tea.

"*Yoi*—good?" I asked, indicating the rice bowl in his hand.

He grunted, assentingly. I told him about my old nurse Tatsu and he gestured at the makings of his meal. "*Taberu*—eat," he said and I joyfully helped myself.

Dad and Mack were studying a Government map of Kahoolawe, and Jackie and I hung over their shoulders. The names of the bays and headlands fascinated me—Hawaiian names with the noble roll of hills and the lift of the sea in them. There was only one English name on the map and it sent a queer feeling through me. The bay at the southern extremity of the island was marked, "Hanakanae, or Smugglers Cove." What avenues of adventure it conjured up.

I studied the island ahead. It suggested a huge wounded beast lying disconsolately in the sea. Raw red gulches showed like rents in its skin. *Pili* grass, blanched by the sun and spray, grew low on its flanks, like mangy fur which had dropped off in spots. The sampan had turned and was running parallel with the coast, about half a mile off shore.

The water of each little bay we passed was brownish red from wind-blown earth that had piled and drifted across the sand, mingling with it, streaking the blue water, as if the island were slowly bleeding from old sores. Goats, diminished in size by distance, crawled over it like vermin.

Yamaichi took the wheel once more and headed directly for the shore. Tall cliffs opened surprisingly into a little bay. While Yamaichi and his assistant dropped anchor and lowered the skiff to take us ashore, Mac stood in the bows studying the island. Was he mad to dream that he, that anyone, could bring life back to it? There was no high mountain to attract clouds, no vegetation to precipitate moisture. A man might give a lifetime to reclaiming this red heap of desolation and make no visible impression.

For a week we lived in some old weather-worn houses huddled under cliffs which had shadows like faded blue garments hanging in their crags. Whitewash flaked off the house walls, spider webs, red and heavy with dust, hung from the rafters, but steadily the island put the spell of its personality on all of us. Day after day we trudged across it and heard, or felt, the protestation of the earth being worn away by the hoofs of goats and stripped of its last rags of vegetation by their sharp little teeth. If Mac decided to lease Kahoolawe, no re-grassing or irrigation could be attempted until the busy little animals were cleared off.

One day we explored the northern end of the island, starting early as there was a promise of wind in the sky. After hours of tramping we reached Kanapo Bay. Here trade-wind-driven seas smoked, in indigo and silver, against land. A thousand feet below, a wild beach showed, littered with mighty pine logs brought from Oregon and Washington by some freakish current which landed them in only this one spot in Hawaii.

About noon the wind began blowing hard. Dust clouds gathered and whirled along, disappearing over the blunt red top of the island until it seemed as if Kahoolawe were burning up and blowing away. Dark red, twisted columns of earth streamed into the sky, blotting out everything until we could only see the earth under our feet. We made our way home by the shore where what remained of the *pili* grass partially bound the soil, enabling us to see a little. Ahead was an angry maroon darkness that grew denser or lighter as the wind waxed and waned.

When evening came the wind dropped and the world opened up again. The tingling mystery enveloping the island was intensified by the rhythm of the sea swelling and receding against the rocky coast. Forever and ever . . . forever and ever, it chanted.

Around ten o'clock, while we were all talking, we suddenly fell silent. We knew in some instinctive way that we were no longer the only people on Kahoolawe. We listened for voices and footsteps; there were none; only the great, muted song of the sea. We went to the door and looked out. Only unbroken blackness.

"Probably a bunch of goat-hunters have landed somewhere," Dad remarked in his cool way.

"They always use these houses," Mac reminded him, his face watchful.

We waited for a while, then extinguished the lantern and walked to the top of the bluff. No flares or signals showed on land or sea, but we knew, as animals know, that somewhere on the island men had landed.

"If it's opium smugglers, it's useless to try and find them, they may have landed in any one of fifty bays," Daddy said. "Let's go back and turn in."

Mac's silhouette showed big and grim against the stars. "Blast it, I won't have them landing on my island," he said explosively, and with those words his long fight to save Kahoolawe was born.

To his astonishment when he went to Honolulu to lease it from the Land Board, the idea met with opposition. After repeated trips over to see people of importance holding Government positions, Mac finally convinced a few of the farthersighted that it would be to the benefit of the Territory to save the island. Finally, a twenty-one-year lease was signed.

As there was no boat communication with Kahoolawe, Mac bought a sixty-four-foot sampan and hired Yamaichi to captain it. Then he arranged with plantation butcher shops to sell them goats at $2.00 a head, on the hoof.

"I estimate there must be at least twenty thousand goats on the island," Mac told Dad. "That means twenty-five or thirty thousand dollars above expenses to add to the forty thousand I've saved up."

After repairing the tumbledown houses and cistern, he built corrals at the southwestern end of the island. All animals drive most easily downhill and the general slope of the land was in that direction. At the end of two months he was ready for the first goat drive. We all went over to help.

With whips, guns, and dogs we moved forward from Moaulu, the highest point of the island. Panic-stricken, outraged, resentful, the goats raced in all directions, pouring down gulch sides, streaming across flats. Bleating nannies, screaming kids, silent angry billies tried to break back.

We raced to head them off on horses shipped over for the occasion. Dust raised by the friction of thousands upon thousands of fleeing hoofs rose and hung in the air like a thin red veil and I thought, with actual pain, that more of Mac's island was being torn away. Through the transparent dust veil came the resounding crack of whips, shouts, dogs barking, and now and then the sharp fatal crack of a pistol which told that some stubborn old billy wouldn't head in the right direction.

After hours of this attack, the majority of goats decided on flight. A dizziness which was exhilaration poured through me as I raced across the hard-packed crimson miles, watching streams of animals pouring toward Hanakanae Bay. Rivers of goats, following the downward-fall of the land, gathered impetus, converged into a living torrent pouring toward the end of the island.

One side of the herd came up against one of the lead fences guiding them toward the corrals. They jammed, tried to turn, were swept on by fleeing comrades. Hundreds broke through the fence, but thousands poured on. A sort of elemental madness seemed to have taken possession of us all. Suddenly Mac began yelling, "Enough, enough," and galloping back and forth he tried to stem the torrent, which the corrals could not possibly hold. Eddying floods of animals poured into the corrals, pushing, packing, fighting to get out and the world was filled with the bleating of nannies and the screaming of terrified kids.

We corralled about four hundred. The sampan could take two hundred and fifty at a load. That meant two trips for Yamaichi, and while he went to Maui the mules and horses could rest.

Drive after drive was staged, for nothing of real importance could be started until the goats were gone. Whenever ranch-work permitted it, Dad took us over to Kahoolawe, but mostly Mac and his handful of men worked alone. As time went on the goats became wilder and wilder and more difficult to drive. Forsaking their old feeding grounds, they lived on the sheer cliffs overhanging the sea, living on weeds and grass growing in crevices.

Then Mac devised a new way of getting them. While men on horseback and on foot prowled along the top of the bluffs, Yamaichi and others sailed along below shooting up at them, while the men on top shot them from above. A thousand animal tragedies took place. Grand old billies with patriarchal beards and spreading horns, on guard to protect their dwindling herds, at the crack of Mac's rifle went hurtling over the cliffs into the indigo shark-infested sea. Nannies burdened with their unborn kids were pulled down by dogs, kids with topaz eyes ran bewildered into Mac's legs. He carried on his task of butchery, loathing it. He was quick to beat off the dogs and speed the mothers to a quicker, more merciful death with the knife he carried in his legging, Island-fashion.

Between goat hunts he and his men worked feverishly to complete a reservoir, and while he worked he watched the persistent efforts of the grass to come back after each rain. Already the decimation of the goatherd was making an impression.

But as the months folded into each other Mac grew gaunt and grim. For two years, except when we occasionally went to visit him, he had only his labor and a desert island for company. He was glad when we appeared, but he refused to leave Kahoolawe for even a short rest or change. It was difficult to keep men on Kahoolawe. They came and went. But Yamaichi and Aina, a Hawaiian, stood by Mac. The dam was completed. Hopefully Mac waited for rain to fill it. It came finally and—the dam went out to sea! Mac built another and it met with the same fate. They had been solidly constructed and he was in despair to understand how such a thing could happen twice in succession. Then he figured it might be because he had used a locally produced cement.

His capital was exhausted for it was costly transporting men and materials by sampan. Cocoanut radio had been broadcasting that there was a bad *kahuna* on the island and labor had become harder and more expensive to hire. He mortgaged his home on Maui and, finally, Kahoolawe, then went to Honolulu to buy mainland cement. The third dam was finally finished, and a retaining wall was added. A cloudburst came. Everyone rushed to see the dam and got there just as the water overflowed the lip. They waited taut and apprehensive for several hours. This time it held.

But Mac was sunk in debt. Banks refused to lend him more money, individuals looked on him as a mad visionary. To meet his interest he was obliged to take a bunch of steers over to Kahoolawe to fatten and sell. Being a good stock man, Mac was loath to take cattle over so soon, but he decided that if he put them on the grass after it had seeded and took them off right after the first winter rain, before the new growth could be damaged, it would not materially affect his program.

But no sooner had he landed the stock than drought came. Months passed, the water in the dam got lower and lower, but the feed held and the steers began to fatten on beans which fell off the *kiawe* trees, and on Australian salt-bush which Mac had planted on the barren flats—a pulpy-leafed soilbinder which equaled alfalfa in food value. The dam went dry. Yamaichi fetched water from Maui in the sampan and Mac, Aina, and the sturdy devoted Japanese carried the kegs through the surf on their shoulders to replenish the water troughs and cisterns. Mac had to realize on his beef steers or lose Kahoolawe.

Winter came. No rain fell on Kahoolawe though it deluged the other un-cursed islands. Then came Mac's temptation. As we suspected, opium was still being landed on Kahoolawe, for distribution to the other islands. Mac and Yamaichi ran into a cache sufficient to take care of most of his debts—if he didn't turn it over to the authorities. Yamaichi was elated, Aina was convinced that the *akuas* had come to Mac's rescue because of his gallant fight.

He came to Maui, the ghosts of the battles he had waged with himself in his wind-burnt face and dust-reddened eyes. "I know I'm a damned fool, but I can't do it, Von," he raged. "You'd think under the circumstances a fellow would reason that it was a God-given break but I'm going to turn the blasted stuff in. I'll hang on for another month. Maybe rain'll come."

We all went over to the island to keep him company for a while and just as we were about to make a pre-dawn landing a tidal wave humped up from ocean bottom unexpectedly. The dingy had just put off with Mac, Dad, Lorna, Jackie, and a young Hawaiian. Errol and I were waiting with Yamaichi and his helper for the next load.

Oily seas tore at the island as the first great wave roared into the bay. Yamaichi cursed as he fought to keep his beloved *Kahoolawe-Maru* from being swept onto the rocks. The ocean began falling back from the cliffs with a smothered tearing sound as the sampan was sucked seaward. Yamaichi's face was agonized in the dim masthead light as he debated whether to save the boat or go to Mac's rescue. Then hearing the gathering roar of the second wave coming he prayed in Japanese to the Gods of Boats. I clutched Errol, beyond feeling or thought. The second wave was milder, but sufficiently terrifying in the dark.

"MakaPhee! MakaPhee!" Yamaichi shouted, his Oriental reserve shattered by the possibility of the man he worshiped being drowned. The masthead light joggled about crazily as the sullen sea swung forward, roared against the island, and fell back. Around us was black confusion stabbed by half-heard sounds and imaginary voices—or were they real ones from those we loved—crying and screaming across the boiling water?

As the ocean began flattening, a faint shout came from somewhere on our right. Yamaichi bellowed, as if he were trying to raise a million dead, gave his helper the wheel and, diving overboard into the tidal sea, began swimming toward the spot from which the shout had come.

After a nightmarish fifteen minutes, the sampan came to her anchorage and when we finally landed we found that Lorna, Dad, and Mac had been thrown onto the lava and scrambled out of reach of the sea. The backwash of the wave had hurled the young Hawaiian out and fatally injured his back. Jackie had been swept away in the skiff, which miraculously had not overturned. It had been her cry that Yamaichi heard. He found her and got her to land. Poor young Kealoha died a few hours later. Yamaichi and Aina were convinced that because the gods had been appeased with a human sacrifice the curse would be taken off Kahoolawe.

But still no rain fell. Mac at last decided to return to Maui with us and see Harry Baldwin, the owner of Grove Ranch and Paia sugar plantation, to suggest that Harry take over Kahoolawe as an adjunct to his other holdings. In a few years it would carry seven or eight hundred head of steers for fattening purposes.

It was not easy to admit after all his struggles that he had failed, and Dad and Mac walked in the garden for hours while he talked. Mac went to see Harry, finally, and he agreed to go and look the island over. Being Island-born he knew its old condition and recognized how much Mac had accomplished in the short time he'd had it. When the day came for Harry to return to Maui, Mac asked him how the proposition looked to him.

"Good," Harry said, in his quiet way. "Hang on. I'll finance you and we'll bring it back together."

Mac had not thought of things taking this turn, and he hesitated to accept the generous offer. "But something inside me that had been dead ever since I made up my mind to give up Kahoolawe, came to life," he told Dad when the partnership papers were drawn up; and he and Harry went on with their work of transforming the Ugly Dustling into a swan.

25. THE HOUSE OF THE SUN

PROBABLY we were the only children in the world who had an extinct crater, twenty-seven miles in circumference and two thousand feet deep, for a summer playground. Each year when the round-up was over, Dad and half-a-dozen *paniolos* drove a hundred steers up Haleakala and through the vast pit to a small forest nestling at the eastern end, and herded them for a while. When the cattle were more or less at home in their new environment, they were drifted up a thread-like trail leading to a lush plateau eighteen hundred feet above the crater floor, where they were left to fatten until the first winter rains fell.

The name Haleakala, House of the Sun, made the mountain a sort of Holy of Holies. On the summit the legendary hero Maui, for whom the island had been named, had lassoed the sun, broken off one leg, and compelled it to move more slowly in order that his mother might have more light and time to braid the mats for which she was famous. And it was the battleground of the Cloud warriors, Ukiukiu and Naaulu, that lent drama to each day.

The twenty-mile trip to the summit was an adventure that never palled. When summer came we prepared, as usual, to take the surplus steers into the crater and camp. This time the always-thrilling jaunt was even more exciting because Jackie, Mac's daughter, was going along for the first time. We were bursting to show her the family crater.

Watching the steers making their way along the dim trail through lava wastes, soaking in the divine loneliness of high altitudes, I wondered if Jackie was getting the lift I always got out of the objects about us. Below, at the six-thousand-foot level,

Trade-wind clouds drifted past, shutting off the lower half of the island. Above, a dome of blue went up to God, and it seemed as if we were the only people on earth.

In spite of our familiarity with the crater, we children always sensed that the maw of the dead volcano guarded some mighty undiscovered secret. At times the conviction was strong and vivid, at other times it was just a hazy impression. On this occasion, whatever-it-was seemed closer than ever before. It was in the shadows of clouds and in the twisted masses of smelted rock through which we were moving. It intensified and emphasized everything—the weary steers, the laden pack animals, the strong figures of the always-gay *paniolos*—and it gave special savor to the knowledge that with the exception of ourselves few humans ever camped in the pit for more than a night.

When the steers were in a stone corral which Dad had built at the foot of Kolikoli, the cone at the left hand of the trail descending into the crater, we walked to the brink.

Immense, silent, rimmed with Cyclopean walls, splashed with barbaric colors, the vast pit lay below. The day was still, but sudden winds came out of the vast blue bowl with gusty swirls and sudden hissing noises, as gases had come in ages past. Across the far rim, in contrast to the color and chaos at our feet, the serene mountaintops of Mauna Kea and Mauna Loa, a hundred miles away, flaunted their snowy caps.

Eagerly we pointed out to Jackie the trail leading down the Sliding Sands, which we would follow after the stock had been rested and we had lunched. Across the pit was Paliku, the little green forest, where we always camped. The seven-mile-wide break in the walls directly opposite where we were standing, which some explosion had blown out, was the Kaupo gap. The ten-mile-wide break to the northeast was the Koolau gap. In a dim human way we tried to realize the power which had blasted out walls of solid granite and hurled them into the sea.

After looking our fill we returned to the corrals, squatted down in the scant shade of the stone walls, and ate lunch. While we nibbled contentedly at hard *poi* and salt beef, we pointed out breast-high stone fortifications standing like sentinels guarding the trail where it descended into a rock quarry just below us. There stone adzes had been fashioned in ancient times. Naked fighters with slingshots and ten-foot *koa* spears had battled to possess that rich prize, and the mountaintop had echoed to shouts and cries. Blood had drenched the cinders we were sitting on and a high spot across the rim of the crater recalled the carnage of long ago: *Puu-ali-o-ka-koa-nui-o-kane*—the Soldiers of the Mighty Army of Kane. . . .

When the stock were rested we began the descent. A delicious sense of remoteness from the world wrapped us as we dropped down the Sliding Sands. Walls towered higher, colors grew more vivid, the silence more impressive. Golden dust smoked up from the thrusting feet of steers and horses pouring down the steep cinder slope. Down, down, down we slid, among lakes of congealed lava, through masses of twisted and tortured rock. Impressively simple cinder cones lifted their heads hundreds of feet above the crater floor and the glittering foliage of Silver Swords flashed on sandy slopes and in blue-shadowed cliffs. Now and then strange cries came from the towering *palis*, as wild goats began moving along the precipitous crags. The afternoon was waning and they were beginning to emerge from caves, where they slept during the heat of day, to browse on the rich feed growing on alluvial flats formed by the earth that winter rains washed down each narrow gulley. Above the sound of hoofs knocking against loose lava chips, or shuffling through hissing cinders, above puny human voices, staggering silence brooded, and as we looked back, the twin cones standing on each side of the trail were diminished to mere dots.

After an hour or so of riding across the crater floor, we swung between a gray and a black cone. They always looked more treacherous to me than the others because over the slight rise between them lay the Bottomless Pit.

While the *paniolos* took the stock on toward Paliku, Dad halted as usual to let us look into the awesome abyss.

"Careful, kids," Dad warned, as we edged forward to the spatter lava the vent had thrown up, forming a natural breastwork. "That rock's rotten as hell. Don't get too close. All the lassos in Hawaii tied end to end wouldn't be long enough to fish you out if you tumble in."

We peered cautiously over the rim. Dad dropped a rock into the black void and we listened. Silence, utter and absolute, followed. Horror always overcame me when I looked into the poisonous throat leading to the innards of the earth. How many thousands of feet down did it go? What awful gases had come out of it when Haleakala was active?

When we had looked our fill, Dad sat down and lighted his pipe. We gathered around him like a pack of puppies, for we never tired of listening to him talk about the crater. He loved it as Mac loved Kahoolawe. It wasn't just a place to him, it was an entity.

"See that odd-looking boulder there, Jackie, with a tail like a pig's," he said, pointing to rock about the size of a watermelon. "It was shot out of one of these cones in liquid form. As it whirled through the air at terrific speed, it cooled, getting more solid as it turned over and over. The little handle is the last bit of liquid that froze in the last whirl. Those stones are called volcanic bombs." And, reaching out, he found one about the size of a potato and gave it to her to take home to start a collection, such as each of us had.

When we started on for Paliku, Dad detoured from the trail so Jackie could get a close view of Silver Swords. Their dazzling beauty on fiery-colored cinder slopes was an unending delight. The leaves, like slim daggers clothed with moth-down, glittered in the rays of the sinking sun. "Silver Swords," Dad explained, "grow in only two places in the world. In the crater of Haleakala, and in a remote spot in the Himalayas."

When we got to the golden-green forest growing under the towering cliffs of Paliku, the tents were set up and the tired steers were browsing happily in imported grasses which Dad had planted to augment native feeds. Horses were rolling and grunting and the smoke of the camp-fire uncurled through the trees.

Jackie asked Dad why Paliku was green and the rest of the crater arid.

"The Trade-wind, laden with moisture from the wet woods above Hana, pours over the cliffs, hits the cold air in here and precipitates moisture," Dad explained. "Also, this is the oldest end of the crater. The lava has begun to crumble and vegetation can take hold."

After a supper of broiled goat, we lay on our blankets in front of the tent watching evening creep into the vast bowl. The sound of horses grazing, the thin cry of goats high on the *palis,* the bubbling of sea-birds in the crags could not dispel the silence. Swinging walls were silhouetted sharply against the calm evening sky, cones reared above cobalt shadows steadily engulfing the floor. At sunset Haleakala seemed kin to the burnt-out craters of the Moon, which it approximates in size. Like them it is filled with majestic peace, accumulated from the ages. The sun hit the twin cones guarding the faraway entrance, blazed for a moment, and slid out of sight.

We all drew closer together. Night began pouring into the bowl, washing the bases of cones which had been vents for the fires which had built up the mountain we loved. Little by little they were engulfed by darkness and taken from our sight.

As a rule we always accompanied Dad and the *paniolos* when they went up Lauulu, the plateau above the crater, to shoot goats and pheasants. We were trained to ride for hours in silence but

if the men had bad luck they would tease us and say, "All time
you kids talk too much, no can get goats."

One evening, when we returned to camp empty-handed, they
ribbed us too much and we declared that next day they could go
and get their damned goats alone. We would ride our horses up
the steep gray cone to the right of the Bottomless Pit and slide
them down like toboggans. Dad agreed it might be sport.

When the men set off, soon after breakfast, we headed for the
Bottomless Pit. It was the first time we'd crossed the crater floor
alone. It felt bigger and more forbidding without Dad's presence.
Lava flows looked treacherous, violence hung over everything as
though at any instant the volcano might rouse itself and blow up
into eternity. To turn back was unthinkable. We'd be the laughing stock of the camp. We suspected that the *paniolos,* in their
mischievous Hawaiian way, would be watching to see if we
would really ride up the gray cone to do horse-tobogganing. In
the rarefied atmosphere, visibility was perfect for miles.

Being the oldest, I led the way, but I felt as if I were getting
smaller and smaller as we drew near the Bottomless Pit. The
black cone, Haalii, was too rough to ride up, but the gray cone
opposite was formed of fine ash which would not rasp our horses'
fetlocks. Somehow none of us wanted to peer into the Bottomless
Pit without Dad, so we detoured and headed for the shortest
slope of the cone we wanted to ride up.

Our horses sank into the loose ash to their knees and we had
to cling to their manes to keep from sliding over the cantles of
our saddles. Every few yards we halted to let the horses rest. As
we got higher up the cone, the floor fell away with increasing
rapidity. In spite of the thundering size of the cinder hill we
were climbing, we felt like ants on a wee hillock when we
looked at the towering walls that ringed us in. They were miles
away, sheer, breath-taking, shutting out the world as completely
as if it had never existed. The last hundred yards was so steep

that we dismounted and led our horses the rest of the way to the top.

For a few moments we were groggy from exertion at that high altitude. When our heads cleared we looked into the three-hundred-foot depression in the summit of the cone. On the bottom were several obviously man-made structures. Smooth water-washed boulders, which must have been carried from distant portions of the island, were piled in rectangular platforms, like small temples. We looked at each other. Had we all gone mad simultaneously? Surely if Dad had known of their existence he would have told us about them as he had told about the secret leper settlement and the hidden caves at Nuu.

A sort of panicky excitement swept us. What had we run into? Was this the mystery we had sensed lurking in this cluttered work-shop of Vulcan? Should we descend into the pit and examine the platforms more closely? None of us wanted to. The little temples might be *tabu*. But would anyone believe us when we returned to camp and told our story? Then the solution came. Being a mainlander, Jackie carried a Kodak. If Dad and the *paniolos* jeered at us, we'd have concrete proof, later, that our story was real.

After taking several pictures, we looked across at the half-visible crater at the top of the black cone, the same question in all our eyes. Possibly Haalii, too, hid structures of a similar nature. We'd go and see. But first we decided we might as well enjoy the horseback tobogganing we'd come out for.

Cinching up our saddles we rode to the steepest side of the gray cone. Our horses bunched up, braced back, and we jammed in the spurs. Once started, there was no stopping. With gathering speed we avalanched down the slope, yelling, while cinders hissed about our horses' legs. It had taken a good twenty minutes or more to get to the top. We landed at the bottom in about a minute and looked back with satisfaction at the yellow trails marking our descent through the gray ash. Even the most in-

experienced eye could see that we'd accomplished what we set
out to do.

Tying our horses to lava fragments, we started for Haalii. Of
all the cones it was the most sinister in appearance. Crimson,
black, purple, and bronze streaked its slopes. Volcanic bombs
strewed the ground about it and the half-glimpsed crater in the
summit looked as if it had been torn off by some recent convulsion. We scaled its steep ragged slopes painfully, stopping every
few yards to get our breath. In places the sides were so steep
that had it not been for lava-encrustations we would not have
dared to stop or we'd have slid back to the bottom. Inch by inch
we edged up, not at all sure that we wanted to scale it but lashed
on by curiosity.

When we finally got to the top and looked into the crater we
were stunned. At the bottom of the four-hundred-foot depression were eleven more of the mysterious rock platforms. Three
at the bottom, the others built into one of the steep, poisonously
colored sides like a series of great steps.

When we got back to camp Dad listened to our jumbled
breathless account. He was silent for a moment. "Instead of hunting tomorrow, I'm going with you kids to look into the cones.
I've been here thirty years and never heard a whisper about there
being any *heiaus* in the crater."

He questioned the *paniolos* but they denied any knowledge
about the matter. It was unthinkable, they insisted, that people
would erect monuments in the terrifying House of the Sun.

Next day when we took Dad up the gray cone he stood in
amazed silence.

"It would take a lot of crazy kids like you to run into a find of
this sort," he remarked. "I'm going down to examine them."

We followed him into the cone while he explored the rock
platforms. The ones in Haalii were better built than those in the
gray cone. Some were twenty feet long, five feet high, and per-

fectly level. Others were smaller. That night Dad questioned the *paniolos* again, but apparently they knew nothing.

"Soon as the snapshots are developed I'll send them to Kakina and tell him to take the matter up with the Bishop Museum," Dad said. "I'm stumped. There've been several thorough surveys of the crater. Hundreds of people have ridden through it, but no one has ever reported these structures. It's possible that uninitiated eyes, seeing them, would not recognize the fact that they're man-made. Hold your tongues when we go out. If this is talked about the whole island will swarm in and destroy clues as to what the structures really represent. A find of this sort, to which no allusion has been made in history or legend, belongs to science."

When the Bishop Museum saw the pictures of our accidental discovery, tremendous excitement was aroused. Kakina wrote, saying that a branch of the Polynesian Research Expedition was being fitted out to come to Maui, and he would accompany it. While we waited for it to arrive we pondered the matter over. "It boils down to one of two things," Dad insisted. "Either they're extra-sacred *heiaus,* or they may be burial places. The name Haalii is a contracted form for the phrase The Passing Place of Chiefs. I'll arrange ranch work so I can go along with the outfit when it comes over."

But he didn't. Shortly before Professor Herbert Gregory was due, a frantic phone call came from the watchman of the Olinda reservoir saying Dad had just come in with a broken arm and collar bone, and had sustained some sort of injury to his hip. He had fallen into a lava hole while he was chasing a wild bull above Puuniniau. He had limped in hanging to his saddle, after he had managed to get himself and his horse out of the hole. A conveyance of some sort must be sent up to take him the last seven miles home. I rushed off with Hauki in the light buckboard. Dad was sallow with pain, but smiling, when we arrived. The broken bones healed but his hip, while it worked, continued to be so painful that the doctor ordered him to stay off horses for a while.

Professor Gregory's two young assistants arrived and went into the crater for preliminary scouting. Kakina was to follow in a few days with the Curator. There was work Dad wanted me to attend to for him, but as soon as it was done he sent Lorna and me into the crater to assist the research party. We rode away blinded by tears. It was the first time we'd ever gone up the mountain without Dad's strong figure leading the way.

When we finally located the scientists' camp, we were floored. Instead of going to one of the places Dad had advised, they'd pitched their camp in a gulley. A small cloudburst during the night had sent down a freshet, flooding their tent, soaking their bedding, and disarranging their gear. They had omitted to tether the horses Dad had lent them and the horses had wandered off. Altogether, they were a sorry sodden pair.

It was too late to change camp that night. Lorna and I pitched our pup-tent on a rise and trenched it. More rain fell. We were dry and comfortable and chuckled over the miseries of the Great Aching Brains, as we labeled the two young scientists. But we were indignant about the horses who had probably wandered off to hell-and-gone.

When we got up we found the two professors, drenched to the skin, sadly eating cold beans. Stretching a tarp, as it was still drizzling, we soon had a fire going and a hot breakfast. The two men sort of figuratively crawled into our laps, like thankful rescued puppies. When they'd eaten, we sent them off on foot for their prowlings and set about getting the camp into shape. Thanks to Dad's training, it was no task. By two o'clock, everything was shipshape, blankets dry, tent gunked out and tidy.

Lorna went off with her rifle to get a goat for supper and I headed for a flat where I knew mushrooms must be coming up after such a rain. When I heard the crack of her rifle echoing in the *palis,* I started back to camp. There were so many mushrooms that I took my shirt off and filled it. When I neared camp there was old Kakina waiting, and, shortly after, Lorna jogged in with a fat kid slung across her saddle and a lost dog, belonging to some hunter from Kaupo, trailing at her heels.

When the tired, dusty professors dragged in we had a decent camp and a savory meal. Just as we were about to sit down, Eole, with Professor Gregory, the Curator, at his heels, rode up. Gregory was a muscular man with merry brown eyes and a big smile. When he smelled goat and mushrooms cooking he rubbed his hands, and his assistants, starved for a good meal, could hardly wait while we dished out heaping platefuls of the smoking stew. Kakina beamed with pride. "Von's girls can take care of themselves," he remarked, and we were filled with pride and with loneliness for Dad.

Next morning Kakina volunteered to go down to Kaupo to interview oldtimers about the structures in the cones, and see if he could locate the lost horses, while Lorna and I took the professors into the cones. Excavations during the following days revealed that both the gray cone and Haalii were burial places. Teeth were found in several of the platforms but extreme expansion and contraction from heat and cold at this high altitude had destroyed the bones. When the professors first began taking down the rocks, Lorna and I felt a trifle hostile, but we soon saw that each stone was charted and its arrangement recorded and we realized they were not vandals tampering with sacred things, but rather were painstakingly gathering up broken threads of the history of the Pacific and were trying to weave them into a significant pattern.

From information gleaned from old residents of Kaupo, by Kanina, and deductions of the scientists the fact was established that the structures were burial places of extra *tabu* chiefs, as Dad had suspected. A sense of gratitude stole through me. The great bowl which was our summer playground had lived up to the mystery we had felt was in it. Haleakala—the Great House of the Sun—guarded forever the Passing Place of Chiefs.

26. PACIFIC POLO

Because Dad had started polo in Hawaii, and established it on Maui, it was a toss-up in our family whether the whack of a mallet or the running fire of hoofs on a track was the greatest thrill. In a horse race excitement is high and brief. In a polo match a person gets wrought up to fever-pitch for a sustained period. Matches year after year between the same teams breed an almost fanatical rivalry and lend an importance to winning incomprehensible to onlookers whose lives are not intimately bound up with those of the players and horses.

From April to August, when the Inter-Island tournaments are held in Honolulu, Aina, Lorna, and I helped to recondition old ponies and school a new crop of blooded youngsters. We vied with each other to see who could turn out the most finished performers. Once a week during the early spring, twice a week as the season neared its close, we rode down to the polo field to watch the Maui teams play.

After Dad's accident, he resigned his captaincy to Frank Baldwin, the most brilliant player on the island, as well as the most rugged fighter. Often after a game was over, Frank and his wife Harriet, close friends of the family, came to the ranch for supper, or we went to their house, to talk over the game and plot methods of attack against Oahu, Maui's bitter rival.

One warm night in July we sat on the front steps at the ranch discussing the approaching tournament. Blue moonlight, sifted with platinum, bathed the island. Plants made happy, sleepy little rustles and across the isthmus the lights of sugar mills twinkled like jewels lost in seas of green cane. Dad and Frank talked and planned.

For years in succession Oahu had carried off the coveted Wichman Cup. The Maui men played a slashing game, were superbly mounted, but the Oahu team had the advantage of playing on their own ground. The Maui ponies had to make the trip to Honolulu on small buck-jumping steamers which took seas in the channels with consequent damage to the animals.

"Damn it, Von!" Frank exploded. "I appreciate the handicaps we play under, but we've got to lick the beggars anyhow. Polo got its real start on Maui, you fathered it, and the cup's got to come home!"

While they sat talking, my mind flitted over the history of Pacific Polo. Christmas Day in 1886, at Hawi on Hawaii, when Dad was a stripling, a dozen sporty young bloods gathered together to celebrate the holiday. The day had passed its peak and the afternoon had begun sagging.

"I say, fellows," Dad had announced, "that game, polo, which is being played in England and America, is right up our alley. Let's take a crack at it this afternoon. The old pasture below the road is grazed short and will serve as a field for a starter. We've got lots of horses and when Major Haley of the 10th Hussars left for England he gave me his book of rules, some balls and six sticks—"

"Meaning those elongated croquet mallets you pack around with you?" someone chuckled.

Dad nodded. "We've told all the stories we know, eaten all we can hold, drunk more than we ought to. Let's get out of doors and have some real fun."

And in this wise, polo was born in Hawaii. The fact that eight mallets were needed and Dad only had six, did not daunt him. Two extra ones were hurriedly fashioned from bamboo and whatever wood was handy for heads. Each team was armed with three good mallets and one makeshift.

The game was a riot. Horses collided, riders were spilled. Insecure malletheads flew through the air. The ball was struck with more force than skill and time lost while Ah Sin hunted for it in the maze of guava bushes surrounding the pasture. Goal posts of a sort had been erected and two *paniolos* and four house-servants were the only spectators. When the ball soared in their direction they ducked, when an accurate stroke whizzed it toward the goals they cheered.

The score for the initial polo match in Hawaii totaled: a goal for each team, a broken collar bone, a dislocated wrist, two bloody heads, seven spills, and one pony with a strained hock. But so great was the success of the afternoon that mallets were written for, two teams organized, ponies schooled in stops and turns, and rules studied.

But like most innovations, after the initial enthusiasm cooled down, a leading spirit was needed to keep the game alive, and Dad supplied the driving force which established polo permanently in the Pacific.

A small fairly level field on Maui, as centrally located as possible for the majority of the players, was leveled and planted with a short tough variety of grass. The fact that the place where Dad then worked was farthest away did not bother him. After being in the saddle from dawn until dusk, he rode twenty miles on Sundays to the polo field, played eight furious chukkers and rode home in the scented island twilight singing *hulas* and leading his tired ponies.

Gradually interest was awakened in the new sport being played on the slopes of Haleakala. Arthur, Harry, Fred, and Frank Baldwin, sons of the leading Missionary family on Maui, came to watch the matches after church and expressed their desire to play, but said as long as the games were held on Sundays the family would not consent to their taking part. Dad called a meeting of the Club, suggesting that the matches be held on Saturday afternoons in order to include the eager youngsters. The matter was put to vote and carried unanimously.

As time went on, the Saturday matches became quite a social

event. Lemonade and light sandwiches were served to lure people to the field, but most of the dashing young players preferred to pop into Jubilee's loose-box between chukkers and take nips from the flask of "cold tea" Dad carried in his hip pocket.

After a few years Maui was thoroughly polo-minded. People from Honolulu came over to watch the game and became infected with the bug. A team was organized on Oahu and challenged Maui. The Maui men took their ponies over in the teeth of an outlaw *kona* gale, which sprung up the day the ship was due to sail. All night long players and grooms were in the bows getting half-drowned ponies to their feet, and forty-eight hours later went gamely into the match on schedule, only to meet with defeat. Since then, with the exception of one year, it had been the same story.

"By Jove, Frank, I see the way out of one difficulty." Dad's voice jerked me back to the present. Frank leaned forward and Harriet's lovely face became all attention.

"Instead of shipping the ponies on the *Mauna Kea* as planned, write to the Oahu team and suggest that the game be postponed until later in August. The big Matson boat, the *Manoa*, is making her first trip to Kahului about the end of the month to get sugar. If the ponies go over on her they won't have to take their usual beating. The Oahu boys are fine sports and they will be glad to do it. If we were in their boots, we'd feel the same way. There's not much satisfaction in winning the way things have been these past few years. If they lick us again, it'll be more to their credit."

The Oahu team agreed enthusiastically. When arrangements were completed Frank urged that Dad come along as the Maui mascot. But postponing the day made it conflict with certain essential ranch work, and it was impossible.

"We'll take Ummie and Aina along then, they can carry the flag for you. Four of the ponies they trained are in our first string."

We felt important and frightfully responsible and the day before we were due to leave, I went off alone to make a *kahuna*
to ensure victory. Step by step I followed the method my dear
old Makalii had taught me. Finding two sticks of the same
length I laid them crosswise so the ends pointed to the four
points of the compass. Seating myself cross-legged I emptied my
mind of everything except the vision of victory. I said prayers
to all the good *akuas,* finishing with the Creator. Then I visual-
ized our team in the center of the crossed sticks and blew on
them from north, south, east, and west to ensure support and
luck from every direction. To make things doubly sure, I finished with a prayer to Christ and Buddha and went home forti-
fied with the belief that nothing could prevent the Maui team
from winning.

When the great lighted ship pulled away from the dock, its
bows filled with glossy ponies, Aina and I stood close together,
waving to Daddy down below. It seemed empty not to have
him along.

The next two days in Honolulu the Maui men, their wives,
Aina and I, spent at the polo fields accustoming the ponies to
new ground, and at night we attended gay parties where bronzed
polo players from Kauai, the Army, Maui, and Oahu assembled
for the week which is the social high of Honolulu.

No one slept much the night before the date of the Maui
game, although everyone went to bed early. Maui must beat
Oahu and beat it thoroughly. The fact that we adored all the
men did not alter the fact that once they were mounted and on
the field they were enemies. For the first time our ponies had a
fair show and our team was in the pink of condition.

The day of the game came bright and clear with a cool trade
wind blowing down from the forested mountains. Two hours
before the game was due to start automobiles began rolling
through the gates of Kapiolani Park and arranged themselves
about the vivid green oblong of the field. Grandstand and

bleachers were crammed. At the end of the field, reserved for
the players, tents had been erected and the anxious heads of
waiting ponies flanked both sides of the long hitching rails.

Before going to the box reserved for Maui players' wives and
friends, Harriet, Aina, and I went to wish our men good luck.
While they joked and laughed with their opponents there was a
purposeful look in their eyes.

When we started back to the grandstand, I dodged down the
line of ponies to hug Coquette, Frank's top pony which I rode
between September and April, and I patted Adonis and Marcus
which I'd trained.

The bell sounded and players began mounting. Ponies fidg-
eted and sidestepped as they never did in ordinary games. The
whistle blew, then the ball was thrown in.

The men scuffled for it. The blue shirts of the Oahu team and
the gold and black of Maui made bright moving spots of color
against the grass. The Oahu Number One got the ball clear and
darted after it. A Maui man raced on his heels trying to hook
his stick, but the Oahu player managed to put another length
between himself and his opponent. A smart click told spectators
that the Oahu Number Two had hit the ball a second time, then
a clash of stirrups rang out as the Maui man overtook him and
tried to ride him off the ball.

"Crowd him, crowd him, I'll get it!" Frank Baldwin shouted,
racing to support his man.

His gold and black shirt billowed in the wind, both teams
thundered in pursuit. Dust puffs, jarred out of the grass, hung
in the air; the gasps of hard-ridden ponies sounded clearly.
While the Maui man rode off his opponent Frank Baldwin overtook the ball, backed it, and wheeled his horse for the Oahu
goal. Like a streak he carried it along the side-boards, clear of
racing horses and riders, and finally it soared and landed between
the Oahu goal posts. A roar broke from the spectators.

The teams jogged back to center field and people talked excitedly in the grandstand. The umpire tossed in a fresh ball and backed out of the scrimmage. As the ball fell, Frank Baldwin and Walter Dillingham, the captain of the Oahu team, crossed stick heads. The Oahu Number Three made a dribbling stroke and edged out with the ball. His mare flattened out and followed it like a dog. Frank dashed out of the scrimmage, looking back for a survey of his men. The Oahu Number Three missed his stroke and Frank rushed on trying to overtake the white streak of ball bouncing on toward the Maui goal posts. Lifting his mallet in a full arm stroke to whack it back, he missed because his pony stumbled. The Oahu support took it on and drove it through the goal.

Cheers rent the air. One to one.

Players wiped their heated faces and assembled in mid-field, and went at it again. Men shouted and swore, ponies grunted and shoved, turned, propped, tore up the turf with deep-digging hocks.

"Keep the ball hanging," the Oahu Captain shouted.

Sticks rapped hocks, clicked against each other. The ball was lost among horses' legs. One of the Maui players found it and sneaked it to Frank, who darted upon it and drove for the Oahu goal. The resounding whack of his mallet was heard all over the field and excited ponies tied to the hitching rails kicked up their heels. Another smack and the ball soared in one of Frank's characteristic strokes, then a deafening roar broke from the spectators. Maui had scored a second goal.

The bell sounded time, automobile horns honked persistently, deliriously. The band struck up *Maui no ka oe*—Maui is the best, and fresh bets were made in the grandstand.

When the second chukker started, everyone knew rough riding was ahead. The Oahu men were savage, the Maui team elated. Frank went out on Coquette. The ball was tossed in and the Oahu team got it. Horses knotted, strung out, raced down the field. The play thundered along the side-boards and across corners of the field. Stirrups clashed, players' and ponies' tempers were tried to the limit. Coquette dodged along the edge of the scrimmage, darted through openings, waiting for a Maui man to get the ball and pass it to Frank.

It finally rolled into the clear. Coquette saw it and leaped into position. Frank drove and, with the click of his mallet, Coquette was gone like a streak, both teams racing in pursuit. Just as Frank lifted his mallet to hit, an Oahu player overtook him and hooked his stick.

"Not this time, blast you!" he shouted, riding Frank out of the way.

The bell sounded time. Teams came in. "At any rate, Maui didn't score this time," one of the Oahu players panted as he slid off his reeking pony. "One for us, two for Maui. We'll soon change that!"

The next chukker was an open game, easier to follow. The ground quivered under the impact of racing hoofs and the reek of sweat-drenched leather drifted to the eager thousands looking on. Muttered commands, savage oaths, the sobbing of ponies, brought the game into our very midst. Neither team intended to lose and were riding more roughly than rules permitted but the play was too fast and frenzied for umpires to keep track of each move.

The chukker ended with a goal for Oahu. Two to two.

When the teams went out for the last chukker of the first half Oahu was up on its fastest ponies. Hoofs drummed, the smacks of mallets meeting the ball echoed like pistol shots. The Oahu man riding Frank off nearly knocked him out of the saddle and brought Frank's pony to its knees. The umpire called a foul on Oahu and a point dropped off their score.

Before a minute Maui scored again. Three for Maui, one for Oahu. There was only a minute and a half left. Then with appalling rapidity Oahu scored twice in succession and the score stood three to three.

The bell sounded time, the band played, onlookers relaxed. The Oahu team was triumphant. Ponies came in with drooping heads, hoarding their energies. Grooms seized the wet soaking horses and scraped them off. Fresh bundles of mallets were brought out and stacked. Teams went into huddles, planning new methods of attack.

The first chukker of the last half began venomously. Team work on both sides was completely disorganized, men played out of position, ponies thrust and fought.

When Frank went out on Coquette in the next chukker I felt weak. Coquette was lighter than most of the Oahu ponies and had taken some bad bumps the previous period she had played, but Maui's victory, if there was to be one, depended largely on her fleet legs, valiant heart, and Frank's spectacular playing.

The ball had not been in thirty seconds before Oahu added a goal to her score, making four for them and three for Maui. Then Frank got away, and headed for the Oahu goal. The Oahu Number One overtook him, flung the whole weight of his body against him and dug him in the ribs with his elbow. The jar knocked Frank's helmet over his eyes. Coquette propped, tearing up the sod with deep-driven hocks. A foul was called on Oahu and a goal dropped off their score. Three to three again.

"Somebody's going to get hurt," Frank Baldwin said tensely. "This is wicked polo."

The next chukker proved the truth of his prediction. The Maui Number Two collided with an Oahu pony and both horses went down, but Maui made a goal a minute later and roars shook the air. Maui four, Oahu three. Half a minute later there was another collision and when the men scrambled up Maui's Number One's arm hung limply. Another foul was called, reducing Oahu's score to two. A substitute was put on the Maui team and playing recommenced.

When the ball was thrown in, Coquette leaped on it. Frank smacked it clear, followed up with an even finer stroke and the ball rose like a rocket and soared between the Oahu goal posts. Maui backers yelled, horns squealed from cars parked around the field.

As the teams rode back to center field, I saw Frank patting Coquette's reeking shoulder. The Maui Number One took the ball, Frank raced to support him, both teams thundering on their heels. The Maui Number One struck and missed. Frank drove, his mallet met the ball squarely but the head flew off and Coquette streaked for the sidelines where men waited with extra sticks.

The Oahu player nearest overtook the ball, backed it, and headed down for his goal. Coquette raced back into the scrimmage, dodging about like an inspired thing. Finally Frank got the ball and was heading for the Oahu goal before the rest of the players realized what had happened. Once, twice, three times he struck it, then pandemonium broke loose as the ball soared between the Oahu goal posts. Six for Maui; two for Oahu.

"Scrimmage, don't let Frank get the ball," the Oahu captain ordered as the teams reassembled in the middle of the field.

Ponies were lathered, sweat dripped off their bellies; only Coquette walked briskly though she was as wet as if she had just come out of the sea. The Oahu team got the ball and scored a point. Three to six.

After the ball was tossed in again, Frank swooped upon it and raced, regardless of position, for the Oahu goal but before he succeeded in scoring an Oahu man overtook him, rode him off, backed the ball, and wheeled in the opposite direction. Within seven seconds Oahu had scored again. Four to six, in Maui's favor, but they were creeping up on us. I sat still, making *kahunas* in my mind.

Then Oahu scored again. Five to six and only three minutes left to this chukker. Then with bewildering rapidity and inspired playing Frank scored another point, and another.

Eight for Maui; five for Oahu. That was better. I got my breath.

When the umpire tossed the ball in, Coquette and Frank leaped upon it. Nobody seemed able to get near them. They were in a class of their own. Frank took the ball down the field with stroke after echoing stroke. It wasn't, it couldn't be possible. But it was. He and Coquette made another goal which gave Maui nine goals against Oahu's five.

The band began playing *Maui no ka oe*—as if it had gone insane. Tears were pouring down the faces of most of the people in Harriet's box—tears of sheer joy. Had ever a man and horse played such polo together? And then, just an instant before the whistle blew, Frank scored again. Ten to five!

The tide had turned, the polo tide which has flowed toward Maui ever since, in that deathless game when Frank and Coquette virtually single-handed made the Maui polo team supreme in the Pacific.

27. REGAL ACRES

ONE SUNDAY afternoon Dad came in laden with golden plover, black-breasted and fat before their Alaskan migration. Sitting down he began ejecting cartridges from his shotgun. "The manager of the Parker Ranch, who is an old friend of mine, has written inviting me to bring you kids over for a month while they're branding and roping," he said, watching us.

We yipped with glee. The Parker Ranch! One of the world's most regal estates, of almost a million acres. The first cattle landed in Hawaii had been turned loose there. On its payroll were men whose fathers and fathers' fathers had worked there before them. Ikuwa Purdy, who had won the world's roping championship at Cheyenne, had been born there. A month at the Parker ranch, plus our own round-up afterwards. Ten weeks of riding, roping, branding, with their attendant fun. It was almost too much good luck.

When we went to Lahaina to board the steamer, such a heavy sea was running that the wharfinger said there was a possibility we might not be able to get away. Inter-Island steamers stopping at Lahaina had to anchor a mile off shore. Between beach and roadstead great swells were bursting with magnificent deliberation and piling over the reef, trailing their long white manes in the sun. The fierce blue spaces of the sea and pure pale spaces of the sky, broken by the shapes of Lanai and Molokai, were enveloped with awesome splendor. Sun-drugged distances waited expectantly and an occasional cessation in the great angry voice of the sea created an illusion that the day halted every now and then to catch its breath.

Sensing great forces flowing around us, I held my body taut

trying to catch the messages moving through the heart of the afternoon. This visit to the Parker Ranch was another turn in the road. Daddy, still bothered with his hip, limped over to inspect our luggage and saddles and bridles, neatly sewed into gunnysacks. His eyes had a remote expression I'd seen in Gan's when she was thinking about things which were past. What was on its way?

When he rejoined us where we sat on piled sugar-bags watching the smoke of the approaching steamer, I reached for his hand. "I feel things in the offing, don't you?" I asked.

"Not particularly," he replied.

"You're dodging," I accused. "Your face looks funny and your mind isn't on what we're doing."

"You spend so much time writing that your imagination runs away with you," he teased, "and my damned hip's raising Cain today." He struck it contemptuously with his fist, in a gesture which was getting more and more familiar. "I can't figure why the blasted thing doesn't let up. It isn't broken or I couldn't ride and walk. Well, to hell with it, when fun's ahead." Drawing the worn silver flask from his pocket, he drank a little whisky and began whistling a naughty *hula*.

The day picked up immediately and by the time the whale-boats began riding in over the rollers, with spray shooting out from their bows, the feeling of change and sadness had evaporated, but I still knew deep inside myself that we were taking off on a new flight.

Dad watched the great white boats fighting with the sea. "In a few years there won't be any more of this," he said, with a sort of regret in his voice. "It's a rousing way to make a landing or departure but," his eyes flashed gaily, "time marches on!"

While the boats bumped and banged against the wharf, now on a level with it, then ten feet below as great combers roared past, we waited for the signal to jump. Suitcases, saddles, crated canned goods, half a dozen hogs with tied feet were heaved to

the lusty sailors. Fat *wahines* squealing with fright flung themselves into brawny upstretched arms, an old Chinaman with
three small grandsons went next, then two sweet little mama-
sans in dainty *kimonos*. Finally we were all safely in and the
steersman put the boat's prow into angry hissing swells.

Going out was more exciting than riding surfboards at Waikiki. Each time the heavy whaleboat met the roaring crest of
a sea it seemed as if we would be swamped. Instead the boat
leaped into the air like a rearing horse, propelled forward by
long flashing oars expertly handled by mighty brown arms. Boat-
men yelled and whooped, mama-sans cowered and hid their
faces, *wahines* yelled, "*Auwe*—woe is me!", pigs squealed.

As we neared the roaring reef, the sailor's faces grew watchful and their eyes wary. Spray like wet bullets, leaving red stinging marks on our arms and faces, hit us. The world seemed
made of boiling white water. Finally, a shout of relief announced
we were safely through.

It took half an hour to get aboard the ship. The sun died behind Kahoolawe, stars came out and a vast velvety night descended on the troubled ocean. Each time the steamer stopped
at a port, everyone came out on deck to see who was going
ashore and who coming aboard. Stewards in white uniforms
served fat sandwiches and coffee to the groups on deck. Port
dropped behind. Mahukona . . . Lapahoehoe. How the sailors
shouted the names—like war-cries, as they fought to keep the
boats under the gangway while black cresting seas went roaring
by. Somehow it seemed appropriate that our first visit to the
Parker Ranch should have such a spectacular prelude.

When we dropped anchor off Kawaihae, we clustered a trifle
uneasily about Daddy. "This may be a bit nippy, the sea's been
coming up steadily," he said in the even tones he always used
in tight places, "but don't be afraid."

We children and the hogs were the only passengers getting
off at Kawaihae but it took twenty minutes to get from the ship

into the buck-jumping boat. We were wet to the skin by the time the last lashing sea rushed us toward the wharf, dimly lighted by a couple of lanterns. Half a dozen Hawaiians helped the sailors to get us ashore.

"That was ripping," Dad gloated.

A Japanese chauffeur, sent by Mr. Wright, manager of the Parker Ranch, came out of the shadows to get our bags and saddles. Cold wind blew down from the snow-clad summit of Mauna Kea, rustling the *kiawe* trees and cocoanut groves around us. Dad told the driver we'd be ready as soon as we'd had coffee and led the way to a shabby restaurant behind a stone wall. The old Chinese proprietor met us and broke into delighted pidgin English when he recognized Dad.

While we drank the hot coffee, cobwebby pictures like tattered fragments of a dream kept brushing me. "I feel as if I'd been here before," I said finally to Daddy.

"You have been," he said, an odd expression flitting over his face. "When you were a toddler and Gwen just a baby, Mother and I spent a night here. Wright, who's a lawyer by profession, had just been appointed executor of the Parker Ranch. He doubted his ability to manage the ranch competently and offered me the managership."

We were stunned with surprise. Dad had been offered the management of the Parker Ranch. How little we knew of his life. How little of the inner man. Never a whisper or mention of this during all the years.

"Why didn't you take it?" Lorna asked, amazed.

"After spending a week in Waimea, Mother said it was too lonely."

Dad's voice was as impersonal as if he were talking about some other person. "Wright had no confidence in anyone else's ability to tackle such an undertaking, so set about learning the cattle business himself and he's done a fine job of it."

I wondered how any woman could fancy she could outweigh

the splendor of limitless acres, blooded stock, and the sweep of life that goes hand in hand with such things when they are on a big scale. It seemed unfair that Dad had had to forfeit his rightful first-place in his profession, like pulling a winning horse in a race. I studied his still face, wondering how many times he'd regretted having to let his great opportunity go by, and my eagerness to see the Parker Ranch changed from curiosity to reverence. These acres hidden in the dark were an altar on which Dad had sacrificed ambition for love. I wondered how many other instances of a similar nature, where Mother and we children were concerned, were buried in Dad's past.

Something lawless and passionate, savage and strong, kin to the forces imprisoned in the earth, stirred inside me next morning when we rode out of the tall trees surrounding the house. The land swept away, a limitless ocean of flowing grass, broken by volcanic cones. Mauna Kea and Mauna Loa filled two-thirds of the sky, and behind the straggling village of Waimea the wet green ranges of the Kohala mountains lifted into the freshly born day. This swoop of country, guarded by slumbering volcanoes, was the cradle of cattle ranching in Hawaii.

The scope of the place was almost beyond comprehension as we moved across the plains to meet the herd which was to be drafted and branded the next two days. Five thousand head of cattle, gathered from the hundred-thousand-acre pasture they grazed in.

Long before we saw them, we heard them. Whenever the wind lessened slightly the atmosphere shook to a great disturbing sound. It made me want to stay close to Dad and in the same instant to spread wings and fly toward the unknown. It made all the people who had lived here in past decades vivid and close. Old Sam Parker, who met life open-handed and open-armed. Old Sam who the instant he got up drank a quart of coffee and downed six soft-boiled eggs and who, an hour later, was shouting for breakfast: steaks cut off juicy two-year-old heifers, slathers of bacon, more eggs, a loaf of bread, and a pint of wild *koa* honey. Old Sam whose death had been mourned throughout Hawaii, a mighty figure of friendship and fun, belonging to an era which had ended. It conjured up visions of Thelma, his beautiful granddaughter who married a man from Virginia and died tragically, far from the Islands she loved. It made me think of Richard Smart, her son, who was being reared in America instead of on the kingdom he had inherited and could have ruled.

We rode over a hill and in the miles-long undulating hollow below a herd of cattle moved forward like a red swollen river. Dots of horsemen galloped at the edges, guiding the animals forward. I tried to grasp the fact that this was only a sixth of the Parker Ranch herd and that this one pasture was bigger than our ranch! As the herd came closer, the great crying grew louder. I tried to absorb the sound, for I knew that aside from the roaring of Mokuaweoweo in action, or when a *kona* gale piled the Pacific into tumbling blue ranges, this was the mightiest sound I'd ever heard.

At that moment the man leading the herd galloped by. He seemed part of the land, fierce and free, holding himself with triumphant carelessness. There was an aura of vigorous beauty about him, the beauty that is in a strong horse or a rough sea. As he passed, with the cattle at his heels, he looked up and smiled. He appeared to be about thirty and had the magnetic vitality which is often the lot of men of mixed race. In him mingled the softness of a Hawaiian, the fire of a Spaniard, and the keenness of a Scot. His eyes were black. His mouth had a triumphant lift to its corners. With a soul as free and strong as his body, he seemed the incarnation of Waimea. Seeing Dad, he brandished his coiled lasso and shouted. "Louis—Aloha!"

"Who is he?" I asked.

"Liholiho Lindsay," Dad answered. "Johnny, the oldest of the family, is foreman. There are a dozen others."

Standing in their stirrups, with coiled lassos in their hands and flowers on their hats, the men were very like our *paniolos* and yet there was a difference. After watching several of them, I analyzed the quality that set them apart. For over a century Lindsay and Purdy men had ridden these plains and mountains, each generation absorbing more of their environment into their personalities. In addition to this, most of them had white blood in their veins which gave them added force without robbing them of Polynesian charm.

When Mr. Wright gave the signal to fall in, my fine gray shot away and I found myself galloping beside a kind-faced *paniolo* who asked if I were one of "Louis's" girls. I nodded. "Swell you come to Waimea. My name is Kamaki Lindsay."

By the time we reached the corrals our friendship seemed a thing of long standing. Lorna and Errol had been just as busy. Errol was wearing old Johnny Lindsay's hat. Lorna was using Kaliko's lasso, and Kamaki had promised to bring me a new horse from his string which he wanted me to try. The fact that Daddy was firmly established in Lindsay and Purdy hearts probably made them warmer toward us than they might have been otherwise, but whatever the cause we were elated to be so swiftly accepted by the hard-riding *paniolos* of the Parker Ranch.

Johnny, the foreman, took young Errol under his wing. While Johnny could not read or write, he knew every animal on the ranch and he knew of the tiniest happening on the vast acres he ruled with an iron hand. In him the Scot dominated his mind, the Spaniard his body. When he gazed over the land entrusted to his care he suggested a fierce Cortez or crafty Pizarro. Lorna's pro-tem *paniolo* was Lauliko, another Lindsay, all Hawaiian in appearance and temperament. I had two escorts, solemn Kamaki and dashing Liholiho.

Temporarily, the life of the Parker Ranch possessed our interest to the exclusion of everything else. Like our own place, it had a polo field, race track, and stables, but on de luxe scales. In addition, there was a golf course, and a landing field for planes was being built. Thirty thousand head of Hereford cattle —most of them registered—eight thousand horses—the majority of them thoroughbreds—grazed off the plains sweeping away to mountains and sea. The ranch supplied remounts to Schoefield, the largest of all American Army posts, and it contributed polo ponies to prominent players all over the Islands. It supplied Honolulu with most of its meat. Each day, activities relating to the different departments filled the atmosphere with bustle while the great round-up went steadily on like a slow-moving tide.

One evening as we rode home old Johnny cantered up beside Dad. "Tomorrow I go up Mauna Kea after three hundred head of young horses for break this fall. I like fine if you and the kids come. Swell fun. Ride like hell."

"I'd like to go, Johnny," Dad replied, "but Wright's planning to take me to Makahalau tomorrow to see some of the stallions and bulls."

Johnny's face fell.

"Take the kids, they can keep up with you."

Johnny's keen old eyes narrowed as if he were weighing Dad's remark. I felt a chill in my heart. Was Dad inferring that because of his hip he could no longer maintain the furious pace necessary to chasing horses down a mountain, or merely assuring Johnny that we could ride stirrup to stirrup with the famed *paniolos* of Waimea?

"Sure I take the *keikis*," Johnny said. "They ride swell."

"I got a letter from Mr. Baldwin today and I have to go back to Maui Saturday. Keep an eye on the kids, Johnny, and don't let them break their fool necks," Daddy said.

Some of the light went out of the spacious evening.

"Why didn't you tell us that you have to go home?" I asked, when Johnny rode off.

"How in hell could I? You've all been scattered to hell-and-gone."

"How long will you be away?"

"I shan't be coming back. Wright's invited you kids to stay on, if you want to."

"Sure, stay, stay," the *paniolos* around us chorused. "Us have good fun with you crazy kids."

"Might as well make hay while the sun shines," Dad advised.

"Would you like one of us to go home with you?" I asked.

"Hell, no, I'll be busy and time'll fly. You're only young once. Soak in this experience. Not many people are invited up here."

Again the sense of change, which had been so strong the day we left home, brushed me. Something was afoot. Dad wasn't putting all the cards on the table. He knew something which he wasn't telling us yet.

"I want to have my cake and eat it, too," I confessed. "I want to go home with you but I hate to cut off my visit here. Liholiho wants me to ride Kanaloa, his black three-year-old. Do you think I can stay on him?"

"You'll find out fast enough," Daddy laughed.

Next morning about four we met Johnny and the eight *paniolos* slated to bring the young horses off Mauna Kea. Liholiho was waiting with his snorty gelding. While he held his head I mounted cautiously, whirled him around a few times, keeping a good grip on the bit, then my tense muscles relaxed for I felt the horse's spirit meet mine and knew I could handle him.

By the time the sun rose we were far up Mauna Kea. Everyone was eager for the fun ahead, and the beautiful young beast I was riding swung along, docile as a baby. "Kanaloa like you more better from Liholiho," Kamaki commented.

"I give to you when you go back to Maui," Liholiho said generously.

"I have lots of horses," I said, while I tried to put my finger on the quality in Liholiho which put him in greener pastures than his brothers. It wasn't his good looks alone, or his dash and fire, but some royal ingredient that made him, as Conrad expressed it, a man of all time.

When we reached the top of the pasture we jogged off in twos, stationing ourselves at proper intervals. Johnny signaled to start driving. At first we only saw a few horses streaking through openings in the *koa* forests, but as we kept pushing them down the slope of the mountain their number increased. The pace got faster and faster. Wind snatched at our hats and our horses fought for their heads, eager to run with the wild youngsters. Unbroken three-year-olds, with tails held high, turned their heads from side to side as they raced, sailed over fallen logs, and flattened out when they struck grassy reaches. The hollow ground rang under the impact of thudding hoofs and the morning echoed to shouts and the cracking of stock-whips. I raced beside Liholiho who watched to see Kanaloa didn't get out of control. "Fine!" he shouted approvingly, when I leaped a big log.

With a dull gathering roar, the horses poured down the rugged mountainside toward distant corrals. The *paniolos* kept crowding in. Now and then some band would try and streak out only to whirl back into the mass of streaming glossy backs when long whips cracked in their faces. The whole mountain seemed filled with fleeing animals, though actually we were only driving five hundred head.

In a seething mass they were maneuvered into wing-fences leading to the main gate of the corrals, whinnying, kicking, squealing. Johnny shut the gates and I scrubbed my hot face with my arm. It had been glorious.

On the way home Liholiho suggested playing lasso tag. There was a heady elixir in the wind, a suggestion of violence in the shapes of Mauna Loa and Mauna Kea whose capes of snow belied the fires smoldering in their hearts. Pairs of riders began racing across the plains, one fleeing, the other pursuing with a swinging rope. I bent low over Kanaloa's rhythmically moving withers as Liholiho took off after me. The thunder of pursuing hoofs, the whine of the circling rawhide filled me with strange sensations, the elemental instinct of flight mingling with determination to elude my would-be captor.

Playing tag on horseback with lassos is a tricky performance, but no game can rival it for thrills. There's the chance your horse may bolt, that the man roping you may misjudge his slack and jerk you off. However, no disaster resulted from our wild half-hour of fun which ended when we picked up the outskirts of the village.

The sun was slanting on the steep green ridges of the Kohala mountains when we slowed down and blue shadows were arranging themselves in the deep gulches in the steep hills. In some way Liholiho's reckless laughter, resonant voice, matchless horsemanship seemed to embody Waimea.

"He's only a *paniolo*, but he haunts me," I said to Dad, that night telling him about Liholiho's reckless laughter and matchless horsemanship.

"Some people fire the imagination," Dad explained. "Liholiho belongs to that breed. He's exciting company, even to another man. You're the spit of me, First Born. I've heard laughter in the dark and wanted to follow it. Plus me, you've got Granddad von Tempsky to wrestle with. It's a large order for a peanut to handle. Ride yourself on the curb. I was here when I was nineteen. There's dynamite in the atmosphere. We had some big times when Old Sam was living."

I listened to wind prowling among the mountains. Strong and wild, it mocked the proper atmosphere of Mr. Wright's house. The spiced wine of Waimea had been here long before its walls were built and would last after they crumbled. I wanted to get my thoughts sorted out and arranged in order and I did it the best way I knew how, by talking them over with Daddy. I had ridden, chatted, and laughed with Liholiho, he had given me *leis,* sung to me, lent me his horses as dozens of other *paniolos* had, only this time it was a tingling adventure.

Dad made no comment until I finished. "If you weren't Island-born I'd take you home with me tomorrow. If you want to write living stuff, you must have all sorts of experiences. At the same time you must appreciate that the real battle in life isn't winning your spurs, it's keeping them bright and shining. I want you to go ahead, be a fool and rush in where angels fear to tread, but at the same time you must keep faith with your gods, whatever they may be, and" he gripped my hand—"stay the same shining thing you are."

"Wait," I gasped, as a rocket fizzed off in my head.

Dad's fingers tightened about mine.

"It isn't Liholiho," I said. "You've given me the idea for a real book at last. Now I know why I felt like a spooky horse when we left home to come here. I was going through a gate into a new pasture, though I didn't know it. I've been bungling along writing about what I felt were stirring things: explorers in polar snows, hunters stalking lions in Africa—"

Daddy chuckled.

"I never realized that Hawaii was dramatic virgin ground which has only been scratched on the surface by outsiders—"

Dad's eyes got eager. "Go after it. You know the Islands from the inside. Write your book but don't show it to me until it's *pau.* You might unconsciously shape it to please me. It may take years of work and heartbreak before you crash the gate. The outside world doesn't even dream of the Hawaii we love. It thinks of the Islands only in terms of ukuleles, surfing, and *hula* dancing." Breaking off, he looked at me with grave eyes. "It's going to be a hell of a job to put the life we take in our stride onto white paper with little black letters."

I nodded.

"I've a hunch you can and will. In a few more decades this phase of Hawaii will pass, as the Monarchy did. It should be preserved for people to know and enjoy. You're equipped to do it for you've been raised in its heart. More than ever I'm glad I brought you to Waimea. You've found your right field. Stay on. Make all the hay you can, while you can. When you come back, I'll send the kids to Hamakuapoko school and instead of teaching them you can devote your mornings to writing."

We looked at each other, feeling happy in a solemn way. The road had turned once more.

"And always remember this, First Born," Dad said, after a silence. "Life's a grand adventure, even when it goes against you."

28. ONWARD

Dᴀᴅ's ᴡᴏʀᴅs haunted me through the succeeding, action-crowded weeks in Waimea. While most of my mind was greedily absorbing material and translating it into story-form, some fragment of my brain kept reiterating, "Remember, even when life's against you it's a fine adventure."

I was sad and glad when we returned to Maui. Always sensitive to atmosphere, the moment I stepped into the grand ramble of our own home, which always pulsated with life, I knew that in some curious way the house had been stilled. The rooms had a feeling of silence and waiting in them which even voices and laughter did not dispel.

Our family reunions were always exuberant affairs, but while we made the round of stables and kennels I had an impression that Dad was speaking and moving in a guarded way, as though his mind were occupied with some matter which muted his joy at having us back.

Next morning after breakfast he said, "Kids, I've news to break to you—"

My heart missed a stroke.

"Shall we go to the Office?" I asked.

"This thing's too big to discuss under a roof. Get your horses."

An apprehensive silence fell on us but we went to saddle up. As soon as we were mounted, the sensation of oppression faded. Riding through the green sunny hills, my regret that Dad had had to forego being manager of the Parker Ranch melted away. It was epic, but our particular Paradise was on the slopes of the House of the Sun. Grasses that Dad had imported from all over the world brushed our horses' legs. The hundreds of thousands

293

of trees he had planted stood proud and straight in the sun like regiments of soldiers drawn up in bluish squads, a guard of honor saluting the work he had done.

When we were high up the mountain Dad halted on a hill. To right and left, above, below, the acres of the ranch spread out like a multi-colored relief map. Acres Dad had loved, benefited, and beautified for future generations. Dismounting he flipped the reins over his horse's head and turned him loose to graze.

When we were all seated in the warm sweet grass he took his pipe out of his pocket, looked at it as if he had never seen it before, then gazed at the towering blue wall of the sea with the most faraway expression I'd ever seen in human eyes. I knew he was wondering how to tell us what he had to. "Well, kids," he said finally, "I might as well let you have both barrels, then we'll collect the pieces and make a new design. Take a deep breath and stick out your chins." He paused, weighed us, and said, "After the first of next year Sam Baldwin will take over the management of the ranch."

The day which had been so deep and still went crashing into splinters. Silence which was suddenly flooded with terror and panic made us all lunge for Daddy. He managed to get us all more-or-less into his arms. It wasn't, it couldn't be true. Dad's twenty-year-long reign was ending. Paradise was *pau*. Our crying made the grazing horses lift their heads. The dogs raced back from nosing in the grass and began licking our faces, then seated themselves in an anxious panting circle. Daddy didn't even try to talk until our first grief abated and we had ourselves somewhat in hand.

"How long have you known?" I asked finally.

"For four months. When Mr. Baldwin talked to me first, I wrote Wright and asked if I might take you kids to Waimea. I didn't want you at home for the last round-up. You're all too young and soft yet for an ordeal as stiff as that. Sam had to be present and you'd have sniffed out what was in the offing."

My mind did a back-flip, my own pain which had been writhing around inside me lay still. "You were here, all alone!" I
could get no farther.

"It was better that way, for all concerned," Dad replied. "At
first, it was a jolt knowing I'm too spavined to manage this place
any longer. I had to think in a straight line before telling you
kids. For some time the Baldwins have been worried about my
game leg. They feel if I don't ride so much it may get well. In
appreciation for the work I've done here, my salary is to continue
and I'm to have charge of the thoroughbreds and be on tap if
Sam needs me."

"Then we don't have to go?" we chorused.

"Not exactly. The Baldwins are going to build us a new house,
which we're to design, in the brood-mare pasture which we all
love best. Sam will move into the old place."

Dad let us rave for a bit.

"Don't rant against life, kids," he said, when we'd let off sufficient steam. "We've sung a fine song here. I'm banking on you
to help me to make our new life as rich as the old. We'll be in
our Paradise, only we'll see it from a slightly different angle."

He waited for us to get rid of a few more feelings.

"Life's worth living, no matter what," he said, after a few
minutes. "There's so much to it. Nature. Friends. Fun. Books
to read. Music to listen to. Coming home at night. Planning for
tomorrow. Dawns and sunsets to watch. Work to do."

An odd little feeling stole through me. Dad had always
worked full blast. There wouldn't be so much to do now and
the dynamite in him might blow up. I glanced at him and felt
reassured. Sitting in the grass, he suggested a perfectly schooled
thoroughbred walking up to the barrier for a great race, con-
fident that he can, and will, win.

"Don't start off on the wrong foot, kids, by looking back and
grieving for the good old days. Jam all you can into each new

one as it comes. After a bit you'll discover that they'll be the good old days of the future. In the meantime keep your chins up and smile and the world will never lick you."

I looked at the sun-soaked mass of Haleakala. Dad was like his trees. Drought or deluge they grew on. They didn't depend only on outer things to help, the push up came from within.

"Now for immediate matters," Dad went on. "Sam is coming to live with us until our new place is built. The poor devil knows he's about as welcome as a snowball in hell, where you kids are concerned. Be decent to him, his family's been generous to us. It's going to be an interesting experience to you kids to learn that it isn't life that matters, it's the spirit you bring to it that counts. Two people can have identical incomes and set-ups. One gets little out of life, the other gets the limit. If you can think of yourself in relation to life, instead of thinking of life in relation to you, you'll get somewhere and be happy. Some people might feel if they were in my boots, 'I've played First Fiddle here and I'm damned if I'll play Second.' After the first jar of knowing I'm no longer up to the riding that a place of this size requires, I realized how lucky I was to have worked for such fine appreciative people who are making it possible for us to stay in the place we love."

He gazed across the ranch.

"The racing stables are to be moved near the new house. Without so much work to attend to I'll have more time to be with you kids. Get what I'm driving at? Happiness is mental adjustment to whatever circumstances surround you."

I remembered. Makalii had said the same thing in different words.

"Make hay with what you have, *as you go*," Dad went on. "I know how passionately you are attached to the old house. Why?"

The kids looked blank.

"I suppose because peace, love, and fun are in it," I said, thinking hard. "All of us, our friends and memories, have saturated it."

"And of course you all *know*," Dad's eyes teased us, "that no other house can ever mean to you what the present one does?"

We nodded with youthful dreariness.

"That's where you're haywire. I'll bet all the horses on the ranch against a spavined mule that not only will you love the new place as much as the old, but even better. It'll be only ours. No other family will have ever lived in it, leaving bits of their thoughts and selves behind to dilute the essence of us."

That was a new thought.

"Making a house a home is like marriage. You must work at it every day it it's to be a perpetual adventure. There'll be a few natural wrenches pulling up stakes. That's part of growth. But sure as God made little apples, our new place will mean more to us than the old."

I weighed Dad. He brought love, laughter, and purpose to life, made you want to forge ahead and find out what the next turn of the road hid. No matter what, he stayed in love with living! He tapped the ashes out of his pipe against his boot and smiled at us. "Will you all work with me to make every day fuller and richer than the one behind it?" he asked.

Would we!

"Okay. Eyes front, chins up, Boots and Saddles, we're on our way!"

29. THE ISLAND OF GHOSTS

B Y THE first of the year plans for the new house were completed and the foundations laid. While it was being built,
the Baldwins, as a further appreciation for Dad's twenty years
of work, sent him and me away, at the ranch's expense, for a
seven months' trip. We visited the States thoroughly, cruised
through the Gulf of Mexico, saw Alaska and Canada. I got my
first taste of the world outside our immediate Paradise and Dad's
hip improved with rest from riding. We had a gala time.

When we got back in the fall the house was ready. The wild-
bull horns were above the new mantel. The ever-increasing crop
of racing trophies decorated the piano. Familiar furniture, rugs,
and pictures lent the strange rooms an atmosphere of home.
The garden, through Aina's efforts, was well under way though
she had taken a job in the Bank of Wailuku and commuted the
thirty miles every day in the car.

We had barely been home an hour before Gwen ditheringly
told us that she was engaged to a man from Portland who had
come to Maui during our absence, and was going to be married
in six weeks. Dad met her beau. He offered no objections, though
he confided to me that he felt uneasy. The man's background
was very different from ours and Gwen was only eighteen.

Her marriage was an elegant affair. Cousin Elena lent her a
rose-point veil which had been handed down through generations on Gan's side of the family, and she was the first bride to
be married in the recently built Baldwin Memorial Church in
Paia.

The first Christmas under our new roof was the last one when
we would all be together. Daddy decided it was Sam's right as

298

Manager to have the tree for the ranch people. Our tail-feathers dragged slightly, but remembering our promise on the day we were told of the changes ahead, we set out to make it a joyous celebration. We invited all the friends the house could hold, decorated the tree, and sat down to the usual lavish dinner. In the midst of it a joyous burst of music came from the dark. The entire personnel of the ranch had sneaked into the garden. At the last minute Sam had felt inadequate to handle our variety of Christmas and had fled to Honolulu. The *paniolos* and everyone had come to be with "the family," as they expressed it. "No matter if no got anny presents. Us have hot-style fun," they exulted and it was the most hilarious Christmas we ever had.

The following spring Gwen and her husband moved to Honolulu. Aina received an offer to go to New York and work. Before the end of the year she wired saying she had married Major Vernon Olsmith. It was only Dad, the kids, and me now and the bonds around us drew steadily tighter. Life kept its rollicking tempo, in a slightly different key. Directly after breakfast the kids rode to school, twelve miles away. Dad went to the stable to superintend thoroughbred affairs and I settled to writing. Over week-ends the house roared with people—Mac, Jackie, the Fitzgeralds, and others came for picnics, swims, and shooting parties. Errol and Lorna brought home young Baldwins of their own age, and although Dad's hip nagged at him the new house was even more hospitable than the old.

One Saturday when Lorna came in with the mail there was a letter from the Bishop Museum. Dad read it. "I've got grand news," he announced. "As a compliment for the discovery you kids made in the crater, Professor Gregory has invited you to go with him on an expedition to Lanai to check up on rock drawings which have been discovered on the island and which may prove an important link in tracing the origins of the people of the Pacific."

Lanai was known to old-time Hawaiians as the Island of

Ghosts. Dad and a few other sportsmen went over to it, off and on, for a week during the autumn. The hunting was splendid; deer, turkey, pheasants, sheep, and hogs abounded. It was off the regular run of Inter-Island steamers and was still a unique spot. The entire island was one cattle ranch, run by a solitary white man, with only Hawaiians to assist him.

"When will we go?" we asked eagerly.

"Gregory plans to leave in ten days. His assistant, Kenneth Emory, and Ken's father, will accompany him, and Kakina's going along. They're arranging for a sampan to take them and their supplies over. If they find petroglyphs are plentiful they'll stay a month. I'll give you kids a dispensation from school and make it right with your teachers. This is something you mustn't miss. See they don't get into mischief, First Lieutenant."

"Aren't you going along?" I asked, my heart sinking.

"Until my damn hip improves I'm not up to all the cliff-climbing and miles of tramping that an expedition of this sort requires."

We rebelled. At least one of us would stay with him. We'd draw lots to see who would remain. There was going to be no more of him holding the fort alone. Seeing we meant it, Dad compromised. "Okay. I'll arrange with Sam to get off for a month and go to Honolulu and visit Gwen and her husband. None of you are going to forego an opportunity like this—because of me!"

"But you'll go nutty with nothing to do but sit around," one of the kids protested.

Dad grinned. "Gwen and I'll manage to have a good time. Besides, remember what I told you. Make hay with things you have, as you go. If you pass up a windfall of this sort you'll fall into the class of people who scrimp the present for the future, and for that sort of people the future never comes. Most people probably think we're crazy acting like a houseful of kids enjoying a perpetual Christmas. But at least we have our fun safely inside us. Whatever happens, no one can take away what we've had. If you don't *all* go, you'll make me feel that I'm a millstone around your necks. If I thought I was that—" And he broke off.

Our three sets of eyes met with the same hurried thought, which Dad deftly banished with his next words. "Though Gwen is married and has a kid of her own, she misses me. This'll be a fine chance for her to have me for a visit. Besides the Morelock girls, when they visited us, offered me free osteopathic treatments for my hip when I could arrange it. So I'll kill two birds with one stone, visit the chick who's flown from the nest and get my game leg pulled."

He laughed and the sadness faded away. Whether or not Dad believed it, he continued to give us the impression that he was convinced he'd hit on some treatment to clear up the mysterious pain in his hip-socket that was gradually making him limp more and more.

The familiar thrill of anticipation and doing things swept through the day. Dad wrote saying we'd be delighted to go to Lanai. Kakina arranged things from his end so the party from the Museum would arrive at Lahaina on the way to Lanai, the same afternoon that the boat coming from Hawaii would stop and take Dad to Honolulu. That way we would all leave for our different destinations at the same time.

To my relief the steamer was ahead of schedule and Dad sailed before Kakina had completed a few last-minute purchases of extra food and supplies. If we had gone first and left Dad on the wharf the keen edge of delight for what was ahead would have been blunted.

As the small sampan the Museum had chartered drew closer to the Island of Ghosts, the place seemed sunk in savage melancholy. No habitations of any sort showed along the coast but every so often a white jet of spray sprang up against the dark sheer cliffs like a lost soul leaping out of the sea.

A little after sunset we reached Manele, the only port-of-call for Inter-Island steamers which visited Lanai four times a year to pick up cattle. Except for a small wharf and a *paniolo* with horses and pack mules, the place was deserted. It was dark before the professor's outfit was packed and we started for the ranch house where we were to spend our first night. As the line of animals plugged up the steep rocky trail I watched the lights of the sampan bucking back to Maui.

After two hours of slow riding, we turned up a dusty road and saw light winking through trees. We dismounted and a voice with a New Zealand accent called out. Our host was fifty-ish, with stern blue eyes peering from under bristling eyebrows, but his manner was cordial. Six enormous Manx cats haunted his legs, sliding off into the shadows and reappearing like fluid things.

Over dinner he said he would provide us with horses and lend us a *paniolo* to make a base camp near the spot where the petroglyphs were most plentiful. After we'd checked the locality and were ready to shift to another part of the island he would lend us assistance and horses again. He suggested that Lomi, an oldish Hawaiian, might be useful in supplying the expedition with information about Lanai, as he'd been born here. We felt elated. Life is always gayer with a Hawaiian around.

Next day we established ourselves at the base of the forested mountain. While the members of the expedition went off on a prowl, Lomi, the kids, and I made camp. Lomi proved excellent company and by the time dinner was ready we were all friends.

Next morning about daybreak we set off to scale the cliffs where petroglyphs were reported to be plentiful. Gregory explained that it was easiest to see them early in the morning when the sun's rays slanted diagonally across the faces of cliffs. Owing to moisture and the growth of almost invisible moss, the outlines might be blurred and difficult to find until our eyes became trained. We clambered over broken rock which had tum-

bled off the *palis,* crept along ledges, and wormed around overhanging rocks. Kenny, who was lean and active as a goat, kept
the lead. Presently he let out a war-whoop. He had found rock
carvings, hundreds of them!

For the next ten days we were busy from daylight until the
afternoon was well advanced. While the light was best we took
dry blades of *pili* grass and carefully scraped the moss out of
the figures which long-dead hands had carved into the rocks.
Then we chalked in the outlines which Kenny photographed
singly or in groups for Museum records.

One afternoon, while he and I were prowling on a hilltop. we
came on a big boulder with three animals resembling goats with
straight horns carved into it. They were arranged one above the
other, each one slightly in advance of the other. We had seen
no symbols even remotely like them. After scratching the moss
out of them, Kenny photographed them. There were no animals
in Hawaii except hogs and dogs, before whites came, but the
slim little figures resembled goats. Kenny was sunk. Possibly all
the petroglyphs were of recent origin.

We fetched Gregory. After examining them he said they resembled antelope symbols carved into a cliff-face at Atamana,
near the Petrified Forest in Arizona!

Every so often our host would ride in to see what we'd found.
He'd given us permission to shoot pheasants, but as we had no
dog to flush them we'd bagged nothing. Each time he came we
hoped he'd weaken and tell us to get a turkey. They swarmed
in the forests covering the steep ridges above our camp and while
we ate canned fare we could hear their derisive gobblings.

In the evenings we sat about the fire listening to Professor
Gregory and Kenneth theorizing why, in the middle of the
Pacific, thousands of miles from the nearest continents, petro-
glyphs should exist duplicating symbols found in the Mayan
Peninsula, Tibet, and other far-off places. Few of the rock carv-
ings had any resemblance to the figures Polynesians carved into

wood or stamped on their *tapa* cloth. But it would all be carefully checked and worked out later, Gregory told us.

Even the cold precise talk of science and the orange glow of
the fire with seated figures around it, could not quite dispel the
peculiar atmosphere of the island. When Lomi and Kenny took
out their guitars and played, using their jack-knives for steels,
the long-drawn-out notes sounded like the voices of forgotten
people calling to one another across time.

Even by daylight when we were sweating and hanging onto
rocks, the same strange atmosphere persisted. The loneliness of
the island, which ordinarily would have exhilarated us, had an
opposite effect. While the great reaches of the Parker Ranch
made you want to shout and go crazy with joy, the isolation of
Lanai made you speak in lowered voices.

One by one we covered the canyons. In some, figures were
plentiful, others harvested nothing. Maunalei, the deepest gorge
on the island, was over two thousand feet deep and its sides were
so sheer that if you were absolutely still you could hear infinitesi-
mal particles of earth sliding down and *listen* to erosion in progress.

When the light was too much overhead for petroglyph-finding
or photography, we searched out house foundations to estimate
the original population of Lanai. Lomi proved invaluable as he
knew the location of every village of olden times. When the estimate was completed we judged that at one time Lanai had had a
population of over fifteen thousand Hawaiians. The present cen-
sus netted a hundred and nine. Contact with Whites during a
little over a century was responsible for the shocking decrease.

"If this continues the Hawaiian race will be wiped out before
many more years," Gregory remarked to Kakina.

I tried to imagine the world without Hawaiians, then stopped
my mind.

One evening while we were having supper, Kakina turned to

Lomi. "Make a *kahuna* so a fat turkey or pheasant will fly into our stew-pot."

Lomi chuckled. "*Opu*—stomach—no like tin *kaukau* enny more?"

Kakina shook his head.

"Okay, tomorrow Errol and me go try catch some fish," Lomi promised. Lorna looked at me, her eyes secret and excited.

Next morning we remained in camp on the pretext of wanting to wash ourselves and our clothes. When the last figure disappeared in the tall waving grass we sneaked off up the mountain. "I'll just shoot one," Lorna remarked over her shoulder as we fought our way through the thick brush covering the steep ridges. The day was hot and heavy. By the time we reached the table-land we were half-mad with thirst. The cool forests were refreshing and we licked moisture off the leaves, then soft-footed on our way with a wary eye out for a solitary horseman making the rounds of his ranch. No one in sight, only the great tawny reaches stretching to the southwest, dotted here and there with red Herefords.

Presently we heard turkeys gobbling. Lorna took the lead and we slid through the brush silently. When we neared the spot where the gobbling had sounded, Lorna straightened up and aimed her gun. I looked around, signaled no one was in sight and she whistled sharply. A turkey cock stuck his head up out of the deep fern and she fired. The bird leaped into the air and began thrashing madly with its big pinions. Rushing forward we flung ourselves on it. Then to our consternation other thrashings sounded around us. Lorna had hit three!

With pounding hearts we finally killed the birds and sneaked into a deep gully with them. Each turkey weighed about thirty pounds, more than seven people could possibly eat in several meals. We felt steeped in guilt but couldn't help giggling, as, hidden by laced branches, we set about plucking the giant birds, burying the telltale evidence in a pit we dug.

When the birds were dressed and laid out they looked like white corpses. I could carry one and the gun, Lorna, who was by now brawnier than I, staggered under the other two. As long as we had cover they would not be obvious but beyond the outskirts of the forest anyone with a trained eye would be able to see what we had—even from a distance. Sheepish with guilt, wobbly with laughter, we started on the long trek back to camp, but when the brush ended we lost our nerve and hid the "bodies" in a wash, covering them with fern leaves to keep them from spoiling.

When Kakina and the professors trailed in for supper I whispered our secret to Kakina. He gave a whoop. "Bring 'em in. It's a sin to waste."

"But supposing the Boss should stop by—"

"We'll have supper—after dark," Kakina chuckled, then he told the other men that we were having "bull-pheasant" for supper. Gregory looked puzzled and Kakina explained.

Gregory's face broke into a wide grin. "The Museum should make you Von girls a permanent part of their personnel," he said.

We ate "bull-pheasant" for days: stewed, broiled, rolled in cornmeal and fried, until we never wanted to see it in any form for ages. Then we shifted camp to the southern end of the island, eager for new territory to explore and fish for a change of diet.

Our new camp was at the bottom of a deep gorge of bronze rock, opening on the sea. To right and left successions of headlands faced the unbroken sweep of the Pacific, rolling up from the South Pole. Kaunalu, the mass of rock flanking the right side of the ravine, was twin-brother to Gibraltar in size and impressiveness. Since it was the fall of the year, *kona* gales were brewing below the horizon and, despite the misleading oiliness of the water, an occasional great swell came traveling stealthily up and burst against the cliffs, filling the rocky walls with muffled thunder.

The tide was out when we arrived. Tempting pools shimmered in the lava at the base of the cliffs, and, after two weeks of dry-camping, our skins shrieked to be entirely covered with water. The instant things were shipshape, we scrambled into bathing suits and hurried to the sea, swelling against ragged rocks and pouring deliciously into those glassy pools. I was about to plunge into one when old Lomi grabbed me. "*Malama pono!*" he said warningly, pointing at a strange jellyfish which I'd never seen before. It resembled a semi-transparent golf ball, with spider-like tentacles, about the size and color of twine, stretching for yards around it. "Burn like hell," Lomi explained, then with the kind-ness of his race he searched until he found a pool which was free of the revolting creatures. He told the men to come on with him, so we girls could swim nude and really enjoy ourselves.

While light flamed on the towering headlands and strange colors crept over the ocean, we dunked joyously, then sat on rocks still warm from the sun while a heavenly breeze dried the bright salty drops off our bare skins and lifted the hair off our necks. When the men returned, shortly after sundown, we had the fire going. Lomi and Errol slipped fish and squid off their spears and we waited impatiently while the tantalizing odor of cooking sea-food filled our nostrils.

At Kaunalu the mysterious atmosphere of Lanai was more noticeable than in any other section of the island. While we worked along cliffs and ledges during the day we were aware of the presence of people who had lived there before us—vital brown people who had gone about their business of eating, sleeping, making love, and rearing children. At night Lomi's and Kenny's music brought them rustling closer until the skin crept on our bodies and someone would heave another *kiawe* log onto the fire to make them retreat into the background.

In the gorges behind Kaunalu was ample evidence of how thickly this end of the island had been populated in the past. Hundreds of rock platforms, which had served as foundations for grass houses, were fitted into ledges and scattered over hill-tops. Polished and rounded stones six or eight inches in diameter lay in the long *pili* grass. Kakina said they were *ulumaika* stones which had been used in the Hawaiian version of bowling. Flat-topped rocks with scooped-out holes in them abounded where children and adults had played the Polynesian game of checkers.

It was inevitable, in such an atmosphere of frowning headlands and surging seas, that talk should drift to old legends and *tabus*. Lomi talked at length of old times when seven-foot chiefs had dispensed wisdom to their people. Professor Gregory, although mainland-born and a scientist, did not pooh-pooh Lomi's tales but absorbed them like a blotter. Encouraged, Lomi began to expand and grow confidential.

One evening when he had ridden to the ranch for a fresh supply of *poi,* he really loosened up. Judging from his manner he had been swigging *okolehao* with his pals before returning to camp.

"Look, you professor-guys," he said, "I tell to you sum-kind that make your hair stan' up. There"—he pointed at the sheer black mass of Kaunalu facing the Southern Cross which blazed above the horizon—"got big-kind things up there."

"Tell us in Hawaiian," Kakina suggested. "I can translate. It'll be better in your own tongue."

"Okay," Lomi muttered, like a person in a trance. "In the face of the great headland, Kaunalu, there are caves with war canoes filled with feather cloaks, helmets, and spears belonging to long-dead chiefs. At noon and midnight, sunrise and sunset, the spirits of the Great Ones who have passed on walk in a mighty procession through towering caverns. The caves are *tabu*. Anyone fool-ish enough to enter them and remain through a sacred hour when the chiefs walk will die or go mad."

I'd heard whispers of the legend, but in that setting the mental picture of the ancient and eerie rite, eternally repeated, made my bones feel as though they were turning to jelly. Lomi looked a trifle belligerently around the circle of seated figures, then seeing the interest and respect in the eyes fastened on him, he relaxed.

"Wait, I'll tell you a true story, which my father told me. It happened many years ago. Always white people have wanted to see and possess the hidden things of our great past. Many of the most valuable have been taken away from Hawaii." His manner, which had briefly hardened, grew sober. "Today it isn't so bad. You museum-men have respect for sacred things. You look at them, write about them, and, mostly, leave them where they belong. But before"—his dark eyes flashed in the firelight—"it was different, and made my people distrust and doubt even those who came for information in good faith."

Reaching out to the firewood stacked beside him, he placed a fresh log on the fire.

"When my father was young, a white man called Blythe came to Lanai. With him was a Japanese and a Hawaiian called Kane-kapulu, who was renegade to the sacred things of his people. It was known all over the Islands that he had a loose mouth." Lomi dropped his eyes. "He was related to our clan which compelled our village to extend hospitality to him and those with him, though we were ashamed to acknowledge him as our kin. When he appeared we knew that trouble of some sort was brewing, and our aging chief Maikai warned us to be on our guard."

Kakina nodded.

"Blythe showed great interest in our manners and customs and told Maikai that he was gathering data to put into a book which would preserve the history and lore of the Pacific. Maikai was bothered because a man of culture was in the company of such a blackguard as Kane-kapulu, but put it down to the fact that being a mainlander Blythe was not a good judge of Kanakas. By degrees Blythe gained Maikai's confidence. The old chief told him legends and showed him places of interest on the Island of Ghosts but his lips remained sealed about the great caves of Kaunalu."

His eyes went reverently to the cliff soaring above us.

"Blythe was a writer and a man of science, but greedy tot data. When he and the aged Maikai came in weary from a day of tramping he urged rum on his host. 'You are old and weak,' he said. 'To drink rum in excess is not good, but a little is medicine.' "

Lomi rubbed his forehead with his arm.

"My father, who was Maikai's right hand, was troubled when he found out that the chief was drinking rum every evening. Rum loosens the tongue. Even upright men with rum in them speak too many words. So it was with Maikai. One night when his heart was warm and expansive with liquor he told his writer-friend about the caves. Blythe confessed that rumor of them had lured him to Lanai and we all knew that Kane-kapulu must have told him. Blythe asked Maikai to take him into the caves, promising not to disturb anything or take so much as a calabash away. Maikai replied that the caves were *tabu,* and no one could take a white man into them.

"Blythe sent a letter by canoe to Maui. Another Island-born white man whom he knew answered it in person. He tried to reason with Blythe and persuade him not to try and enter the caves, but Blythe was mad to be the first white man to see the hidden treasures he wanted to write up.

"From then on it was a battle. Though Blythe was a *malihini* —stranger—he knew how to devil a Hawaiian. Maikai professed to be a Christian, and still believed in *tabus* and all that rot? Maikai, who was six feet tall and who had the frame of an ox, was scared of something he couldn't see and had no proof even existed? Who had ever seen a spirit? *Tabus* were just old women's tomfoolery. Maikai knew, better than anyone, why such tales had been started—to prevent vandals from looting valuable material which belonged to Hawaii. All he, Blythe, wanted to do was to go into the cave and list what was there for his book."

Lomi sighed and a long sea broke shudderingly along the rough coast of the island.

"One night the white man who came over to join Blythe spoke with my father. 'Maikai has agreed to permit Blythe to enter the caves of Kaunalu,' he said in an uneasy voice. 'Because Blythe comes from America he will not be dissuaded even by another white man. Blythe is what he represents himself to be, a writer. He will leave things unharmed and not attempt to carry anything away. I shall go to the cliff when he lowers himself over but I will not violate the *tabu* by going in. I want you to go with me to Kaunalu tomorrow. Blythe has persuaded Kane-kapulu and the Japanese to go into the cave with him and help him to list what is there '"

Lomi glanced over his shoulder and hitched closer to the fire.

"My father and the other white man went with Blythe and his party to Kaunalu shortly after sunrise. Kane-kapulu looked pea-green now his time was on him. Blythe had paid him handsomely when he agreed to bring him to Lanai and run the matter of the Kaunalu caves to earth. But no man, however low, is really happy when he betrays the sacred things of his forefathers for money.

"The old chief had impressed on Blythe that he and his companions must not remain in the caves after eleven-thirty for the chiefs walked at noon. 'If you remain when they make their mighty procession death or madness will result,' Maikai told him in a shaking voice.

"Just before starting the descent Blythe glanced at his watch His feverish excitement did not instill much confidence either in my father or in the white man who was Blythe's friend. Men of science and letters are apt to forget everything when they get started on some subject which interests them.

"It took sixty minutes to lower Blythe and his two companions and would require another hour to haul them up. That left about fifty minutes for explorations."

Lomi looked at us all sitting spellbound about the dying fire.

"My father and Blythe's friend waited tensely for a tug on the rope when the sun approached the zenith. None came. The sun climbed to its height. Shadows contracted. What had happened? Probably nothing. My father said prayers. Shadows began lengthening again. The sun began dropping toward the sea. Uneasily the white man and my father conjectured. Possibly all was well. Probably the cave was large with many chambers filled with the glory of the ancient days of the Pacific. Likely Kane-kapulu and the Japanese were sharing Blythe's enthusiasm and they were listing everything. . . .

"When my father and his white companion could conceal their fears no longer, the rope which had been limp in their hands came to sudden life. Relief swept through them, believing the nightmare was safely over, but it had just begun."

Lomi paused dramatically and I felt as if we were all seated over the deep mystery of the past.

"When they pulled Blythe over the lip of the cliff his eyes were out of focus. He sat down limply, propping his head in his hands. Then he tore up. 'I saw Them!' he screamed. 'Believe it or not, I *saw Them!* God, what giants of men.' His face twisted. 'The caverns were filled with canoes, feather cloaks, helmets, paddles, *tapa*-cloth, spears. We began listing. Things were going full blast when I noticed that the atmosphere of the cave had grown noticeably colder. I glanced back at the opening to see if the day had clouded over. Then Kane-kapulu and Nakamura froze—' He broke off, gulping for air."

Lomi's eyes and manner were feverish.

"I'm telling you straight," he insisted, "just as my father told me. Blythe looked as a man who, unbelieving in such things, had seen ghosts. He kept tearing up handfuls of grass as he talked. 'Kane-kapulu and Nakamura fell on their faces as if they'd been knocked on the head with sledge hammers. Then I saw Them— the Great Chiefs Who Walk. I tried to remain upright. I wanted to record the phenomenon, but some terrific force knocked me flat. They kept filing past. . . . Such fellows, such unbelievable giants. Then something went off in my head with the hiss of a rocket and I lost consciousness.

" 'When I came to, Kane-kapulu and Nakamura were lying where they had fallen. I went over to them. They were dead. We've got to get help. We've got to get those poor beggars out and give them decent burial. They can't be left in that terrible cave. Say I'm mad. Laugh if you want to. I know what I know. *I saw the Chiefs walk!* I thought Maikai's tale was tosh. Island drivel. As a result—two men are dead. I killed them. I shall feel like a murderer as long as I live!' "

Lomi's voice ceased. The dark throbbed and folded more closely about us and our spirits heard the dispersing rustle of unseen people who haunted the gorges of Kaunalu. A long sea hissed against lava outcroppings and spilled with crystal notes into quiet pools.

"Gosh, what a story," Mr. Emory said.

"I've heard fragments of it before," Kakina announced in his resonant voice. "Tomorrow I'll show you two graves in a small swale back of Kaunalu. For over forty years they were kept in good condition. Blythe was well-oiled with this world's goods. When he died his relatives did not trouble to care for them. New England is a far cry from the Island of Ghosts, and the courts agreed with Blythe's relatives that the request of an unbalanced mind should be ruled out."

Lomi looked at Kakina with grateful dignity. *"Mahalo*—thank you—you know I have spoken the truth."

In the flickering firelight Kakina's eyes, wise with the lore of Hawaii, met Lomi's, and he nodded.

30. CHAOTIC FLIGHT

OUR DEPARTURE from Lanai at the end of the month was delayed twelve days by a *kona* gale that isolated us from all communication with the other islands. Terrific seas tore at the coasts, wind bellowed overhead, and rain smoked against the earth. Our host was away in Honolulu but his strapping nephew insisted that we stay at the ranch house. Every afternoon we went for a gallop in the storm and in the evenings sat about the fire talking. Had it not been for the knowledge that Dad was at home waiting for us we would have enjoyed ourselves thoroughly.

But I had opportunities for long talks with Kakina about the growing problems which I sensed were sneaking up on me. Dad's hip was getting steadily more painful and, barring some miracle, would probably continue to do so. To spare him any unnecessary distress I had largely assumed the role of disciplinarian where the kids were concerned and as a mere sister my authority was often flouted.

The freedom we'd been allowed had made us self-reliant but it had drawbacks in other directions. Lorna was a daredevil youngster, muscularly hard as nails and, with the exception of Dad before his accident, the most finished rider and horseman in Hawaii. Thirteen-year-old Errol was at a stage of development where he considered advice or counsel of any sort as a personal affront to his wakening manhood. Under the self-control which my position as Dad's right-hand man compelled me to maintain, I had a high temper which blew up inwardly when I felt the kids were going off at half-cock and a battle always left me physically shaken.

"Yes," Kakina agreed one evening, "you're up against a pretty stiff problem. At present you're so occupied trying to steer a straight course for your Dad's sake that you don't realize that you may easily run foul of reefs yourself."

"In what way?" I asked.

"Well, sister dear," Kakina replied, fixing me with his dark steady eyes, "from Von you've inherited a tremendous capacity for love, not only for persons and places but for life itself. You rush at it, without weighing it—"

"Do I? I thought my judgment about most things was pretty good."

"To a point. Beyond that, time will show." He laid his gentle kindly hand on my arm. "I always have the impression when I'm with you kids that I'm moving among kegs of dynamite which may go off in any direction. You're all chips off the old block. Your Dad's a great person and it's up to you all not to let him down."

"As far as it's possible, I'll never let Dad down. Now or ever," I said, swallowing the pain in my throat.

"You probably will, here and there, but that doesn't count in the final score as long as you keep heading generally in the right direction, as your Dad has."

Looking at him I felt humble and immature. He was a great man. He did not sit in judgment of others and tell them how to think and live. He believed in them and had a Hawaiian's tolerance and understanding of human frailties.

"Von and I have been pals since we were striplings," he went on. "Bar none, he's the finest all-around human I've ever known. I'm going to tell you something, and in doing so, don't feel that I'm betraying his confidence, only arming you for what lies ahead."

A tremor went through me and I took a deep breath of air, fragrant with the scent of spider-lilies in the rain.

"When Von wrote saying he was sending the three of you

over here, he asked me to keep an eye on you without trying to guide or restrain your actions in any way, then report to him how you managed yourselves."

"Did we—" I could not finish, thinking of the poached turkeys.

"You've all behaved well, but you Vons are a wild lot. Whether you youngsters make bull's-eyes out of your lives, or smash up, is a fifty-fifty gamble. Probably it'll be a bit of both. But when your Dad checks out, as we must all do eventually, remember a lot of people will be watching to see whether or not he was right in taking off the lid where you kids were concerned.

"Keep a tight rein on yourself and on Lorna and Errol, as far as it's possible. I know you're in a spot. You aren't their mother but have to try to exert a mother's influence and control over them. They naturally resent and buck it. But whatever happens, feel free to S O S me if you ever need me."

When we got home I went into a huddle with Dad, without betraying Kakina, and hashed our immediate family problems over pretty thoroughly. Dad agreed that Errol was getting out of hand and decided he must be sent to the Military Academy in Honolulu for a year or two to knock his ears down.

While Dad's hip had been temporarily benefited by the osteopathic treatments, his health in general was not good. At night, recurrent attacks of bronchial asthma left him so spent and depleted in the mornings that, often, he was unable to get to the stables before noon.

"I'll tell Errol," I said, eager to spare Dad any unnecessary jolts, but I shrank from the job. Errol and I had tangled horns in private on scores of occasions. While we were devoted as a family we were fierce individualists, resenting advice or control from anyone but Dad.

"I shouldn't let you take this on," Dad protested.

"It's my turn to do some of the dirty work, you've had a life-time of it."

"Okay, I'll shift this load onto your shoulders, they're younger and stronger than mine. I'm getting—"

"You'll never be old if you live to be a hundred," I cut in.

"I'm not in heart, but I'm a bit spavined and wind-broken." He smiled and squeezed my hand. "I'll let you take the gaff this time. Thanks."

Errol received his doom in white-lipped silence. I tried to explain to him that he must learn to see our life in Paradise in relation to the rest of the world. He watched me in a curious, unmoved way while I talked, but I was relieved there was no open rebellion. Arrangements were made with the Academy, his passage engaged, but the morning of the day he was due to sail I found a note on my dresser saying that he would not come home until we promised not to send him away. Paradise was enough of the world for him.

Rushing into Dad's room, I showed him the note. After reading the brief scrawl, he grinned. "I ran away once when I was a kid," was his only comment.

Sera came in with morning tea and Lorna joined us. Dad asked Lorna if she knew where Errol had gone. She said no, she had got up about two, helped him to catch Manuwainui, packed some food, and got his gun for him. That was all.

"I'll bet he's in the crater," Dad announced.

At breakfast Dr. Will Baldwin came tearing into the driveway in his long car. His son Dwight, a pal of Errol's and Lorna's, also due to go to school in Honolulu, could not be found.

"I'll send a *paniolo* into the crater and track the young rascals down," Dad promised, but I knew from his eyes that he regarded the affair as a joke.

During the succeeding eight days while *paniolos* were trying to locate the missing boys, Dad was more like his old self than he had been for ages. Life seemed to have regained zest and impetus, as though he were reliving his own youth through his wayward son.

"Hell, let the kids have their thrill, they'll come home when their food supply runs out," he said.

News of the runaways had flashed over the island. Each afternoon people came in hordes for tea and the latest bulletin. *Paniolos* sent into the crater came back and reported that they saw the boys' tracks but could not find them. Fitz, the Irish veterinarian, Mac, over from Kahoolawe, were of the opinion that when Errol came in he should have the hiding of his life.

"You forget that an old crock like me can't thrash the daylights out of a husky kid of thirteen," Dad reminded them.

"I'll do it for you," Mac offered belligerently.

"It's up to me to handle my kids, old man—the best way I can. My son should have been born when I was in my prime, but he was the last of the litter."

After ten days the runaways were brought in by a ruse. While we were at tea the French doors into the living room opened and Errol came in, his face pale and set. When he saw Daddy seated at the round table, drinking a highball, his eyes widened. "Charlie told me you were ill—so I came home. When I saw cars parked all over the garden, I thought—"

Reaching for his crutch Dad rose, held out his hand, and Errol gripped it. They headed for Dad's bedroom and stayed behind closed doors for an hour. What they said is only theirs and God's business, but Errol won, as far as leaving Paradise was concerned, and for the time being was easier to handle.

However, shortly afterwards the *paniolo* in Lorna set her kicking over the traces. Without our knowledge she organized an expedition of herself, Errol, young Edward, and Lawrence Baldwin to go up Haleakala to rope a notorious wild bull. It was unheard of that a bunch of youngsters in their early 'teens, expert riders and ropers as they were, should attempt such a stunt. The first news Dad and I had of the affair was a phone call from Harriet Baldwin. Her boys had just come in with Lorna and

Errol. They had been roping wild cattle. No one was hurt but they were white as ghosts and badly shaken.

"I'll be right up," Dad said.

I got the car for him and he smoked off. It was better for him to go alone, he would feel more in the stream of life again and at the helm of our ship. I needed to be alone and think.

Life for all its appearance of serenity and stability was getting away from us, going too fast, like an avalanche roaring with gathering speed down a long slope. Dad's health, the kids' sprouting pin-feathers, my writing that seemed to be getting nowhere, were jumbled up in my mind. In an attempt to clear my head I looked at the long familiar outline of Haleakala showing above the dark trees, and the mountain seemed to send down a message to my soul.

As oldest of the rising generation, and because I was Dad's right hand, it devolved on me to make some effort which would swing our lives back into line. While we had sufficient to live on from Dad's salary there wasn't much over. What we needed was enough money to go to America and see some bone expert who could check his increasing lameness, or get at the source of the trouble and ease the pain which was sapping his vitality. If he were on his feet physically he could cope with the problems which were stalking us. He was losing ground and probably knew it. There were times when he was his old flashing self, but mostly he was like a tide which has been at flood for a long time, then slowly begins ebbing.

I looked at the brave blue day. The air sparkled and was buoyant with sunshine. Ranked around were the hills, trees, and pastures of the Paradise we loved. We had slathers of friends and the devotion of the many races which had played a part in our lives. I mustn't get in a panic. I must keep cool and fight. Fight and write. Maybe my books would be the key to unlock the door I wanted us all to go through.

When Dad and Lorna drove in, my mind was clear. Dad's

eyes had an odd expression when he got out of the car. Lorna's face was drained of all color.

"Where's Errol?" I asked.

"Riding home. Come on, old girl," he said, addressing Lorna, "It's okay. I'm not angry. You're punished enough."

"What happened?" I asked.

"Bill was killed," Daddy said. "And Lorna nearly was." His manner was strange, then I remembered that Bill was the last horse he had ever roped a wild bull off, the bull which had been responsible for his hip injury. Opening the back door of the car he lifted out a bloody bullhide and laid it on the grass. I felt as though an invisible curtain had come down in my mind, announcing the end of an act.

Later I got details. The children had gone up and located the outlaw they were after. Each wanted the honor of roping him. Eleven-year-old Lawrence got his lasso about the animal's horns but tangled in the slack. Lorna rushed in to save him and his horse from being gored. In the stress of the moment she had been forced to rope from below. The bull wheeled, charged, and disemboweled Dad's roping horse. Lawrence cut himself free and Errol and Edward came racing back.

For a few minutes it looked as if the bull would get Lorna but she kept cool and dodged around the dying horse, eluding the bull's charges, and when the right moment came made a dash for a small wash and hid in it. In the meantime Errol and Edward got their ropes on the bull but Lorna had to kill Bill, still kicking on the blood-soaked grass.

"I won't punish her for taking my horse without permission," Dad said, when we talked the matter over. "It was a jolt for her to tell me Bill had to be sent on his way. Plucky little devil, if she'd had an ounce less presence of mind she wouldn't be here."

For a few days Lorna was a sad object and haunted Dad like a lost pup. But Dad never dug up corpses. When a thing was *pau* it was never referred to again, and he helped her to tan the great brindled hide to use as a rug for her bedroom floor.

My resolutions to devote every spare instant to writing did not dim though life seemed to have, outwardly, regained a normal tone. I finished "Fire," my novel about the Parker Ranch, and sent it off to New York secretly, hoping I'd have the joy of telling Dad when the acceptance came. Then I started another, "Ripe Breadfruit."

Weeks passed. My hopes began to soar. I haunted the Post Office on steamer days, riding my best horse, Happy, with a *lei* on my hat, boots polished, spurs shining, looking as I fancied a successful writer should. Of course, the bulky, incoherent manuscript that was the original book came back. When the postmaster handed me the package I couldn't believe it. Perhaps the editors only wanted some changes. God wouldn't let me down. He knew that aside from wanting to win my spurs as a writer, I mostly wanted to make enough money to take Dad to the Mayo brothers. Often he had to use two crutches now and only at race-meets when we won some big event did he throw them away and limp down on his game leg to weigh us in, forgetting pain in his joy at seeing another trophy come to our house.

I rode Happy into the hills, undid the bulky manuscript. There was only a rejection slip. When my tears of disappointment were all shed, determination swept me. "I won't be beaten!" I thought and went at the story again.

Next time it went off I *knew* I'd done it, got the sweep of Hawaii onto paper. Every few months I'd ship either "Fire" or "Ripe Breadfruit" to New York. Being young and foolish I'd broadcast the fact that I was writing books, and each time a novel went off or returned I ran the gauntlet of ribbing friends and relatives who took it for granted I'd never make the grade.

Repeated rejections fanned my determination. I would do it! Sell books. In New York. Nothing would stop me. Had it not been for my desire to make a bull's-eye quickly, for Dad's sake,

I would have probably worked more slowly and done better, but urgency resulted in a welter of words that defeated their own purpose.

When Dad was on the eve of leaving for Honolulu to see if further osteopathic treatments might ease his pain, I gave both manuscripts to him. When his letter came I was transported to such heights of bliss that I got Happy and raced among the hills for hours. No house was big enough to hold such joy. Dad knew Hawaii, and he never cheated. He told me I still had lots to learn, but that I had a great feeling for life, and the ability to put the smell and feel of Hawaii onto paper. It was only a matter of mastering my tools and sticking to my guns. I put the letter away with other treasures in the little camphor chest Gan had given me.

When Dad returned, temporarily benefited, we went over the books together, rewriting parts of them, discussing turns of the stories. When they were in the best possible shape, Dad surprised me with a new typewriter to replace the thrashing machine I'd been using. With him fighting beside me, I felt invincible and whacked away, utilizing every split instant when other duties did not claim my attention.

My bedroom with two sets of French doors and many windows made a sort of indoor garden on sunny days. It became the family camp ground. Princess Ruth's four-poster, which we had all been born in, occupied center stage. On one side was Gan's camphor chest, on the other my desk. While I typed, Daddy read or played the melodies he used to wake us up with on Sunday mornings at the old ranch, tinkling old love songs and Beethoven melodies. Sometimes Japanese or Hawaiians came in to discuss their problems with Dad. Or Errol and Lorna roared in with noisy young Baldwins to visit. When Mac, or the Fitzes, dropped in for tea, it was served on the table by the couch where Dad lay nursing his bad leg.

I learned to write while the piano was going, and while the

kids were yelling with laughter, or while Dad regaled them with funny stories. I knew there was solace for him sitting on the edge of my work and the kids' adventures. On days when he was able, he went to the stables, and if he couldn't, Benny Rawlins, the head jockey, came and they talked horse-matters.

Dad was my dictionary and encyclopedia. If I wanted to know how to spell a word, I asked him; if I wanted some fact about Hawaii, he had the data on tap. This way he was in the thick of the turmoil every instant, vicariously living at top pitch because nothing else was possible to a man of his nature.

While the kids and I never put it in words, we knew his tide was steadily ebbing, and we conspired to keep life gay, crowded, and overflowing as it had been all the way. Often I wrote with great lumps in my throat. "Oh, please, God, let me sell one while he's with us," I'd pray while I worked, "so we can all share the fun. Or give him a 'Dispensation,' he's given so many to us. Make him well again—miraculously. Or let him go, if he must, on a flood tide, not the ebb!"

31. THE LAST RIDE

IN A last effort to keep from submitting to being a cripple, Dad had an iron bar put up in the alcove of his bedroom. He hung from it with his bad leg for five minutes daily, hoping to limber up the joint which was becoming more and more solidly set in the socket. He had an extra-high mounting block made which enabled him to get on a horse with the minimum of effort and contrived a sort of sling from the pommel to ease his leg, gamely joking about the indignities inflicted on his free proud soul. But the steady contraction of the joint made straddling a big horse increasingly difficult and he was finally reduced to riding a small half-Shetland pony.

It always gave me a shock to look down, instead of up, at Dad when he was riding with us. Our fiery mounts were contemptuous of the pony and nipped him if we didn't watch and he paid back with deft kicks. When Dad rode with us we went mostly at a walk. His big saddle with a sling instead of a lasso at the pommel looked forlorn and it never seemed quite real that he wasn't on a powerful horse leading the way.

But somehow he managed, even when he was poking slowly along on the chunky pony, to envelop himself with an air of adventure. E. W. Christmas, a Royal Academy artist whom Dad had snatched into our midst from the Wailuku hotel, became a member of our family. He had a bad heart which prevented him from taking violent exercise, but on Sundays in autumn the two gallant old fellows would set off with shotguns across their saddles to bag a few pheasants. Having an excellent pointer to flush and retrieve the birds, they usually returned with several brace and, smelling of feathers and gunpowder, would sit in front of the fire drinking highballs and telling rather ribald stories.

Daddy never lost the mysterious *élan* he had inherited from his dashing Polish ancestors. Even when pain and ill health compelled him to move slowly and carefully, you were aware of the passion and energy of his spirit. When Father Christmas, as old E.W. was called in our family, and Dad sat together before the fire after an afternoon of hunting, you didn't think of two old men. They were two scamps giving their devils a scamper with Bacchus, while they plotted fresh mischief which scattered laughter and fun. Father Christmas had a biting wit, but behind it you sensed the genius which had gone into his great painting "The Christ of the Andes," which brought him a gold medal and international fame. Dad retained his ability to make any occasion a party when he foregathered with even one other congenial person.

When they got pleasantly bunned, the hours seemed to pass like lazy stock wandering happily over a rich sunny landscape. I knew from the relaxed expression in Dad's eyes that alcohol had temporarily eased the pain of his hip, and from the smile-wrinkles clustering up Father Christmas' face that he'd forgotten the white powder he had carried in his poison ring for so many years.

Listening to their conversation was like looking at some boundless view. Father Christmas recalled his years on the great South American pampas. He spoke of glittering Rio and the green Amazon, of *gauchos* he'd drunk *mate* with, and of liquid-eyed Señoritas. Then Dad would talk of the days of the Monarchy, of Kalakaua's court, of *hulas* he'd danced, or races he'd ridden and . . . of bulls he had roped.

In their widely different spheres Dad and Father Christmas had both lived constructively and done things which would live on. They had tackled life joyously, taken spills, got up, dusted themselves off, and gone on. They'd laughed at defeats, been merry and understanding with friends, but most of all they had stayed in love with life and relished every step of the way.

When an evening of this sort broke up with one or the other saying, "Well, you old ruffian, we'd better roll in," I'd whisper a quick prayer. "Please, God, let Dad go with a splash of splendor. Don't let him peter out and end his life in a damned bed." Dad was not really old, he was only sixty-two, I'd tell myself. He had the vitality of an ox. Surely medical science could do something to cure him.

On one such Sunday night I determined to see the family doctor in private. An X-ray was being installed in the Paia Hospital. Maybe it would reveal what was wrong. Next day I saddled Happy and rode down. Being on horseback instead of in the car always made me feel more optimistic. A brave wind bled out of the east and trees shivered happily in the sunlight as clean cool air poured through their branches.

The nine miles melted away under Happy's long stride. By the time I reached the great white building set in fields of jade-green cane, I felt buoyant once more.

The doctor who'd taken care of the family for the past five years said he'd been intending to take X-rays of Dad's hip as soon as the instrument was installed. It would enable him to see the root of the trouble and perhaps make it possible to remedy it. In another week or so we'd be on the trail.

The pictures were taken and the doctor said as soon as they were ready he'd phone. One morning he called me and asked me to come down alone. I had to wait until Dad left for the stables, then I rushed away.

The doctor was in his office waiting for me. His face was grave, his eyes sad. He looked at me without saying anything, then gripped my arm. "How brave are you?" he asked.

I wondered if I had enough breath to reply, then said, "I don't know, I'll have to find out."

"Sometimes doctors feel like executioners," he said in his low level voice. "My dear, your Dad can never get better. Only worse. Half his pelvis is tubercular. The knowledge must be kept from him. There's no telling what a man of his temperament might do in the face of such knowledge. You mustn't even tell Errol or Lorna. Being kids they might muff the job."

I felt as if icy seas were pouring over me.

"If you can live with, and keep, this under your hat you may prolong your Dad's life. He can't see the plates. I'll substitute others. The trouble goes back to the fall he had when he roped his last bull. His hip socket was slightly cracked and the continued irritation of hours in the saddle kept the bone in an inflamed condition." Picking up the X-ray plates, he held them up, but they blurred before my eyes.

"If he went away immediately—"

"It's too late."

"How long—"

"It's difficult to say. Years possibly. Or the condition may gallop."

"He'll be in pain all the time and get less and less able to do the things he loves?"

The doctor nodded. In the utter silence of the room I felt as if I were under a drug that made me numb and sleepy. It wasn't quite sleep or waking, but a sort of in-between world filled with mists and shadow pictures of what Dad's life had been, and would be. . . .

Going to the cabinet, the doctor poured out a stiff jolt of whisky from his private store and handed it to me. I downed it and it recalled the first big race I ever rode in Honolulu, and my first drink of hard liquor, a wee shot out of Dad's flask because I was shaking so hard. In my memory I could hear his encouraging voice. "Take this. A nip'll steady you. The instant you're on your horse you'll be cool and ride straight."

I was entered in another event, the stiffest of my life. I must keep my head, obey all the rules of sportsmanship, and not fail the person I loved best on earth. I smoked a cigarette and got up to go.

"I'll show some plates to Von and tell him what I can of his trouble. But I'll wait a day or so. I don't feel quite equal to it yet. The rest's between us."

In times when life puts thumbscrews on you, wells of strength rise up. Half my mind was numb, the other was working at top speed. For the first time I must act a part, and never slack on the job for an instant. Temporarily I could pretend I was in a haze wrestling with some big scene in my new book. After a few days I'd adjust to the new set-up and realize that the landslide I'd sensed *was* under us and avalanching down invisible slopes with gathering speed. Beyond that I could not see. The kids and my future were not the problem, it was the immediate present that must be safeguarded and kept beautiful.

Life ticked on its way like a muted clock that never ran down. The kids rode to school in the mornings and returned with friends in the afternoons. Dad visited the stable when he was well enough, or Benny consulted with him in my bedroom. After lunch, Dad rested. Around four o'clock friends dropped in for tea. The house was always full over week-ends. Twice a week, if Dad was up to it, he drove to the hospital for violet-ray treatments which the doctor thought might help. I wrote reams of unfocused stuff which I had to destroy. Father Christmas painted when he was well and in the evenings yarned with Dad over bumpers.

I wrote to Aina in New York and, without giving away what I knew, suggested that if she and her husband could arrange for leave they ought to come out. They came, and we had a rich month. One of us stayed with Dad and the other two took Aina and our new brother-in-law into the crater, to chase wild bulls, over to Kahoolawe and to see cattle shipped from Makena. But we made the trips short and spent most of the time with Dad.

Next it was Christmas, then the Fourth of July. A rodeo outfit, the first from the States to visit Hawaii, arrived on Maui, and
Dad had them all stay with us. The kids rode in their show at
the Kahului track and Dad looked on like an eager boy. Lorna
carried off most of the honors to the delight of everyone, including the visiting horsemen.

Autumn crept up with breathless days of beauty and the sea
grumbled warnings of *kona* storms to come. The family doctor
went to the Coast for a trip and a young Russian took his place
for the time being. One day after Dad had been to the hospital
alone, he called us together. He was dressed in his best boots and
breeches and there was an excited glitter in his eyes. After down-
ing a stiff highball he got up. "Saddle Playboy for me, we're going for one more real ride."

Playboy was Jubilee's old colt, fleet, spirited, a handful to ride.
The kids and I went to the corrals, feeling solemn and empty.
Great gods walked silently through the afternoon. We all suspected that Dad was convinced he'd never get any better and
was going for one last family fling on horseback while he still
could.

Mounted on our best horses, with the pack of fox terriers running ahead, we rode up among the hills, then started home at
full speed, dashing down steep gulleys, tearing across flats, Dad
in the lead. Watching his rigid back, I knew no matter what he
might be suffering he was happy to hear again the wind in his
ears and to feel a proud horse stretching out under him.

We halted once to wind our mounts and Dad sat gazing across
the broad acres of the ranch. His eyes had a faraway expression,
not of sorrow, but rather a sort of fierce exultation. Playboy was
lathered, but wild to go on, and kept shifting restlessly from foot
to foot.

It took all the strength of will the kids and I could muster to
keep from breaking down. Dad was on his old throne, a horse's
back, and the afternoon and island were rejoicing with him. We

must not spoil his high moment with tears. When the horses got their breath, Dad jammed in the spurs and raced on, while we galloped at his heels. I recalled the many times we had "broken the record" from the summit of Haleakala to the house; the thrill of each time knocking a few minutes off our time without overriding the horses.

I knew, as Happy leaped under me, that Dad was re-riding old races, captaining the polo team, roping bulls. . . . The tears stinging my eyes hurt like blood but behind was a boundless gladness that he was having it all once again—first-hand. When we got home, he was green with pain and drenched with sweat.

"Wasn't it ripping, kids?" he said, and for a moment looked like a god again. We helped him off and he leaned against the fence for a bit, then asked, "Where's that old reprobate, Christmas? Dig him up. I want to give my devil a run."

In a numb way I knew more was afoot than was apparent. Was it possible he'd found out the real nature of his malady? But the new young doctor had his case history and specific instructions, undoubtedly. Maybe it was only an upsurge of spirit conspiring with body to refuse to surrender to circumstances without at least one last splendid revolt.

The kids and I sat in on the fireside devil-running, feeling poor because our lives were only in their beginnings and we had no assurance that the years would yield *us* such a harvest at the end. Hosts of incidents lost in Dad's and Father Christmas's pasts —trivial, humorous, touching—quickened to life. Problems which once had been urgent, tricky crossings, quick decisions, the fragrance of youthful loves, mirth and friendships, moved in a stately pageant across the bright leaping firelight, reminding me of Browning's lines:

> *Grow old along with me,*
> *The best is yet to be,*
> *The last of life, for which the first was made!*

While Dad and Father Christmas reminisced, people we had never known drew closer to the hearth, swelling the ranks of other people who had lived, loved, and walked out of the picture. Glowing Helen, little Gan, Ah Sin, gentle Makalii, and swaggering Hauki. The clink of castor oil and gin bottles being beheaded with legging knives on Saturday afternoons of long ago, the lilt of Pili's accordion, the shrieks of Moku's wife when she crashed the dinner party for the British officials, sans clothes, came out of the shadows again.

I wondered if emotions and events persisted in the universe when the last traces of them vanished from a specific person's memory. If so, what a host of happenings must cling to Dad for their last refuge before they were annihilated forever.

The end came swiftly and suddenly. Father Christmas was called to Honolulu to paint a picture. A morning or so after he had gone, Dad sent the three of us off on errands which involved an hour or two. I was deputed to take Lord Malcom Graeham, who was visiting us, to see the Hereford bulls which had taken prizes in the last County Fair, Lorna was sent off with a message to Benny, Errol dispatched to Makawao to get something.

While Lord Graeham and I were inspecting the wine-red lumbering bulls, Adaji, the house-boy, came running through the paddock, looking as if *obakes* were on his heels. "Come quick— Mr. Louis!" he sobbed. Dad had had a fair night. No asthma, no heart-spells, which resulted if the spasms were bad. I tried to get details but Adaji was incoherent. Tearing to the car, we rushed home and I dashed into Dad's room.

He was seated at his desk, a little bent over, with a glassy far-off look in his eyes. Sera, the cook, was wringing his apron, the other servants huddled on the steps. Snatching up the always-loaded hypo, I shot Dad in the arm. A strange little whistling murmur came from his back. Then I saw. . . .

On the front of his undershirt were two smoke-edged bullet

holes, dully fringed with red. The pistol which had mercifully
released many an animal from the bondage of age or wounds,
lay on the floor. I put my hand over the lung wound through
which Dad was partially breathing and Lord Graeham helped
me to get him to his bed. The bullet holes were bluish and only
slowly bleeding. Both had gone clear through him. Graeham
muttered, "God—twice with a forty-five!"

I told him to get ice, phone the doctor, radio Kakina. The
servants were useless. When he left, Dad gripped my hand.
"There's a note on the desk for you kids—"

"Time for that later—"

"Read it," he ordered.

I wadded a towel against his worst bullet hole and went over
and picked up the brief scrawl.

"I'm spavined, broken-winded, and have stringhalt. Just another old horse sent on his way before life's a curse instead of a
joy. You kids understand.

"DAD."

I laid the note down reverently and went back to him. He
grabbed my hand and all the things people say with their minds
and not their lips were in his eyes.

32. THE RAIN OF THE CHIEFS

RAIN roared triumphantly on the roofs and savagely assaulted the island, filling the night with an immense rending sound. The scent of drowned soil rose and mingled with the fragrance of clean water slashing from the sky. Elemental lawless force was in the sound and smell of the colossal downpour, a hint of majestic hosts assembling, of pulses pounding and feet hurrying to a converging point. Our house, which had always echoed to the strong sound of men's voices and jingling spurs, was silent. Daddy was dead and the *Alii* rain was falling to salute him.

Our worship of him and the worship of thousands of others had not been misplaced. In Hawaii, only when a member of the Royal Family dies, do torrential rains fall, signifying that the Gods are saluting the new anointed member joining their ranks. Something wild and joyous, something passionate and strong, stalked triumphantly through the streaming dark. Dad's gay valiant spirit, which had been chained for five years in a crippled body, was free again, and the drenched garden and island were chanting a paean of victory.

I was conscious of Kakina's strong frame filling the open door facing Haleakala as he watched the falling rain. After an instant he came over and laid his kind heavy hand on my shoulder.

"Sister dear, do you want to be alone for a few minutes?"

I nodded. He left the room and I looked at the still form on the bed. By an oversight the young doctor had not been told to keep the real nature of Dad's ailment secret. When Dad discovered what was wrong, he'd decided quietly what he'd do. For two days and nights his body refused to die. Doctors gath-

ered from all over the island declared he could have pulled
through, if he'd wanted to. . . .

How could I grieve? With outflung arms he had voluntarily
leaped across the abyss between Here and There, as he leaped a
horse over a stone wall, without doubt or fear that he'd make
a landing.

I must go out and tell the people who had thronged our house
and garden for two days, waiting, hoping, that it was all *pau*.
Brown and yellow people, white people, whose lives had overlapped Dad's wide splendid one. Work on the island had been
practically at a standstill for forty-eight hours while Dad hovered
between life and death. Friends had rushed to Maui from other
islands in sampans to be with him at the end.

I knew what the rest would be. He would be buried in his
riding clothes. Personages high and low who had peopled our
Paradise would remain to pay him tribute with the unashamed
tears of Hawaii which would fall as heavily as the *Alii* rain that
roared like drums on the roof. *Leis* of flowers he loved best
would be heaped on his bier. Hawaiian songs, concluding with
Aloha, the love he had given so lavishly to life, would be sung
at his grave.

My overstrung sensibilities responded to some stirring quality
in the deluge. The strong voice rushing out of the sky was saying something over and over. My faculties, trained by Makalii,
strained to understand the message in the liquid silver spilling
through the dark and smoking against the earth.

Illumination came. Paradise in the hereafter? What did it matter? We'd enjoyed it here on earth, a Paradise which must end
with the man who created it. Our gorgeous era was over, but the
flag of gaiety and gallantry which Dad had hoisted must never
be let down as we, his fledglings, flew on to whatever destinies
awaited us in the years unrolling ahead.

GLOSSARY

akamai: ah-kah-my: smart.

akuas: ah-ku-ahs: gods.

alanui o Lani: ah-lah-noo-ee-oh-lah-nee: Highway to Heaven.

anana: ah-nah-nah: praying to death.

ape, or ape-ape: ah-pee-ah-pee; indigenous plant with leaves six feet in diameter.

alii. ah-lee-ee: chief.

aloha: ah-loh-ha: love.

auwe: ah-oo-weh: woe is me, alas.

ele-makule: el-lee-mah-koo-le: old one.

haupia: how-pee-ah: arrow-root and coconut pudding.

hau: how: indigenous tree of Hawaii.

haanau: hah-now-oo: to give birth, be born.

haole: how-lee: white person.

hele: heh-leh: to go.

hele mai: heh-leh-my: come here.

heiau: hay-ow: temple.

he'i: hay-ee: octopus.

hemo: heh-mo: take off.

holoholo: hoh-lo-hoh-lo: to ride or go.

holoku: hoh-low-ku: Hawaiian version of Mother Hubbard introduced by Missionaries.

huhu: hoo-hoo: mad.

ilima: ee-lee-mah: native yellow flower used in *leis* for Royalty.

Inia: ee-nee-ah: Pride of India tree.

ipu: ee-pu: container, or bed-chamber pot.

335

kao: kow: goat.

kawao: kah-wah-o: wax-berry shrub.

kaakonokono: kah-ah-ko-no-ko-no: indigenous grass.

Kilo-kilo o Haleakala: kee-lo-kee-lo-o Ha-leh-ah-kah-la: We sing of Haleakala, or the song of Haleakala.

kahuna: kah-hoo-nah: priest or sorcerer.

kolohi: koh-lo-hee: naughty, bad.

kahili: kah-hee-lee: feather ceremonial emblem.

kaukau: kow-kow: food, eat.

kamani: kah-man-ee: indigenous tree.

keiki: kay-kee: child.

kiawe: kee-ah-weh: mesquite, introduced to Hawaii by Spaniards.

kiú: kee-you: electrical wind local to Haleakala.

koa: koh-ah: beautifully grained native wood.

kona: koh-nah: southerly gale.

kolea: koh-leh-ah: plover.

kokua: koh-koo-ah: help, assist.

kuleana: koo-lee-ah-nah: small, inherited holding.

kukui: koo-koo-ee: candlenut tree.

kulu: koo-loo: indigo shrub.

kulolo: koo-low-loo: coconut and sweet potato pudding.

lanai: lah-nigh-ee: open-air sitting room.

lauhala: lau-ha-lah: pandanus leaf used in weaving hats and mats.

laukahi: lau-kah-hee: variety of lamb's tongue, used in Hawaii for drawing boils or sores.

lauki: lau-kee: native weed, excellent for fattening cattle.

lei: lay: wreath or garland.

lei aloha: lay-ah-lo-ah: wreath of love.

lilikoi: lee-lee-koy: passion-fruit.

lomilomi: low-me-low-me: to massage.

limu: lee-mu: edible seaweed.

lolewaewae: loh-lee-wigh-wigh: breeches, or pants (leg-coverings).

luau: loo-wow: native feast.

maile: my-lee: sweet-smelling vine used for making garlands.

makaloa mat: mah-kah-lo-ah: sacred mat for chiefs to sit on.

mana: mah-nah: spirit essence.

mahalo: mah-hah-low: thanks.

mahalo nui: mah-hah-low-noo-ee: thanks a lot.

makule: mah-koo-lee: old (corrupted form).

malo: mah-low: breech-clout.

mamo: mah-mo: native bird (Drapanis Pacifica) whose yellow feathers were used in making leis and cloaks.

maninis: mah-nin-ees: tiny black and white striped fish.

me ke aloha pau ole: meh-keh-ah-lo-ha-pow-oh-lee: my love for you will never end.

mele: meh-leh; chant.

meles: meh-lehs: chants.

moemoe: moy-moy: sleep.

malihini: mah-lee-hee-nee: stranger.

malama pono: mah-la-mah-po-no: take care, watch out.

mauka: mow-kah: toward the mountains.

makai: mah-kai: toward the sea.

Mynah: or myna bird: (Hindu *maina*) a common Asiatic bird (Acridotheres tristis) of the starling family.

Naulu: nah-oo-loo: wind local to mountain of Haleakala.

Newa: Nee-wah: Southern Cross.

Noholoa: No-ho-law-ah: North Star.

Nivi: nee-oy-ee: Chili pepper.

Niiuhi: nee-oo-hee: Tiger Shark.

O-o: Oh-oh: native instrument for tilling crops.

O-o: Oh-oh: native bird (M. nobilis), feathers used to make cloaks, etc.

ona: oh-nah: drunk.

opihis: oh-pee-hee: edible limpet.

opu: oh-poo: stomach.

okolehao: oh-koh-lee-how: intoxicating native drink made from the root of the *ti* or *ki* plant.

paa'u: pah-oo: trailing skirt used by native girls in old times for horseback riding.

palapalai: pah-lah-pa-ly: fern used for covering *luau* tables and making *leis.*

paanini: pah-ah-nin-nee: cactus.

papaia: pah-pi-yah: paw-paw fruit.

pau: pow: done, finished, through.

pali: pah-lee: cliff.

paniolo: pah-nee-oh-low: cowboy.

pelekane: peh-lee-kah-nee: Britisher.

pilikea: pee-lee-kee-ah: trouble.

poi: poy: native food used in place of bread.

pili grass: pee-lee grass: used for thatching huts.

pua-kawao: poo-ah-ka-wow: wax berry, resinous shrub, growing above 7,000-foot level.

pualeli: poo-ah-lel-ee: milkweed, excellent for fattening stock.

puune: poo-oo-nay: corner bed common to Hawaiian homes.

tabu: tah-boo: forbidden.

tapa: ta-pah: paper-like cloth made in Polynesia, used for women's and men's garments before Whites came to the Pacific.

taro: tah-row: root like large gray potato from which *poi* is made.

ti: tuberous root from which *okolehao* is made.

tu-lai é: tu-ly-aye: Throw your strength! Pull hard! (as in rowing).

Tutu: too-too: grandparent.

ukiukiu: oo-kee-you-kee-you: misty rain and wind local to Haleakala.

ulua: oo-loo-ah: cavalla, or carangus fish.

ukulele: oo-koo-lel-ee: miniature guitar.

ulumaika: oo-loo-my-kah: bowling stone.

wahine: wah-hee-nee: woman.

wahine u'i: wah-hee-nee-oo-ee: beautiful woman.

wana: wah-nah: edible sea-urchin.

welakahao: wel-ah-kah-how: stuff stuff, hurrah.

wanaao: wah-nah-ow: ghost dawn.

wikiki: wick-ee-wick-ee: quick, quickly, fast.

PRONUNCIATIONS OF NAMES OF LOCALITIES IN TEXT

Aala: Ah-ah-lah: park in Honolulu.

Ainahou: Eye-nah-how: old Cleghorn estate at Waikiki.

Hamakuapoko: Hah-mah-ku-ah-poko: district on Maui.

Haalii: Hah-ah-lee-hee: Black cone in crater of Haleakala.

Hana: Hah-nah: district on Maui.

Hawaii: Hah-wy-ee: largest island.

Hawi: Ha-vee: plantation on island of Hawaii.

Haleakala: Hah lee-ah-kah-lah: House of the Sun; extinct volcano on island of Maui.

Hanakanae: Hah-na-ka-nigher: bay at south end of island of Kahoolawe.

Honaunau: Ho-now-now: City of Refuge in district of Kona on island of Hawaii.

Hilo: Hee-low: largest city on island of Hawaii.

Honolulu: Hoh no loo-loo: capital of Islands on Oahu island.

Honomanu: Ho-no-man-oo: valley of island of Maui.

Hualalai: 8,000-foot-high extinct volcano on island of Hawaii.

Iao: Ee-ow: valley on island of Maui.

Iwelei: Ee-wah-lay: old red-light district on island of Oahu.

Kahului: Kah-hoo-lui: port on island of Maui.

Kahoolawe: Kah-hoo-lah-wee: island to southwest of Maui.

Kanaio: Kah-nigh-o: district on island of Maui.

Kailua: Ky-loo-ah: chief port-of-call for district of Kona.

Kalepolepo: Kah-lep-o-lep-o: old koa house on island of Maui.

Kolikoli: Koh-lee-koh-lee: highest cone on summit of Haleakala.

Koolau: Koo-lau: gap in north wall of crater of Haleakala.

Kanapo: Kah-na-po: bay at north end of island of Kahoolawe.

Kauai: Kah-wy-ee: fourth largest island of Hawaiian group.

Kau: Kah-oo: district on south end of island of Hawaii.

Kanae: Kee-ah-nigh: valley on island of Maui.

Kaupo: Kow-po: district on island of Maui.

Kealakekua: Kay-ah-lah-kay-koo-ah: bay on island of Hawaii where Captain Cook was killed.

Kilauea: Kee-lah-way-ah: active crater on slopes of Mauna Loa about 4,000 feet above the sea.

Kehekenui: Keh-hay-kah-noo-ee: district on island of Maui.

Keonehaehae: Kee-o-nee-hay-hay: Sliding Sands trail leading into crater of Haleakala.

Kipahulu: Ki-pah-hoo-loo: district on island of Maui.

Kohala: Koh-hah-lah: district and mountains on island of Hawaii.

Kula: Koo-lah: district on island of Maui.

Lanai: Lah-nigh-ee: one of the smaller islands of Hawaiian group.

Lapahoehoe: Lah-pah-hoy-hoy: port on island of Hawaii.

Lahaina: Lah-hi-nah: port on island of Maui.

Lauulu: Lau-oo-loo: plateau above crater on north-eastern end of crater of Haleakala.

Lua-lai-lua: Loo-ah-ligh-loo-ah: twin blow holes on island of Maui.

Makawao: Mah-kah-wow: district on island of Maui.

Kawaihae: Kah-wy-high: port on island of Hawaii.

Kaunalu: Kow-nah-loo: Gibraltar-like headland on southern end of island of Lanai.

Makena: Mah-ken-ah: port on island of Maui.

Manoa: Mah-no-ah: sacred valley on island of Oahu.

Maui: Mow-ee: second largest island of Hawaiian group.

Makahalau: Mah-kah-ha-lau: district on island of Hawaii.

Manuwainui: Man-oo-wy-noo-ee: deep canyon on island of Maui

Mahukona: Mah-hoo-koh-nah: port on island of Hawaii.

Mauna Kea: Mow-nah Kay-ah: (White Mountain) 13,825 feet above sea-level, on island of Hawaii.

Mauna Loa: Mow-nah Law-ah: (Long Mountain) 13,680 feet above sea level. Active volcano on island of Hawaii.

Manele: Mah-nel-ee: port of call for island of Lanai.

Mauna Lei: Mow-nah Lay: deep canyon on island of Lanai.

Molokai: Mo-low-ky-ee: island on which the Leper Settlement is located.

Moaula: Moh-oo-lah: tallest mountain on island of Kahoolawe.

Mokuaweoweo: Moh-ku-ah-way-oo-way-oo: active crater on summit of Mauna Loa.

Nu'u: Noo-oo: district on island of Maui.

Nuuanu: Noo-ah-noo: valley on island of Oahu.

Oahu: Oh-ah-hoo: third largest island in Hawaiian group.

Ohia nui: Oh-hee-ah-noo-ee: Big Ohia, pasture on Haleakala Ranch.

Ohia lili: Oh-hee-ah-lee-lee: Little Ohia, pasture on Haleakala Ranch.

Paia: Pah-hee-ah: small plantation town on island of Maui.

Pali-ku: Pah-lee-koo: tall cliffs in crater of Haleakala.

Pokakumoa: Poh-hah-ku-mo-ah (rocks like chickens): gulch on island of Maui.

Puualiakakoanuiokane: Pu-ali-ah-kah-ko-ah-noo-ee-o-kah-nee: point on rim of crater of Haleakala.

Puuniniau: Poo-oo-nin-ee-ah-oo: conspicuous cone on side of Haleakala.

Ukupalakua: Oo-loo-pah-lah-ku-ah: ranch on island of Maui.

Waikapu: Wy-kah-poo: (Forbidden Waters) valley on island of Maui.

Waikiki: Wy-kee-kee: famous beach on island of Oahu.

Wailuku: Wy-loo-koo: (Bloody Water) valley and river on island of Maui.

Waimea: Wy-meh-ah: district on island of Hawaii.

Waiopai: Wy-oh-pie: district on island of Maui.

1. *ahaguro:* black stain used on teeth when loved ones die.
2. *Bakatari:* swear word.
3. *Banzai:* hurray.
4. *Byoki:* sick, ill.
5. *obakes:* ghosts.
6. *chimaki:* beans and red rice wrapped in lily leaves.
7. *hari-kari:* suicide; seated cross-legged a man disembowels himself.
8. *hi-yah:* Japanese expression of relief.
9. *Shobu-no-Sakhu:* Boy Day, May 5th.
10. *Sayonara:* "Since it must be so" (Japanese farewell).
11. *Taberu:* eat.
12. *Yoi:* good.
13. *san:* Mama-san, Papa-san: like Mr. or Mrs.